RING OF STEEL

REBEL VIPERS MC BOOK 2

JESSA AARONS

RING OF STEEL

This book is a work of fiction. The names, characters, places, and incidents are all products of the author's imagination and are not to be construed as real. Any similarities are entirely coincidental.

Ring of Steel Copyright ©2023 by Jessa Aarons. All rights are reserved. No part of this book may be used or reproduced in any manner without written permission from the author, except in the case of brief quotations used in articles or reviews. For information, contact Jessa Aarons.

Cover Designer: Charli Childs, Cosmic Letterz Design

Editor: Rebecca Vazquez, Dark Syde Books

TABLE OF CONTENTS

WARNING	VII
DEDICATION	VIII
PLAYLIST	IX
PROLOGUE	1
CHAPTER ONE	7
CHAPTER TWO	15
CHAPTER THREE	23
CHAPTER FOUR	31
CHAPTER FIVE	41
CHAPTER SIX	47
CHAPTER SEVEN	55
CHAPTER EIGHT	63
CHAPTER NINE	71
CHAPTER TEN	83

CHAPTER ELEVEN	93
CHAPTER TWELVE	99
CHAPTER THIRTEEN	105
CHAPTER FOURTEEN	111
CHAPTER FIFTEEN	117
CHAPTER SIXTEEN	125
CHAPTER SEVENTEEN	135
CHAPTER EIGHTEEN	141
CHAPTER NINETEEN	151
CHAPTER TWENTY	159
CHAPTER TWENTY-ONE	173
CHAPTER TWENTY-TWO	181
CHAPTER TWENTY-THREE	191
CHAPTER TWENTY-FOUR	197
CHAPTER TWENTY-FIVE	205
CHAPTER TWENTY-SIX	211
CHAPTER TWENTY-SEVEN	217
CHAPTER TWENTY-EIGHT	225
CHAPTER TWENTY-NINE	233

CHAPTER THIRTY	241
CHAPTER THIRTY-ONE	249
CHAPTER THIRTY-TWO	261
CHAPTER THIRTY-THREE	267
CHAPTER THIRTY-FOUR	275
CHAPTER THIRTY-FIVE	281
CHAPTER THIRTY-SIX	289
CHAPTER THIRTY-SEVEN	297
CHAPTER THIRTY-EIGHT	305
CHAPTER THIRTY-NINE	315
CHAPTER FORTY	325
CHAPTER FORTY-ONE	333
CHAPTER FORTY-TWO	345
CHAPTER FORTY-THREE	353
CHAPTER FORTY-FOUR	367
CHAPTER FORTY-FIVE	375
CHAPTER FORTY-SIX	383
CHAPTER FORTY-SEVEN	395
CHAPTER FORTY-EIGHT	403

CHAPTER FORTY-NINE	413
CHAPTER FIFTY	423
CHAPTER FIFTY-ONE	433
EPILOGUE	443
ACKNOWLEDGMENTS	448
ABOUT THE AUTHOR	450
OTHER WORKS	453

WARNING

This content is intended for mature audiences only. It may contain material that could be viewed as offensive to some readers, including graphic language, dangerous and sexual situations, murder, abuse, and extreme violence.

This book is for everyone who needs that extra hug to brighten your day. We all deserve love. No matter what form it comes in, we all deserve it.

Stay strong and shine on, you crazy diamonds!

PLAYLIST

CLICK HERE TO LISTEN ON SPOTIFY
My Chick Bad – Ludacris ft. Nicki Minaj
Sunshine & Whiskey – Frankie Ballard
Can't Take My Eyes Off You – Lady A
Fooled Around and Fell in Love – Miranda Lambert ft. Maren Morris, Elle King, Ashley McBryde, Tenille Townes, Caylee Hammack
Make You Feel My Love – Ian Flanigan
Beers And Sunshine – Darius Rucker
Stay With Me (Brass Bed) – Josh Gracin
Body Like a Back Road – Sam Hunt
Show You Off – Dan + Shay
Follow Your Arrow – Kacey Musgraves
The Joker – Steve Miller Band
Already Callin' You Mine – Parmalee
Man Of Steel – Brantley Gilbert

PROLOGUE

STEEL

TWO YEARS AGO

"You did what?" Whiskey yells so damn loud, these cinder block walls might crumble. We're in an interrogation room in the back halls of the county courthouse. There are no windows to the outside and the floor's a concrete slab. The room's brightly lit by four large, fluorescent tube lights and I'd normally be super annoyed by the buzzing they're making, but I won't be in this room much longer.

"I took the deal."

"You took the deal?" Is he deaf? Maybe all the yelling has affected his own hearing.

"Yes." I had to.

His energy instantly deflates, and he drops back into the chair on the other side of the table I'm handcuffed to. "Why the fuck would you do that?"

"I couldn't let this go to trial and drag the club's name through the mud. That's not how things work." He knows this. It's the reason I did things the way I did.

"But you—"

I interrupt him before he can say something to make life worse for the both of us. "Stop. You can't say shit like that here. We've got ears." I tilt my head back, nodding toward the two-way mirror behind me. I know there's at least three people in the room behind the glass.

"Fine," he huffs and runs a hand over his beard. "What's the deal?"

I lean forward and fold my hands on top of the table. "Twenty-four to thirty-six months. Possibility for early release with good behavior."

That gets Whiskey's hackles right back up. If he's not careful, he'll give himself a heart attack. "What the fuck? You could be in prison for three years? What kind of dumbass lawyer did we hire?"

"Dude, calm the fuck down. I need you alive on the outside of these walls when I get out. And it could only be two years total. That's better than the twenty I'd get if we go to trial. You know those dumbass feds would lock me up for longer if they could. Doing it this way, I get the say on my time."

"Fine. Where you being held?"

"In state, at New Lisbon Correctional. I made it part of my agreement that I picked a place close to home. It's just over an hour away from the clubhouse." Not that I want any of my Brothers to visit me in prison, because no one needs the problems that could cause. I simply wanted the peace of mind of being in an area I know.

"So, will you have a felony on your record?" I think this incarceration's going to bother Whiskey more than it will me. I get why, but he really needs to take a damn chill pill.

I nod. "I'll be on parole when I get out early, then yes, I'll have a felony."

"If you only would've—"

I cut him off again. "Stop. Not here."

"But what about Opal?"

That's the worst part of all this. Opal, my two-year-old daughter. I won't be able to see her while I'm locked away. I won't let her come here to see me through a piece of plexiglass or behind metal bars. She's too young to understand why we won't be able to hug or that there's a time limit on our visit.

"Ring said he'll watch over her and do stuff with her, and he promised to bring her to family functions at the club. Just because her mother's a whore, don't mean Opal can't be around everyone while I'm gone."

"Sydney won't be a problem. We'll make sure Opal gets whatever she wants and needs. You too. We'll keep your account full, but if you need anything, just call Mountain or Ring."

"Thank you." This is why I'm proud to be part of the Rebel Vipers MC. We watch out for each other when someone needs a helping hand. And I'll need it the most over these next two years.

"I should be thanking you." Whiskey meets my eyes, dead on.

I bust a chuckle, trying to break the tension. "When I get out, I expect one hell of a welcome home party. There better be lots of fuckin' hot club girls waiting for me."

That gets him smiling. "It's a deal. I'm sure all the girls will be happy to lend you a hand . . . or two."

Knock knock. I guess the guys in the monkey suits didn't like us talking about club girls and me getting laid. The door opens and FBI Agent Emanuelle walks in, followed by my lawyer. "Alright, gentlemen, time's up."

If Whiskey could kill someone with just a look, Agent Emanuelle would be dead. He really doesn't like anyone in uniform, especially those who go back on their word. And Luke Emanuelle has turned out to be one of those people. He put up a big stink about how he thought I should be let go, but once he was assigned as the head agent in charge of my case, his protests stopped. His attitude did a full one-eighty and he was all on board with locking me behind bars. What a jackass.

"Time for me to go?" I ask.

"Yes, it is, Mr. James," my lawyer answers. Now, this man has been a saint. After I laid everything out and told him what I wanted to do, he worked a damn miracle. In an effort to avoid the long process of arraignment, a trial, and sentencing, he managed to get me the deal I wanted in two days.

I hold up my wrists and Agent Emanuelle unlocks my cuffs from the chain attached to the table. I stand up, wrists still cuffed in the front, and turn to look at my Brother. "Look after my little girl and I'll see you in two years."

He stands. "You got it."

I walk out the door and head toward my life for the next twenty-four months. Orange jumpsuits and three-hots-and-a-cot . . . here I come.

CHAPTER ONE

STEEL

END OF FEBRUARY

Clang. The sound of my cell door opening wakes me up. I roll over on my cot and see one of the day shift guards standing in the open doorway. "Rise and shine, James. You've got a meeting with your P.O. this morning."

I swing my legs over the side of the shitty mattress and jump down to the floor. "Can a guy get some privacy to take a leak?" I chuckle, knowing I won't be given time to do anything. I just like to push buttons to test what someone's attitude is like.

"No time. You know the drill. Turn around, hands behind your back." He holds up the handcuff chain and shakes it in my direction. This guard is one I've only seen recently, so my guess is that he's super new to the job and wants to do everything by the book. I know my time here is counting down, so having an issue with someone like him isn't worth it for me. I turn and he snaps the cuffs around my wrists.

I back out of my cell and turn to head for the stairs. My cell is on the second level of the cell block, all the way in the furthest corner. We meet a second guard at the end of the mezzanine and head down the stairs, then through the empty rec room. Once outside the secured area, we make a bunch of left and right turns, almost like going through a maze. If someone was stupid enough to try and escape this place, they'd probably get lost in these halls.

We stop in front of an open office and I see my parole officer sitting at his desk. "Come on in. Have a seat." I drop down into the single plastic chair, and the guards back out into the hall. "Sorry to have you brought in so early, Colt, but I've got some good news for you." He grabs a file folder off the pile on the corner of his desk and opens it up.

"Good news? What's that? I'm still in here, ain't I?" I laugh at my own joke, but this time, the guy I'm talking to laughs back with me.

"Not for long. That's why I wanted to meet with you, to inform you that your release has been scheduled for sixty days from now. That'll be the end of April." He lifts the top piece of paper in the file, flips it around, and slides it across the desk so I can read it.

There's a whole shitload of words typed all formally, but the thing that catches my eye is the circle of yellow highlighter at the bottom. The words 'Date of Release' are in bold font and underlined, then circled with the bright fluorescent ink. Holy shit! I knew the time was coming, but seeing it with my own eyes is shocking.

"This for real?" I look up and ask. In a place like this, I know it won't be real until I'm on the outside of the block walls, riding away into the sunset.

"Oh, it's real. The judge and warden signed off last night. I would've pulled you in then, but I didn't get the email until thirty minutes ago. I've got some paperwork for you to look over and sign, then we'll meet again in a week." He grabs the paper back and starts separating everything in the file into two different piles.

"Why a week?"

"You get a week in case you want to schedule a meeting with your lawyer. Because you had a plea deal, I suggest you don't sign your formal release papers without showing them to your lawyer first. Something I recommend just to cross your t's and dot your i's."

Makes sense, I guess. "I'll call him this afternoon. Is there an exact date yet? I noticed the date says April, but the number is blank."

"Due to scheduling purposes, the exact date won't be determined until the week before. I do know that it'll be the end of the month. Sixty days from today is April twenty-seventh, so it'll be anytime in that seven-day window." He puts the smaller pile of papers into a large manilla envelope, then slides it across the table. "These are your copies. Show them to your lawyer. When you're ready to sign, let a guard know and they'll get you in front of a notary to make everything official. Any questions?"

"I don't think so." I shake my head, still a little unbelieving of everything happening so quick.

"Alright. Guards," he calls out, "he's all yours." The two men appear back in the doorway as I stand up and walk their way.

"Let's get you back to your block." The nicer guard leads the way.

I get back to my cell block just in time for all the other cell doors to start rolling open. The block I live in has an open-door policy during the day. We're allowed to walk around the open rec room with everyone. We can watch television, play cards, read books, and make phone calls. From nine in the morning until seven at night, twenty-three other men and I are nothing more than mice in a bulletproof glass cage.

The guards get me back to my cell and unlock my cuffs. I walk straight to the shelf above the desk and pull down the cardboard box I keep all my court papers in. While inside this place, I like to have all my paperwork within reach. I drop the folder in the box and slide it back onto the shelf.

"Howdy ho, neighbor." I turn to see my cell neighbor, Ray, standing in the doorway. "What'd they pull you out so early for?"

I step toward him and we fist bump before heading for the stairs. "I had a meeting with my P.O. He gave me my release paperwork."

"No shit? That's awesome, man. When you heading out?"

"Sixty days, give or take. I gotta call the club and get them to send my lawyer for the paperwork." We jog down the stairs and head for the payphones in the corner.

"You still serious about me coming to visit the club when I get out? I've got about six months left myself, so I won't be out long after you." I met Ray the day I got here. He's a few years younger than me and has been my cell neighbor since day one. He's three and a half years into his four-year sentence for armed robbery. We got to talking one day about where we're from and how we got here, and we instantly clicked. Talking to him felt like I was back home with my Brothers.

"When you get out, you bring your wife and kid and come to the clubhouse. I already told Whiskey that I invited you to visit, and he's open to meeting with you. After that, it's all on you. I can only get you as far as the door, getting in the club is determined by your actions."

"Sounds good to me. I'll leave you to your call." He heads to talk to some of the other guys.

I pick up the payphone and dial the numbers I need to make the collect call. The line buzzes a few times, until I hear the click that someone picked up on the other end. "Hey, Steel. How's it goin' in there?" It didn't take Ring long to answer. It never does. No matter what he's doing, whether it's something for the club or when he's at the brewery, he picks up.

"It's going really good actually. That's why I'm calling. I need you to do a favor for me."

"A favor because of something good? That sounds kinda fishy. What'd you need?"

"Call my lawyer and get him to come down here to look over some paperwork. I just found out I'm getting out in two months."

"TWO MONTHS! Holy shit, man! That's not good, that's great!" I can tell he's happy for me. "Yea?" I can hear him talking to someone on his end. "Hey, Whiskey. It's Steel . . . He says he's getting out in two months . . . I'll tell him."

"Dude, can't you tell him that when we're off the phone?" I jest. It feels good to be razzing and joking with my best friend.

"He approached me, so no, it couldn't wait, ya asshole," he mocks back.

"Fine, fine. Tell me how things have been there. What kind of shenanigans have you guys gotten yourselves into?" I haven't actually seen any of my Brothers since I got here, but I talk to someone at least once a week.

"Whiskey went and got Duchess knocked up. She dropped the bomb on him on Valentine's day."

Whoa! That's something I didn't see coming. I was shocked enough when I heard he took an Old Lady, but a baby? That brings things to a whole other level. "How's he handling everything? Babies change things big time."

"He's been a papa bear on the prowl ever since. He won't let her go anywhere without him and she's about to lose her damn mind. It's the funniest thing I've ever seen."

"I bet he has. If Duchess is anything like you say, I bet she'll keep his ass in line." From what I've heard about her, and how she handled being kidnapped, I have no doubt she's the perfect woman for our President.

"She sasses back at him when he needs it. It's great," he laughs. "Oh, and speaking of Duchess, you should've seen her with Opal last weekend. I took her to the bakery for a cupcake and Duchess let her into the back to decorate her own. By the time we left, her cheeks were tinted pink from all the frosting she ate. Then, she was so hyped from all the sugar, she was up way past her bedtime."

That cracks me up even more. God, I miss my little girl. Opal is four years old now and I hate that I've missed all this time with her. When I get home, I'll be spending all the time I can with her, no matter what her bitch of a mother says. "You spoil her rotten, Ring. You bring all that trouble on yourself."

"It's all worth it for the little girl cuddles, just you wait and see. She's so excited for you to get home. I wish she was here so you could tell her the good news yourself."

"It's alright. Let's wait to tell her 'til after I meet with the lawyer and get the ball rolling. I don't wanna get her hopes up, just in case something happens to delay it." The last thing I need to do is lie to Opal when coming home is so close.

"I'll wait to tell her. But listen, I've gotta get going. A new distributor just walked in the door and I need to give him a tour. I'll call the lawyer when I'm done. Is that alright?"

"All's good here. I'll call again when I know more."

"Stay safe, Brother." Ring says the same thing at the end of every call.

"Always" is always my reply back, then the line goes dead.

Now, it's time to wait. Sixty days and I'll be on my way back home.

CHAPTER TWO

PENELOPE

END OF MARCH

"I still can't believe she's gone. What do I do now?"

"I'm going to miss her too, honey. But I'll help you with anything you need." I look at my aunt and can see this is eating her inside, just as much as it is me.

My mother is dead. We're standing in the open hallway of the cemetery's mausoleum, watching as the funeral home attendant talks with the groundskeeper, getting ready to slide her coffin into the block wall. I had originally thought about burying my mom like people usually do, but when I met with the funeral director to make plans, something about this area spoke to me. Knowing she won't be under the ground when I come to visit her made me feel a lot better about the whole process.

My mom and Aunt Jane are the only family that I had. I'm twenty-six years old and now it's just my aunt left. I grew up not knowing who my dad is. When I was younger and asked my mom about him, she would say she didn't know his name and to never bring it up again, so I eventually stopped asking.

"Let's let the gentlemen do their work and head back to the house. People will be coming soon to pay their respects and I want to freshen up before they arrive."

I don't want to leave Mom here alone. I haven't been away from her since she got sick two years ago. "But . . ."

"Don't give me no sass, little lady. It's time to go." She loops her arm through mine and pulls me toward the parking lot. We get into my minivan and I drive away before I chicken out and run back to the building.

It takes about twenty minutes to get home, and as soon as we park in the garage, Aunt Jane gets out and practically runs into the house. What's the big hurry? No one's here yet. We chose not to have anyone else with us at the cemetery, but put in the obituary that everyone was welcome at the house afterward.

I shut the garage door and head into the house. When I walk in, she's coming down the hall, holding an envelope in her hand. "What's that?"

"It's a letter from your mom. She wanted me to give it to you when the timing felt right. I'm giving it to you now, but don't open it until everyone leaves." She holds the envelope out, but I'm afraid to take it from her.

"Then why give it to me now?" I finally grow some balls and grab it. My name's written on the front in a swirly script. Toward the end, the cancer made her muscles weak, but somehow, her handwriting never changed.

"Well, partially so I don't forget, but mostly because I wanted you to know she left you something. Everything she did was for you." How cryptic.

I walk into my office and put the letter in the desk drawer. I don't know what it says, so I'll read it when I'm alone.

A few hours later, the last guests leave and I head for my office. I pull the envelope out and decide to sit on the extra wide chaise lounge chair in the corner. Something tells me I'm going to need comfort when I read this.

I carefully rip the envelope open and pull out the folded pieces of paper. Whatever she had to say took two pages.

> *My Penelope,*
> *If you're reading this, that means God decided it was time to call me home. The cancer has been ruling our lives for the last few years, but now we're both finally free. Now you can spread your wings and get back to living your life, instead of being stuck under my dark shadow.*
> *It also means your aunt thought you were*

ready to read what this letter says. Please don't be mad at her for saying she didn't know. I only recently told her and I made her promise to keep my secret. I'm not really sure there's a right way to say this, so I'll just drop the bomb and come back to explain after.

I lied to you. I do know who your father is. I didn't realize I was pregnant with you until after I'd moved away to college and I struggled with what to do. To put it simply, I was scared. By the time I built the courage to tell him, you were almost a year old, and then I chickened out. I thought that if I just kept pushing it under the rug, I could raise you all by myself. I had your aunt to help me and we were doing just fine.

Holy fucking shit! She lied to me? I never saw this coming. I thought this letter might've been her saying what she wanted me to do with the house, not to drop my damn birth father on me. Who is he?

If you're still reading, I can imagine that you've probably said a few choice swear words. And I can say I don't blame you one bit. I'd hate me, if I was in your shoes.
Nothing will make up for my mistakes, but hopefully one day you'll forgive me. Even if it's

in the distant future. So dear Penelope, please be mad at me. I honestly want you to be upset. What I did was so very wrong and it crushed my soul a little bit every day for keeping this from you.

If you'd like to know who he is, go into my closet and find the black shoebox on the top shelf. It's tucked in the back corner, way up high, somewhere I hoped you'd never go searching.

You were always such a good little girl. You never argued with me, never peeked at Christmas presents early, and always told me when you snuck in after curfew.

I should've trusted you with this information a long time ago, but it was my own issues holding me back. If you find him, and he wants to get to know you, please give him a chance. His lifestyle may be a bit unorthodox, but for the short time he was in my life, he was an amazing man.

I'm sorry, again, for not being there to tell you this myself, but know that I'm watching over you as you take this next journey in your life. I love you to the moon and past the stars. Mom

I throw down the letter and take off running down the hall. My socks slip on the hardwood and I almost bust my behind when I try to turn into her bedroom. I need to know what she's been hiding in this shoebox.

I swing the closet door open, pull the chain to turn the light on, and freeze. I came running in here on a mission, but seeing all her things right where she left them hits me hard. Am I going to do this? Is this the right thing to do? Should I go looking for a man I know absolutely nothing about? What if he's really an ax murderer or something? She said he was an amazing man, but then why didn't she say anything before now? What is an 'unorthodox lifestyle'?

Finally getting over myself, I take a few steps into the closet and reach up for the box. It's not heavy at all. It almost feels empty, but I give it a quick shake and hear things sliding around inside.

Turning off the light and shutting the closet, I crawl onto my mom's bed. Maybe being in her space will make it feel like she's here with me. I lift the lid and peek inside, almost like something's going to pop out at me. All that's inside is two ticket stubs for a county fair and a picture tucked inside of a plastic sleeve. It's like the ones you usually find inside a photo album, but this is just one picture.

I pick up the picture and first notice a very young version of my mother smiling bright. She looks so damn happy. She was always so happy, though, no matter how much pain she was in. Next, I turn my attention to the very tall man standing next to her with his arm around her shoulder. They look mighty comfortable being all up in each other's bubbles.

What he's wearing is what really draws me in. He's got on what looks like black boots, some really dark-colored jeans, a bright white t-shirt, and a black leather vest with patches on it.

The picture isn't clear enough to show what they say on the front of his vest, but someone standing just to his side has their back turned to the camera. The vest has a giant skull and snake patch in the middle and I recognize it immediately. Anyone who lives within a hundred-mile radius knows what that patch means. My father's a biker in the Rebel Vipers Motorcycle Club. Their clubhouse is in a town thirty minutes from where I've lived since I was five years old. My father has been this close for most of my life and I never had a clue.

I flip the picture over and see my mom's handwriting again. *Me and Jethro. County fair.* There's no year, but I'm going to guess it was the summer before she left for college. What if she was pregnant with me in this picture? I guess there's only one way to find out. I know where I'm going to visit this weekend.

Jethro, whoever you are, you're about to be in for the shock of your life.

CHAPTER THREE

RING

What a crap-tastic morning. It's eight a.m. on a Sunday morning and I'm getting ready to pull fucking guard shack gate duty. I haven't had to do this since I was a Prospect, and I don't miss it one bit.

Last night, the club celebrated Duchess's birthday and it was one hell of a kickass party. But because of the giant ass mess everyone made, both inside and out back, all the Prospects will be busy cleaning up all day. That means I drew the short stick and get to sit in the shack and watch the gate until they're done. If I see them lollygaggin' and dickin' around, I'm bound to whoop some Prospect ass.

I slide on my cut, throw my backpack over one shoulder, shut my bedroom door, and head downstairs. I swing through the kitchen to grab a few leftover cupcakes and my morning dose of caffeine. Everyone gives me shit because I don't drink coffee.

That's right, I hate coffee. I start every day with a twenty-ounce bottle of Mountain Dew. And if I don't get it, I'm such a bear, I don't even like dealing with myself.

"Morning, early bird." This comes from Hammer as he walks in the kitchen.

"What you doin' up this early? I would've thought you'd still be passed out with your woman." That earns me a punch to the arm so hard, I almost drop my cupcake.

"Don't even get me started with that shit. You know she's still not givin' me the time of day," he grumbles as he ducks into the pantry. When Hammer pops back out, he's digging into a box of Cheerios.

"Still? It looked like you were having a decent conversation when I went up to bed." Knowing I had an early morning, I ducked out when things were still in full swing.

"Ha! You musta just missed the fireworks." He heads for the coffeemaker and drops in one of those fancy ass pods, then pushes the button. The damn thing lights up like a fucking spaceship. "Wings and I were talking just fine until Jewel decided to be her usual skanky ass self and started rubbing all up on me. I pushed Jewel back on her ass, but it didn't matter to Wings. She started going off on me about how I'm a player and a manwhore and I'm not worth her time. She stormed to her room and wouldn't let me in to talk."

Damn. That woman's got one hell of a temper. "I'm sorry, man. Maybe try again today?"

"Nah, I think I just need to back off her for a bit. Nothing I've done so far has worked. I'm gonna go out to the shop and bury myself in that rebuild I'm working on." The coffeemaker dings and he grabs the tumbler. "What're you up so early for? I thought the Prospects were on clean-up duty?"

"They are, and that's why I'm up. Whiskey asked me to do guard shack duty 'til they're done. He asked, so here I am. Back on pissant duty."

"Shit. There could be worse things. I'd rather be sitting out there by myself than picking up all the trash in the backyard." That gets us both laughing.

He's got a point though. I don't miss cleaning up after all these messy ass bikers. Some of them can be standing next to a garbage can and still drop their shit on the ground, just because they know the Prospects will have to clean it up.

Prospecting for the Rebel Vipers MC is no walk in the park. My worst day as a Prospect was when I was forced to climb inside the compactor across the road, at the recycling center owned by the club. I had to use the pressure washer to clean all the grease and grime inside until the machine sparkled. By the time Mountain said I was done, I think the machine was cleaner than the day it was installed. And I smelled like a rusty can for a whole week afterward. Receiving my member patch was the happiest day of my life!

"Alright, I gotta get out there. Later." We bump fists and I head out.

I make my way across the parking lot and see Tiny kicked back in the shack. He's got his feet propped against the wall and he's playing on his phone. Time to have some fun.

Slowing down my steps, I walk to the wall adjacent to the door, lift my boot, and kick the wall as hard as I can. Well, not really as hard as I can. Don't need to be busting any siding today because I'd be the one stuck fixing it.

WHAM! CRASH! "Holy fucking shit!" And I lose it. I'm laughing so damn hard, I almost fall over. "Hey, asshole. What'd you do that for?"

"You were more into your phone than you were watching the road. Thought I'd give you a wake-up call." I give him a shove on the shoulder, and he pushes right back.

"I was watching the road just fine. I got a text from Whiskey, said to stay here 'til you came out." He goes into the shack and comes back out with a backpack. "See ya later. Don't have too much fun out here. It's been a quiet night." And he's off.

I yell at him as he jogs away, "Don't fuckin' jinx me, Brother. I was hoping for an easy day." I toss my backpack into the shack and sit in the open doorway.

What's with the backpack? Lemme tell you, it doesn't take people long to realize that ninety-nine percent of your time sitting out here is spent doing absolutely nothing. You sit on your ass and twiddle your thumbs. Unless you have to open the gate to let someone in or out, you're bored, so the smart ones bring stuff to do to occupy their time.

Some guys bring books to read, some will do crossword puzzles, and Tiny . . . well, Tiny likes to crotchet. He's been a member for almost as long as I have and he's one of the biggest, burliest, meanest guys ever. But don't ever make fun of his crocheting. He'll whoop your ass from here to kingdom come. His granny taught him how and he doesn't care who knows it.

Personally, I like sudoku. I also brought my laptop out so I could answer some emails for the brewery. If I get some stuff done today, it's less I'll have to do in the morning when I get into my office. I'd rather spend time on the production floor than cooped up behind my desk.

It's a quiet morning and after I finish my emails, I tuck my laptop away and step outside to stretch my legs. That's another shitty thing about this duty—I hate sitting for long periods of time. I'm used to being on the move and I hate when my ass falls asleep. Sliding my sunglasses down over my eyes, I stretch my arms up over my head, cracking my back and instantly feeling ten times better.

It's almost noon and there's only been a handful of vehicles that have driven past. I'm liking the peace and quiet, though I may have spoken too soon.

I step outside the opening in the fence and see a white minivan come flying around the curve. It slams on the brakes and comes to a screeching halt. Damn. Sounds like they need to have their brakes replaced, and soon.

The van is still stopped in the middle of the road and I can just barely make out that it's a woman sitting in the driver's seat. It starts to roll forward slowly and turns left into the driveway. This isn't a familiar vehicle, so my radar immediately kicks in. Glancing around the area, I don't see anything out of place.

Once she's parked, I start walking toward her, circling the van from the back. I try to look through the back windows, but the tint makes it hard to see. I snap a picture of the license plate and send it to our club tech-wizard, Cypher. Finishing my circle, I get to the driver's door and knock a knuckle on the glass. It immediately rolls down, and I drop my hands onto the window sill and lower my head to get a good look at my visitor.

Hot damn! She's drop dead gorgeous. She has chin-length, wavy blonde hair, and her eyes are a crazy swirl of green and brown. They look like a tornado of colors.

Neither of us have said a single word, but I notice that she's staring at my hands. Most people do when they see all my tattoos. There's not much of my skin that isn't covered in ink. I wonder if this pretty little lady has any ink for me to find. *What the hell?* I need to get with the program here.

I cough to get her attention and she snaps her head up, almost like she wasn't aware she was staring. "Can I help ya, darlin'?"

CHAPTER FOUR

PENELOPE

I got a later start today than I planned, but life sometimes has a funny way of doing that. I know I set my alarm last night, but it never went off.

I hustle to get my ass moving and get dressed in record time. It's a surprisingly nice spring day for the beginning of April, so I walk out the door in black sparkly leggings, a Badgers hoodie, and my black Adidas. No reason to get dressed up to go to a place I doubt has a fancy dress code.

The drive itself is actually really nice. The trees are starting to bud and spring has officially sprung. March came in like a lion, but it sure left like a lamb.

I drive around a curve and what I see to my left makes me slam on the brakes. The height of the chain link fence, topped with barbed wire, shocks me. I'm going to go out on a limb and say this is the place I was hoping to find. The Rebel Repairs sign to the left is another indication that I'm at the right place.

Realizing I'm stopped in the middle of the road, I look around to find a place to park. I see a very tall man appear in the driveway just ahead, standing next to a small building of some sort that is set back into the fence line.

I look him up and down and notice he's completely dressed in black. His boots, jeans, t-shirt, leather vest, sunglasses, and even his hair is black. Another thing I notice right away is he's covered in tattoos from his neck down to his knuckles. I'm not close enough to see any detail, but every bit of skin I can see has something inked on it. I wonder if they continue under all his clothes.

Penelope, I scold myself, *now is not the time for those thoughts. You're here for a reason, and it's not to ogle this man.*

I lift off the brake and turn left into the driveway approach. There's enough room for my van to be off the road, but I can't pull ahead too far because of the closed gate.

When I get the van in park, the guy starts walking toward me. He walks all the way around my van before knocking on my driver's side window. I hit the button to lower it and he drops his giant paws on the window sill. Now, I can see the details of his ink a lot better.

The guy coughs, and when I look up at his face, I'm struck stupid again. Holy shit is he hot!

"Can I help ya, darlin'?" That snaps me out of it.

"What's your name?" I squeak out.

"Ring," he says, pointing to his chest. Sure enough, it's embroidered on his vest.

"I need to talk to someone in charge."

"Why's that? I can't just let anyone in here. You may be very pretty, but that's not enough sometimes." He finally breaks into a half-smile and chuckles.

Oh . . . he's trying to be flirty with me.

I pull the picture of my mother from my purse and hold it out to him. He grabs it, looks at it, and walks away. "Wait!" I open the door and get out to chase him down. "You can't take that."

He stops at the hood and pulls a phone from his pocket. "Whiskey. You need to get out here . . . No, I can't describe it if I tried . . . Okay." And he hangs up but is still staring at the picture in his hand.

I walk around him and get as close to him as I dare. "Give me that," I snap and yank it from his hand. We're now locked in a silent stare off, neither of us moving.

"What the fuck is so important that you make me leave my sick pregnant Old Lady?" This bark comes from another guy wearing a leather vest, but his is over a white t-shirt. The vest says 'Whiskey' and that he's the President. I'm not exactly sure what that means, but I'm guessing he's the one in charge.

"I'm looking for someone."

"Who's that?" he asks.

"This guy." I hand him the picture and his eyes about pop out of his head.

"Where'd you get this? Who's this woman?" He points at the photo, his demeanor not happy or friendly.

"I need to know where he is." I'm not telling him anything until he gives me the information I need. I know it's not rational, but I don't care.

"He's not here unless you tell me what the fuck is going on in this picture," the man named Whiskey roars in my face.

"Well," I take a deep breath, "I need to know where he is because I think that man is my father."

"He can't be your father!" The tall blonde man yells, running his hand through his long hair. He pulls a ponytail holder out of his pocket and ties half of it up.

"Why not?" I throw back.

He shoves the picture back in my face. "Because this man is my Pops."

Shit on a shingle. Could I have a brother? I never even thought of that.

"Let me ask one more time, before I boot your ass off my compound. Who's this woman?"

I yank the picture back. "She's my mother. She died and left me a letter saying that this man is my father!"

The gasp that comes out of both men would've sucked the air out of a room if we were indoors.

"I'm sorry to hear about your mom," the guy in all black says with what I can tell is empathy.

"Thank you" is all I can say back.

"Are you sure?" the blonde one questions. His attitude went from grouchy bear to quiet tiger. Still dangerous but gentle for the time being.

"Honestly, your guess is as good as mine. Like I said, I just found out myself this week. I grew up not knowing who my father was and this is the only explanation my mom left me. I recognized the patches on the other guy's vest, in the picture, and decided to come here and give it a shot. I hope I'm in the right place." I try to keep my eyes on this guy, but there's something about him that's eerie. Not in a scary way anymore, but in a connected way, like we should know each other.

"Oh, you're in the right place. I'm just not sure how you being here is gonna go down. If what you're saying is true, and we have the same Pops, he's gonna blow a damn gasket."

"Why? Maybe I should just leave then. I don't need to be around someone who doesn't want me here." I go to turn away, but what he says next stops me in my tracks.

"Hell no, you can't leave. You've got a niece or nephew coming soon and I want you to be here to meet the baby." He tucks his hands in his pockets and rocks back on his boots. "Please?"

"Yea, we're all family here. What's one more?" Ring chuckles.

Well, shit, I didn't know bikers had such manners. I look between both men, trying to gauge if they're being sincere. "What's your name?" I ask the one who says he's my brother.

"Road name's Whiskey," he taps on his vest like Ring did earlier, "but my real name is Connor Hill." He holds his hand out and I shake it. Then he pulls me in for a hug, and I stand there, frozen.

Hugging? Can I hug a stranger? He doesn't seem to be in a hurry to let go, so I wrap my arms around his back and squeeze. He's probably a good foot taller than me, and a lot bulkier, so my arms don't even reach all the way around his waist.

With my head turned to the side, I see the other giant of a man smiling at us. Damn, it makes him even hotter.

Whiskey finally lets me go. "Shoot, I didn't even ask your name." That breaks the tension again and all three of us laugh out loud.

I wipe a few tears that escaped and meet his eyes. "I'm Penelope Jet Thompson, and I live in Henderson."

"Jet?" Ring looks shocked. "Your middle name is Jet?"

"Yea, why? I know it's different, but I like it."

Whiskey pulls his phone out of his vest pocket, taps on the screen a few times, and raises it to his ear. "If your mom gave you that middle name, you're definitely my sister."

"Why?" I ask again.

"Hey, Pops . . . Yea, Ring and I are out front and need you to come outside . . . Okay, five minutes." He looks at Ring and nods.

"Why don't you hop back in your van and pull it inside the fence, drive up to the right and park by the light pole." He points through the fence toward the big building which I'm guessing is their clubhouse.

"If I go in there, will someone answer my damn question?"

"Everything will make sense once you get inside. I promise." The man called Ring grabs my hand and walks me to my door, then pulls it open for me to hop in. I pull it shut as he jogs over to the little shack and steps inside.

The fence slides open just wide enough for me to drive through. I pull ahead, park at the end of a row of what looks like all Harleys, and shut off my van. I sit there for a minute, just taking in the line of bikes and the way the sun makes all the chrome shine.

I notice some movement on the porch in front of me, so I look up and see an older version of the man in my mom's picture. What's in the water out here? Are all the men this big and burly?

I grab my cell phone and the picture and get out of the van.

"What's goin' on out here?" the man in front of me asks, looking between me and Whiskey.

"Pops," Whiskey starts, "This is Penelope. She has something she needs to show you."

"Hi there," he replies. Turning my way, he crosses his arms and stares down at me. "Whatchya got for me?"

Glancing down at the picture, I take a deep breath, then finally get the courage to speak. "My mom left me this. I think this is you." I look up and hold the picture out to him.

He takes it in one hand and staggers back, almost losing his footing. Whiskey rushes to his side and grabs his other arm.

"Careful there, Pops."

"Where'd you get this?" The man has his attention zeroed in on me.

"Like Whiskey said, my name is Penelope." I rub my hands together, unsure of what to do with them. "I found it in an old shoebox that my mom had hidden. I grew up not knowing who my dad was, but based on that picture, I'm thinking it might be you."

I watch as this behemoth of a man flickers his eyes from the picture, then to me, back and forth several times. He tucks the picture in the front pocket of his vest and closes his eyes.

My legs are shaking like a newborn calf. I have no clue what's going through his mind. I look to Whiskey and Ring, but they both shrug.

Taking a deep breath, I push up my sleeves and prepare for battle. "If this is too much for you, sir, I'll just go. I'll leave if you don't want me here."

I don't even make it one step back when I'm scooped up in another suffocating hug. This time, my feet even leave the ground.

"Holy crap on a cracker. You look exactly like your mother." He sets me down and drops his hands onto my shoulders. "What's your name, sweetheart?"

Looking into his eyes, ones that look a lot like mine, I know he's my dad immediately.

"Penelope Jet Thompson."

"She gave you my name," he whispers, almost like he didn't mean to say it out loud.

"Your name?" That must have been what the guys were referring to.

"My club name is Mountain, but your mom said it was silly. She wanted to know my real name, and when I told her it was Jethro, she laughed in my face, sayin' that was even sillier. For the two months that I knew her, she called me Jet."

How did my mother end up pregnant after only knowing this man for two months? "You only knew her for two months? Is that when the picture was taken?"

Mountain's face drops. He pulls the picture back out and hands it back to me. "The day that picture was taken was the last time I saw her." He sounds sad when he says this.

"Were you together? Did you love her? Why'd you never see her again?" I have so many questions and this man is the only one with any answers. I hope he does, anyways.

"Oh, honey, we have so much to talk about."

CHAPTER FIVE

RING

I watch the van pull into the compound and am completely blown away. I said she was gorgeous before, but holy fucking shit. Seeing her up close, gorgeous doesn't even begin to explain what she is. She's a tiny ball of sunshine. When I walked her to her door, I had to grab her hand. It was like she called out to me, and my body instinctively responded.

"What the hell just happened?" Whiskey knocks me from my daze.

I hit the button to shut the gate and turn back around. He's standing in the parking lot, staring at her van as it parks. Only I know his staring and mine are for totally different reasons.

"I have no clue, man. That shit's crazy though. You've got a sister." And I'm going to lose my head if I'm not careful. It's going to take some planning if I want to get to know my President's sister as more than just his sister.

Wait a minute . . . I've known this chick for less than fifteen minutes. Do I want to know her that way? Hell fucking yes, I do. It may take some time, but eventually she'll be mine.

"Pops is gonna go ballistic. And what's Blue gonna say? Shit, Duchess is gonna be so excited. She and her baby hormones will eat this shit up with a spoon."

We're almost to the clubhouse when Mountain comes out the front door, approaches the van, and just stares. With the shade from the front overhang, he probably can see her through the windshield. Penelope gets out and walks toward him, almost like she's floating.

"He's not yelling, so that's a good sign," Whiskey chuckles.

"Not yet. Knowing him, he'll wait 'til she leaves, then the powder keg will blow."

Whiskey and I stand back as Penelope and Mountain introduce themselves. Whiskey rushes over to steady Mountain when he sees the picture, but steps back when all seems to be smoothed out.

After wrapping her in a tight hug and lifting her off her feet—something I'm instantly jealous of—he sets her back down and they keep talking. Penelope explains who she is, then Mountain tells her his real name. He doesn't share that with many people, so she's obviously special to him right away.

"Were you together? Did you love her? Why'd you never see her again?" Penelope's questions come out like bullets from a machine gun, fast and straight to the point.

Mountain smiles and shakes his head. "Oh, honey, we have so much to talk about."

"What's going on out here?" We all turn to see Blue and Duchess standing just outside the front door. They're both staring at Mountain and Penelope with a mix of confusion and anger.

"You should be inside resting, little momma. I left you on the couch for a reason." Whiskey wraps himself around Duchess like she's going to blow away. That man is pussy whipped.

"I'm perfectly fine and you know it. Now, don't try and butter me up. Your aunt asked you a question. Who's that girl all huddled up with your Pops?" She pushes him back and plants her hands on her hips. She may not have a kid yet, but she's got the mean mom stare down perfect.

"Well, um . . ." He can't seem to find the words. "She's my sister."

"SISTER!" both women yell.

Mountain loops his arm over Penelope's shoulder and leads her closer to us. If she could disappear through concrete, Penelope would melt right into the ground. She looks scared shitless.

"Blue, I'd like to introduce you to Penelope."

"Hello," Penelope waves to the ladies, but they just stand there, staring at her like she's got two heads.

Mountain drops his arm and slides up next to his wife. "It seems that a few years after Roxy left, I went and made myself another kiddo. Didn't know she existed until five minutes ago, but she's here now, and I want you to make her feel welcome."

He's trying to sound gentle, but I think that was the wrong thing to say, because Blue explodes.

"What in this world makes you think that I wouldn't welcome and love on another one of your children? I think I've done a pretty damn good job of it for the last twenty years, haven't I?" she barks.

And this is where the mountain crumbles into an anthill. "Yes, you have, and you know I love you for it. It's just that this is different."

The steam rolling out of Blue's ears is enough to power a locomotive.

"Well, no kidding, you big idiot. She's a grown ass woman and I won't have to ground her like I did your crazy ass son."

"Hey! I take offense to that," Whiskey butts in.

"Shut up," Duchess snaps, "and don't talk back to your aunt." Pregnancy hormones and standing up for woman power. No, thanks.

I pull off my sunglasses and tuck them in the collar of my t-shirt. I scoot around a few of the bikes to get up on the covered porch next to Penelope. Her body language is screaming that she needs some support, so I tuck her into my side. Her shoulders are bunched up and tight, and she's got her fingers tied into knots.

I can tell the argument going on in front of her is getting to be too much, but I'm holding her to be a little selfish, too. I want to be the one she leans on. She grabs hold of my cut and clutches it so tight, her knuckles turn white.

"Guys, hold up. Let's not do this this way. Let's go inside and talk in the office? I'm sure everyone has questions, but the yelling needs to stop," Duchess pipes up like the kickass President's Old Lady she is and takes charge.

The rest of the group heads inside and I'm left standing with Penelope. "Come on, I'll take you in and let you get to know your family."

I open the screen door and she tugs on my cut again. "Can you come with? Please?" She looks around the main room and her eyes bug out. "I don't know if I can do this."

"Yes, you can. You were brave and came all this way. I'll stay by your side if that's what you want." If I thought convincing Whiskey to let me get to know his sister would be tough, it looks like I'll have a mountain to blast through now, too.

But if Penelope wants me by her side during all this, I'm more than willing to take whatever my Brothers throw at me. I'm not going anywhere.

CHAPTER SIX

PENELOPE

I stay tight to Ring's side as he leads me through this big, open room, and I look around in awe at the amount of space. It's ginormous. There's a couple pool tables to the left, a long bar in the middle, a whole bunch of couches in front of a television the size of my living room wall, and some cafeteria style tables along the side wall. And the people . . . it looks like I'm inside that biker show that everyone loves to watch. I guess I am in a way, just no characters here. These guys are the real deal.

We head to the right and down a hallway. When we get almost to the end, I see an open door to the right.

"Whiskey's our club President and this is office," Ring explains, pointing at the open door.

"Sounds like I've got a lot to learn." I try to laugh, an attempt to break the tension, but it comes out more like a wheeze.

Ring squeezes my shoulder. "I've got ya. Anything you don't get answers to in there, I'm more than happy to help with."

"Thanks." I duck my head and untangle myself from his arm before walking into the office. I take one step in and all the talking stops. Everyone just stares at me. Maybe coming here wasn't such a good idea.

"Well, since everyone's decided to play mute, let me break the ice and introduce myself," a tiny redhead says as she marches toward me. "My name's Kiana, but everyone calls me Duchess. That big lug over there," she throws a thumb over her shoulder, pointing at Whiskey, "is my Old Man. I'm currently a few months pregnant, so I guess that means you're gonna be an aunt." She's a little spitfire. I think we'll get along just fine.

"It's nice to meet you. Thank you for inviting me in." I hold out my hand, intending on a handshake, but just like everyone else, she grabs for me and wraps me in a hug.

"No handshakes allowed here. We're a hugging family, so get used to it." She lets me go and leads me to a chair in front of a giant wood desk, then she sits in the chair next to me. "That lady over there," she nods to another tiny woman standing just to our left, "is Mountain's wife and Old Lady, Blue. She's also Whiskey's aunt from his mother's side, but I'm sure that'll all be explained here shortly. And you know the two giant behemoths behind the desk are Mountain and Whiskey. Don't let their size or angry mugs fool you—on the inside, they're squishy teddy bears."

"I'll be the first to admit this is super crazy. I only found out about having a dad this past week." I turn my head and see that Ring has placed himself in front of the now closed door, directly behind my chair.

"Ring, you can head out now if you want," Whiskey offers as he drops down into his chair.

"I'm good right here. She asked me to stay, so I stay." He's got his arms crossed and one boot kicked over the other.

"Whatever. Everyone staying, pick a seat. I think we're gonna be here for a while."

Mountain and Blue drop onto the couch against the left wall.

"Why don't you start with whatever you feel comfortable telling us? Whatever blanks need to be filled in, I'm sure Pops can try to help." Whiskey leans back in his chair, hands folded on his chest.

Here goes nothing. Or maybe everything. There's no going back now. "Well, like I said before, my mom just passed away—"

"Wait! Sandy's dead?" Mountain leans forward, dropping his elbows to his knees.

"Yea. I told Whiskey that when I got here." I look around the room.

"Sorry, Pops. I musta missed that when I called you. I was too shocked with the new sister thing," Whiskey states. Can't say I blame him. This is a lot.

"It's okay. Can you tell me how she died?" Mountain asks.

"She had cancer for just over two years. It started when she had an abnormal mammogram, but then they discovered it had metastasized into her lungs and liver. The doctors said she could try to fight it, but her chances weren't good. I tried to convince her to fight, but her mind was set on going out her own way. She started a pain management regiment and lived for twenty-six more months, which was longer than the doctors said." I feel my tears start to form, so I stop talking and close my eyes.

I feel someone grab my right hand, so I squeeze tight. I look and see Ring has moved another chair to sit at my side. I try to give him a smile, and he squeezes my hand back.

"I'm so sorry to hear about your mom." Duchess whispers. I turn to her and she's got tears rolling down her cheeks. "My parents died when I was a teenager, so I totally feel your pain. If you ever need to talk, I'm here. Okay?"

"Thank you." This time, I get up and wrap her in a hug. She's still sitting, but I can tell she needs it.

"Sheesh. Totally not where I thought today was going. I half expected to be in a cat fight when I saw this pretty young thing all hugged up with my man." This comes from Blue, and her humor sends the rest of us into full-out laughter. I even think I hear Duchess snort. Glad to know I'm not the only one with that silly habit.

"Do you still have that picture, Penelope? I think Pops should see it," Whiskey asks.

"I already saw it, son. That picture was taken the last day I saw Sandy. We went to the county fair with a whole bunch of people. We'd just gotten off the Ferris wheel when she whipped a camera out of her purse and forced Brick to take our picture. She said she wanted to remember that day forever. I guess now I realize why. I never saw her again after that day." Blue kneels up on the couch and wraps her arms around his shoulders. His arms are stuck under hers, but he leans his head into hers, showing her his appreciation. They really are in love.

"She moved to Milwaukee to go to college, so my guess is that's why you never saw her again. I was born there, and we didn't move back to Henderson until I was five," I offer.

"And you're how old now?" Mountain asks.

"Twenty-six."

This gets his hackles all drawn up. "You mean to tell me you've been this close for over twenty years and she never told me about you? What the hell was she thinking? This is bullshit!" Every sentence gets angrier and louder.

"In her letter, she said she was scared that your life was a bit unorthodox. She didn't realize she was pregnant until after she left and when she was going to tell you, she chickened out. But she encouraged me to find you and hopefully get to know you."

"I guess I can't be too mad at her for that, but I can say I'm still furious about everything else. I would've given anything to know about you when you were growing up." Mountain and I lock eyes. "I promise you, I would've done right by you."

"I don't blame you one bit. I asked her so many times who you were, but she always shut me down. I'm not very happy with her myself at the moment."

"If you didn't know who your dad was, how did you end up here at the clubhouse?" Duchess questions.

"I saw the patches on the vest in the picture and recognized the club name. I couldn't read the name on the front of his vest, but the giant skull and snake was hard to miss."

Mountain stands up and walks toward me. "I'm sorry. I need to get some fresh air." He drops a kiss on my head and he's out the door.

The room is silent. I think it's time for me to go too, so I get up. "I need to leave too. I need some time. This is too much."

Whiskey jumps up and comes around the desk. "Can I have your number before you leave? I'd like to have a way to get ahold of you. I don't wanna lose you now."

I pull my phone out of my pocket and wake up the screen. "That'd be fine. I can maybe call, so I just don't randomly show up at your gate next time."

Blue laughs at that. "That's how I got roped in to being here. I showed up and never left."

"Me too." This is from Duchess.

Whiskey grabs my phone and starts tapping away. I hear a ding from somewhere, so I'm guessing he sent himself a text. "Here ya go. You're welcome anytime. No need to call ahead. I'll give your info to the Prospects who watch the gate and they'll let you in."

I'm still astonished by what the ladies said about showing up here. "Really? You never left?"

"Oh honey, you've got a lot to learn about these men. They're a different breed around here." Duchess loops her arm through mine and leads me toward the door.

I look back and see Ring is still sitting in his chair. He's got a smirk on his face and he winks at me. Before I can stop her to say goodbye, Duchess has me out the door and halfway down the hall.

"Would you be able to come back next weekend? We're having my gender reveal party on Sunday, and now that you're family, I'd love for you to come," Duchess says as we walk outside. "Then you can meet more members of the club, who are basically family too."

"Are you sure? Will Mountain want me here?" He got up and left the room so fast, I don't want to come back and step on his toes.

"I'm one hundred percent sure. Mountain has had a rough last couple years." We get to my van and stand next to it. "I don't know if you noticed he has a little bit of a wobble in his walk?"

"I guess I didn't look close enough to tell." I wonder what happened.

"Now, this happened before I got here, so my details may not be exact, but a little over a year ago, he was in a motorcycle accident. He had to have surgery because his leg was crushed, so they removed it from just above the knee. He wears a prosthesis most of the time, but occasionally you'll see him rolling around in a wheelchair." That makes her giggle. "That's mostly when Blue makes him, because she can tell when his leg's bothering him, and he's being pigheaded."

Stubborn? I know that emotion very well. "Looks like I got one thing from him then. I'm as stubborn as they come."

"Ha! Stubborn should be both Mountain and Whiskey's middle names." Duchess and I laugh together.

If nothing else, I know I'm going to like being friends with this one. She handles these guys like a pro.

CHAPTER SEVEN

STEEL

I'm counting down the days. I know it's probably not the smartest thing to do, because things around here can go to hell in a handbasket real fucking quick, but I met with my lawyer yesterday and got my release day signed on paper.

Two weeks.

Fourteen days.

Three hundred thirty-six hours . . . give or take.

When I get back to the clubhouse, I'm looking forward to drinking beer, eating real food, and fucking as many club girls as I can. And in that exact order. Beer, food, and pussy for at least two whole days. I think I deserve that much for having to live in this cement shithole for the last two years.

Yes, I know it's technically my fault that I'm here, but that also means I get to say what I do when I get back out.

Two years ago, when I took that gun out of Whiskey's hand, I never thought things would go this far.

Whiskey and I are cruising down the highway in his truck, heading home from a meeting with our gun buyer in Chicago. We aren't even hauling any merchandise on this trip. It was just supposed to be a simple one-day, there and back. We're maybe twenty minutes from home when our mirrors start swirling with red and blue lights.

Whiskey moves over to the right lane and the lights follow us.

"Shit. He's coming for us," Whiskey grumbles.

"Looks like it." As we pull over, I look back and see a sheriff's Explorer stop right behind us. "At least it's our county. Maybe it'll be someone we know."

"At least this wasn't a full run, otherwise we'd be up shit's creek without a paddle."

"Do you have your handgun on you, or is it in the lockbox?" I turn and doublecheck to see that the back seat is in its proper position and hiding the gun lockbox we have behind it. We may not be running guns right now, but we definitely aren't riding without protection. Even if it isn't in immediate reach.

"Fuck!" Whiskey throws the truck in park and tries to reach behind his back without moving too much. "I've got mine in the back of my jeans. If I get caught with that, I'm fucked. It's got the serial numbers filed off."

That's not good. I peek back again to make sure the deputy isn't headed our way yet. The coast is clear, but not for long. "Slide it out real slow and give it to me. We can't have you getting arrested for this."

"What? No way. You're the VP and shouldn't get caught with it either," Whiskey grits out.

I snap. "Don't fucking argue with me, Whiskey. Give me the damn gun. You're in line to be President soon and you can't lead the club from behind bars. Just give me the gun."

Hie eyes bug out, but he finally starts moving and gets the gun pulled from his waistband. He slides it across the center console, and I move my left arm behind my back, tucking it in my jeans.

Hopefully, we don't need to get out of the truck, but with cops, you never fucking know. They get one look at our cuts and a lawman who thinks he has something to prove will try anything he can to get us in cuffs. Ninety-nine percent of the time, our lawyer has us out within an hour, but one can never be too careful. I may be this club's Vice President, but in a situation like this, Whiskey's freedom is more important.

"Here he comes." Whiskey rolls down his window. "Can I help you, officer?"

"Do you know why I pulled you gentlemen over?" This guy looks like he got hit by the ugly train, and he sounds like a giant douche canoe. Gentlemen? What's that bull crap?

"Nope, can't say I do. Was I speeding?" Whiskey questions.

"Sir, we got a call from a concerned driver that a vehicle matching yours was driving erratically. I was behind you for a little bit and saw you swerve pretty fast to make a lane change, about a mile back. Is there a reason for that?"

Oh, for Pete's sake, this idiot is just out looking for trouble.

"I made a lane change to get around a slow driver, but I don't think it was anything too crazy. I apologize and promise to move slower next time." Whiskey's trying to answer nicely, but I can tell he's not liking this guy any more than I am.

"That may be, but can I see both of your licenses, registration, and insurance, please? Gotta do my job ya know. One can never be too careful these days." Yup, giant douche canoe.

We pull out our wallets and Whiskey hands everything to the deputy.

"I'll be right back. Don't be driving off now." He taps the door and walks back to his vehicle.

"What a fucking idiot," I mutter.

"No shit. Driving erratically, my ass. He probably ran my plates and saw the opportunity to try and be a big dog. Fuck that."

"Calm down, Brother. We don't need him finding a reason to start something. Let's just wait to get our stuff back and we'll be home in no time."

Fifteen minutes pass by and the guy still hasn't returned. That's when I see the second SUV pull up behind us. Next thing we know, there are four deputies standing behind us with their guns drawn.

"What the hell is this?" I wonder out loud.

"No damn clue," Whiskey replies.

Then the intercom kicks in. "DRIVER, TURN OFF THE VEHICLE AND EXIT WITH YOUR HANDS UP. PASSENGER, SAME THING. OPEN YOUR DOOR AND LET ME SEE YOUR HANDS!"

Whiskey looks at me. "Here goes nothing."

"Catch ya on the flip side." We bump fists and get out of the truck.

I'm immediately pushed up against the truck bed and patted down. The deputy starts at my shoulders and pats down until I feel him hit the gun. Fuck! This isn't good.

"Well, well, what do we have here?" He lifts my cut and t-shirt, then pulls the gun from my waistband. "Looks like someone's carrying without a permit. Is this gun registered to you?"

"I invoke my right to remain silent." I ain't saying shit without my lawyer. This cop can kiss my ass.

My arms are wrenched behind my back and he snaps the handcuffs way too tight, but I don't say a word. I'm pushed into the back seat of the second SUV and the door slams shut. We sit there for another half-hour while they search Whiskey and the truck, but I know they won't find anything.

After twelve hours of interrogations, where suit after suit comes in to ask questions, and I don't say a word except to ask to see my lawyer alone.

But they make one big mistake before letting him in—they send an FBI agent into the room to ask more questions and he's not a happy camper. Agent Luke Emanuelle wants me out of here almost as bad as I do. He starts cussing up a storm about how the traffic stop was bogus and that we never should've been pulled from the truck. I almost like this guy for how pissed he is on my behalf, but the tides turn quick when he's pulled out because my lawyer gets here.

After ensuring that the cameras are off, and that we're really in private, I spill the beans to the lawyer. He's been on the club's retainer for almost ten years now, so he knows what we really do. He knows where we go and what we haul around, but we pay him enough to get us out of situations like this.

Unfortunately for me, being in possession of a firearm with a tampered serial number is a big no-no in the eyes of the law. And since I'll go to my grave with the knowledge that it was really Whiskey's gun, I make a deal with the state's attorney's office and admit that the gun was mine.

Carrying a handgun without a permit is normally just a misdemeanor and a fine, but when you add in the tampering, an unregistered firearm, and that we're in an MC, sometimes it's best to cut your losses and make a deal with the devil. I made my deal, so here I'm sitting, two years later, ready to get the fuck out and go home.

A few months into my two-year term, Luke Emanuelle came to visit me. Only when he got here, he informed me he was no longer an agent with the FBI. Apparently, he'd been having issues with the bureaucracy and red tape for a while, so not long after I went away, he quit. When I asked why he was visiting me, he said he wanted to know what it would take to join our club. I almost fell out of my chair from laughing so damn hard. When I saw the look on his face, and that he wasn't laughing with me, I realized he was dead serious.

After talking for a few hours, I gave him my blessing to go talk to Whiskey. When he left, I called the clubhouse and had to convince my Brother that I didn't have brain damage and was telling the truth. A few months later, I got word that the club had accepted Luke as a Prospect and things were going well. Now, two years later, Luke is a full patch member known by the road name Trooper. An ex-FBI agent in a motorcycle club . . . what a crazy, fucked-up world we live in.

I can't wait to see my Brothers, my baby girl, my mothers, Dad, and even my bratty little sister. Oh, did you catch that? Yes, I said mothers, as in plural. I come from what you'd call a unique relationship. My mother, Janie, who carried me for nine months, is bisexual. She and her wife, my other mother, Helen, wanted to have a baby, but since in vitro fertilization is so damn expensive, they went an alternative route to making a baby.

They found a male friend to "donate sperm" to them and he agreed. But don't ask me for the specifics because there are some things a person doesn't need to know about their parents. Then—wham, bam, thank you, sir—nine months later, I came into this world kicking and screaming.

I want to go home and get back to my unconventional, crazy, loud, awesome life. Fuck what I should or shouldn't do, my countdown starts now.

Thirteen days, twenty-three hours, and fifty-nine minutes . . .

CHAPTER EIGHT

RING

"Can that be included in my order from last week?"

"I'm gonna add it to your purchase sheet and leave a note for shipping to double check it's on the truck. Don't worry, Bill, you'll get your summer order in plenty of time. You know I'm good for my word." This isn't a customer I can afford to not bend over backward for. He was our first out-of-state customer to order beer from Moraine Craft Brewery when the guys first started it almost fifteen years ago.

"I know you are, Ring, and I appreciate it. We've got customers already asking for the summer brew, so I look forward to the delivery. And I'm sorry for calling you on a Saturday. Time got away from me this week."

"It's no problem. You have my number because we appreciate your business. I have to get going though. We've got a party to prepare for tomorrow, so I've got lots to do." It's more like if I don't get off this phone and finish loading the beer to take to the clubhouse, Whiskey's going to kick my ass.

"Alright, well, have a great party then. Talk soon."

"Have a good weekend, Bill. Bye." I hit the red button and slide my cell in my cut pocket, then it's back to loading the truck.

Tomorrow is Duchess's gender reveal party, so I'm loading a few extra kegs and cases to our usual order for the clubhouse bar. The pregnant lady may not be able to drink right now, and she's not very happy about that, but it doesn't mean the shit-ton of people coming can't indulge a little in her honor.

I stack a few cases of our leftover winter lager on the dolly and roll it across the shipping area and out the doors, loading it onto the refrigerated truck we use to deliver locally. Since we don't allow just anyone on the compound property, I took it upon myself to do the deliveries to the clubhouse.

Moraine Craft Brewery is a club-owned business, started by Mountain and Bear before I was in the club, but these days, it's my baby. I started working here after graduating high school, learning the ins and outs of making beer while getting my foot in the door at the club. I saw the other members who worked here and learned that it's more than just a club—it's a family. And as an eighteen-year-old kid who had just gotten himself booted from the foster home I'd been living in for the last year, I was in desperate need of family.

I don't consider myself someone who needs a family, because it's something I've never had, but being accepted by the club was what I wanted. I busted my ass at the brewery and proved myself as an asset to the club, and now, eight years later, I'm an Enforcer for the Rebel Vipers MC and the man in charge of the entire brewery.

I roll the last keg onto the truck and slide the door shut. After closing the garage door, I stop in the shipping office to leave the note I told Bill I'd pass along, then head down the hall and duck into my office to update the system to note everything I took for the clubhouse. Never thought I'd be the type of guy who sits behind a desk and completes spreadsheets, but it comes with the territory, I guess.

"Knock knock." I look up and see Hammer standing in the doorway.

"Hey, man. How'd you get out of the clubhouse? I thought every free hand was to be there to help set up for tomorrow?"

"Yea, I managed to piss off the party planner and get myself kicked out."

"Wings still won't give you the time of day, huh?" Poor guy. He's trying.

He drops into the chair in front of my desk and crosses one boot up on the other knee. "I asked her one simple question, 'Where do you want the gift table?' She exploded and told me to get the fuck out. Every time I think I get one step forward, she shoves me back to the starting line."

"Sorry to hear that, but what are you doing here then?"

"I figured I'd stop here and see if you needed help loading the beer for the clubhouse."

"You're about thirty minutes too late. I already finished, but thanks for the offer." Saving the form, I shut down my computer. "You can follow me back to the club and help unload the order though. Maybe if you look busy, Wings will see you're trying to be helpful. Can't hurt to try."

He pops out of the chair and heads straight for the door. "You got it, man. I'll follow you back." With that, he's gone. I guess it's time to get this show on the road.

I climb up into the truck's driver seat and make my way to the clubhouse.

I wonder if Penelope is there helping get stuff ready. I haven't seen her since the day she showed up, but it sure doesn't mean I haven't thought of her in the last week. A woman like her is not easily forgotten. I just wish I'd gotten her number before she left. She exchanged info with Whiskey, but I'm not going to push my luck and ask him for it. Duchess mentioned inviting her to the party tomorrow, so that'll be my chance to get some time with her.

Buzz buzz buzz! I feel my phone vibrating in my cut pocket. I hope it's not another work problem. I don't have time for that right now. I pull it out and see Sydney's name on the screen. Shit! What does she want?

"Hey, Sydney, what's up? Is Opal okay?"

"Yes, she's fine. I'm calling to see when you're coming to get the brat next weekend. I've got plans and need to know when you'll be here." Of course, she has plans. She doesn't care about anyone but herself.

"I wasn't planning on getting her until after Steel is home in two weeks."

"Two weeks? But I've got plans next weekend. Can't you come get her anyways?" Sydney's voice gets under my skin and on my nerves.

"Fine. You know I'll take her any time. When do you need me to pick her up?"

"Be here before five on Friday. Then you can drop her off at daycare on Monday."

"That's fine. Tell Opal I'll be there on Friday." I hang up and toss my phone onto the passenger seat. What a selfish bitch. If it weren't for Steel and my promise to him to watch over Opal, I'd be happy to never see that bitch ever fucking again. I love Opal like she's my own, but I wouldn't wish that woman as a mother on my worst enemy. And that's saying a lot coming from a guy who grew up without a mother.

When Steel gets back home and settled into life, I think we need to see what we can do to get Opal living with us full time. She loves being at the clubhouse and I'd be more than happy to help raise her. Steel's my best friend and I'd do anything for Opal.

As I pull up to the gate, it slides open and I drive through the clubhouse parking lot. Spinning the truck around, I back it along the right side of the building, then jump out and see Hammer drop the lift on the back.

"Thanks for the help, Brother." I throw him a fist bump.

"No problem. Anything to keep me busy and out of the main room," Hammer chuckles back.

"That's why I backed the truck up here on the side. We can roll everything through the back door and straight into the kitchen. No need to step foot in the main room."

"Smart man."

"Can't help that I'm smarter than you."

"Shut up, jackass. I don't see you trying to get a woman."

"I already met who I want. I'm just waiting for the right time," I toss out without thinking.

That stops Hammer in his tracks. "You found someone? Who is she? Please tell me it's not one of the other club girls. We don't need them running around thinking they're gonna take over. I can see some of the others trying to latch on to someone because of me trying to get with Wings."

"No, I'm not that stupid. But this might not be much better."

"Who the hell is she?" His eyes about pop out of his head when the answer hits. "No. Don't tell me you're gonna go after Whiskey's sister."

I rub the back of my neck and kick a tire on the beer dolly. "Yea, it's Penelope. She was only here for a few hours, but I couldn't leave her side."

"Dude, I don't know what you're thinking opening that can of worms. You're gonna have to deal with Whiskey *and* Mountain. Good luck with that." Hammer chuckles and shakes his head.

"I've told myself that a few times now. But I think she's worth it."

CHAPTER NINE

PENELOPE

I walk into the clubhouse and am blown away by what I see. The entire main room looks like a green and black bomb exploded inside. There are balloons, streamers, and paper lanterns hanging everywhere. Every table has a tablecloth draped over it, and everyone has either a green or black button pinned to their shirt.

Lost in taking everything in, I miss Duchess heading straight for me. "Oh my gosh. I'm glad you're here." She hugs me tight. "I need you to help me from murdering Whiskey. He's turned into a damn nuisance."

I hug her back. "Why's he being a nuisance?"

We pull apart and she drags me by the arm into what I now know is the kitchen. Dang, this room's huge. It looks like something you'd see in a fully functioning restaurant.

"Your big brother seems to think that because I'm pregnant, I can't do anything. *'Duchess, sit down.' 'Duchess, put your feet up.' 'Duchess, you need to rest for the baby.'* AAGH! He's gonna need to rest when I kick him and break his stupid leg." The look on her face when she imitates Whiskey is hilarious. She scrunches her eyebrows and crosses her arms, wagging her pointer finger like she's scolding a child.

"I'm sure he's just trying to be protective. This is your first kid, right?"

She walks to a stainless-steel refrigerator and uses both hands to pull the giant door open. "Yea, this is our first, but that doesn't give him an excuse to be clucking around like a mother hen. I can't even get up to pee without him standing outside the door, worrying if something's wrong." She grabs a couple bottles of water and pushes the door shut with her hip. Then she holds out one to me, and I grab it.

"Maybe he'll calm down when he realizes what's happening is normal. I've never been pregnant, so I don't know what you're going through, but I'm a nurse and have done quite a few rotations in OB and labor and delivery. Having a baby is one of the most natural things a woman does."

"You're a nurse? How come you didn't say that the other day?"

"Not sure there was a time in the conversation for it to come up. After high school, I went to tech school and got my associate degree. I became a registered nurse, then did some more online schooling to get my bachelor's degree. I worked at the hospital until my mom got sick. She needed around the clock care, so I stayed home with her."

"Dang. I know you said she died, but I didn't know you took care of her." Now, she looks sad. Shoot, that's not the emotion she needs to have today.

"Hey, no pouty faces allowed. Today's a happy day. If I promise that we'll talk more about missing our moms another day, will you please turn that frown upside down before someone comes in and thinks I'm being mean to you?"

That gets us both laughing. "Girl, the last thing I need is Whiskey thinking something's wrong. No more sad face, I promise."

"INCOMING!" someone yells out before the kitchen doors swing open and two women come barging into the room. One of them is carrying a big, white rectangle box. "Baby cupcakes coming through."

"It's about time you got here, Lynn. I was beginning to wonder if you were lost." Duchess helps the woman slide the box onto the island.

"I've been here for ten minutes already, but Angie wouldn't stop feeling up Whiskey's giant man muscles and unlock the van door to let me get the box." She rolls her eyes. "She honed in on your man and they're outside talking each other's ears off. I had to steal her purse to get the keys."

"That woman's bat-shit crazy. Penelope, this is one of my employees, Lynn. Lynn, this is Whiskey's sister that I told you about." Duchess points between us. "And this one in the corner is Stiletto. She's one of the club girls."

"Nice to meet you both. What's a club girl?" I ask.

"How do we describe that without making it sound horrible?" Duchess looks at Stiletto.

"Ha! I don't think there's a nice way to explain what I do here." Stiletto jumps up on a stool and turns my way. "Basically, being a club girl means I'm here for anything a member needs. Anything from cleaning to bedroom activities."

"You sleep with the members? Like all of them?" What kind of place is this?

"Oh goodness, no. I only do stuff with the men who are unattached. I don't mess around with men who have an Old Lady or girlfriend. Some of the other club girls do that nasty shit, but not me," Stiletto says with a straight face.

I turn to Duchess. "And you're okay with this?"

"Honestly, it's not my favorite thing, but it's the way things are done in this lifestyle. Every couple deals with things differently, and Whiskey and I have a no club girl agreement. He doesn't want to wake up missing any important body parts, and I'm more than happy with just him."

"Wow. That's crazy."

"If I was bold enough to be with someone in the club, I'd probably beat a bitch if she even looked at my man," Lynn growls.

Duchess laughs at her. "That's why you'd never be able to handle this life. You can come here to visit and look all you want, then you go home to your accountant husband."

"Hardy har-har. Stanley knows how to rock my world just fine, thank you very much," Lynn sasses and walks out of the kitchen.

Just as she disappears, another woman comes walking in. This one looks like she could be Duchess's twin. "There you are! Time to get this show on the road. Ring just got here with the target and the guys are setting it up in the backyard. Blue sent me to find you."

"Yay!" Duchess claps her hands. "Oh, Penelope, this is my little sister, Tempy. Everyone around here calls her Wings." She loops her arm through mine and leads me outside. "This is Whiskey's sister."

"Damn, you look a lot like him. That's crazy," Tempy says as she follows us.

When we step out on the back patio, I'm stunned again. Every new area of this clubhouse amazes me even more. This patio looks like a fairytale mixed with black leather and hot as hell men. "What's in the water out here?"

"I wondered that myself," Duchess giggles. "They don't make them small around here, that's for sure."

I swear, I don't think I've ever seen this many huge men together in my whole life. They all look like they swallowed a linebacker whole. It's muscle city out here.

Duchess is suddenly yanked from my side, and I turn to see her being kissed like her life depends on it. Whiskey handles her super gently, but they look like they need each other to breathe.

I catch myself staring, so I turn to give them as much privacy as they can get while standing outside. A yard full of fifty plus people isn't super private, but they don't seem to care. Looking out, I step off the patio and onto the grass.

"Hey there." I spin around again and see Ring coming out the back door. He sees the lovebirds now whispering to each other and chuckles. "Ignore them. Eventually, she'll get sick of his hovering and join the rest of us normal people."

"I think it's cute. A bit much for out in public, but still cute."

"What? You don't wanna be kissed like someone owns you? I think you'd like it if I did it." Ring steps super close to me, and I lift my head so I can keep looking in his face.

"You . . . you want to kiss me like that?" I'm dumbfounded.

He nods. "I wouldn't do it if you didn't want me to, but I'd very much like to kiss you."

I'm speechless. I stare up at him with nothing to say. My brain's still trying to catch up—who goes from saying hello, to saying he wants to kiss me? Duchess wasn't kidding when she said these men here are a different breed.

I drop my eyes and whisper, "Does that mean you'd want to own me too?" I don't think I can look at him when he laughs, telling me it was just a joke.

"The owning part can come later."

I lift my head so dang fast. "What does that mean?"

Ring runs his pointer finger down my forearm, and I follow it with my eyes. Goosebumps pop up and the tiny hairs stand on end. I feel my whole body tingle as he threads our fingers together. "It means that the second I'd kiss you, you'd be begging me to make you mine."

I think it's time to bring this conversation back down to Earth, since this isn't something I should be talking about with someone I barely know. "A little sure of yourself, aren't you? Maybe a little cocky?"

He lifts our linked hands, kissing my knuckles. "Not cocky. Though I've been told I've got a nice one of those." The smirk on his face is in full force. "It's just that when I see something I want, I don't stop 'til it's mine."

I pull my hand from his and wipe the sweat on the back of my neck. "Oh, boy."

I think he can feel my discomfort, so he changes the subject, thank goodness. "Let's go find you a spot for the show, then I have to go check the target one more time. Okay?"

I look where he's pointing and see a giant bullseye painted on a square sheet of plywood. It's way out in the grassy area, probably a couple hundred feet out. "Check it for what?"

"That's how we're gonna find the gender of your niece or nephew. I'll shoot it with my rifle, and it'll explode with either green or black powder. Green for a girl, black for a boy."

"Aren't they supposed to be pink or blue? I've seen stuff like this done in online videos, but never with green or black."

"Those are our club colors, so it was Whiskey's one request for this shindig." Ring snickers.

"I guess so." We walk toward a row of picnic tables and I see Mountain standing in the sea of leather and denim. He sees me and ducks out, heading our way.

"See you later." Ring winks and heads off as I walk toward Mountain, meeting him halfway.

"Hi, there." He gives me a quick hug. "I'm sorry I walked out like that the other day. I needed to get my head on straight before I said something I couldn't take back." He looks ashamed of himself and that's the last thing I want.

"Nothing to apologize for. I understand the need to act out. When I got home that day, I had a tiny pity party and broke a few plates."

That makes him laugh. "Sounds like you got my temper."

"I think I did. Mom never got mad at anything. I'd get upset, and she'd just wait me out." Shit. This isn't where I want to start crying.

"A few plates, huh? You should get Blue to tell you about the day Whiskey got his first speeding ticket. I broke every plate and bowl we had. Blue yelled at me as I swept up the mess, then she made me take her to the store and bought the most expensive set she could find."

"Sounds like something I'd do."

"I'm glad to know that you have a little of my spark. Makes things even better, if you ask me."

"I like it too," I agree and smile up at him.

Whistle! "EVERYONE PAY ATTENTION!" We turn to Whiskey standing on top of a picnic table and head that way. "Duchess and I would like to thank everyone for coming today to celebrate our little biker on the way. We decided to find out the sex by doing some crazy DNA test thing, so as soon as the results came in, Ring and Mountain took over."

I look at Mountain. "You know what it is, don't you?"

Winking, he mimes zipping his lips.

"Ring's gonna shoot that target down there and it'll explode with green for a girl or black for a boy." Whiskey climbs down and clutches Duchess's hand. He uses his free hand to lift her chin as he leans down to kiss her. So cute.

Ring appears from the crowd and sits down on the bench, behind a rifle set up on the table, then he looks around the group and finds me. He winks, and I smile back. "Give me a count down and let's see what this baby is," Ring shouts out.

The group starts to chant, "FIVE! FOUR! THREE! TWO! ONE!"

BANG! The target explodes in a cloud of black dust.

"IT'S A BOY!" Everyone cheers, and there's so much talking and congratulating, I'm not sure anyone can really understand what anyone else is saying.

Suddenly, I'm smushed in the middle of a Duchess and Blue hug. They start to jump, and I get wrapped up in the excitement, hopping right along with them.

"Woman, stop jumping like a damn kangaroo. You need to keep that baby inside you for five more months." Whiskey stomps up behind Duchess and pulls her away from us. "I can't leave you alone for one minute before you're getting yourself in trouble."

"I'm not doing anything wrong!" she snaps and walks away. Quickly, she stops, spinning back our way to face Whiskey. "If you think a little jumping's gonna hurt the baby, then no more sex for you. You shake me more with your dick than I did with those tiny hops."

"Oh, no, you don't. I won't stop loving on you 'til the doctor says so. Only then will I keep my hands off you." He places his hands on her sides, cupping her barely there, tiny bump with his giant hands.

Blue wraps an arm around my waist. "Let's let the love birds have their thousandth argument of the day. Would you mind helping me carry out some of the food? It's nice enough that we can eat outside."

"Lead the way." I wrap my arm around her, and we head inside.

"With a boy on the way, it'll be nice having you around. You help balance the number of men versus women we have around here," Blue tells me as we pull bowls and dishes out of the fridges.

"I'm happy to help boost the woman numbers. Seems like all the testosterone around here needs some lady vibes."

"I'll take all the estrogen backup I can get." Blue cracks me up.

CHAPTER TEN

PENELOPE

The party has been going for a couple hours now and I've met a lot of people. It'll take me forever to remember everyone's names, but they've been super welcoming. And some of these guys are an absolute hoot.

When I met Smoke, the club's newest patched Brother, he swept me off my feet . . . literally. He was sweeping up some chips he dropped and I wasn't watching where I was going. I tripped over Smoke's boot and he saved me from landing on my backside. The whole room started clapping when Smoke scooped me up and spun, like we were doing some sort of tango.

I met Kraken when I caught him sneaking gummy worms to some of the younger kids. I went into the kitchen to make popcorn, because the pregnant lady was craving some, and I found him digging in the pantry with three little tagalongs. I learned he's addicted to the gummies and carries a pack in his cut pocket at all times.

I've talked to Ring a few times and he keeps acting super flirty. Every time he gets close, he touches me one way or another. At one point, he slid his hand across my back when he walked past. Later, he ran his fingers down my arm when next to me at the bar.

Every time he touches me, my skin feels like it's alive. Should I be feeling like this? I've only been here twice now, and both times have been out of the ordinary situations.

I just found my father and surprise brother, and barely know anything about them past the basics. Should I really be thinking about a friend of theirs like this? Should I be wondering what it's like to take him up on his offer to kiss me like he owns me?

I'm starting to feel a bit overwhelmed by all these good family vibes floating around. I'm not used to being around this many people. My family was just my mom and aunt, and now, I've got an entire club of bikers accepting me in. It's a bit too much.

My hands are starting to get sweaty, and I can feel my heart beating fast. I look around and try to find an empty corner I can duck into and catch my breath.

Everywhere I look, there's a group of people, laughing, drinking, having a great time. I see a woman come out of the bathroom and realize that's my perfect escape. I weave my way around and duck into the bathroom, and as soon as I'm through the door, I lean against it and close my eyes. After a few deep breaths, I feel myself calm just a bit.

Realizing I might not be alone, I open my eyes to check my surroundings. The bathroom's painted a light green color. There are three stalls and a few sinks spaced out on a large vanity, with a mirror hanging above each. I'm not sure what I was expecting for a clubhouse bathroom, but this wasn't it. This definitely has a woman's touch.

I make a pitstop to take care of business, and just as I finish washing my hands, the door opens behind me. Ring pushes it open just enough to get through, then flips the lock behind him. He turns back my way as I toss the paper towel in the garbage.

"Crazy meeting you here." Ring winks, leaning back against the door.

The smirk he's got painted on his face flips a switch in my head and I lunge toward him. The instant attraction I feel for this man is too much. There's no use in holding back.

I throw my arms around his neck and kiss him like I need his air. I feel his hands grab the back of my thighs, and next thing I know, my feet leave the floor and I'm wrapping my legs around his waist, never stopping our kiss.

Ring takes a few steps and backs my ass up onto the countertop. With my arms still around his shoulders, he lets go of my legs and grabs hold of my head with both hands. His thumb nudges my chin, and I tilt up to deepen our kiss.

I open just a bit and use my tongue to tease the seam of his lips. He takes that as a green light and dives his tongue into my mouth. We fight each other for dominance, and I quickly realize who's in charge here . . . and it's not me.

His hands slide down to my shoulders and his lips follow their path. Ring kisses down my neck, and I shiver. He hits a magic spot I didn't know I had, and I let out a moan so desperate, even I can tell I liked it.

"You like that?" he growls, licking the same spot.

"Yes" is all I say.

"Let's see if we can find more spots like that." Ring pulls back, and I miss his mouth immediately.

Before I can ask him to come back, he grabs hold of my belt loops, pulling me off the counter. I'm back standing on my own, but not for long. His fingers make quick use of opening the button and zipper, then he spans his giant hands over my hips and slides the denim down my legs.

Ring stands up to his full height and spins me around. I slap my hands down and look up, facing the mirror, seeing his large form dwarfing me from behind. I'd known he was significantly larger than me but seeing us like this is so much more.

Keeping our gazes locked, he pushes my hips against the cold porcelain, and I let out a tiny squeak. He smirks at me. It's almost like I'm watching what's happening to me from an outsider's perspective. In my head, I know it's us, but seeing us in the mirror is like I'm a voyeur to someone else's private times.

His hands slide down my arms until they're covering my own, pinning them down. "Keep your hands right here," he whispers in my ear.

I nod, still watching our reflection.

Ring pulls his hands away, leaving me leaning forward on my own. His legs are bracketing mine, so I feel him shifting behind me. I'm essentially stuck in this spot.

He runs his fingertips down one of my butt cheeks, then suddenly has two handfuls of my flesh. The shock makes me jolt forward and I raise one hand to the mirror, stopping my head from hitting it.

"Did I say you could touch the mirror?" he barks, loudly.

"No, I—" I try to speak, but he interrupts me.

"I told you, hands on the counter. That's okay. We'll just skip ahead to the fun part."

He lets go of my ass and the grind of his zipper opening echoes throughout the room.

"Fun part?" I ask, turning my head to catch his eyes for real, not just in the mirror.

"Oh, yeah, this'll be fun for the both of us," Ring says as he toes off his boots. Once they're kicked off, he pushes the denim down and kicks them back.

I still have my head turned toward him, so I see the huge bulge barely being contained by his boxer briefs.

"Like what you see?"

"Uh-huh," I answer with no shame.

"Then you're really gonna like this." He grabs hold of the elastic band and pushes his briefs down his legs. When he stands back up, he's not the only thing at full attention.

Holy fucking shit is his cock huge.

"Well, thank you for the compliment." I turn my head to the mirror, and he raises an eyebrow at me. "Yup, you said that out loud."

Ring steps up behind me, so close I can feel his hardness slide along the crease of my backside. When his chest is flush with my back, I feel the weight of his erection press against my spine. He lifts my shirt over my head and drops it to the floor.

"Are you gonna take yours off?" I inquire. If he gets to see my goodies, I should get to see his.

"If you'd like." Ring slides his leather vest off and lays it on the counter, then he strips off his t-shirt and drops it on top of mine.

"Why'd you drop that but put your vest on the counter?"

"It's called a cut, and I guard that thing with my life. It doesn't touch the ground unless I'm still wearing it."

"Oh" is all I can get out before he leaps into action.

He threads his fingers into the string of my thong and pulls it until it snaps. I feel the material pull against my other side and the bite of it on my skin. Then he grabs the other side and does the same. This time, he pulls the material and it glides right off. Now, I'm standing here with no panties and my pants around my ankles.

Ring threads his hand up into my hair, basically holding the back of my skull, his other hand I can feel is wrapped around his member. He pushes it down to rub between my open legs. He rocks his hips forward and his cock slides against my tender parts. I hiss out at the feeling and close my eyes.

Ring pulls on my hair a bit harder, tilting my head to the left. "Open your eyes and look at me," he demands as he nips the side of my exposed neck.

I open them and am stunned. I've never seen myself like this before. I don't make a habit of standing in front of my bathroom mirror in only my bra, being manhandled by a dark, god-like man.

He's dark everywhere. I was right in guessing that he's covered in tattoos. The black lines start at the sides of his neck and flow down both of his shoulders, then meet in the middle to span his pecs. I can't see if there are any on his torso, but I'd bet there are.

Still looking in the mirror, I can see his biceps flex and it's almost like the pictures are moving. I can see some flashes of dark on his legs, but not enough to get any detail. My attention's about to be gone, though, because his hand slips around to my front and his fingers disappear into my folds.

"Just as I thought. You're soaked for me." He finds my hard clit and pinches it, causing my center to spasm. "I need inside you. Are you protected?"

"Yes. The pill," I moan.

Green light again and he thrusts forward, sliding his dick into my opening in one push.

"Shit!" I pant.

"God, you're hot and tight. Made just for me," he grunts out.

Not stopping his thrusts, Ring pushes my head forward and folds me in half. My arms slide out to the sides and I grab the edges of both sinks, holding on for dear life as Ring starts slamming into my opening like he's on a mission to find gold. Maybe he is.

His cock slides in and out of me, and my insides start to quiver. I feel an orgasm start, but I've never come this fast before. Not even by my own hand.

"I'm . . . gonna . . . come . . ." I try and say over the rush of air being pushed through me, since my chest is crushed to the counter.

"Fuckin' come for me," Ring yells. "Now!"

I explode and scream.

"Hold on, 'cause I'm not done." He keeps thrusting through my aftershocks, and I'm still pulsing between my legs. "That's it. Just like that. Keep squeezing my cock. Fuck yea."

I turn my head to the side and look up in the mirror. I can see him behind me this way. I think all his muscles are bulging at this point. He's looking down at where we're joined and pumping his hips into mine. His hands have a tight grip on my hips and he's using me like his personal toy.

Ring's eyes find me in the mirror. "You're gonna make me come with this tight pussy, aren't ya?"

I nod as best I can in this position, but my movements from his thrusts override my efforts.

CHAPTER ELEVEN

RING

Damn, her pussy is tight as fuck. Her body shakes and I know she's about to come again. And it's a good thing too because I can feel my legs start to tighten and a shiver runs up my spine. "Wanna come with me this time?"

"Oh, please," she begs.

"Here we go." If she thought I was fucking her hard already, she's sadly mistaken. I kick into overdrive, thrusting forward, over and over. Her pussy starts to squeeze, and before I can take a full breath, we're both coming. I hear her scream, but the sound that comes out of me echoes around the bathroom like a siren. It's a mix of a bear and a loud "fuuuuuuuckk" that I shout.

I pump a few more times before collapsing on top of Penelope. I slam my hands down next to her head, my chest heaving up and down, trying to catch my breath.

"Damn, woman. I can't wait to do that again," I groan.

Penelope freezes. She pushes up, knocking me back, and I double-step to avoid falling on my naked backside.

"What the hell?" I reach for her again.

She spins around and slaps my hand away. "No. Don't touch me."

"Whoa, there, little filly. What's wrong?" I ask.

Bending over to pull her jeans up, she tugs hard, ripping a belt loop. "Shit! These are my favorite pair."

I take a small step, afraid to spook her. "It's okay. I'll buy you another pair."

She gets her pants buttoned and zipped, then looks around the room again. She scoops up our shirts, throwing mine at me and I slip it on.

"I don't need you to buy me anything. I can pay for my own things," she mumbles through the material as she pulls hers on.

"Did I do something wrong? I thought you wanted this just as much as I did." I'm confused. What's happening here?

She stops turning and faces me head-on. "I do. I thought I did. I don't know." She keeps rambling. "This is just so much at once. First, my new giant family, then, all the emotions with missing my mom. You keep flirting with me and we've only known each other a week. Who tells someone they want to kiss you like they own you? I don't know which way is up." She runs her hands through her hair.

I understand the overwhelming feeling, but I need to know if she regrets this. I don't regret anything. Hell, I'm standing here half ass naked, dick hanging out, while she second guesses our tryst. "So, you regret fucking me? Is that what you're saying?"

Penelope meets my eyes. "I don't regret it. I just think this happened too fast. I came in here to go to the bathroom and you appeared. I don't know what came over me, but I need to go home."

I bend over and scoop up my underwear, step into them, then I slide my jeans on, leaving the front undone. I grab hold of her hands and pull her close. I bend down just a bit so we're eye to eye. "I want you to listen to me good. Okay?"

She nods.

"I regret nothing. What we did was meant to happen, and I hope it happens again. I get that you're freaking out but understand that I like you. I like you and would like to know you more. Do you understand?" I need her to understand that this isn't just a one-time thing.

"You like me, like me?" Her hazel eyes are wide open and sparkling, looking like she's shocked by my admission. That makes me smile. "Isn't it too soon? It's only been a week," she whispers.

"Things around here happen at warp speed sometimes. Fast in our world doesn't work the way it does out there. I don't wanna blink and miss whatever this is." I pull her close again and she snuggles into my chest. "I'm not asking you to be my Old Lady and wear my cut yet. I just wanna know you better, and hopefully, make it out alive when your father and brother find out about us."

"Crap!" She pulls back. "What are they gonna say about this? I can't have them mad at me. They're practically all I have left."

I drop a kiss on her head, then grab my cut from the counter, sliding it on. "We'll figure it out one day at a time. For now, let's get you out of here so you can go home, if you still hafta go." But she's got one thing right—I'll have to go about this very carefully.

"That's probably best. I need some peace and quiet."

"You get used to it after a while. Becomes just another thing," I tell her with a shrug. "Why don't you get going and I'll hide in here for a bit."

She nods. "Okay." She gets on her tippy toes and kisses my cheek. Before I get a chance to grab her back, she scoots around me and heads for the door. She looks back one more time before walking out.

"There you are!" I hear through the door. It sounds like Duchess is right outside.

While I bend over to put my boots back on, I lean against the door, listening for when the coast is clear.

"I got a little overwhelmed by all this and needed a break, so I locked myself in there to take a breather. I guess I lost track of time playing on my phone," Penelope explains.

Duchess laughs. "I've been there. Locked myself in our room just to get away from all the manly voices and crude language."

"Yea, that's probably it. Would you mind if I ducked out? I need to get home and be alone for a while."

"That's perfectly fine. How about I call you tomorrow and plan a time for you to visit during the week? Most everyone works and it'll be quieter."

"That sounds perfect."

"Good. I'll steal your number from Whiskey's phone and call you."

I don't hear them anymore, so I pull the door open just a crack. The girls aren't in front of the door anymore, so I know the coast is clear. Avoiding anyone who may have seen her come out before I did, I duck down the hall into the kitchen to grab some snacks and a few beers, then head up to my room for the night. I need the night to myself to figure out a plan for what to do next.

CHAPTER TWELVE

STEEL

END OF APRIL

Today's the day. The day I get to escape this fucking hellhole. And before you ask, no, I'm not exactly escaping per se. I've thought of doing that exact thing many times, but today's the day I get to turn in this hideous ass prison uniform, put on my street clothes, and walk out the front gates. I get to climb on my Harley Davidson and ride my ass back home. Back to the Rebel Vipers clubhouse to get my life back to normal, or as normal as my lifestyle can be.

"Colt James," the overhead speaker kicks in, "grab your things and head for the door."

I pick up my lone carboard box and walk out of my cell for the last time.

"See ya soon, Steel." Ray is standing outside of his cell, so I drop my box and hold my hand out. He accepts it, pulling me into an obligatory bro-hug, back slap combo. "It's not gonna be the same without you here."

We pull apart and I grab my box again. "You'll see me soon enough. Don't forget to bring the family and come see the club. I've no doubt you'll make a great Viper." I give him one last nod, then head down the stairs and straight for the first door on my journey out of this place.

I spend the next couple hours going through the release process. I sign a few forms and get my real clothes back, happy to see they still fit. My t-shirt is tight in the arms and chest, but that's a good thing—I bulked up a bit in the last two years. It would've been simple to take the easy road and get fat and lazy, but I used my spare time wisely. I did so many damn push-ups and sit-ups, even I think I look fucking good.

"Alright, Mr. James, this is where we say goodbye." This comes from the lady officer sitting behind the front desk. She was the first person I saw the day I was brought here, so it's fitting she's the last I see as I leave.

"No offense to you, ma'am, but I hope I never see you again."

That makes her laugh. "Right back at you. Have a good day, young man."

I don't feel that young, but I guess twenty-nine isn't exactly old either.

Buzz. The door unlocks and I push it open. Freedom.

Damn, it's bright out here. It's going to be a long ass ride home with the sun in my eyes the whole way.

Keeping my head down, I head for the final gate keeping me locked up. Another buzz goes off and the gate slides open.

"Brother!" I hear someone yell and I look up. Holy fuck! The parking lot is filled with black, chrome, leather, and what looks like the whole Rebel Vipers MC. I expected a few of my Brothers to be here, but the whole club? I'm a fucking lucky bastard to have a family like this.

Ring is the first to hustle toward me, so I drop my box again and practically pick him up when he jumps at me. "Did you miss me, lover boy?"

He slaps my back a few times and I let him down. "I missed you way too much for a straight man. Just don't be trying to kiss me, you freak. I don't need to know what you've been doing in there to keep yourself entertained."

That makes the whole group of my Brothers bust out laughing.

I make my way around, shaking hands and saying hi to everyone who rode all this way to see me.

There are a few guys who I notice are missing. "Where's Whiskey, Trooper, and Buzz? Am I missing anyone else?"

Mountain holds out his hand, and I shake it. "Buzz had to keep the shop open, but he'll be back by the time we get to the clubhouse. Whiskey stayed back because he's waiting for a call from Monty to set up the next pickup.

And Trooper pulled Enforcer duty to watch things while everyone was gone."

"Totally understandable. Life still goes on when I go get myself locked up," I chuckle.

"That it does, son. Alright, boys, time to load up and get the hell out of this shit-hole!" Mountain yells the last part.

Ring steps to the side, and I see my girl standing there, shining even brighter than the day I bought her. "Well, hello there, beautiful. I've missed you." I straddle the leather seat and reach up to grab the handlebars. "How'd you get my bike here?"

"Brewer rode it here and is riding back with Mountain in the van." Ring climbs on his bike and immediately starts fiddling with one of the saddle bags. "Here, bro."

I look over and see he's holding one of my black bandanas. "Thanks, Brother." I grab it, lay it across my tank, and fold it into a long strip before I wrap it around my forehead. Now I feel complete.

"LET'S RIDE!" Mountain hollers, then the ground starts to rumble.

One by one, bikes start to kick on. I turn the key, hit the start button, and my girl fires right up. The rumble vibrates through my body and I instantly feel at home. I look around at my Brothers and raise my right hand. Spinning a circle with my pointer finger in the air, everyone revs their engines. That's when we start to roll.

The ride to the clubhouse takes just over an hour, but it passes in a blur. I take in my surroundings, like I imagine a blind man would after getting his sight back. Everything I see is familiar but still different at the same time. I got locked up in March, and now it's April, so the time of year is the same, but it's still crazy. Crazy that I'm finally out of prison. I imagine it'll take me a little time to get used to the freedom.

It really sinks in that I'm free when I ride through the front gates of the compound. I've missed so much over the last two years and I can't wait to settle back in.

We roll through the lot and back our bikes into a row, right at the edge of the front porch. It almost looks like a damn parade of black and chrome. Everyone climbs off their bikes and head straight inside. I kick out my kickstand, but just sit back on my seat. I almost don't want to get off my bike.

"Steel." I look to my left and see Ring next to me, still on his bike as well. "You okay?"

I take a deep breath and look around the front yard. "I am now."

"Good. I'll give you a minute. See ya in Church." And he's gone.

I sit outside for a few minutes, just taking advantage of the quiet. I haven't heard anything this silent in quite a while. It's almost tranquil. The only sounds I hear are the birds chirping and my own breathing.

Finally, I stand up and swing my right leg back off my bike. I stretch, then head inside. I see a few women talking at the bar but pay them little mind. Instead, I head straight for Church and shut the door behind me.

The room goes silent as Whiskey stands up from the head of the table. "Aren't you a sight for sore eyes!" It's weird seeing him in that chair, but him being there just proves one thing—taking the fall for him and serving those two years was worth it. He wouldn't be where he is had he got locked up instead. Now, he's got himself an Old Lady and a little one on the way.

"Good to see you, Mr. President." That gets the volume kicked back to loud. Everyone laughs and I hug Whiskey. We separate and he turns back to the front of the table, grabbing something from the table and holding it out to me.

It's my cut. Hell yea!

I slide it on and tug the front, pulling it tight to my chest. Now everything is complete. Time to get down to business and find out what's been going on while I've been gone. Time to rejoin my Brothers and get back in the swing of being their VP.

I sit in my chair next to Whiskey, kick my feet out, and cross my ankles, taking everything in. I listen until it's my turn to share what I've been up to.

CHAPTER THIRTEEN

PENELOPE

"So, what's the story with him?" I ask the other girls as we watch the doors to the Church room shut. I didn't see the new guy's face because I just came out of the kitchen, but I saw his back as he crossed the room.

"That's Steel," Duchess answers. "I've never met him, but him going to prison was a crazy thing. He actually took the fall for Whiskey and never gave him up." She shakes her head, still staring at the closed door.

Tempy leans forward on her stool and reaches over the bar, grabbing a bottle of vodka. "Yea, it was crazy when it went down. The guys were in a constant uproar for months. One day, he and Whiskey went on a run, but only Whiskey came back."

Wow. "What happened? Why'd he take the fall for something Whiskey did?"

"He did it because he's the club's VP, and even though Whiskey wasn't President yet, he knew he would be soon. Steel took the fall to save Whiskey from spending time behind bars. That's just the kind of Brother he is," Tempy replied.

"I'm guessing that's a good thing, to protect the other Brothers?" I've been around a few times in the last month, but I've got a lot of things to learn about how the club works.

"It's one of the best things you can do for another Brother. Short of saving someone's life, taking the fall for them is right up there." This comes from Duchess. "I hate that he had to be gone for so long, but I owe him big time."

I spin my stool to face her. "What do you mean?"

"Had he not taken that gun from Whiskey, I never would've met him. I owe Steel one heck of a big hug, or maybe a million." She puts her hand on her barely visible bump and has a faraway look on her face. "I wouldn't have this little guy on the way. I came here to find my sister and found so much more."

"I can understand that." Much like mine, her life changed so much by coming here. This place seems to change lives.

"Not to put a damper on the emotional moment, but now that everyone's back, we need to get stuff set out in the kitchen. I'm sure they'll be hungry by the time they're done in Church." Tempy hops up and heads behind the bar.

Duchess laughs. "Those guys would be hungry even if they ate five minutes ago."

"What's there to do yet?" I ask.

Duchess slides off her stool. "I wanna stir everything one last time, then everything else is self-serve. Wanna give me a hand?"

"That's why I'm here after all. Put me to work," I respond as we walk in the kitchen.

"That's not the only reason you're here," she turns toward me, "is it?"

Oh boy, she looks worried. We can't be having a sad, pregnant lady. Whiskey would have a coronary if he saw her right now. "No, no. I was just kidding. I'm here because I want to be. I like being here with everyone."

"Thank goodness. I don't want you to think we only want you around to be free labor. We have plenty of Prospects for that." Duchess opens a drawer and pulls out a handful of metal mixing spoons. She walks to the pass-through window and pushes the button, raising it up, opening the counter area that resembles a cafeteria style serving area. The Brothers can pass by the other side to fill their plates and never step foot in the kitchen.

"No worries. But enough of the guy talk, tell me how you've been feeling. Is the morning sickness gone yet?"

"I think it finally is." Switch the talk to her baby and Duchess lights up. Her face is now sporting the biggest smile I've seen from her yet. "I haven't thrown up in a week and I couldn't be happier. I can tell I'm getting tired a little earlier, but my doctor said that's part of the second trimester symptoms."

"How far along are you now?"

"I'm just about at the four-month mark. Your brother knocked me up on New Year's Eve." Duchess drops a spoon in front of each slow cooker and we start on opposite ends, stirring the various foods in each one.

"That's crazy. So, what's your due date?"

"September twenty-seventh."

"No way!" What a small world. "That was my mom's birthday!"

She drops her spoon, splashing some spaghetti sauce on the counter. "No kidding? That's so cool. The little man will have a great birthday buddy watching him from heaven." Duchess wraps me in one of her amazing hugs I've grown to love so much.

"She'll be the best guardian angel any kiddo could ask for." I sniffle just a little, missing my mom in moments like this. She would've loved Duchess.

"When's your birthday?"

I go back to stirring the barbeque. "It was just recently actually. April sixteenth."

"Why didn't you say anything? We would've thrown you a belated birthday party. We love parties around here. These guys will use anything for an excuse to have fun. My birthday was April first. We had a party the night before you came here that first day."

"Honestly, I wanted to forget it. This was the first one without my mom, and so close after she died, I just wanted to ignore the day. I stayed in my pjs all day and watched movies. It's what we did every year for my birthday. Even if it was a school day, she'd call me off and we'd stay home, just the two of us."

"She sounds like an awesome mom."

"She was. Minus the whole 'you don't have a dad' thing," I try to joke, but it falls flat.

All the pots are mixed, so she pulls me to a stool by the island. "We all make mistakes. We're just happy you're here with us now. Next year, we can celebrate our birthdays together. That sound good to you?"

"I'd like that."

"And I'm definitely glad to not be the newbie anymore. The guys have someone new to bug all the time."

That makes me smile. "I can handle anything they throw at me. So far, they've all been giant puppy dogs."

"Oh, just you wait. You haven't been here during a full-blown Brother party yet. Just wait until you catch a club girl giving one of them a blowjob in the middle of the main room. Then you'll see them at their wildest."

My jaw drops open. "In the middle of the room? With everyone watching? Why would they do that?"

"Some of the guys don't care who sees them. It's just the way things go sometimes. Those are the parties that the

Old Ladies and families stay away from. We just don't need to be seeing those kinds of things."

I shake my head. "Well, if I'm ever here during something like that, I'll hide out with you. I've seen enough naked backsides while being a nurse, I'd never be able to look someone in the eye again if I saw that."

Duchess claps, excited. "We can hang out in mine and Whiskey's cabin and have some girl time."

"I'm all in." Girl time sounds good to me.

CHAPTER FOURTEEN

RING

"What have you crazy fuckers been up to?" Steel asks, kicked back in his chair at the head out the table, next to Whiskey.

"Oh, you know, just kickin' back and relaxin'. Nothing too crazy." Hammer throws out a wisecrack.

Everyone's laughter makes the room sound like a crack of thunder. It's buzzing with energy. Having our VP back has put all my Brothers in a very good mood. I'm glad to have my best friend back. We've been a pair of troublemakers since he joined the club a year after I did.

Bang! Whiskey bangs the gavel. "That's enough of the jokes, you idiots. You can do that after we're done here. We got stuff to catch Steel up on. Essentially, this damn Chaos Squad shit we seem to be stuck in."

The mood in the room goes dark real fast. Grumbles circle the table, and I can feel my temper kicking in. "Those fuckers picked the wrong club to mess with. I'm still waiting to burn someone," I growl out loud.

"Tell us how you really feel, Brother," Whiskey spits out.

"What? Like you don't feel the same way. They took your Old Lady's sister, then got her too."

Thump. Hammer's fist hits the table. "We need to figure out who these fuckers are. I'll never get her to feel safe if we don't kill them all."

"Who's she?" Steel asks. He's really out of the loop.

Everyone else knows exactly who he's talking about. We've all heard them arguing one time or another these last few months. They need to figure their shit out soon, or just hate fuck each other and get it out of their systems.

Hammer's too focused on his fist to answer, so Whiskey does it for him. "Our Brother has decided to get his head out of his ass and unofficially claim Wings. Only problem for him is she wants nothing to do with him anymore."

"Damn. That sucks. When did this happen?"

Kraken joins the titilating conversation. "Dude was banging only her before she got snapped up but didn't have the balls to admit his feelings 'til after she was gone. Then when she got herself back home, she didn't want him any more than the shit on her shoe."

"Enough!" Hammer barks. "I'm working on it. I'll break her down one of these days."

"Does that mean she's not a club girl anymore?" Steel asks.

"Hell no, she's fucking not. Hands off, asshole."

Steel throws up his hands, like Hammer's words can jump across the table and hit him in the face. Knowing Hammer and his swing, I wouldn't be surprised if they could. "Not trying to take your girl, just asking a question."

"On to more pressing issues," Mountain pipes up from the far end of the table. "Steel, how about you fill everyone in on your job while on the inside."

Here we go. Time to learn about the day Steel served up a dish of Rebel Vipers payback for our former President, Mountain.

The look on Steel's face is one of pure evil. His eyes turn dark and his face shows no emotion, except if you look super close and know what to look for. He has a small twitch in his upper lip, almost like a tiny snarl.

"He got what he fucking deserved. It took me a couple weeks to gain his trust, but after that, he was all mine. One day while eating lunch, I made sure to ask him real loud to borrow a magazine I knew he just got in the mail. I was sitting in my cell when he came in thinking we were gonna shoot the shit about bikes. I pulled him forward, and he tried to fight back. Try being the key word."

I look around the room and everyone's captivated by Steel's words, like they're experiencing it themselves.

"I let him struggle a bit and punch me a few times, so I wouldn't walk away too clean. Eventually, I had enough and slammed his head into my bunk. It bounced off the metal like a fucking basketball. Except the blood flowing was making one hell of a mess. I yelled and hollered and pretended to be hurt. Then pulled a shiv I made, stabbed myself in the leg with it, and put it in his hand."

Smoke lets out a whistle. "Shit. Then what?"

"Well, newbie, then the guards came running and handcuffed me. Once they saw the shiv in his hand, and the blood pouring from my leg, they scooped me up and rushed me to the infirmary."

Mountain speaks up again. "Thank you, Steel. You didn't have to do that, but I'm sure glad you did."

Steel nods back, "Anything for you. Shane Miller was a vile worm for hurting you the way he did. He got what was coming. I'm just mad I couldn't make it last longer."

"He's dead and that's all that matters." Whiskey leans forward and grabs his beer to take a swig. We normally aren't allowed to have alcohol in Church, but since this isn't a normal meeting, that rule was let loose just this once.

"There was one good part of my day though." Steel smiles. "I made sure to do it on a day I knew Dr. Green was coming to work his prison rotation. I expected him to be the one to stitch me up, but I got an even better surprise. The nurse he had with him that day was hot as fuck."

"Please tell me you got to tap that ass," I joke while trying not to laugh too hard.

"I fucking wish. The ass she had on her would've fit my hands perfectly," he says while holding up his hands, probably imagining what she looked like.

"Maybe you should call Green. Now that you're home, you can go find her," Brewer chips in.

"Maybe I will, just so I can bring her here and show her off to you losers," he jokes back.

"Enough talk about you and your horny pecker. There are plenty of club girls here who I know are more than happy to help you with your needs. Worry about the booty woman another day." Whiskey points toward the wall between us and the main room. "There's food and a party waiting for you out there, so let's end this meeting and get to it."

Bang! He slams the gavel again and everyone stands up.

I'm out the door, grabbing my phone from the box and heading straight for the bar. I see Penelope chatting with Duchess and Wings and I want to be as close to her as possible. If I want a repeat of the other day, and more, I need to keep her within arm's reach. I don't need any of my Brothers getting any dumb ideas to try and snag her.

"Hey there, stranger," I whisper, standing just to her side.

"Hey, Ring. How are you?" she asks. Huh? She doesn't seem to be as worried about being close to me today. When she rushed away from me last time, it was like her shoes were on fire.

"I'm even better now that I see you're here." I look at Duchess, but she's too engrossed in her conversation with Wings to pay us any mind. "Have you put any thought into what we talked about?"

Her body is still facing forward, but she turns her head my way, smiling. "You mean about getting to know me? Or kissing me like you own me?"

Oh, she's being cheeky. I do want to get to know her better, but more kissing sounds good too. "Are you flirting with me?"

She crosses her arms, then shrugs one shoulder. "And if I am? What you gonna do about it?"

"We'll have this conversation when there aren't so many ears around. Once the party really starts, you and me can duck away. Sound good?"

"I think I can handle—" Her whole body jolts. "What the hell?"

I spin ninety degrees to the right and see Steel standing behind her with a handful of her ass cheek.

"Hey there, beautiful. Wanna come up to my room and keep me company?" Steel asks, still grasping her back side. I don't really blame him for not letting go right away—she's got one fine ass.

Penelope spins around and slaps his hand away. "No, thank you, and please don't touch me."

CHAPTER FIFTEEN

STEEL

I'm making my way around the room, getting more handshakes, back-slapping hugs, and just catching up with my Brothers. It's so good to be back and I can't wait to get into the swing of things.

One of the things I've missed the most is the availability of the club girls. There's one that I noticed as soon as I walked out of Church. I don't recognize her, so I'm guessing she's somewhat new to the club.

Mmm, fresh meat. Not that I mind sharing the club girls with my Brothers, but sometimes you just need to find a woman who doesn't give in so easy. I like a challenge every once and awhile.

We definitely won't be strangers for long because she looks exactly like my type. She's got blonde hair, the color of the sun, that flows to just above her shoulders. It's a little tousled and wavy, reminding me of after-sex hair. If her hair looked like that after we did the dirty, I'd be proud of myself. She's wearing a gray long-sleeve t-shirt and skin-tight blue jeans. She looks to be about five-foot-five or so, and has a perfectly round ass to fill my hands. What I wouldn't give to get acquainted with that tush.

So, that's just what I do. I make my way across the main room and get as close to her as I can. When I grab a handful of her ass, she jumps sky high.

She squeaks out, "What the hell?"

"Hey there, beautiful. Wanna come up to my room and keep me company?" She's standing at the bar with Ring, Wings, and another shorter redhead wearing a club cut. The name on the front says 'Duchess', so I get my first glimpse of the woman who knocked my President on his ass.

If Duchess's eyes could pop out of her head, they probably would. She opens her mouth to say something, but before she can make a sound, the woman spins around and slaps my hand away.

"No, thank you, and please don't touch me," she snaps, and Ring busts out laughing. I don't understand what's so damn funny.

Wait a minute, why does she look so familiar?

"Aww, come on now, babe. You may not know me yet, but you also know that girls like you aren't allowed to say no to the Brothers," I reply. Club girls may be protected, but they've also got their uses to the Brothers.

"I'm not your babe and I'm definitely not a club girl." Now, she's got her arms crossed and the look on her face is one that would scare away a lesser man. Too bad I'm not a weak, wet noodle.

Holy fuck, now I remember her. I'm left speechless. I know her. Her hair's a lot shorter than it was the last time I saw her, but I'd never forget her face. It's been visiting me in my dreams for the last year.

"Steel," Duchess says in a tone that lets me know I've done something very wrong, "this is Whiskey's sister, Penelope."

Oh shit! "Sister? I heard about a sister but didn't realize you were here." I guess I missed that part during Church. Fuck. Wait, how did I meet Whiskey's sister while I was in prison? Does he know?

"I know you. You're that guy who got stabbed. I didn't know you were the same guy everyone's been talking about." She finally remembers my face.

"You're right, that's me. Just a lot better dressed than when we met. No more orange and gray jumpsuits." What a damn small world. "Did you know you were Whiskey's sister back then?"

"No, I didn't know Mountain was my dad until last month." Her attitude has as much fire as the blazing hot sun. That's it. I know what I'm going to call her. It's just too perfect.

"Chill out there, Sunshine. The guys said Whiskey had a sister, but I didn't know it was you. I'm sorry I assumed you were available, but you can't blame a guy for trying. It's been a while since I've been around." I shrug, trying to act nonchalant and undo my mistake. Whiskey's my President and I don't need to be pissing him off.

Ring is still chuckling like a damn monkey and I'm about to kick his ass. But my new sunshine beats me to the punch, turning to him and getting right up in his face. "You think this is funny? It's funny that he grabbed my ass? After what we did together?"

Ring stops laughing and snaps to attention. I don't know exactly what's happening between them, but I can guess, based on their current standoff, they must have hooked up. I bet it was hot as fuck. Damn, I wish I could've been in on that action. Maybe they'll invite me to join them.

"Not exactly, but you gotta see a little humor in it. He did it without knowing it was you," Ring answers her.

Interesting. Ring isn't usually one to answer to others. He keeps private things close to his chest.

"So, you don't care that your best friend touched me? You're okay with that?" Now, she has her hands on her hips, ready to keep reading him the riot act.

"To be honest, I think it's kinda hot. Want him to join us next time?"

The look on her face is priceless. Her mouth drops, her cheeks turn bright red, and her eyes volley back and forth between Ring and me.

"Join us? Like all together?"

Ring goes to answer but is halted by Duchess. "Shush your mouth. Incoming." Our small group gets quiet when Whiskey joins the circle. He makes his way behind Duchess and wraps his arms around her waist, kissing her on the cheek.

I never would've guessed that this badass could be so mushy over a woman. "Hey, Steel. I see you've met Duchess. And this is my sister, Penelope."

Based on everyone's quick quietness, and stopping Whiskey from hearing what we were talking about, I'm guessing Whiskey doesn't know anything happened between Ring and Penelope. Interesting.

It must have been very recent if the news hasn't spread far yet. Secrets don't stay secrets very long around here. The clubhouse may be fairly big, but with this many people living under one roof, sneaking around isn't easy.

Penelope glares at Whiskey. "He grabbed my ass and tried to get me to fuck him! He assumed I was a club girl."

Now that I see them so close together, the similarities are shocking. They have the same hair color and snarky attitude. Nature sure won this round. Mountain has some powerful swimmers!

He reaches out and slugs me in the arm. "Dude, you can't be doing that shit. Pops would put your own boot up your backside if he heard that shit," Whiskey scolds.

"Well, I know that now, but I didn't know her and assumed wrong," I say, trying to defend myself.

"You always were a horny bastard. Why don't you go find one of the club girls? They're a much safer bet for your wellbeing," the asshole chuckles.

"Nah, I'm good right here," I retort. I won't say it out loud, but there's no way in hell I'm letting this woman get too far out of my reach.

I want to know everything about her. And I'll get to know her, even if it kills me. I also will be getting her under me, in my bed, as soon as possible. Maybe even in between me and my best friend.

He and I definitely don't like each other in more than a platonic, Brotherly way, but we do happen to enjoy sharing a woman. Seeing a woman thrash around, receiving pleasure, is right up our alley. I'm a self-proclaimed voyeur. That's not saying I don't get aroused when I'm alone with a woman, but I'm more than okay to share her, so we can give her as much satisfaction as possible.

"But I gotta tell ya, Prez, your sister and I have met already." I need to get this out in the open. Can't be hiding shit from him, especially if I want to get more than friendly with her.

"Oh yeah, when?" Whiskey stops kissing up on his Old Lady and zeros all his attention on me.

"When I was stabbed, she was the nurse that day in the prison."

Whiskey's eyes go wide. "You mean the one you mentioned in Church?"

I nod. "The very same."

"We'll discuss that later," Whiskey snarls at me, then turns his attention to Penelope. Hopefully, he gets wrapped up in that news that he forgets I just told the whole club I wanted to fuck her.

"The same what?" Duchess asks.

Whiskey ignores the question, focusing on Penelope's news drop. "You worked at the prison? Why didn't I know this?"

"I only did it for one day. It was back when I worked at the hospital. The doctor's usual nurse was out sick, so he asked me to help out for the day." She looks shell-shocked, her eyes wide as saucers, and she's talking fast.

CHAPTER SIXTEEN

PENELOPE

So, Steel's the guy I stitched up the day I helped at the prison. He's also the reason I never went back. Dr. Green asked me to assist him a few times in the last year, but the feelings I felt for one specific prisoner kept me from returning.

I was in no place in my life to be tempted by the smooth words of someone who was incarcerated. But he's not locked up anymore, and to make things even crazier, he's a member of the same club as my father and brother.

Whiskey asked me a question, so I try to unscramble my brain. "I only did it for one day. It was back when I worked at the hospital. The doctor's usual nurse was out sick, so he asked me to help out for the day." I think I'm in shock.

"Do you still work at the hospital?" asks the guy I now know is Steel.

"Nope. I quit to take care of my mom."

"Oh, that was nice of you. Is she feeling better?" He doesn't know.

"Dude," Ring butts in, "her mom just passed away. That's how she came here."

He wraps an arm around my shoulder, and like my body has its own brain, I snuggle close to him. He gives me a squeeze.

"Fuck," Steel swears. "I'm sorry, Sunshine. I can't seem to keep my foot out of my mouth today."

"Why are you hugging on my sister like that?" Whiskey barks, taking a step toward us, probably trying to intimidate Ring.

Ring stiffens. "I can explain."

Before he can say more, Duchess wiggles her way in between the guys, then pulls on my arm.

"Whiskey, leave them alone. He's just being nice." I let go of Ring and duck out of the way.

"But—," Whiskey tries to keep going, but she shoots daggers at him, making him shut up quick.

"Nope, not right now. Today's meant for celebrating Steel being home. Now, I'm gonna take our girl here and show her the baby's room. Put your dicks back in your pants. Today isn't for arguments." With that, she leads me down the hall, then outside.

"Thank you. I'm not exactly sure what just happened, but it got to be a lot really fast." I take a huge breath, the fresh spring air feeling amazing. This is my favorite time of year. The newness of everything, and the regrowth of life makes me happy.

"Don't thank me. Those men may be adults in age, but when they get a burr in their backside, they turn into toddlers."

"I didn't know Steel was the guy I treated back then. I only knew his legal name, and I never knew he was in an MC." How did I get to this place? I started the day crushing on one Brother, then I find out Steel's here too. And they like to share? What's happening?

The door opens and Stiletto comes out behind us. "What's going on, ladies?"

"I had to get this one away from all the man attitudes in there, so I'm gonna show her my newest nursery purchases." Duchess gives her a hug. "Wanna join?"

"Sure," Stiletto replies, so we head across the backyard to their cabin.

When we go inside, Duchess leads us into a room filled with cardboard boxes.

"Whoa! Did you rob the Babies R Us?" I laugh. There's a stack of boxes of diapers in the corner taller than me.

"This is all your brother's doing. I asked him to go with me to make a gift registry, but that was a huge mistake. When he realized we weren't actually buying anything, he started throwing stuff in the cart."

"Doesn't he realize a baby shower is for other people to buy you stuff?"

That makes her laugh. "Apparently not. He said we don't need other people to buy things for our baby. He got all puffed up and went on and on about being a man and being able to support his family on his own. All that macho man bullshit." She shakes her head.

Sounds like Whiskey, at least from what I've seen so far. "So, will you not have a shower then?"

"Oh, I'll have one. I'll just put a note on the invite for guests to bring things to donate to charity or something." She waves her arm at all the boxes and bags scattered around the room. "We don't need any more diapers or onesies or another changing table, so we might as well do something meaningful with what I know people will try to give us."

"Maybe you could donate to the hospital. Remember how I said I did some rotations in labor and delivery?"

"Yeah," she says and nods.

"Well, the NICU is always in need of baby gear. A lot of times the families who have their babies early don't have stuff yet. The department takes donations to help them."

"And I bet having a baby being in NICU is super expensive," Stiletto remarks, "so I'm sure they could use lots of help."

"That's an awesome idea! Tempy's planning everything, so I'll have her put on the invite that we're gonna donate stuff to the hospital. Thanks, Penelope."

I wave her off. "No need to thank me. Just thought it sounded like a great cause to help."

"I agree. You tell the club that someone needs help and they'll dive in full force. If this works well, maybe you can suggest they do a poker run, too. They always try to pick something new to donate to," Stiletto suggests.

Duchess picks up a stuffed bear and sits in a wood glider in the corner. "I'm liking this idea. We're lucky to be blessed with a life where we can take care of our baby, but I know there's a lot of people out there who need help."

"Okay, enough of the sad talk. You brought us here to talk baby stuff, so show us what you got." It's time to turn this conversation to a happy place.

"You're right." Stiletto agrees as she drops to the carpet and pulls a box in front of her while I sit next to her. "Let's see what your Old Man thinks you needed to have." She pulls out the cutest onesie with a dinosaur on it.

"That's adorable." Stiletto hands it to me, and I just hold it in my hands, imagining a tiny baby wearing it. I wonder if he'll have blonde hair like Whiskey and me, or fiery locks like his momma.

"I can't wait to have kids."

That gets Duchess's attention. "You want a baby? Don't you need a man to help with that first? Wait, do you have a boyfriend or something we don't know about?"

I shake my head so hard, my hair fans out. I pull a ponytail holder from my jeans pocket and tie it back, and while my shorter hair doesn't all stay up, the bulk of it's out of my face. "No mystery husband or boyfriend out there. I've been single for just over a year. I was seeing another nurse when I worked at the hospital, but he got a better job in Minnesota."

"He just left you behind?" Stiletto asks.

"Not left behind. My mom was sick, so I couldn't leave her. We hadn't been together for super long, so it was more a mutual break-up."

"Is there someone here in the club who you might have your eye on?" Duchess raises an eyebrow, giving me a silly smile.

"No idea what you're talking about." How would they react to my thoughts of being interested in two men?

"Now that I think about it, you looked pretty cozy in Ring's arms when he stepped in for you in front of Steel."

I feel my cheeks start to heat up, so I duck my head and stare at my hands. "Maybe I like two guys," I whisper.

"What'd you say?" Stiletto scoots closer. "Did you say two guys?"

"Two guys? Did you take what Steel and Ring said seriously? There's something you're not telling us." Duchess is in full interrogation mode. She caught onto the thread of what I didn't say and she's pulling it to unravel all my secrets.

"Fine. I'll tell you, but you have to promise this goes no further until I figure it out myself. Promise?"

"Pinkie promise," comes from Duchess.

"My lips are sealed." Stiletto mimes zipping her lips and tossing the key.

"It started the day Steel was stabbed. I spent a few hours with him, and we flirted a bit. I had no clue of the club connection, or that I was connected myself, so a little harmless flirting was no big deal. But when I got home that night and thought about him, I realized it wasn't a good idea. I mean, he was in prison and I had no idea when, or if, he'd get out. That wasn't a direction I wanted to take my life in, so I never went back when Dr. Green asked me. I never saw Steel again until today. He grabbed my ass, I spun around to yell at him, and recognized him immediately." Phew, that was a lot.

"What's the deal with Ring? When did you start liking him?" Duchess questions.

"That began the day I showed up here looking for the mystery man in my mom's picture. Ring was at the gate when I pulled up. I thought he was hot, and he flirted with me from the get-go. Then, at your gender reveal, he was super flirty again, telling me he wanted to kiss me and get to know me. One thing led to another and I may or may not have jumped his bones in the ladies' bathroom." I spit out that last sentence so fast, I hope they don't understand my gibberish.

"Wait a damn minute. When I found you leaving the bathroom, right before you said you were leaving, you fucked Ring? Like you just had sex with him? Where was he? I didn't see him." I think Duchess picked the wrong career. She would've been a killer detective.

"He was still in the bathroom when we talked. He was waiting for me to leave and clear the path, so he could sneak out. I didn't want people seeing us together yet. I'm still unsure about it now, especially realizing I like both guys. What do I do with that? I can't date both of them."

"Why not?"

"Duchess! I can't date two Brothers at the same time! That's crazy!"

"You do know they have a habit of sharing women, right?" Stiletto throws in.

"Yeah, they told you that earlier," Duchess reminds me.

"Sharing a woman to fuck is one thing. Sharing a woman to be in a full relationship is way different. I'm not gonna fuck Ring, then try to date Steel. They're friends, and I'd never put them in that position. I don't think I could pick between the two, so I'll just bow out and pick neither."

"Maybe you should ask them if they're serious about the sharing thing. You said Ring wanted to get to know you, so maybe Steel will be the same, then you wouldn't have to pick. You could have them both." Duchess rocks in her chair.

I look to Stiletto. She's been here the longest of us all. "Do they really share woman like that? Have sex together?" I just thought of another potential problem. "Do they like each other that way, too?"

That question sends both women into a hysteric fit of giggles.

"Oh goodness, no. Not that there's anything wrong with men liking each other that way, because to each their own, but not them. There are a couple other guys in this club who I've got suspicions about, but I can promise that Steel and Ring don't like each other that way." After the chuckles stop, Stiletto continues, "They're both straight as an arrow. Sharing a woman is a kink they both happen to have, something about voyeurism or some shit. I'm not sure of the specifics."

I can't help but feel a little jealous of her knowing this much about them. I know I asked, but I still feel a little twinge in my heart, thinking about them with someone else. "Have you ever—"

Stiletto shakes her head. "Nope, never together. I'm not gonna say I've never done anything with either of them, because that'd be a lie, and I like you too much to lie to you. But you need to remember, even though I'd like us to be friends like I am with Duchess, I'm a club girl here. I've slept with several of the Brothers."

"Yup. She's even been with Whiskey," Duchess says.

"What?" I'm shocked.

"It seems weird, but now, I don't even think about it anymore. It's better that way for everyone."

"I may be here to take care of the members, but like I said in the kitchen last time we talked about what I do, I don't touch men with attachments. To me, that now includes you." Stiletto grabs my hand.

Looking down at my lap, I shrug. "I'm not really with either of them. Technically, they can do whatever they want, with whoever they want."

"Nope, doesn't matter to me. I know you're interested in them, so I'll stay out of the way. Now, that doesn't mean there won't be other club girls who'll try shady shit. We've got some real pieces of work around here."

Duchess gives her advice. "There will be a few to watch out for, but if the guys are really serious about you, they'll turn them down. They're both really good guys. You might be surprised by what happens if you let them in."

I was torn up enough about just liking two men separately. Now that I have the idea of them sharing me bouncing around in my head, it's making me a little dizzy. Then you throw in these sneaky club girls they're talking about, I'm even more spun around. What do I do now?

"I guess I've got a lot to think about, huh?"

"We're in your corner. If you need to talk, just call. You've got my number now." Duchess stands, so I jump up and give her a hug.

She's given me plenty of hugs since I showed up here, I think I owe her a few in return.

CHAPTER SEVENTEEN

RING

It takes a pretty damn good reason for me to be driving my truck instead of riding my bike, but today's trip into town is worth it. I'm on my way to pick up my little buddy, Opal. Steel has only been out of prison for a few days, so he doesn't have a truck yet.

When he got locked up, he had me sell his so it wasn't just sitting around. He's getting his new ride next week, so until then, I'm on Opal pick-up duty. He would've come with me, but he's expecting a call from his parole officer and doesn't want to miss it.

I pull into the parking lot of Sydney's apartment complex and park in a visitor spot. I hop out and take a look around the area. This place isn't anything fancy, but it's the best Tellison has to offer. Steel pays Sydney way more than his child support regulated amount, so she can afford living here.

I head to her door and knock a few times.

"Coming," I hear through the door.

The door swings open and I see Sydney looking like she just got run over by a train.

"What the fuck is wrong with you? Why are the lights off?" I bark.

Sydney snaps back, "Chill the fuck out, dude. I was taking a nap."

I push her out of my way and stomp inside. Flipping the light switch, I don't know if what I see is any better. There are pizza boxes and fast-food bags cluttered on the coffee table and several beer bottles scattered around the room.

"Where's Opal? She shouldn't be living in this filth." I keep looking around, getting angrier with every nasty thing I find. The counters are covered in dishes and it looks like no one has cleaned in weeks.

"She's in her room taking a nap. We had a late night," Sydney sighs.

"I'll go get her," I grumble and turn to head down the hall.

"Why are you here? I heard Steel was out. Shouldn't he be here to get her?" she follows me.

"Not that it's any of your business, but he's busy, so I offered to get her. Back the fuck off, bitch."

"Whatever" is all she can think of for a comeback. What a dumb one she turned out to be. She tricked Steel into knocking her up, and she thinks her shit don't stink.

I push Opal's door and see her room is a little cleaner than the rest of the apartment, but not by much. My anger soars sky high, and I spin around to face Sydney and back her up against the wall. "I'm taking Opal with me and you won't see her again 'til you get this pigsty cleaned up."

"You can't do that," she whispers.

"Try and stop me." I spin around to see Opal start to wiggle in her bed. I gently scoop her up in my arms, and even still asleep, she wraps her tiny arms around my neck, snuggling into my warmth. "Text me when this place is cleaned up and maybe I'll bring her back. Until then, fuck you," I say through clenched teeth, then get out as fast as I can.

I open the back door of my truck and slide Opal into her booster seat.

"Papa?' she mumbles through a yawn.

"Hey there, little lady." I tuck a wild piece of her hair behind her ear. "You ready to go to the clubhouse?"

That wakes her up all the way and she wiggles in her seat. "Yes, please."

I snap her buckles and shut the door, then walk around to the driver's side and hop in. The drive back to the clubhouse takes ten minutes and we spend the drive singing along to "The Joker" by Steve Miller Band. It's Opal's favorite song. Ever since she was a baby, any time this song came up on my playlist, she would bop her head and sing along as best she could.

We pull into the compound and I park to the left, in front of the repair garage. It's closed because today's Sunday, but I've got an oil change scheduled for tomorrow morning, so the guys will get it done right away.

I get out and round the back to get Opal out. As soon as I have the door open, she leaps out at me, taking me by surprise. "Whoa there. How'd you get unbuckled?"

"I did it myself," she giggles, so proud of herself.

"Next time, you need to be careful. I don't want you to fall."

"I won't fall. You catch'ted me." This girl will turn me gray before she's ten.

"This time I did, but please be careful, okay?"

Opal grabs my cheeks with her tiny hands and drops a kiss on my nose. "Yes, Papa." No one in this world, besides this tiny human, would dare do something like that to me. I wouldn't let just anyone touch me like that. Except maybe this one sunshine lady I know.

I set Opal down and shut the truck door. Before she can go running for the clubhouse, I squat down in front of her. "Opal, I've got a surprise for you inside. Do you wanna go see it?"

"Is it the new pony movie?" She gets all bouncy on her feet again.

"Nope, no ponies. This is even better. Your daddy's home from his trip." Not knowing how to explain to a two-year-old that her dad was going to prison, we decided it was best to tell her he was away for work. When she's a little older, Steel will fill her in on the details.

That sends her into a screech loud enough to scare the birds. "MY DADDY'S HERE!" And she's off. She turns and runs as fast as her short little legs will allow. My longer steps make it to the screen door before she gets there, so I hold it open, allowing her to run right in.

"Hi, Opal." Duchess is sitting on one of the couches, doing something on her phone.

Opal runs right for her, vibrating with excitement. "Did you hear? My daddy's here!"

"I heard. That's so cool." Duchess picks her up, setting Opal next to her on the couch. She then looks my way. "Steel's in the kitchen with your friend. I'll keep the princess occupied here while you go check on them." Duchess winks.

My friend? Who is she . . . the lightbulb goes on and I realize who she's talking about. Steel's in the kitchen with Penelope, and it might not be the best thing for Opal to be barging in on.

"Thanks for the heads up." Opal has her nose buried in Duchess's phone, so I walk toward the kitchen.

I push the swinging door open just a bit and peek into the kitchen. What I see has me hurrying in and locking the door behind me. Steel and Penelope are at the other end of the kitchen and he's got her up on the countertop, head buried between her legs. Her head is thrown back in ecstasy, eyes pinched shut. The sounds coming out of her mouth make my jeans instantly uncomfortable.

Steel grunts and shakes his head back and forth, causing Penelope to explode. She starts to scream but stops herself by biting her fist. I press my palm down on my bulge, trying to stop from coming in my jeans at the sight of her taking her pleasure. This is exactly the reason I don't mind sharing a woman. And seeing this particular woman get her rocks off underneath the prowess of my best friend, I don't think I've ever seen anything hotter.

"Damn, woman. I think you squeezed my ears off," Steel chuckles, still kneeling on the floor.

"I think that was the hottest thing I've ever seen," I growl. That gets both their attention.

Penelope squeals and jumps off the counter, tripping over her feet and knocking both her and Steel to the linoleum. Steel and I bust out laughing.

CHAPTER EIGHTEEN

PENELOPE

I came to the clubhouse this morning to spend some time with Mountain. He and I spent a few hours huddled together at the kitchen table, sharing pictures and stories about the last twenty years of our lives.

To say I'm growing to love him is an understatement. He has this temperament and way of saying things that puts me instantly at ease. I can see why my mother was attracted to him, which on the flip side of the coin makes her leaving him that much more confusing. I obviously don't find him attractive like she would've, but I can see the allure he'd have to a young, single woman. It's no wonder Blue gave in to his whims after three days. That woman is a force of nature and I can't see him forcing her to do anything she doesn't want to.

I grab a soda from the fridge and make my way back through the kitchen. I intend to go sit in the main room with Duchess, when I'm almost sacked in the face by the door swinging open.

"There you are." Steel. He found me. I haven't been ignoring him on purpose, but I haven't gone out of my way to find him since getting here.

"Yup, here I am." I take a sip of my soda, but as soon as I get the cap back on, Steel grabs the bottle and sets it on the island.

He steps forward, one boot at a time, backing me further into the kitchen. "Were you hiding from me?"

"No," I whisper, keeping my eyes locked on his. Steel has this glint in his eyes, unlike one I've ever seen. His eyes are a caramel brown, lighter than Ring's but they still hold this little bit of darkness. Around the edges. It's like he has a swirl of every shade of brown, all mixed together.

"Then why are you back here all alone?"

I bump into the countertop at the back of the room. "I was visiting Mountain, then was about to hang with Duchess."

"Well, now, you can hang out with me." He steps into my bubble and cages me in, setting his hands on the counter on either side of my hips. "Is this okay?"

I'm not one hundred percent sure what he's referring to, but I'm really liking the way he's making me feel. Most people would be intimidated by such a large man pushing them around a room, essentially backing them in a corner, but I find it stimulating.

My heart is beating fast, and my breathing is just a little harder.

I grow a little bold and lift my right hand to set it against his chest. "Is what okay?" Slowly, I drag my fingertips down the smooth leather of his cut, tracing the stitching running along the center edge.

Steel drops his gaze to watch the path my hand is taking down. "Is it okay that I'm this close?" When my hand hits the bottom hem of his cut, he grabs it and lifts it to his lips, kissing my palm.

Then he kisses me. No passing 'go'. No collecting two hundred dollars. Just full force pushing himself into my space, kissing me.

I grab hold of his shoulders and pull him even closer. Our chests slam together, and he uses the breath I take to his advantage. My lips open just a sliver, and he attacks. He slides his tongue forward against mine and we fight for air and steal each other's at the same time.

Shifting our stance a little, I grind my center into his left leg, using the hardness of his muscles to gain traction. I feel my center throb and have a feeling if this continues all hot and heavy, he's going to make me come without any other stimulation. His hands are still gripping my hips, and I feel his fingers pressing into my back.

Steel must feel my waist squirming because he backs his hips away just enough to stop me from rubbing against him, taking away my rapidly approaching need to come.

I break our kiss. "Why'd you stop?" I complain.

He starts kissing down my chin. "You can't come from just my leg."

I let my head lay back, giving him more room to continue down my neck. "When you come . . . it will be . . . because of . . . my tongue," he whispers between kisses.

Steel licks along my collarbone, until he hits the strap of my tank top. I took my sweatshirt off earlier today, so I've been just hanging out in a pair of denim capris and an orange, chunky strap tank.

"Oh" is all I manage to pant out.

"Oh, is right, Sunshine." He lifts his head and meets my eyes again. "You'll be coming with my face buried in your heat."

Dropping one more scorching kiss on my lips, he pulls back, pops my button open, and unzips my capris. He pushes the material down over my hips and butt, then lifts me up to sit on the counter. Kneeling in front of me, he pulls the denim off over my shoes and tosses it aside.

"Yes, please," I beg as he begins nipping and kissing up the inside of my legs.

Steel takes one last lick, then sits back on his haunches. "Not until you agree to my terms."

I look down at him and frown. "Why do you keep stopping?"

"Because I need you to listen and do what I say," he retaliates.

I rest my elbows on my thighs, leaning forward, getting my face closer to his. Maybe I can sneak a kiss and get the ball rolling again. "What do you need to say?"

"I know what you're doing and it won't work. Sit back right now and listen," Steel rumbles.

His voice makes my whole body feel like I was struck my lightening. I sit back but keep my eyes on him. Ring and Steel don't have many physical similarities, other than being super tall and bulky, but their attitudes are a lot more alike than I thought. They're bossy when it comes to extracurricular activities and it makes me burn.

"Sorry."

"No need to apologize, Sunshine, but I do need you to listen very carefully. Okay?"

I stay silent and nod.

"Now, I know you've done something with Ring, but I'm not exactly sure what. We'll talk about that later, but I need you to know that sexually, he and I are a lot alike. We need to be the ones in charge when we're with a woman. He and I can have a conversation without even talking, so if you see us looking at each other when we're with you, just know that it's nothing bad. That make sense?"

"You were serious about wanting to share me? Like for more than in bed?" I question. I need to make sure this isn't a one-time thing. After my talk with Duchess and Stiletto, I decided to just let anything that happens with the guys happen naturally. I wasn't going to initiate anything with them, but if they came to me, I wouldn't push them away.

Steel nods. "I'm dead serious. One day soon, we'll get you between us in bed, but before I go any further, I need you to agree that going forward, this is all three of us. I won't butt in if what you're feeling for Ring is stronger than what you feel for me. I'll step back and let you two be."

I know he told me to sit back, but the tenderness and sincerity in his voice makes me need to touch him. I reach forward and pull his head to me, placing a gentle kiss on his lips. I let him go and sit back. "I know we haven't had time to talk since you came home, but I need you to know I'm all in. I've thought a lot about it this week and I decided to just let things happen. I want to see how this goes."

The smile that grows on his face is hard to describe. I guess the best way to explain it is simply that it makes him beautiful. He probably wouldn't describe himself as beautiful, but to me, he is. "You know Ring and I have shared women before but committing to a relationship is new for the both of us. We've talked about it a little this week, but the three of us have a lot to learn about each other."

"I'm all in," I whisper.

"Good," he says back.

Then things get hot again quick. Still kneeling, he starts kissing my chest through my tank. His hands grab my panties, tugging them down. I shift my hips so he can get them off while I'm still seated, and once off, they go flying somewhere over his shoulder.

Steel pushes my knees apart and dives into my lap with his face. He instantly latches onto my clit and shoves his tongue between my folds. I grab his head, running my hands over his buzz cut, not having anything to hold onto. He takes my silent hint and shoves forward even more. Steel shakes his head back and forth and I detonate.

My orgasm sneaks up on me like a damn earthquake. My whole body shakes and I let out the start of a scream before I can stop it. I bite my knuckles to muffle the noise, forgetting until just now that we're in the open kitchen. Anyone, including my dad or brother, could've walked in on us. Not that being with Steel is anything to hide, but there are some things you don't need to share with your family.

Steel leans back, laughing a little. "Damn, woman. I think you squeezed my ears off."

"I think that was the hottest thing I've ever seen," a voice comes from somewhere.

I look up and see Ring standing on the other side of the room, so I squeak and leap off the counter. Too bad I forgot Steel is right in front of me because I land on top of him, sending both of us to the floor.

Steel wraps me in his arms, keeping me from getting away. I'm still trying to get my brain back on track from that quickly exploding orgasm when I feel my body start to shake. I quickly realize it's from Steel laughing. His laughter is like a roll of thunder, shaking everything in its path, including my whole body.

I peek up and see Ring laughing right along with him. He's got a hand braced on the kitchen island, keeping him from joining us on the floor.

Ring finally stops chuckling enough to speak again. "Looks like you two are getting to know each other well."

Steel sets me aside and climbs up to standing, then pulls me back to my feet. "We sure are. Aren't we, Sunshine?"

I avoid both their eyes, quickly sliding my underwear back on. I kick off my shoes, then pull my capris on.

When I'm back to normal, I meet their eyes. "Are you two really serious about this?" I wave my hand around in a circle, referring to us three.

"Dead serious." Ring walks toward me, grabbing my right hand.

"Serious as a heart attack." Steel closes in threading his fingers with my left hand.

I take a deep breath and take the final jump off the waterfall. Here goes nothing. Crashing into the water below, I let the feeling of serenity wash over me. There's no going back now. I nod and agree, "Okay."

Ring pulls me close and drops a kiss on my lips. I battle with his tongue for a minute before I'm yanked back and spun to face Steel. He kisses me with just as much vigor and heat. We separate, all catching our breaths.

"I hate to be the one to break up the party," Ring speaks up first, "but Opal's here. She's so excited to see you, Steel."

"What?" I pull away from both of them. "You just did that with me when you've got someone else here to see you?" What the hell? He's got another woman? "How many women do you two expect to be sharing?"

Steel crowds me and grips my hands. "Opal's my four-year-old daughter. I haven't seen her since right before I went to prison."

And I'm handed my first steaming pile of humble pie. "Oh my gosh, I'm so sorry. I'll just go home now. You have more important things to deal with."

CHAPTER NINETEEN

STEEL

"Oh my gosh, I'm so sorry. I'll just go home now. You have more important things to deal with." I've got Penelope's hands clasped in mine. I can tell she's feeling pretty uncomfortable right now, so I try to ease her nerves.

"No, stay. I want you to meet her." If the three of us are going to give this relationship a real shot, Opal needs to be a very big part of that. We would basically be a family of four right off the bat.

She still looks unsure. "Are you sure?"

I squeeze her hands, then draw her in for a hug. "I'm sorry I didn't mention having a kid before. When I'm around you, my brain seems to short circuit to inappropriate things."

That makes her giggle. "It's okay," she says, then she pulls back.

Ring reaches for her hand and pulls her toward him. "If I may?" he asks to butt in.

"She's all yours . . . for now." I wink at Penelope.

"Opal's the happiest and friendliest little girl in the world. She's gonna love you. Come meet her and see for yourself."

Penelope takes a deep breath, and the tension rolls off her shoulders. She looks more relaxed. "Okay, but if she doesn't like me, then I'll go."

Like that'll happen. I ain't letting her run far. "Whatever you say, Sunshine."

I head for the kitchen door, but when I push on it, it doesn't budge.

"I locked it. I don't think certain someones would appreciate finding you two the way I did." Ring laughs.

"I was a little preoccupied," I flip the lock, "so thanks for that."

"Any time you two wanna do that again, just let me know."

"Again?" Penelope gasps.

"Maybe in one of our rooms next time." I throw her a wink and head out to the hallway. I've got another very important girl to see.

My footsteps are quick as I make my way to the main room. I see my little girl before she notices me. She's sitting at one of the dining room tables with Duchess, completely immersed in what I'm guessing is a coloring book. Her nose is lowered, and her tiny hand is scribbling away.

She's so much bigger than the last time I saw her. Ring sent me several pictures over the years, but having her in front of me makes everything real. God, I missed her so much. Her hair's a dark brown, just like mine, and it looks to be super long. Just another thing to make it real that she's not a baby anymore.

Duchess looks up, seeing me, then nudges Opal with her elbow to get her attention. Opal looks up and notices me standing across the room. I'm just standing there, staring at her like an idiot. I was so excited to see her, but now that I'm out here, I'm frozen.

"DADDY!" Opal's face lights up. The smile that crosses her face is infectious. She drops the crayon she was using, slides off the bench, then runs straight for me.

I drop to my knees and hold my arms wide open, waiting for her to get to me. She's running so fast that when she hits me, I fall back and land on the floor. Seems like I'm sitting on the floor a lot today.

I wrap my arms around my little girl and hug her as tight as I can without squishing her. She may be bigger than the last time we were together, but she's still a tiny thing. I nuzzle her super tight, just soaking in all her pure goodness.

A hand drops to my shoulder and I look up to see Ring and Penelope standing next to us. Ring pats me once more then backs up. Having his support while I was away was the best. He stepped in for my little girl, and I don't think I'll ever be able to repay him.

Opal's shaking, so I untangle her arms from my neck, pulling her back to see her face. "What's the matter, baby girl?"

Her tiny brown eyes are swimming with tears. "I missed'ed you so, so much," she sniffles.

I drop a kiss on her forehead. "I missed you, too."

She wipes her eyes, then puts her damp hands on my cheeks. "You're back."

Nodding, I choke back a tear. "Yes, I am."

"Do you hafta leave again?"

"Nope." I shake my head, still under her small hands. "I got home a couple days ago and I get to stay home forever."

She drops her hands, sitting down in my lap. "Oh, thank goodness. Papa said you were here, and I got so excited. That was after I almost falled'ed out the truck."

"Oh, really? Next time, you tell Papa not to let you fall."

Opal looks over at Ring and giggles. "He catch'ted me and helped me down."

Ring comes forward and kneels down in front of us. "I'd never let my munchkin fall."

Opal finally notices the beautiful woman standing behind Ring. She looks up and points at Penelope. "Who's that? Is she your friend, Daddy?"

"Yes, baby girl. That's Daddy and Papa's friend, Sunshine. You wanna meet her?" I ask.

Opal climbs out of my lap, then walks over to her. "Your name's Sunshine? That's so cool." She's in total awe. I really can't blame her—Penelope's drop dead gorgeous.

Penelope kneels down to get level with the rest of us. "My real name's Penelope, but your daddy's silly and calls me Sunshine."

And with that, the name is official for me. From now on, no matter what happens between us all, she'll be my Sunshine. I'll talk to Ring about this at some point to make sure the name is okay with him.

Shaking her head, Opal looks back at me and rolls her eyes. Looks like we've got a little diva on our hands. "He's the silliest," she says, sticking her tongue out at me before returning all her attention to Sunshine. "Do you wanna be my friend?"

Sunshine smiles at her. "Of course, I'd love to be your friend."

Pouncing forward, Opal knocks her back, giving her a big hug. "Oof," Sunshine grunts. "You're such a big girl. How old are you? Eight?"

Opal climbs back to her feet. "No, you silly. I'm only this many," she answers, holding out a hand with four fingers up.

Sunshine over-exaggerates her shock, holding a hand to her chest. "Only four? No way, I don't believe it."

Opal nods her head, looking at me and Ring. "Yes way. Ask my daddy and Papa. Right? I'm four."

"You got that right, little lady. You just turned four and a half." Ring nods at her.

I laugh at myself, at all of us really. The room's filled with places to sit, but we're all chilling on the floor. "Alright, enough of this silly four business. Let's get up off this floor. Your daddy's too old for this."

Ring climbs back to his feet and offers a hand to pull Sunshine up. I guess I'm on my own. I get back on my feet and crack my back. That hour ride was hell on my whole body. It'll take a bit to get used to riding long distances again.

"Sunshine," Opal pulls on her hand, "will you come color with me?"

Sunshine looks between Ring and me, not knowing what to do. She looks torn, and she's starting to get a little overwhelmed again. "Oh, I don't know. I think you need to spend some time with your daddy. It's time for me to go home and do my laundry."

Opal looks sad. "Oh, okay. Will you come back and play with me?"

I butt in, trying to get her back in a happy frame of mind "We'll see what we're doing the next time Sunshine comes to visit. Is that okay?"

"Okay. Next time." She hugs Penelope's legs, then runs over to Ring.

Ring scoops her up over his shoulder, carrying her like a sack of potatoes. That sends her into another round of infectious giggles. "Let's go color your dad a picture."

"Yay!" she screeches, banging her fists on his back. "Giddy up!"

I grab Sunshine's hand, drawing her attention away from the two crazies now galloping around the room like ponies. "Is everything okay?"

She nods. "Yea, it's just a lot at once."

I kiss her knuckles. She's looking up at me, so I drop a quick kiss on her lips. "I know you want to leave, so I'll let you go. But just know, next time I see you, we'll be finishing our conversation from earlier."

That gets her flustered. "Finishing?"

"You heard me. You may have *finished*, but I sure as hell didn't. And I know exactly what I'm gonna be thinking of tonight when I go to bed."

Her eyes go wide. "Ummm . . ."

She doesn't know what to say, and I think it's adorable.

How the hell did I get here? This isn't how I thought things would go when I got home. I expected to be fucking my way through the club girls, getting my dick wet with any pussy I could dip into. I had no idea I'd be chasing this ray of sunshine, willing to wait for her to be ready for me and my best friend.

I reach behind her, pulling her phone out of her back pocket. I swipe the screen to wake it up, then enter both mine and Ring's numbers. I also start us all a group text chain. "You don't need to say anything else. We'll text you later." I slide the phone back in her pocket, spin her around by the hips, tap her butt cheek, and give her a little push toward the door.

She starts walking, waving to us.

"Bye, Sunshine!" Opal yells out.

"Bye, Opal," Sunshine replies, looking shellshocked. Like she's caught in the middle of the twilight zone.

I know it's going to take her some time to get used to everything, but we'll get her there. One day at a time.

CHAPTER TWENTY

PENELOPE

What a day. I went to the clubhouse to see my dad and left with two boyfriends. If that's what you want to call it, because I'm not sure what to label what we are right now.

Steel backed me into the kitchen and took control of my thoughts. He didn't let my insecurities stay in the light for very long. I've been forced to be in control of everything for so long now, letting him tell me how things were going to go was a breath of fresh air. I had no idea it'd feel like this, but my drive home has given me a little time to think everything over.

I get home and look around the living room. Seeing all my mom's things laying out is almost a double-edged sword. On one hand, it's nice to have her belongings as reminders of her good times. But then on the other, it's almost too much. I think I need a fresh start.

I go down to the basement, find some empty totes, and bring them back to the living room. Sorting through some of her things, I separate what to keep and what can be donated to charity. Moving into her bedroom, I realize this is a project I'll need to save for another day, because it's getting close to dinner time and I haven't eaten anything today.

Pulling the totes into her room clears the living room just a bit, and my heart feels lighter. I head to the kitchen to heat up some leftovers, then eat, load the dishwasher, and head up to my bedroom. After a quick shower, I put on a loose-fitting t-shirt and crawl into bed. I settle myself in the middle, where I'm propped up by a massive pile of pillows, then use the remote to fire up Prime to play an episode of *Bones*. I started bingeing this a few weeks ago, but with everything that's been going on, haven't been able to watch in a while.

Seely and Bones just smooched under the mistletoe and he thanks her for the gum when my phone dings on the nightstand. I pause the show, but before I can even grab my phone, it dings again. Whoever it is sure wants my attention.

Swiping the screen, I see a group text titled 'My Men'. Steel must've done that when he took my phone earlier.

Steel: Hey there, Sunshine.
Ring: I'm here too. ;)

A winky face emoji? I didn't know guys used those. Before I can answer, they keep going.

Steel: Dude, don't use those dumb faces. She's gonna think we're losers.
Ring: Shut up! She knows I'm not a loser. Don't you, beautiful?
Me: You two are crazy! What are you doing?
Steel: I don't know about that other fool, but I'm checkin' on my girl. How are you?
Ring: Same here. I hope things today weren't too much.
Me: You're both too sweet. I'm doing good. I'm glad I got to meet Opal.
Steel: She loved you.
Ring: She wouldn't stop asking questions after you left.
Me: I'm sorry I rushed out. I wanted to stay, but just needed time.
Steel: I understand. It was a lot at once.
Me: It was a lot, but I can handle it.
Ring: She definitely can handle a lot. You should've seen how she handled my dick.

Whoa! That's a total change in topic. Not that I should be surprised. These guys seem to have a libido that flips on like a switch.

> **Steel:** I'm jealous I haven't gotten to be inside your pussy, Sunshine.
> **Me:** Totally not where I saw this convo going.
> **Ring:** Is it okay to talk like this?
> **Steel:** It's the truth.
> **Me:** Yes Ring, it's fine. Steel, I'm kinda sad I didn't get to help you back.
> **Steel:** I call dibs on getting you first next time.
> **Ring:** You can't hog her all to yourself. You need to share!
> **Steel:** Screw you asshole. You got to have your dick in her hot pussy. I only got to feel it.
> **Me:** Boys, boys. I'm starting to feel like a piece of meat over here. LOL!
> **Steel:** Woman, you're one hot piece of meat. One I can't wait to fuck and taste again.
> **Ring:** Now I'm a little jealous. I didn't get to taste her pussy.
> **Ring:** I bet you taste amazing.

They keep going. I can't get a word in edgewise, not that I'd even know what to say. I don't know what I taste like.

Steel: She tastes just like her name. Pure Sunshine.
Ring: I can't wait for my turn.
Steel: Don't worry, Brother. We've got a lifetime to get our share.
Ring: Very true.
Me: Lifetime? Isn't it too soon to talk like that?
Ring: No way!
Steel: Absolutely not!
Ring: A lifetime isn't long enough in the biker world.
Steel: He's right. When a biker claims a woman, it's for eternity.
Me: Claims?
Steel: You got that right. We're gonna claim you one day. I just know it.
Ring: Remember our chat about kissing someone like they own you?
Me: Yea. You said we'd take time to get to know each other.
Ring: And we will, just now that includes three of us.
Me: You said things happen at warp speed.
Ring: I did. I also said I wouldn't make you

my Old Lady yet, but we want you to know that's where we want things to go.
Steel: I know it's quick, but we want to learn everything about you.
Me: There's so much we don't know yet.
Steel: I take full blame for that. I've been a bulldozer since I saw you again.
Ring: Who can blame you, man. She's hot.
Steel: That she is. I'm starting to get hard just thinking about her pussy.
Ring: You ain't alone. I've been at half-mast since I walked in the kitchen earlier.

And now, they're talking about their erections. Conversation one-eighty again. A girl could get whiplash from these two.

Me: You're both hard because of me?
Steel: Hell fuckin' yea.
Ring: I don't think she realizes what she does to us yet.
Steel: Maybe we should show her.
Ring: You read my mind.
Me: What are you talking about?

That's when two pictures pop up. I see two sets of abdominal muscles leading down to two bulges, hiding behind boxer briefs. The picture from Ring is black cotton and lots of black ink covered skin. The one from Steel is blue cotton pushed low, with just the curve of his dick peeking out the top. It's like he pushed it down just enough to tease.

> **Me:** That's not fair! You're both horrible teases.
> **Steel:** If we have to wait to get you, you can wait for us.
> **Ring:** What he said!
> **Me:** Fine. Just know I may spend the rest of the night staring at these pics.
> **Ring:** You should touch yourself.
> **Steel:** Do it! Please?
> **Me:** Not when we're texting. That's crazy.

I still have my phone in my hand when it starts to buzz and Steel's name pops up.

I swipe the green icon to answer. "Yes?"

"You can't tease us like that, Sunshine," Steel growls.

"Yea. You can't talk about touching yourself and not expect us to take part." Ring's voice comes in clear.

"How are you both on one call?" I know they're both at the clubhouse, but I didn't know they were together.

Steel answers first. "Our rooms are next to each other. After your message about looking at our dicks, I popped in Ring's room."

"We've got a door connecting our rooms. Made it easier to watch the little one while Steel was gone," Ring replies.

"That's convenient," I say because I don't know what else to say.

"It's perfect for moments like this." This is from Steel. "Tell us how you touch yourself while thinking about us."

"Tell us how you detonate when you get your clit pinched. I know it worked perfect for me," Ring rumbles.

"I bet that was hot as fuck," Steel echoes.

"I don't know if I can."

I hear some shuffling through the phone, then Steel speaks up. "Sunshine, what are you wearing?"

"A t-shirt," I whisper.

"No panties?" Ring asks.

"No."

"Goddamn it," Steel swears. "I wish you were with us."

"Sorry" is all I can say back.

"Nothing to apologize for. Put your phone on speaker and we'll talk you through this." This I can tell comes from Ring.

I don't know how I know whose voice is whose, but there's something in each of their tones that my mind can distinguish.

I click the speaker button, laying my phone on my chest. "Okay, it's on speaker."

"Good."

"Perfect," both voices boom through my room.

"Now, I want you to push your blankets down to your knees. I want your pussy out in the air." Steel.

"Then slide your right hand down your stomach." Ring.

"Use your fingers to spread your folds. I want your clit to peek out." Steel.

"Are you wet for us?" Ring.

I swipe my slit with one finger and find myself soaked. "So wet."

"That's perfect, Sunshine. Now, use your fingers and start rubbing yourself." Steel.

"Find the spot that gets you hot. I know you've got one. I've touched it." Ring.

"Okay." I push my fingers a bit to the right and focus my attention on the bundle of nerves I know gets me going. I'm making some sounds because both guys let out grunts through the phone.

"Fuck, that sounds hot." Steel.

"Now, take your left hand and slide a finger inside your throbbing pussy. I want you to feel yourself squeeze your fingers, like you did my cock." Ring.

So, I do. I lower my left hand and rub around my opening, gathering some of my wetness to lubricate my digits. I use two fingers and push in as far as I can. This isn't the most comfortable position, but right now, I could care less. The way I'm feeling, I could be folded like a pretzel and not give two shits.

"I can hear your grunts through the phone. Keep going." Ring.

"I can't wait to get inside you, Sunshine. I need to feel you suffocating my dick with your pussy." Steel.

"That's right. I can't wait to see you getting fucked and taking your pleasure. Just thinking about it is making my cock hard as fuck." Ring.

I can feel my orgasm starting to build, so I try to warn them. "I'm gonna . . . it's starting. "

"Come for us. I wanna hear you scream." Ring.

"Let it fly, Sunshine. Come for us." Steel.

As if my body was waiting for both of their permission, like they hold the strings to my pleasure, I explode. "FUCK!" I yell.

"That's right."

"Good girl." My ears are ringing a little, so it sounds kind of tinny.

"Holy hell. I didn't know I could do it like that." I wheeze, trying to catch my breath.

That gets me two sets of deep chuckles. "I knew you had it in you, Sunshine. You're perfect for us," Steel says through his laughs.

"Not just anyone could handle the both of us, but you're doing great so far." The confidence coming from Ring makes my heart beat a little faster.

I take a few seconds to catch my breath, then sit up, catching my phone as it falls to my lap, and swing my feet over the side of the bed.

"Where are you going?" Ring asks. "I can hear you moving."

I pad across the cool wood floor, then flip the bathroom light on, squinting against the bright lights. "Just going to wash my hands. I can't sleep feeling all sticky." I set my phone on the vanity.

"That's a good idea. I think we need to go wash up ourselves," Steel groans.

What? I freeze, hand midair, reaching for the faucet. "Why do you need to wash up?"

"Did you think we were gonna listen to you diddling with yourself and not partake in the fucking hotness?" Ring chuckles.

"Fuck, Sunshine. You had me so fuckin' hard, I had to take myself in hand and play along," says Steel.

"I didn't know you were doing that. You're in the same room. I didn't think you'd do that together." I'm shocked.

That makes them both laugh out loud again.

"Sunshine, if we're gonna fuck you at the same time, we definitely have no problem jacking off in front of each other. The weirdness of that went away a long time ago," Steel explains.

"Don't worry, I wasn't looking at him when I was imagining you sliding up and down my dick. I had my eyes closed, picturing you," Ring tells me.

"I was imagining Ring bending you over and you sucking my dick at the same time. UGH!"

"Dude, stop with that shit. I'm gonna get hard again," Ring barks.

They're both going to get me going again. Maybe even tempt me to drive back to the clubhouse so they can do the things they're talking about. "That's enough. I can't listen to this anymore. You're both horrible influences." I pick up my phone and lean a hip against the counter.

"Alright, I think that's our sign to let you go," Steel speaks up.

"Fine, be that way then. Just don't forget us when you close your eyes," Ring teases.

"You two are too much." I snicker a little, just imagining them pouting, not wanting me to forget them.

I can tell I'm going to have my hands full with these two. But the more I think about it, the more I love the idea. Who would've thought I could be so captivated by two burly, hot guys? Not me, that's for sure.

"Good night, Penelope," Ring growls. "Call us tomorrow, okay?"

"I will, I promise. Good night, Ring."

"Sunshine? You still there?" Steel asks.

"I'm here."

"Just making sure you didn't hang up without saying good night to me."

"I'd never forget you," I promise.

"Good to hear. Good night, Sunshine."

"Good night, Steel." And the line goes dead.

What an interesting evening. Not how I saw things going, but I'm not disappointed. I can't wait to see what's next for us. I may not be ready to be their Old Lady, not really sure what that all means yet, but I look forward to learning.

Maybe I should talk to Duchess. She's been a good ally so far, and I trust her to give me the truth on how things could be. I'll text her tomorrow and see when she can meet to talk.

CHAPTER TWENTY-ONE

RING

I turn my head and squint at the clock sitting on the nightstand. Three-twenty-seven a.m. My alarm will be ringing in three minutes.

Lying in this cheap motel bed makes me miss my pillowtop, king size mattress at home. I know it makes me sound like a damn pussy, but when you grew up like I did, you learn to appreciate a good place to lay your head

Plus, being in this bed means I'm that much farther away from Penelope. I didn't have time to see her before I left, so I texted her to let her know I was leaving town for a few days. She thanked me for letting her know, told me she'd miss me, and that I needed to be safe. I told her she was the reason I'd be making it home in one piece. She replied by sending me a picture of her feet kicked up on what I'm guessing is her front porch railing. She said she expected me to be sitting with her next time. I promised her that I would.

Being on a run for the club is something I've gotten used to over the years, but I've never had anyone at home to explain my going away to before. It's almost a mixed blessing—I'm happy I've got someone waiting for me, but it puts that devil on my shoulder to be extra careful in everything I do.

We left the clubhouse at noon yesterday and took the three-hour ride north at a leisurely pace. We got checked into the motel, then found a bar to eat dinner and have a few beers. Everyone hit the hay early, knowing we had a god-awful wakeup time.

Beep beep beep beep! The alarm on my phone goes off, so I sit up and throw my feet over the side.

"Fuck. Why does it have to be so damn early?" Wrecker groans from the bed next to mine.

"'Cause the sunrise doesn't care about your damn beauty sleep," Mountain grumbles from the pullout sofa in the corner.

I leave the complaining ninnies behind, grab my backpack, and head for the bathroom to take a piss and change. After I splash some water on my face and dry it off, I'm about to walk out when the door flies open.

Mountain comes hobbling in. "You about done? Old bladder needs to take a leak."

I grab my stuff and skirt around him. "Sorry for holding up the senior citizens." He laughs before slamming the door in my face.

"What time did you get in?" I ask Wrecker.

"Rolled in and shut my eyes at midnight. Tiny left to join the others at the hangar," he answers through another yawn.

"We've got a long day ahead of us, so get some caffeine in your veins."

Wrecker heads for the tiny coffee maker sitting on the dresser. "You sure you don't want any of this nectar of the gods?" He laughs, waving a foam cup in my face.

I swat his arm and sit to put my boots on. "Fuck you very much. Everyone knows I can't stand that swill."

"You're the strangest one of us all," Mountain adds as he comes out of the bathroom. "How can you drink soda so early in the morning?"

"Because I can." I reach for the mini-fridge and open it to grab the bottle of Mountain Dew I put in there last night. I crack the seal and take a swig of the citrusy goodness. "Ahhhhh!"

"Enough making out with your bottle, we need to get rolling. This is a bigger shipment than usual, so we really need to keep an eye out for trouble," Mountain alerts and walks out the door.

Since Mountain still doesn't ride, we detached the semi-truck from the trailer and he's driving that. Wrecker and I fire up our bikes, and we ride out.

It's a two-minute ride to the private air strip, where we park inside one of the hangars. We don't always stay the night before pick-ups, but this time we decided to because of the early drop-off time.

"Morning, fellas," Tiny greets us with a nod behind his high-powered binoculars.

"Where are the boys?" I ask.

Tiny cracks his neck and stands to stretch while Mountain takes his place in the chair. "Cypher took Smoke for a walk around the perimeter. Now that the sun's starting to peak, I wanted the newbie to see the area better."

I slap him on the shoulder. "Good thinkin', man. This whole new team line-up can throw things off, but I'm good with everyone. What you think?"

"I'm good with it. Having the youngins mixed with us old fogies is good. The club needs guys like them for the future."

"Who you calling old? I'm only thirty. You're the ancient one."

"Forty-five isn't ancient. We'll leave that title to the dinosaur over there." We both turn to look at Mountain.

"Fuck you both." Mountain flips us off while keeping his eyes peeled through the binoculars.

"How's it looking out there?" I ask him.

"Plane just popped in my sights. Time to get this show on the road." Mountain gets up and sets the binoculars on the seat of Wrecker's bike.

Wrecker heads for the door opener and hits the button. The door slowly raises, folding in half as it goes up. The plane we've been waiting for taxis its way down the runway and we wait for it to roll our way.

The area this private air strip is located in is totally secluded. It's why this location was picked. The runway is surrounded on all four sides by trees and farm fields. Unless you knew it was here, you'd drive right past it. You can't even see any of the buildings from the road.

It takes a few minutes, then the plane is fully inside the hangar and it slowly shuts down. When the side door drops open, four men come climbing out and head our way.

"Good morning, boys." Monty makes his way toward me, and I greet him with a firm handshake.

"Morning. How was the flight?" Mountain asks while shaking Monty's hand.

"All's good on our end. Any issues here?"

"Nope. We've got eyes outside," I reply. I may trust Monty because of what he does for the club, but one can never be too careful about the information they share. He doesn't need to know the specifics of who we have outside and where they are.

"Perfect. Let's get this unloaded and we can all be on our way." Monty nods at the men behind him and we all get to work.

Between their four guys and me, Wrecker, and Tiny, we get the plane unloaded and the semi loaded in less than an hour. Once the plane's empty, they taxi out to refuel while Tiny and I get the load secured in the trailer. The guns we run get brought to us in wood crates, but we take them out and load them in the semi-trailer by hand. It's almost a human conveyor system. Everyone has their job and we get it done quick.

The guns get hidden in bins of scrap metal that we bring with us from the club's salvage yard. Each bin has a false bottom or hidden center, depending on what we need to hide in it or the size of scrap in it. It's like a game of *Tetris* with hunks of metal and guns.

The plane takes off just as I pull the trailer's door closed and snap the seal on the latch.

I pull out my phone and see it's six-fifteen. I send a simple 'Done' text to Whiskey, then slide my phone back in my cut.

"Mountain, you stay with the truck. Wrecker, Tiny, let's do one more walk around the field and meet up with Smoke and Cypher. When we get back, we'll head out," I order then walk out of the hangar and head left, while the others go right.

Now that Steel's back home, and we've got Smoke as a full-patch Brother, the club had to restructure our

Enforcer teams. As one of our four head Enforcers, the guys on my team are my responsibility. We go through a change every few years, and it's just part of the constant ebb and flow of club life. As we get new Brothers, and as others step back to take simpler roles, everyone has to adjust.

"Hey, Ring." I take a corner around another hangar and see the back of Smoke's cut. He's watching out toward the road. Damn guy has eyes on the back of his head.

"How'd you know it was me?" I ask as I step up next to him.

He looks my way and just winks. "That's for me to know and you to wonder about."

I laugh along with him. "It's time to get on the road."

"Let's roll." We head for the hangar and load up for the long day of riding we've got ahead of us.

Smoke and Mountain climb up into the semi, and Tiny, Cypher, and I straddle our Harleys. When the semi drives out of the hangar, Wrecker shuts the big door, then comes out a side door to climb on his bike. We split up to ride two bikes in front and two behind the semi.

We ride for three hours until we need to stop for fuel and food, then we're back on the road pretty quick for the final stretch south. We pull into the docks in Chicago just before five at night. The guys on Scotty's team have the truck unloaded and swap our full bins for empty ones. That's how the trade-off works. The company he works for has their own ins and outs, but Scotty's our main contact for drop-offs.

Just about two hours later, we're on our way back out, headed north. The plan is to find another motel to stay the night in, then we'll get some dinner, rest for the night, and drive the rest of the way home tomorrow morning. We should be home by early afternoon.

Then I can find Steel and see what he has planned for the night. Hopefully, he's open to taking our woman out. We need to take her on a proper date and get to know her better. Sometimes the clubhouse isn't the best place to be when you want some alone time. Maybe we can take her to The Lodge for dinner, then head back to the clubhouse for a night of sweaty, dirty conversations where we get to know her body even better.

CHAPTER TWENTY-TWO

STEEL

Ring left on a run yesterday, so I'm up shit's creek without a paddle. I called my crazy ass baby momma to find out when to drop Opal off, but Sydney hasn't answered her phone. Tomorrow's supposed to be my first day back working at Rebel Repairs, but if I can't find someone to watch Opal, I'll have to delay going back.

"Hey, Opal," I peak in the bathroom, watching her splash around in the tub.

She looks up at me and I laugh. She has two handfuls of bubbles and is holding them to her face, giving herself a pretty impressive beard.

"Look, Daddy. I'm Santa!" She's so happy with herself.

"You sure are. How about after your bath we go downstairs and see Duchess? I have to work tomorrow and need someone to watch you."

"Where's Papa?" Her lower lip quivers. Oh no, here come the tears.

I rush forward and kneel next to the tub. "No tears." I rub her cheeks, trying to make her sadness go away. "Papa had to leave for a few days. He'll be back in two days."

"You promise? Two days?" That makes her frown turn into a small smile.

"I promise." My chest feels heavy, knowing my daughter wants Ring so much, but I guess that'll be part of getting back into the routine of being home. It's an adjustment for all of us. "I'd love to spend the day with you, but I have to work for a few hours. After I'm done, we'll do something fun. That sound good?"

Opal nods, sending the bubbles on her chin dropping to the water. "Sounds good to me." Now that she's smiling again, I can take a full breath.

When she's all washed and rinsed, I drain the tub and wrap Opal in a towel. I carry her out of the bathroom, then drop her on my bed. She bounces around a little, causing her to giggle. We work together to pick out the perfect jammies, then head for the door.

I don't see Duchess in the main room, so I take a wild guess and take my little pony on a piggyback ride headed for the backyard. The lights are on in Whiskey and Duchess's cabin, so it looks like I guessed right.

"Giddy up, Daddy." Opal squeezes my neck.

They must've seen us coming, because Duchess and Sunshine come out the front door just as we stop on the deck.

"What's up, Steel?" Duchess asks.

"SUNSHINE!" Opal screams in my ear. "Lemme down, Daddy. Lemme down."

"Hold your horses." In an effort to not drop her, I slowly let Opal slide down my back. "Sorry for interrupting your evening. I came to ask you a favor, Duchess."

Once Opal's feet hit the deck, she pushes around me and is at Sunshine's feet. She kneels down and the two of them are instantly having a whispered conversation.

"What's up?" Duchess draws my attention back to her.

"Ah, shit," I rub the back of my neck, "I hate to be a bother, but I'm supposed to start working at the shop tomorrow, and a certain someone won't return my calls to arrange me dropping Opal off. I wanted to know if you could watch her for a few hours in the morning. At least until I can check in and get caught up on business stuff."

Duchess looks back at Sunshine, who's now sitting on the deck with Opal in her lap. Seeing my little girl so happy in the arms of my woman does something crazy to my heart. This feeling is one I'll definitely need to get used to, I guess. I'd give anything for this to be a sight I see for a very long time. Maybe Ring and I can convince Sunshine to give us a few more babies. Whoa, where'd that come from?

Trying to get back to Earth, I give Duchess my attention again.

"I'd love to watch her, but I've got a doctor's appointment at nine. I'm sorry."

"I'll watch her." We both turn to see Sunshine lift Opal to her feet, then stand herself. "I didn't mean to eavesdrop, but this one mentioned you going to work, then I heard you ask about tomorrow."

As much as I'd love for them to spend the day together, I don't want Sunshine to feel pressured into it before she's fully ready. "Are you sure? After the other day—" I start, but she cuts me off.

"I wouldn't offer unless I was sure."

That gets Opal excited. "Please, Daddy? Can Sunshine play with me tomorrow?"

I scoop Opal up and hitch her on my side. "If it's okay with you, it's okay with me."

"YAY!" Opal waves her arms above her head, then hugs my neck as tight as her tiny arms can.

"I'll head in and let you guys work out the details." Duchess waves and goes inside.

Sunshine steps closer to me. "What time do you need me here in the morning?"

With Opal still in one arm, I use the other to grab Sunshine's hand and pull her even closer. "Is eight okay?" I ask, looking down at her.

"Eight's good with me." She smiles back, then gives her attention to my arm monkey. "You better get a good night's sleep. We're gonna have lots of fun tomorrow."

Opal practically jumps into Sunshine's arms, making all three of us laugh.

"Goodnight, Sunshine." She hugs her, then goes limp, causing Sunshine to let her down, then she's off at a full sprint for the clubhouse's back door. She looks back to see me not running after her, so she climbs up on a picnic table and waits for me.

"She's adorable." Sunshine squeezes my hand.

I look down at her, then spin her so her back is to the clubhouse. I lean down just a bit, hoping she picks up on my intention.

Sunshine lifts her chin and closes her eyes, giving me the green light. I start out gentle, just pressing our lips together, then go in for a quick taste. I trace her lips with my tongue and dive in when she opens up. Knowing we can't get too carried away, I end the kiss, but pull her in for a full hug. I put my feet a step apart and tug Sunshine to step in between my boots. I wrap my arms around her shoulders and give her all my heat.

"Mmm, I like this," she mumbles into my chest.

"Me too," I drop a kiss on her head, "but I need to get the little one up to bed."

Sunshine unwraps her hands from my back and sets them on my stomach, not looking up at me. "You're such a good dad."

I untangle our arms and lift her chin to look at me. "Thank you" is all I can say before I kiss her one more time.

"See you bright and early." Then she's gone, back inside the cabin.

"Bedtime," I holler and jog toward Opal. She jumps up and runs inside. I chase her all the way inside, then up the stairs to our room.

Opal crawls in her bed, and after hugs and kisses, and two asks for a glass of water, she's out. I get ready for bed, then crawl under my covers wishing I had Sunshine next to me. What I wouldn't give to be able to hold her all night long.

I look at my phone and see it's eight-thirty. Sunshine's late. Opal and I are sitting in the main room, eating breakfast, and waiting for Sunshine to get here.

I wonder where she is. I texted her a few times, but haven't gotten an answer. Trying not to get too worried, I decide to just wing it. If something came up, I'll do what I can in the shop with Opal by my side.

"Alright, little lady. Let's head to the shop. Looks like you're hangin' with me today." I get up and toss our garbage.

"But where's Sunshine?" Opal stomps toward the door. "I want her to sit me."

Her grumpy words make me chuckle. "I'll try to call her once we get outside."

We make our way across the parking lot and enter the garage through one of the big bay doors. I set Opal on a stool, giving her some sockets to play with and organize.

Just as I pull my phone out to call Sunshine again, the front gate rolls open and her van drives in. She parks at the far end of the lot, gets out, shuts the door, then runs our way.

"I'm so sorry I'm late. There was a wreck on the highway and I had to detour and take back roads." Sunshine pants, trying to catch her breath.

"It's okay. I tried to call, but you didn't answer."

"Oh, shoot." Sunshine digs through her purse, pulling out her cell. "It's on silent."

I grab her for a quick hug. "No big deal. I'm happy you're here."

She gives Opal all her attention. "What's the plan for today?"

Opal zeros in on our still joined hands. "Is Sunshine your girlfriend?"

I freeze and look at Sunshine. She gives me a smile and small nod, so I'm guessing she's okay with where this conversation seems to be heading.

"Yes, she is. Is that okay?"

"What about Papa? She's his friend too." Her face is very serious for a four-year-old.

I nod. "She's both mine and Papa's girlfriend." I don't know how else to explain it to her.

"Is it okay to be both their girlfriends?" Sunshine lets go of my hand and sits on the stool next to Opal.

"It's okay to me." Opal shrugs, then goes back to lining up her sockets.

Sunshine and I look at each other, dumbfounded. I guess Opal could care less that the adults in her life are all in a relationship with each other. The girls head inside so I can get my work day started.

I find Wrench kneeling next to a Sportster and head his way. "Hey, Wrench. How are things around here?" While I was away, Wrench took the reins around the shop.

He stands, wiping his greasy hands on a rag. "Everything's been really good actually. I've got everything business wise in the computer system, but daily, all's still the same."

"Sounds good. Listen, I wanted to run something by you. What do you think about sitting down soon and splitting up the responsibilities around here? Now that Opal's getting older, I want to have a little more flexibility on my schedule. And since it seems like you've got stuff running smooth, I want to let you keep doing what you're doing."

That gets Wrench excited. "That'd be awesome."

"You've done this place good, and I don't wanna bulldoze back in and ruin things. We can work together."

"I'm all for it."

"Good. I'll let you get back to it." I head for the office and get lost for a few hours in what seems to be endless paperwork. It's amazing how much business has come through our doors in two years.

It's four o'clock before I realize the day got away from me. My stomach growling reminds me I didn't stop to eat lunch. I head inside and up to my room, and what I find melts my heart just a little. Opal is napping on my bed with Sunshine lounging next to her, doing something on her phone.

"Hey," Sunshine whispers, slowly getting off my bed.

I shut my bedroom door, grab her hand, and pull her into the bathroom. Pushing the door shut a crack, I back Sunshine against the wall. Lifting her by her thighs, I kiss her, silently thanking her for being here for me today.

Sunshine loops her arms around my neck and kisses me back, following my lead.

"Sunshine?" We pull apart when we hear Opal calling from the bedroom.

"That's our sign to stop," Sunshine laughs.

I set her down and open the door all the way. "We're right here."

"Daddy! I didn't know you was here."

"I just came in." I plop down next to her on the bed. "How about we take Sunshine out to dinner?"

"YES!" She jumps up and leaps to the floor.

"I'm hungry. Where we going?" Sunshine scoops her up.

"Pizza?"

"I love pizza."

"What kind?"

"Pep-roni and extra cheese."

"Me too."

"Papa likes yucky green stuff on his pizza. He gets me my own."

"Well, I guess it's a good thing I'm here. We can get a big pizza to share."

"Awesome!" Opal's in heaven while I watch them go back and forth, deciding our plans for the evening.

"Is that okay?" Sunshine asks from my side.

I put my arm around her shoulder and chuckle. "Sounds perfect."

CHAPTER TWENTY-THREE

RING

By the time we were done eating dinner, everyone decided they wanted to skip staying in another motel and ride straight home. It's just after six in the morning when we get the semi closed in the salvage yard and pull into the compound parking lot. We all back our bikes into their respective spots and walk like a bunch of slugs into the clubhouse. Mountain heads for the kitchen, Smoke goes out to the back patio, and I follow everyone else upstairs.

I intend to nose dive into my bed, but stop in the middle of the hall when I notice Steel's door open a crack. That's unusual. I peek my head into the room and smile at what I see. My tiredness goes away in a flash and I'm immediately wide awake.

Steel's lying on the far side of the bed, facing the door, like he's watching over the room. Penelope's in the middle, spooned in his arms, her back to his chest. Then there's Opal, spread out like a starfish on the half of the bed closest to the door.

I step into the room as quietly as I can, locking the door behind me. That gets Steel's attention and his eyes are open when I turn back to face the bed. He lifts his left hand from where it's resting on Penelope's hip and waves me forward.

Using the adjoining door, I duck into my room to kick off my boots and pull down the blankets. I make my way back to Steel's room and gently scoop up the still sleeping Opal. She's out like a light, so I hurry into my room and get her tucked in my bed. I turn on the stand fan in the corner, to make some noise, then shut the door behind me.

That child could sleep through a tornado if you'd let her. She usually doesn't wake up until someone makes her, so I'm not worried about her possibly interrupting what I've got planned for the rest of my morning.

I lean back against the door and just look at the scene in front of me. Steel's running his hand up and down Penelope's arm, but she's still sleeping soundly.

"You gonna join us?" Steel whispers.

"Hell yea, I fuckin' am," I murmur back.

I pad across the room, then crawl up the bed from the end. Lying on my left side, I scoot as close to Penelope as

I can. Steel still has his hand on her arm, so I lift my right hand to push a few strands of hair off her beautiful face.

She starts wiggling a bit. Her face nuzzles into my hand, and I lean in to kiss her awake. Penelope returns my kisses, but I still don't think she's fully awake.

I know the second she wakes up and realizes something's going on around her because her whole body goes still and her eyes fly open. My lips are still on hers, so our open eyes are really close. She tries to jerk back but can't move a centimeter because of the bulk behind her.

"Oh!" she shrieks, sitting up between us.

"I don't think so, Sunshine," Steel chuckles behind her, then I join in making the whole bed shake.

"You're staying right here." I pull her arm, laying her back down.

She settles on her back and looks back and forth between Steel and myself. It's like she can't decide where's the right place to look.

Steel makes the decision for her. He grabs her by the hip and rolls her onto her left, so she's facing him. "Good morning, Sunshine," he says, then he kisses her.

I shift myself closer to her, wrapping my right hand around her waist and slipping it up the front of her shirt, spanning her entire ribcage. I grind my hardening dick into her ass and the dual friction causes her to groan into Steel's mouth.

"It's okay," I whisper in her ear. "Just feel what we're doing to you."

She wiggles her backside into my growing bulge, making me groan back at her.

Her head rolls back so I lift myself, allowing her to stretch back. Steel's kissing down her throat, and I can feel his hands roaming her body. I just hold her close to me while he gets better acquainted with our woman. He's slowly learning all the drop-dead gorgeous parts of her.

Steel stops kissing her chest to sit up and grab her by the arms, pulling her from my grasp. He lifts her onto his lap so she's straddling his legs and they're face to face. "Do you remember what I said the other night in our texts?" Steel threads his hands in her hair, directing her head to the side so he can continue kissing her neck and chest.

She doesn't answer him, so I kneel at her left side and use my finger to turn her chin my way. She meets my eyes but looks lost in her bliss. "Answer him," I whisper before kissing her.

"I don't remember," Penelope says against my lips, in a harsh breath. It sounds like Steel hit a sensitive spot.

"I said," he untangles himself from her arms resting on his shoulders, "that I'd get to be inside of you first when the three of us were together. Do you remember that?"

She looks back and forth between us again, her cheeks rosy and her eyes still wide open. Her hair's a wavy mess and she already looks like she's been ravaged, but we're just getting started.

Finally, she looks back at Steel but reaches out her left hand to find mine. I link our fingers together and give her my demand again. "Answer him, Penelope."

She nods. "I remember."

"Good. Ring was a selfish fucker and got you to himself, so this time, I get to be inside your fuckin' pussy first." The bed shifts when Steel lifts his hips, grinding up into Penelope.

She grips my hand super tight, closes her eyes, and stretches her neck back, making her whole upper body look long and lean. Steel uses this position to his advantage and buries his face in her cleavage. I don't blame him at all—she pretty much just pushed her round tits into his face.

If Steel's going to get to be inside her first, I decide her kisses will be all mine for the next few minutes. I wrap my right arm around her waist and pull her out of Steel's lap. She yelps as I toss her back down onto the bed and crawl on top of her. My arms are on either side of her head and my knees are bracketing her hips. I have her completely covered.

"I need my kisses before we start getting you naked." And that's exactly what I do—I kiss her like I own her, exactly like I told her I was going to. Whether she believed me or not, I don't know, but I'll prove it to her regardless.

I feel the bed move but don't stop to find out what Steel's doing. That's until he grabs me by the back of my cut and pulls me off her.

We're both now standing at the foot of the bed, staring at a disheveled Penelope lying on the rumpled sheets. Steel growls his approval, "Damn, Sunshine. You're hot as fuck."

CHAPTER TWENTY-FOUR

PENELOPE

The mattress shifts underneath me, but I'm focused on keeping my breath while kissing Ring, I forget everything around me. That's until he's yanked off me and I'm left lying in the middle of the bed.

My two very strong, sexy as hell men are standing side by side, at the foot of the bed, just staring at me with hunger in their eyes.

"Damn, Sunshine. You're hot as fuck," Steel growls out like he's part grizzly bear.

"You got that fuckin' right." Ring matches his deep tone.

"What you two gonna do about it?" I don't know where my boldness comes from, but I just go with it.

I trail my left hand from my stomach up to my breast, giving my nipple a teasing pinch through my clothes. That snaps both guys out of their trances and they each grab one of my feet, pulling my socks off. Steel then drops one knee on the mattress, leaning forward to undo the button on my shorts and unzip the denim.

Ring knocks Steel out of the way with his shoulder and tugs the material down by the bottom hem, removing my shorts altogether. Shit, that was hot.

All I can do is lie here and hold on tight to the sheet. The way these two are manhandling me, I'll be lucky to be left in one piece when all's said and done.

Steel untangles one of my hands from the cotton and pulls me up to sit in front of them at the edge. My feet touch the cool wood floor and I instantly have four hands pulling and yanking my t-shirt over my head. My bra is unhooked in the process, leaving me sitting in just my panties.

I guess they must like what they see, because they both freeze, just staring at my chest. It's my turn to take the next step.

I lift both my hands, touching each of their stomachs to push them back a step, and stand up. I work my hands under the material of their shirts, and they unfreeze to shrug off their cuts. They both step away to hang their leather on hooks on the wall but are back in front of me just as fast.

Steel tries to take his shirt off, but I stop him with my hands, grabbing the cotton myself. I've been wondering what he's hiding underneath his colorful t-shirts. Unlike Ring, who is always dressed in all black, Steel isn't afraid of a little color. This shirt, for instance, is a dark crimson red, almost the color of blood.

I slide my hands up his chest, pushing the material up with my wrists. When I reach his shoulders, he lifts his arms, letting me pull the shirt off all the way. I toss it to the left, not caring where it lands. At some point, Steel had unbuttoned his jeans, so I can see the elastic band of his boxer briefs riding above his waistband. Those are a dark red color as well.

"Did you match your clothes on purpose?" I tease him.

"He's been known to do that." Ring laughs.

"Shut up, asshole." Steel keeps his eyes on me but jokes back at his friend. "I like colors, so sue me. I'm sick of orange and gray."

I look him up and down, taking in all his sexiness. I try to meet his eyes, but I see he's now looking to his left at Ring. They seem to be having a silent conversation about something good, because they've got mirroring smug smiles.

Next thing I know, Ring's tugging me so my back is to his chest and I'm facing Steel.

"Like what you see, Sunshine?" Cocky fucker.

I nod and let my hands start exploring. His chest is sculpted, each muscle defined and rock hard, and his pecs are scattered with just a dusting of dark hair, making his skin super soft.

I make a simple observation. "You don't have much ink." His entire right arm is covered in a sleeve of black and gray pictures from his shoulder down to his wrist. But every other surface is just plain skin.

His chest flexes as he chuckles. "I'm not like my friend behind you. I don't have an addiction to needles."

At the mention of Ring behind me, my body becomes aware of what he's doing to me. Ring's hands are sliding around my ribcage and reaching my front to grab handfuls of my breasts. He presses his entire body into my back, holding me tight to him.

"I don't have an addiction to needles," he says as he kisses down my shoulder. "I have an addiction to you."

"I know Steel's real name, but not Ring's," I blurt out, closing my eyes. I don't know what made me think of it in this specific moment, but it's something that's been floating around in my head like a little annoying gnat these last few days. I knew we'd talk about it eventually, but I guess now's the time.

Steel's still in front of me, so when I gain the courage to open my eyes, I see his smirk. He finds my random question outburst funny.

"We probably should've had this talk a few days ago, huh?" He steps forward, pressing his chest into mine, pushing me back against Ring.

I let out a laugh and exhale at the same time. "Probably."

"Because of our first meeting at the prison, you know the name on my ID is Colt, but next to my moms, no one calls me that."

The name suits him. Strong but still a little wild.

"Can I call you that?" I smile up at him.

"Woman," he growls, "only when I'm balls deep in your pussy."

"Don't let him fool you." Ring nuzzles into my neck. "This lunatic would respond to you calling him late for dinner."

I turn my head to look back at Ring. "And what's your real name? You've already been inside me and I still don't know."

"Real name's Ryan. Ryan Bell." He puffs out his chest and has this look on his face that's hard to describe. It's a mix of 'don't mess with me' and 'I dare you to question it'.

I grab one of his hands with mine and give it a squeeze. "I like it. Does Ring have anything to do with your last name?" It's a simple assumption and I hope it's not the reason he's looking kind of defensive.

"Yea," he replies. "It started as a stupid nickname when the Brothers heard my name, and it stuck. I hated it at first but I've grown to like it."

"Well, I don't care what anyone else thinks, I like it." I turn my face for a kiss, and he devours me. I can feel the pride radiating from his chest and into my back.

"I don't care what our real names are, you call us whatever you want behind closed doors. But know this,"

Ring grabs a handful of my hair and tugs my head back, moving his kisses down to my neck, "one day soon, your name will join the ink on my body."

I close my eyes and my whole body shivers. The thought of him getting my name tattooed permanently onto his skin makes me break out in goosebumps.

"I think she likes that, Brother," Steel says between dropping kisses on my chest, reminding me that I'm still the center of a very hot man sandwich. "And as much as I like the idea of getting her name inked on our skin, we need to get this train moving. I need to be inside her, and fast."

Before I can speak, both guys pull away, leaving me standing alone. I hear shuffling behind me, so I turn my head to see Ring pulling his shirt off. I was right, he's covered in tattoos, even on his chest. His stomach's free of ink, but that looks to be the only thing empty. He pushes down his jeans, taking his boxer briefs down with them. His all-black clothes reveal his skin decorated in black designs. But right now isn't the time to look too closely because his dick standing at attention requires all my attention.

I go to reach for it, but my arm's pulled back and I'm spun to face Steel again.

"Me first," he demands before kissing me stupid.

He turns us and the back of my legs hit the end of the bed. He lifts me, then crawls the both of us up the bed, with me holding onto him like a spider monkey. My head hits the pillow, but his kisses never stop.

Steel lowers himself, trailing kisses over my chin, down my neck, and across my chest, going south until he reaches my now very damp panties. I can feel my center dripping with all the excitement from the attention of my two men. He tugs the material off somehow, and I'm not sure what he does, but next thing I know, they're gone and his tongue's buried in my folds. It's only been a few days since he did this the last time, but I missed it.

I feel something cool and wet swipe across my right nipple, and I open my eyes to see Ring's mouth close around my pebbled peak. He sucks as much of my tender skin into his mouth as he can, causing my back to arch up. One of his hands reaches across and pinches my other nipple, causing me to groan out.

My sounds must get Steel's attention because his tongue goes into hyper-speed. I feel a finger circling my opening, and as soon as it pushes up inside me, the several points of stimulation drive me wild. I scream out loud as my orgasm crashes over the edge.

Ring moves his mouth to mine, to silence the noises I'm making. That's when I remember there's a sleeping little one in the next room. Shit, can't wake her or this whole thing is over.

"You taste so sweet," Steel nips my inner thigh. "Wanna taste, Ring?"

That gets Ring's attention, and he stops kissing me to look down. "If I start now, you won't get inside her first."

"Well, then fuck you, I need in this hot pussy." Steel inserts a finger back in my center, making me squirm again.

I push his hand away and grab his shoulder, pulling him down on top of me. "Fuck me now, Steel."

CHAPTER TWENTY-FIVE

STEEL

Have you ever wanted something so bad, you could almost feel yourself touching it? Like your fingertips just gliding over the item, touching it for the first time? Well, that's how I'm feeling about Sunshine right now. My skin's itching to reach out and grab her. I've been craving this woman for over a year, and I finally get to be with her. If you would've told me the day I met her, that I'd be standing here, staring at her naked body, I would've said you were out of your damn mind.

I guess the time for thinking is over. She pulls me down on top of her. Sunshine holds my eyes and whispers, "Fuck me now, Steel."

"Whatever you want, Sunshine." I prop myself up on my left elbow and use my right hand to lift her leg and wrap it around my back. This opens her center just enough that I can tilt my hips to find her pussy with the tip of my dick. My cock's like a heat-seeking missile, zeroing in on her opening right away.

I push forward slowly, rocking a few times. sinking inside her wet depths a little at a time. "Holy fuuuuck," I hiss out between gritted teeth. I get all the way in, and she's so tight, I feel myself on the verge of coming.

But I can't let our first time end like this. I know it's been a long time since I've fucked anything other than my own hand, but for this woman, I need to man up. She deserves my very best, and she'll fucking get it in spades.

I rock back on my heels and pull her legs up to rest over my hips. I grasp her ass and get to rocking myself in and out of her pussy. I don't want to go too fast and blow too early, but I keep a steady pace so we both get what we want and need. I need her to remember this day for the rest of our lives. Remember the day we finally got what we've both been wanting for so long, even if we didn't think it was something we'd ever do.

Sunshine lifts her hands and grabs the pillow above her head, holding on for dear life. Her whole body is rocking on the mattress, bouncing her tits up and down. And I'm not the only one who notices—Ring has all his attention locked on her.

Ring looks at me and I nod, giving him the go ahead to dive in on those bouncing beauties. The second he puts his lips back on her nipple, her eyes fly open, meeting mine. She looks shocked, like us both still touching her is beginning to sink in for the first time.

"Yea, baby, that's right," I grunt through my strokes. "We're just getting started."

"Oh, please," she pants, now holding Ring's head with one hand and reaching for me with the other. I grab her left hand with my right and lace our fingers together, giving her whatever support she needs.

Honestly, I can't believe I'm still this hard and fucking her. I think it's time to switch things up a little, so I tap Ring on the shoulder to get his attention. He releases her tit with a pop, and I see he's left a few red spots behind. Nice, I can't wait to leave a few of my own.

Thinking of marking her has suddenly gotten me even hotter. Maybe Ring was on to something about tattooing her name on our bodies. Maybe we can convince her to get our road names inked on her somewhere. Maybe where only we can see.

"Whatchya got in mind?" he asks.

I grab hold of her hips again, slowing down the rhythm of bouncing against each other that we've got going. I drop my pelvis back, sliding out of her wetness, and lift her legs to one side, rolling her along with. Slapping her ass, I smirk.

"Why'd you stop?" she whines.

I tap her backside again. "Roll over. I want you on all fours."

"Fuck yea," Ring picks up what I'm throwing down and practically throws her around like a ragdoll.

He tosses all the pillows on the floor and scoots to sit against the headboard, pulling Sunshine to kneel in front of him and arranging her on her hands and knees. This is when she understands what we're trying to accomplish with this position.

Sunshine zeros in on the fact that her head's now in Ring's lap with his erection in front of her face. The woman's suddenly on a mission and gets to work. I stand back and watch her lick up his dick. As soon as she's occupied with pleasing him, humming away, I get myself back in the game. Spreading her knees, I get as close to her as I can, then push myself back inside her channel.

This time, I slide in just a bit easier. It's almost like her pussy has formed to fit me perfectly. She's tight enough to give me pressure in all the right places, but not so much so that she'll send me straight into coming too fast.

I bracket her hips with my hands and slam myself in and out of her over and over. I feel her jolt when I'm so far inside her, I hit her cervix and can't go any further. That spurs me to try anyways, so I kick myself into overdrive and let my freak flag fucking fly. I'm only paying attention to what's happening to her pussy and my dick.

That's interrupted just a bit when I hear Ring start to chant. "She's gonna . . . make me . . . come. Keep . . . doing . . . that!"

So, I do. Ring starts grunting, and I see the second he explodes. He grabs her head with both hands and fucks his hips up into her mouth. I hear her choking on everything he's making her swallow. Fuck, that's hot.

I feel the tingle race up my spine, and before I can blink, I'm exploding. I come so damn fast, I couldn't stop myself even if I tried. And that sets off Sunshine's orgasm.

"Colt!" She tries to scream my name, but it comes out more like a grasp for air.

Her pussy starts to suffocate my dick and I force myself not to be pushed out of her heat. I keep my grip on her hips super tight and push myself as deep as her pussy will let me. I wait for her muscles to stop pulsing, then I pull her up on her knees.

Hearing her use my real name was better than I could've imagined. Other than having to tell Sydney my real name because it's on Opal's birth certificate, I've never told any other woman I slept with my real name, and now I know why. No one deserved to know it until this woman. She's the only one worthy of knowing the real me.

Wrapping my hands around her stomach, I soak up her warmth, letting all of us catch our breath.

"Damn," Sunshine lets out a giggle, "I almost died."

Ring runs a hand over his head and lets out a hard exhale. "I think I went to heaven for a second."

I laugh with them. "Oh, I for sure did. She almost squeezed my dick off there at the start."

"And now, it's my turn." Rings gets a very serious look on his face, and that's my cue to get out of his way. Round two, here we come.

CHAPTER TWENTY-SIX

RING

Steel's holding Sunshine against his chest and she has the most blissful look on her face. I don't exactly know what blissful means, but this is the closest I can think to describe the smile that's radiating from her.

Maybe he's got something going in calling her Sunshine all the time. If she keeps looking at us like that, I'd be more than happy to jump on that name bandwagon. It'd be the perfect name for us to use when we claim her as our Old Lady. But right now, it's time for me to get some of our Sunshine's pussy. See, the name's perfect.

"And now, it's my turn." I drop my smile for a blank expression, hoping my woman knows I mean fucking business.

"She's all yours." Steel backs away from her and lays himself out to my left, propping himself like he's ready to watch the show.

I'll give him a show to watch all right.

Sunshine's still kneeling, just staring at me, like she's not sure what to do next. I rearrange myself so I'm lying flat on my back, one leg on either side of her. Before I can reach for her, she pounces at me like a lioness in heat. In a way, she's exactly that.

Her hands land on the mattress next to my head, and I wrap my arms around her back, forcing her to let her whole weight lay on me. Sunshine moves her legs to bracket my hips, opening herself to my dick. I take that as a sign and lift her just a bit to let my dick find her opening.

I slide my hands down to her ass and use them as handholds to control our movements. I slide my cock into her pussy and pull her down on me.

"Shit," Sunshine swears and drops her forehead onto my shoulder.

Now that I have her in the exact position I want, I start moving, pumping my hips up and down, sliding in and out of her wet, warm pussy. And just like my body lost control the last time I was inside her, my brain has no control of what happens next. I keep my grasp of her backside and start pumping in and out of her heat. Over and over and over.

"Fuck, she's tight," I swear out loud.

"I told you." Steel pops up next to my head.

I can feel Sunshine's head turn a little to my left, so I let her adjust her torso a bit, but I don't let her go too far. I keep my hold on her and use the mattress's bounce to help in our bodies' need to keep rocking together. We find the perfect pace and I let my momentum keep us moving.

"Oh, goddammit," Sunshine swears through a breath as she kisses Steel.

"That's our good girl. Keep feeling him fuck you. You can do it." It's almost like he's cheering her on. "Look at me, Sunshine."

"I can't," she whines.

I don't know what's happening between them, but since neither of them are stopping me, I keep plowing into her.

Feeling her pussy squeeze me is really what I imagine heaven's like. When she had her lips wrapped around my cock, I thought I was never going to come down from floating, but this is just as good, if not a million times better.

"Open your damn eyes!" Steel barks. "There they are. Now, I want you to put yourself back fully on top of Ring and let him see your pretty eyes sparkle. Got me?"

"Yes," she nods.

Steel kisses her one more time, then lets her go, backing off the bed. I see him stand and start to jack himself off.

More power to him, but that's not what I care about right now. The woman now back in my face is where my mind belongs.

She drops her forehead to mine, and I tighten my arms around her. I can feel my orgasm building, so it's time to make her come first. I bend my knees and set my feet flat on the bed, legs spread enough to give myself the leverage I need to fuck her so damn hard, she gets everything I can give her.

Her eyes are locked on mine, so when she whispers my name, "Ryan," I know this is it.

I'm no more than a dozen pumps in and her whole body tightens. This is it. I slam into her three more times and we both come. My sight goes blurry, and I can't catch a full breath, but I keep going, giving her every drop of me.

This woman is it for me. She's who I've been waiting for, and I won't stop giving her every part of me until our last breaths.

My brain goes a little fuzzy again, but when I can finally take a full breath, I blink my eyes open. That's when I notice for the first time that the whole room is glowing with sunlight through the window. I don't know how long we've been going at it, but it's been long enough for the sun to be blazing.

"Now I think I'm dead," Sunshine mumbles, sliding off me to lay to my left. "You both killed me and I'm dead."

I use whatever energy I can muster to move over, saving her from taking a tumble off the side of the bed.

"My legs feel like Jell-o." Steel worms his way in next to Sunshine, so we're now back in the same positions we were when this all started.

"Did you come again?" Sunshine asks Steel.

That makes us both laugh. "I sure as hell did. Seeing you take your pleasure made me hard as fuck."

"Phew. If that's any sign of how things are gonna go for our future, sign me up."

Both Steel and I roll on our sides to bracket her.

"Woman," I make her look at me, "if you thought we'd let you go after this, you were sadly mistaken." With that, I kiss her with everything I have. "I told you I was gonna kiss you like I own you, and I damn well meant it."

"He's right. You're ours now." Steel pulls her face his way, then kisses her too. "But what's this kissing to own her business? What's that mean?"

Sunshine looks at me, smile on full blast again. "It was Ring's pick-up line. He grabbed my hand and said he wanted to kiss me like he owned me."

I kiss her once more, then lay back. "She caught Whiskey kissing all up on Duchess and was shocked at their PDA. Telling her I wanted to kiss her like I owned her was my way of letting her know I wanted to do the same to her without doing it in front of her father."

"Fuck, we still gotta bite that bullet. Don't we?" Steel plops down, scrubbing his face.

"What bullet?" Sunshine sits up between us, pretzel style, her nakedness still on full display.

Not that she's ever seemed to be ashamed of being naked in front of us but seeing her like this makes me happy. I want her to be comfortable, no matter what condition we're in. In or out of the bedroom.

"Just wait 'til your brother and dad find out about this little situation." Steel makes a circle in the air with his finger.

"We're gonna be dead meat," I chuckle.

"Oh, shit," she whispers.

"Shit is right," Steel and I respond at the same time. That makes all of us laugh.

Knock knock! Pounding on the door quiets the room real fast.

"Steel? You in there?" Fuck, it's Whiskey. Speak of the devil and he appears.

CHAPTER TWENTY-SEVEN

SUNSHINE

Steel: Don't forget about us.
Ring: I second that.
Me: I never could!
Steel: Good. I can't wait until you're back home.
Ring: Drive safe, Sunshine.

I smile at my phone.

I've only been gone for five days, but both guys check in with me several times a day. When I told them I was taking a last-minute road trip to help my aunt move, they both let me know they were going to miss me being away.

I stopped at the clubhouse with the intention of killing four birds with one stone, telling Ring, Steel, Mountain, and Whiskey that I would be gone for a week. Of course, I didn't tell all of them at the same time. We barely avoided Whiskey finding the three of us together, so I wasn't going to drop that bombshell right before I left.

When we heard Whiskey on the other side of the door, Ring jumped off the bed, scooped me up, and carried me to hide behind the bathroom door. Him showing his brute strength, muscles all bulging, would've been hot had we not been hiding from my older brother.

"Are you in there?" I snap out of my daze and look up to see Aunt Jane standing in the kitchen doorway, smiling at me.

I shake my head, then slide my now locked phone in my pocket. "I'm here. Just looking at my texts." I grab another plate from the box on the table and unwrap it from the newspaper, adding it to the stack on the counter.

"And what was so interesting that you got lost in la-la land? Was it a boy you were talking to?" She carries a box to the kitchen, setting it down next to the one I'm emptying.

I haven't exactly been open with her about what I've been doing while spending all my time at the clubhouse. She knows all about me finding my dad and a surprise brother, but I haven't mentioned anything about finding a guy I was interested while there, much less two guys.

"Maybe it's a guy," I keep my head down, grabbing another few plates from the box, "or two."

I continue unwrapping, hoping she didn't hear the last part, but I'm not that lucky.

"Two? What do you mean two?" I try to ignore her question, but she takes the newspaper from my hand, pulling me to sit in a chair next to her. "Spill the beans, Penelope."

I take a deep breath and let it all out. "It seems I've gone and fallen for two guys who are Brothers in the club. One I met the day I went to the clubhouse. Ring is super gruff and stoic but has a sweet side when I can get him to smile. And there's Steel, who I actually met a year ago when I filled in for a sick nurse at the prison. He got released and came home a few weeks after I started hanging out with everyone. We reconnected and the sparks flew. Oh, and he's also got the most adorable four-year-old daughter. Opal's so happy all the time and her joy is infectious."

I watch her face the entire time I word vomit everything and don't think she blinks once. "Oh my. That's a lot to take in."

"You're telling me." I nod, understanding her shock.

Jane places her hands on top of mine on the table. "Do they make you happy?"

Her simple question makes me smile. "Just thinking of them makes me happy. Is that weird?"

That makes her laugh. "It's a little weird, but if these two make you happy, that's all I care about. I just wish I could've met them before I moved all this way away." She pats my hands one more time, then lets me go to lean back in her chair.

"I'm sorry. You just dropped this moving announcement on me pretty quick and I didn't know how to process all the newness at once."

"I'm sorry about that. I wanted to tell you sooner but didn't want you to feel like I was leaving you all alone. It's just that when Phil asked me to move in with him, I jumped at the opportunity."

"I don't blame you one bit. Moving here was right for you."

Honestly, I'm so happy for her. After what her ex-husband did to her, she deserves all the happiness. About five years ago, he came home from work, a week before Christmas, and told her he wanted a divorce. No warning or anything. Her world was shaken. When she met Phil, she found her laughter again.

They've been doing long distance for a while, but now that my mom's gone, he finally got the courage to ask her to move down to Milwaukee to be with him full-time. I asked him why he waited so long, and he said he knew she'd never leave my mom while she was sick. He'd never ask her to do that. That's when I told her she had to move for him.

So, here we are less than a week later, unpacking all her things in his kitchen. Once she knew I was on board with her moving, we had her apartment packed in three days. Day four was all driving. And today's all about unpacking. I'll be driving back north tomorrow.

I know it'll be exhausting, but I really miss my new life. I haven't told Steel and Ring I'm heading back already, but I want to surprise them by just showing up at the clubhouse. I know that it'll probably out all of us to Whiskey and Mountain, but the more I think about it, the less I care. I'm not ashamed of us, so we need to just rip off the Band-Aid.

"And what's right for you? Can you keep up with two men?" she asks with a wink. "That's a whole lot of testosterone."

That makes me giggle like a schoolgirl. "If the rest of my life is anything like the other day, I think I'm gonna like being with them both. They rocked my world so hard, I was seeing stars."

"You go, girl!" That earns me a high five.

"It was all good until Whiskey knocked on the door looking for Steel." I shake my head, remembering the look on their faces.

"How'd that go down?" Jane props her head up in her hand, elbow on the table, totally invested in my adventures.

"The three of us were in Steel's room and Opal was sleeping in Ring's room. Unbeknownst to us, she woke up and made her way downstairs. Whiskey came upstairs to let Steel know she was down there. Ring and I hid in the dark bathroom, the door open just a crack, listening to their conversation."

"So, he had no idea you were in there?"

"After he went back downstairs, we all got dressed and I snuck downstairs and out the back door. Ring walked me to my van, kissing me like I was leaving for a year, then I left. As far as I know, he never knew I was there."

"Based on what you've told me about Mountain and Whiskey, I think they'll come around to the idea eventually. Remember that you're just as new to them as they are to you. I can't imagine what it's like to find out about a child you never knew you had."

She makes a good point. This is new for them too. "I just hate hiding a new relationship. We may all be happy in our bubble now, but it needs to grow out in the open. I decided when I get back, I'll tell the guys I need to tell my dad. I think he'll be the more understanding one."

"That's good. Just don't forget to invite me to the wedding," she chuckles, getting up from her chair.

"Wedding?" I stare at her like she's lost her mind. "It's way too soon to think about that."

She stands next to me and tucks a loose strand of hair behind my ear. "Sweetheart, love is whatever you make it. If these men are what you want, don't let them get away. Promise me that, okay?"

I acknowledge her thoughtfulness with a smile. "I promise."

"Promise me one more thing, then the rest is all up to you. Don't do what your momma did and run away because of a silly thought she never should've had. Hold tight to your men and that little girl, and don't let go. If they make you this happy just talking about them, I can only imagine what it's like in person."

CHAPTER TWENTY-EIGHT

STEEL

Before I got a chance to invite Sunshine to my sister, Meredith's, high school graduation, she told us she was leaving town for a week. Her aunt was moving and she wanted to help. Seeing that her aunt's the only relative she has left on that side of the family, Ring and I both told her we supported her decision.

I was working in the garage when I saw her van pull in the lot. When she said she was making the long drive, I told her I wanted to give her van a once-over to make sure everything was safe. She tried to refuse my help, but I told her I wouldn't let her leave without knowing everything was up to my safety standards.

I snuck a heated kiss before tapping her on the ass, sending her inside to say goodbye to everyone. Then I called Ring to let him know she was looking for him, so he dropped everything and came to see her before she left.

We've been in constant contact with her all week, but she hasn't told us exactly when she'll be back. I hope it's soon. I've got the whole weekend off work, and will be child-free after tonight, so I'm looking forward to spending as much time with my Sunshine as I can.

I knew sharing her with Ring was going to be easy, but it surprises me at the most random times. Seeing his name pop up in our group chats doesn't make me jealous at all. It makes me happy to see that he makes Sunshine happy. I wouldn't trust her happiness with just anyone else. She's our top priority, after Opal, of course.

Opal and I are sitting in the bleachers of the local high school, surrounded by probably a thousand people, cheering for their graduates as they collect their diplomas.

"Meredith Marie James." I see my baby sister climb the stairs and our whole row jumps up, yelling and clapping. She looks over to see us and smiles so big.

Meredith may be twelve years younger than me, but that never stopped us from being close. She texts and calls me and I always answer her as soon as I can. Being away from her these last two years was just as hard as being separated from Opal. Both girls are my pride and joy. Now, I get to add Sunshine to the mix.

We sit for another hour as everyone else gets their time in the spotlight, then when the ceremony's over, we head to my moms' house for a family dinner. To some, it may seem weird for my dad's family to be celebrating such a big milestone at someone else's house, but it's actually quite normal for our blended family.

Even though my dad was technically used as a sperm donor, his name's on my birth certificate, I have his last name, and visited him whenever I wanted. When he married his wife, Kathy, and had Meredith, we pulled them into our family circle.

We're spending the night at the moms' house so Opal and Meredith can have a long-awaited sleepover, so once I get them settled in their room with popcorn and a movie, I head back downstairs for some much-needed adult conversation. When they started talking nail polish colors, I couldn't duck out fast enough.

Janie and Helen are sitting at the dining room table, each with playing cards in hand. I take my seat and grab the cards they dealt out for me. Looks like tonight's a go-fish night. Don't let the child's game fool you, these women are as conniving as thieves. They take no prisoners, no matter their opponent or game.

"Who's Sunshine?" Mom Helen asks. I guess there's no beating around the bush tonight.

I keep my eyes on my cards. "She's about to be my Old Lady." When no one calls any cards, I give them my attention. Best to tell them everything. "She's Mountain's daughter and she's new to the biker world, but Ring and I are gonna claim her together and make her our Old Lady. You'll meet her soon."

"It's about time you grew up and settled down. I was beginning to think you'd switch teams and just shack with up Ring," Mom Janie says and laughs.

"Mom!" I'm stunned.

"We know you don't really swing that way, but stranger things have happened. We've got a friend who—"

Before she can continue her story, I cut her off, getting the game started. "Do you have any sevens?"

"Go fish," they both chuckle. My life is filled with crazy women, and I can't imagine it any other way.

I park my truck in front of Sydney's apartment the next morning to drop Opal off. Sunshine sent us a good morning text saying she was on her way home, so even though I don't know exactly when she'll be back, I want to be ready for whenever she calls.

I finally went and got myself a new truck this week, so I no longer have to rely on others to pick up or drop off Opal.

I got myself a patriot blue Dodge Ram 2500 Crew Cab. If I was a weaker man, I would've punched Whiskey and Ring when I pulled in the compound after coming home from the dealership. They both were giving me shit, saying their Chevys were better than my Dodge. I laughed back and said when they needed to be pulled out of a ditch, I wouldn't help them.

"Daddy, do I have to stay here?" Opal whispers as I lift her from her booster seat.

I keep her in my arms and kiss her cheek. "You spend the weekend with your mom, then I'll ask her if you can come back next week. That sound like a deal?"

"Okay." She doesn't sound especially happy, but this is one of the downsides of co-parenting.

When Sydney first told me that she was pregnant, I laughed in her face. I knew I was always careful with wrapping my dick with all the club girls, but apparently, letting her supply the condom one drunken night wasn't a good idea. After I got it out of her that she'd poked holes in the whole box, I lost my damn mind.

I didn't trust that the baby was even mine until we had a DNA test. On the off-chance the baby was my blood, I was in the delivery room for her birth, but just stood in the corner to watch. The nurses took our blood right after Opal came into the world, and three hours later, the results proved she was mine. Then, and only then, did I agree to sign the birth certificate and give her my name.

When they left the hospital two days later, I drove Sydney to her new apartment. Unbeknownst to her, she'd been kicked out of the club and was never to be allowed back on the premises. She screamed at me for hours after that, but I didn't care. She lied and connived to get knocked up by a Brother—she couldn't be trusted ever again.

Until I saw Sunshine again, I never really put much thought into trusting another woman enough to want to claim an Old Lady. Now, it's all I can think about.

Knock knock! I bang on the door, but there's no answer. I try the handle and find the door unlocked. When I swing it open, the whole apartment is pitch black. I flip the lights on and walk in with Opal still in my arms.

"Where's Mom?" Opal asks.

"No idea, munchkin. Let's get you a movie started, and I'll go look for her."

What I don't tell her is that I've got a bad feeling. Ring mentioned the last time he was here that the place was a mess, but what I'm seeing now is indescribable. The apartment's spotless. There isn't a plate or bottle or pizza box in sight. In the four years she's lived here, I don't think I've ever seen Sydney put everything away. Something's going on, and not knowing what I'm going to find down the hallway, I want Opal distracted.

I set her down on the couch, turn the television on, and start one of her favorite pony movies. She snuggles down with her blanket, focused on the screen, so I start my search of the apartment.

I use my boot to nudge Opal's bedroom door open and see all her stuff neat and tidy. Knowing my girl, this wasn't her doing.

The bathroom door's open, but I flip the switch, seeing nothing out of place.

At the end of the hall is Sydney's room. The door's completely shut, so I open it, and my worst fear is confirmed. She's lying in her bed, face up, with a needle in her arm. There's a rubber tourniquet still wrapped around her bicep.

I check for a pulse, even though I know it's useless, but I still have to try. Her lips are blue, and her skin is ice cold. Looks like she's been this way for a while.

I knew Sydney smoked a little weed occasionally, but this is so much more than that. This is major drug use. Not knowing what's in that syringe, I don't touch anything.

I may hate the woman, but I'd never wish this on anyone. If I knew she needed help, I would've at least tried to be civil with her.

What am I going to tell Opal? This is too much. I pull out my phone to call Ring. I need back-up. I need the club.

CHAPTER TWENTY-NINE

RING

When I woke up this morning and saw I had a text message from Sunshine, I jumped out of bed and started my workday early.

I don't have much to do today, but I still want to get everything done before she gets back. Steel is dropping Opal off at her mom's, so the three of us adults will have the whole weekend to ourselves.

I may have the reputation for being a moody asshole biker, but that doesn't mean I can't miss my woman like crazy when she's gone. It just goes to show that a good woman really can make a man better than his original self. I talked to Steel about taking Sunshine on a proper date and he was on board. Maybe if we can crawl ourselves out of bed for a few hours this weekend, we can finally show her off in public.

This morning I'm making a quick inventory list of things we need in The Lodge, the club's restaurant and bar. In addition to the brewery, The Lodge is part of my business responsibility to the club. A few months ago, I found a great manager to help be the face of the restaurant and bar. Having Abby's help has been a godsend. She just moved here from Kansas and needed a job and a fresh start.

After checking the last box, I shut off the storage room lights and head for my office. But before I can even make it two steps down the hall, my cell phone rings. Pulling it from my inner cut pocket, I see Steel's name on the screen. Hopefully, he's calling to say Sunshine's back and we can get our weekend started early. I'd be a damn happy camper.

"Did Sunshine call you?" I ask, not even bothering to say hello.

"I need you, Brother." Steel sounds lost.

I run for my office, drop the clipboard on my desk, grab my keys, and am out the back door before speaking. "What's wrong? Is it Opal?" God, I would be lost without that little lady.

"It's Sydney." He lets out a harsh breath. "She's dead."

I freeze mid-step. "Say that again."

"She's dead. Needle in her arm. I need you to call Whiskey and Trooper. I don't know what to do."

"You got it. I'm on my way. Hold on, Brother, I'm coming."

"Thanks" is all he says, then the line goes dead.

I swing my leg over my Harley and get settled in my seat. I hit Whiskey's name and call him right away.

Whiskey answers before it rings twice. "What's up, Ring?"

"We've got a problem. Steel just called me from Sydney's apartment and said she's dead. All I know is he found her with a needle still in her arm. He asked me to call for you and Trooper."

"What the fuck!" he yells. "I'll round up a few guys and meet you there." *Click.* He hangs up on me too.

It's time to ride. I fire up my bike and fly out of the parking lot. It's only a ten-minute ride to the apartment, and by the time I park, I hear more motorcycles coming down the street. Whiskey, Trooper, and Hammer ride up behind me.

"Any more details?" Trooper inquires while climbing off his ride.

"Nope. Just got here myself," I answer as we walk to the front door.

It's open just a crack, so I gently push it, not sure what I'll find inside.

Opal jumps up from the couch and runs for me. "Papa! What you doing here?" I scoop her up and hug her tight.

I set her back down on the couch and sit next to her. She waves to the other guys, but I need to know what she knows, if anything. "Where's your daddy?"

"He's in Mom's room," she says, pointing down the hall.

Trooper and Whiskey walk in that direction, disappearing from our line of sight. Needing to keep her distracted, I start her movie back up, then follow my Brothers to see what's going on.

I take one step into Sydney's bedroom and go still. Holy fuckin' shit. Steel was serious when he described her. There's not much to say about a dead person in general, but the rubber hose wrapped around her arm and the empty syringe sticking out of the crease of her elbow is an obvious explanation of what happened here.

"Did y'all know she was doing drugs?" Trooper asks us.

"No clue," Steel replies. He looks to be in shock himself.

"Me neither," I say, wrapping my arm around Steel's shoulder, trying to be supportive. None of us liked this bitch, but for her to do this was straight up fucking selfish.

"Call it in, T," Whiskey growls. "See if you can get your buddy, Thomas, to do us a favor and keep this as quiet as possible."

"You got it. But we all need to get out of this room for now. And make sure not to touch anything." Trooper pulls out his phone and is talking and walking.

We all follow, me in the rear of the line. I tug the door shut a crack and head for the living room. What I see there makes me freeze again.

Steel's standing in the middle of the kitchen, wrapped around Sunshine like he needs help standing. She's rubbing his back, whispering in his ear. She notices me and smiles my way. Sunshine holds out her hand and I join their little circle.

She pulls back from Steel and looks back and forth between the both of us. "Let's grab Opal and take her outside to the van. She shouldn't be in here when things start happening."

"I don't know where you came from, Sunshine, but thanks for being here," Steel chuckles, kissing her quick before scooping up Opal and hanging her upside down, making her giggle.

I lace my fingers with Sunshine's and kiss her. "When did you get here?"

She looks out the front door and points that way. I turn and see Duchess standing outside with Whiskey. "I had just pulled into the compound when the clubhouse doors flew open and that group came running out. The guys jumped on their bikes and Duchess just climbed in my van. She told me to drive and told me the little she knew on the way here."

"Thank you for coming. I'm sure you had better things you wanted to do today than deal with this mess." This is Sunshine's first real show of the crazy things that can happen in a club like ours. We may have never dealt with a drug overdose before, but dead bodies are a common occurrence in club violence.

She pulls on our still joined hands, getting my full attention. "You have nothing to thank me for. I'm here for you, Steel, and Opal. The three of you needed me and I was on my way before even knowing it. I'm here." Sunshine kisses my hand before pulling away and heading outside.

I stand there, staring at her as she walks away. I don't know how we got this lucky, but if she can give us blind faith like this, I can't wait to see what else she has in store for us. If I didn't have so much trust in her already, I'd say she was too good to be true.

"Ring." Trooper walks in the apartment with his friend, Deputy Thomas, behind him. "Before we get the body dealt with, why don't you go grab as much of Opal's things as you can. I doubt she'll ever have a need to come back here."

He's got a point. I didn't even think that far ahead, but it looks like Opal's going to be moving into the clubhouse with us now. In the back of my mind, I always wished that would happen, but not like this. It may be morbid to think this, but maybe Sydney being dead is best for Opal. She can now be surrounded by a family who loves her and would do anything for her. She's better off with a group of bikers than she was with her druggie mother. Good fucking riddance.

I head to Opal's room and look around. She doesn't have any luggage to pack things in, so I just pull stuff out of her dresser drawers, setting everything in piles on the bed spread. When I have all her clothes piled up, not that she has a lot to begin with, I gather the blanket's four corners and lift everything up in a makeshift sack.

It's not until I'm outside do I realize there's no way I can carry this with me on my bike. I must look lost because Sunshine yells out my name. Turning her way, I see she's got the tailgate of her van open and she's waving me her way. I cross the small parking lot and set my bundle down in the van.

"I knew keeping this van would come in handy one day."

"I've been meaning to ask why you had this thing. Isn't this something soccer moms and grandmas drive?" I give her a little nudge with my hip, joking with her.

She pushes back with both hands, but I don't budge. "Very funny, asshole. This was my mom's van. Having the cargo space made transporting her to her appointments a lot easier. Sometimes we had to go across the state to see different specialists. Just because she didn't want the chemo, didn't mean she didn't get as much care as I could get her."

I tug her into my chest and just hug her. I don't know what to say to make things better, so I show her my care by squeezing her tight. It hasn't been that long since she lost her mom, so whenever she needs someone to lean on, I'll give her my giant shoulders without a second thought.

"I need to get the rest of Opal's things." I push us apart a step. "Wanna give me a hand?"

She nods. "Lead the way."

We make two more trips inside to grab Opal's toys and movies, then load everything in the van. Steel puts Opal's booster seat into Sunshine's van, explaining to her that she gets to ride back to the clubhouse with the ladies.

Opal's so excited to be riding with Sunshine and Duchess, she doesn't even notice the coroner's van drive into the lot, or the gurney being wheeled into the apartment. She doesn't ask one question about the various police and sheriff's vehicles in the parking lot. Sunshine is showing her that there's a DVD player in the back of the headrest, so Opal's attention is on whatever cartoon is playing, not having another care in the world. That's how her life should be. She's four and is about to have her life thrown for a loop.

And if the feeling in my gut is correct, we're all in for a bumpy ride ahead. I can't put my finger on it exactly, but something about this whole drug situation makes my hackles rise. I don't think this is a single incident. Something's not right and I don't like it one damn bit.

CHAPTER THIRTY

SUNSHINE

It's been just over a week since Sydney overdosed on what we learned was an extremely high dose of heroin. The coroner put a rush on her autopsy and Whiskey had her blood results in his email three days after Steel found her.

Doc was out of the clubhouse when the email came through, and since Whiskey knows I have my nursing degree, he asked me to look at it and explain all the medical terms for him. He called it 'medical mumbo jumbo' but it was funny to see him try and read some of the words on his computer screen. A lot of medical words are based on foreign languages, so he sounded like a kid just learning how to read.

Opal has been doing a lot better than I first expected. I know it's still too soon to know how this will affect her in the future, but as of right now, her mom being gone isn't her biggest problem. Now, that's not to say everything has been smooth sailing. In fact, Opal and Steel have been butting heads at every turn.

Nothing he says makes her happy. She argues back at everything he tells her to do. She won't eat, brush her teeth, or get dressed without throwing sass his way. I can tell Steel's getting frustrated with her attitude, but I also can see the pain he tries to hide behind his eyes. Having her push back so hard is chipping away at him little by little.

She may not listen to Steel, but if Ring or I ask her to do something, she's on it immediately. It doesn't matter who else is in the room, when Ring or I come in, Opal runs to one of us. Yesterday, Steel had somehow managed to convince her to eat her lunch at one of the tables in the main room. I stood in the shadows behind the bar and watched him barter with her to take a few bites. I knew if she saw me, she'd want my attention, so I just stayed out of his way.

Steel knew where I was the whole time because he kept catching my eye and teasing me with flirty winks. After I tucked Opal in her bed last night, he pulled me into the bathroom and showed me how much he appreciated my silent support. He gave me two orgasms with his fingers before slamming his hard dick into my sopping wet channel, fucking me until neither of us could breathe.

"Sunshine." I look up from my tablet to see Opal standing in the doorway between Steel and Ring's rooms. Opal was taking a nap in her and Steel's room and I'm reading a book while lying on Ring's bed. Both guys are working today, so I volunteered to spend the day with our little lady.

"Hey. Did you have a good nap?" I pat the bed, and she climbs up to lay next to me.

"I guess." She sighs.

I try and hold back my smile, because when she gets that grumpy look on her face, she looks exactly like Steel. She's his mini-me and I find it adorable as heck.

"Want to see what I got in the mail today?" I've been wracking my brain, trying to think of ways for Opal and Steel to have something to bond over. An ad popped up on my newsfeed a couple days ago, and as soon as I saw it, I knew it was perfect. Two-day shipping later, the Prospect, Sam, brought my package in with the rest of the clubhouse's mail.

There's a company that sells temporary tattoos that look so real, I was sold just by the tutorials on their website. The designs they sell are actually pretty badass. Instead of unicorns and rainbows like most little girls would like to have, these temporary tattoos are designed by actual tattoo artists. I got a pack that had a mix of biker theme designs. There are a skulls, flames, and even a set of letters to spell words.

My question gets her attention. "Is it for me?"

"It's for both of us. Let's go down to the kitchen so we have more space." I set my tablet aside, grab the package from the nightstand, and we make our way downstairs.

"What is it?" Opal asks, looking at the black bubble envelope. I lift her up onto the kitchen island, letting her swing her tiny legs over the edge.

"I got us some tattoos so we could look like your daddy." I slide the plastic designs out of the envelope and her eyes go super wide.

"Those are awesome. I want that one." She's pointing at the drawing of a basic skull. "My daddy has one of those on his arm."

Her recognizing the design makes me smile. It makes me happy to think that even though she's been pushing him away on the outside, on the inside she's soaking everything in. Hopefully, doing something like this will be the first step to her accepting everything he's trying to give her. Anything I can do to help them, I'm more than happy to do.

"I think you'll look so cool with a tattoo like your daddy." I go to the sink and dampen a sponge to do the design transfer, then drag a stool with me to sit in front of Opal.

"I want it on this arm." She holds out her right arm, the same arm Steel has his tattoo sleeve.

"You got it." I peel back the plastic sheet and place the paper on her forearm. Pressing the sponge to the paper, I let the water do its magic. I count to sixty like the directions say, then test a corner of the paper. When the design is stuck to her skin, I gently peel it all the way off, leaving a perfect smiling skull behind.

"So cool." Opal is mesmerized. "Can I do one next?"

"Sure. Which one do you like?"

"Can we do my name?" she asks, pointing to the sheet with the letters on it.

"Only if you help me. I don't know how to spell your name," I tease her. I know she knows how to spell her name. Before all the recent craziness, I heard her tell Duchess all her letters.

"You gotta cut them out. I'm not allowed to have scissors."

I search a few drawers for scissors, then get to work cutting out the appropriate letters. It's a good thing her name only has one of each letter, otherwise we'd have a problem.

"I'll stick them to your arm, but you hold the sponge this time."

Opal nods, watching me placing the tiny pieces of paper in a row down the side of her bicep. Once everything is stuck to her skin, I place the sponge on her arm, and she grabs hold of it. "I got this."

I count down again, then peel back the paper to show her the letters.

"It's my name!" Her whole body bounces on the island with excitement. She's so proud of herself.

"Where's your name?"

Opal and I turn to see Steel standing on the other side of the island. Either he's a stealth ninja or our attention was extremely focused on her new ink.

"It's on my arm, Daddy." Opal scoots across the island on her butt. She sits down in front of Steel and holds her arm out for him to see. "I have a skull like you do!"

"Would you look at that. You sure do." Steel holds his forearm out next to hers and she runs her hand over his skull.

"We're matching."

"That's awesome. Where'd you get these from?"

"Sunshine got thems in the mailbox." Opal stands up on the island and jumps into Steel's arms.

For the first time in a week, I see a genuine smile on his face. It's one tiny step in the right direction, but I'll take it. The mission may not be fully accomplished, but the rocket has taken off.

Not wanting to interrupt their tattoo conversation, I clean up our small mess and put the remaining designs back in the envelope. I have a feeling these tiny temporary tattoos just might be the key to opening the connection these two will need in the near future.

"Will you eat dinner with us?" Opal asks me from her daddy's arms.

His smile is hopeful, but I can tell he's leaving the decision all up to me. As much as I'd like to spend another night here with them, I think these two need to have some time to themselves.

I walk around the island and scoop her into my arms, giving her a big hug. "Not tonight. I have to go home and pay some bills."

Opal squeezes me back so tight. "But I want you to stay with me."

"I'm sorry, but not tonight."

She stops trying to squish my neck, pulling back just a bit. "You come back tomorrow then."

I hand her back to Steel and tap her on the nose. "We'll see about that." I have no reason not to come here tomorrow, but I don't want to make any promises since I currently don't have any set plans.

"Whatever." She wiggles in Steel's arms until he lets her down, then she runs out of the kitchen, leaving us to laugh in her dust.

Steel tugs me close and drops a quick kiss on my lips. "I don't know what you said to her in here but thank you. I haven't gotten a hug like that from her in too long."

I tug him down to me by the back of his neck, kissing him back a little harder than he kissed me. "It's a girl secret," I tease him.

That makes him laugh out loud, full smile on display again. "Girl stuff. As if I don't have enough of that in my life with two moms and a sister. Now, I got my kid and my woman teaming up against me. I just can't win."

"Some things are just best left unknown."

"You got that right. I'm outnumbered big time."

"Now you know how I felt the first day I came here. I was surrounded by men and leather and way out of my element."

"I'm bummed I wasn't here, but I'm glad Ring snatched you up before any other Brothers got any ideas. If I came home and saw you with anyone else, I would've thrown down to get you to be mine."

Looking into his eyes, I see the truth radiating back at me. He's dead serious, and I find it kind of hot. Okay, maybe more than kind of. It's totally full-blown hot. That's how I know I made the right decision to do anything I could to bring Steel and his daughter back together. These people are my people now.

CHAPTER THIRTY-ONE

STEEL

"That's wrong!" Opal screeches, pulling her head from my grasp.

To stop her from taking a tumble off the bathroom counter, I drop the hairbrush on the floor and the ponytail holder I was holding ends up in the sink. "Dammit," I swear under my breath.

"That's a bad word, Daddy," she scolds, eyeing me in the mirror like I'm a monster.

Honestly, that's how I'm feeling right now. I'm trying to get Opal's hair tied back into two braids, but I'm failing big time. I have her long hair parted down the middle, but my giant sausage fingers can't seem to make a braid to meet my munchkin's standards. I've never braided a single thing in my life. I watched a couple videos online, but twisting three simple strands is out of my realm of expertise.

"I'm sorry. I won't say it again." I pick up the hairbrush, and when I look in the mirror, I see a pair of hazel eyes in the reflection. Every time I see those beauties, it takes me a second to remember that she's mine.

"Sunshine!" Opal sees her in the mirror too, and for the first time today, her face lights up.

Sunshine steps in the bathroom with us and leans a hip against the vanity, focused on Opal. "Are you playing hairdresser with your daddy?"

Seeing her give all her attention to my little girl does something to me. I'll be honest, it does make me a little jealous because I want to be Sunshine's first thought. But it also makes me happy to see that she obviously cares for Opal. I may sound like a fucking bastard, because my child no longer has a mother, but if I could've picked someone to raise a child with, it'd be Sunshine. I thank whatever's out there for giving me my daughter, but her mother? Fuck that bitch. She never deserved Opal.

"He sucks at braids," Opal whines.

Sunshine gives me a look I'd describe as half stink eye, half smirk. She wants to be mad at me because she knows it was me Opal heard that 'bad word' from, but she wants to laugh because it's funny as hell. In the range of the bad words I use daily, 'suck' is pretty low on the list.

"Do you want me to do your hair?" Sunshine asks.

Opal's eyes go wide. "Yes, please." And they're off, talking about things I'll probably never understand.

I drop my ass on the edge of the tub and just watch the show. Sunshine has her hair undone from my mess, brushed, and in braids in the blink of an eye. She uses her fingers like hooks, pulling little pieces of hair back, twisting everything together. Opal ends up with two braids that look like they're attached to her head.

Sunshine turns Opal's back to the mirror and pulls a small mirror from her purse. "What do you think? They're called French braids." She holds the mirror in front of Opal's face, so she can see a reflection of the back of her head in the big mirror.

"Wow! Thank you." Opal launches into Sunshine's arms, and they hug each other tight.

I stand up to try and join the sweet moment, but the second Opal realizes I'm still in the room, she loses her smile, drops to the floor, and runs into the bedroom.

"Shit." I wish I knew what I was doing wrong. What does my little girl need that I can't seem to give her?

"It's okay, Steel. Let's go see what's the matter." She grabs my hand, pulling me toward the sniffles coming from the tiny bed in the corner of my room.

Knowing this will probably take a while, I sit on the floor and lift a corner of the pony blanket covering Opal's body.

"What's the matter, baby girl?"

"Nuffing," Opal mumbles between hiccups.

I give the blanket a little harder pull so I can see her face. "I know something's wrong. You can tell me. I won't be mad."

Opal takes a big breath and sits up, like whatever she has to say is super important. "Will I still get to see Papa?"

Why would she think she couldn't see Ring? "Of course, you will. He lives here at the clubhouse too."

"When you was gone, he played with me. Can he still do that?"

"Absolutely. You can see him every day."

"He won't leave like you did?" And there's our problem. For some reason, she seems to think that because I'm back home, he's going to go somewhere.

"Why do you think he's gonna leave? Did someone say that?"

"No," she sniffles, "but he left the other day for work and that's why you left."

"Oh, honey." I scoop her off the bed and stand her in the circle of my legs. "I told you the day I got home that I wasn't going away again. Neither will your Papa. We may leave for club stuff for a couple days at a time, but never for a long time again. I promise."

"But why did my mom leave me forever?" She throws herself at me, crying even harder. Talk about conversation switch-up.

I look up, trying to find Sunshine, and I see her leaning against Ring, his arm holding her to his chest. Sunshine has tears in her eyes and Ring gives me a nod of support. They're leaving this up to me.

I tug Opal from my neck, sit her on the bed, and look her dead in the eyes. "Your mom was sick. She just needed to go to heaven." I don't know how to explain the truth, so I leave it vague for now. She'll learn the harsh truth when she's older, but for now, she needs to be in the dark.

"Can I still see Papa?" And the topic takes a whole one-eighty again. I guess she's done talking about her mom, thank the fucking lord.

"Any time you want. I'll always be here," Ring speaks up.

Opal notices that he's in the room, so she runs to him and he picks her up. "I'd miss you."

"Back at ya, little lady," Ring chuckles.

I get off the floor and sit at the end of my bed, then pull Sunshine to sit next to me. "Not that I mind, but why are you here so early? I didn't know we'd be seeing you today."

"I'm going to breakfast with Duchess, Whiskey, Mountain, and Blue. They're all running a little behind, so I wanted to come see you all while I wait. Is that okay?"

"Of course!" Opal answers for all of us, making everyone laugh.

Since she's here, I think Ring and I need a few minutes with our woman before she runs off. But how to get the little lady out of the room? Oh, I know. "Opal, why don't you grab the pictures you colored last night and head downstairs to give them to Blue and Duchess before they leave?"

"Yay!" She gets excited, grabs them off the desk, then takes off.

If I didn't trust everyone in this clubhouse so much, I wouldn't let her out there on her own. But after the other morning, I've no doubt that Opal can handle herself with my Brothers. In the time it took Ring to sneak Sunshine out, and me to get dressed, Opal had managed to talk Kraken and Whiskey into eating Fruit Loops with her. I found them sitting at one of the kitchen tables, milk mustaches on all three. I wish I'd gotten a picture of that for blackmail.

"Now that she's occupied for a few minutes, how about we show our woman a good morning?" Ring shuts the door, then steals her breath with a kiss.

"I'm in."

I walk behind her and realize what she's wearing. She's got on a tight black t-shirt and a floral print, long, flowy skirt. Perfect for a time like this. But before I can do anything, Ring spins her around to face my desk in the corner and lifts her up onto the top, settling her on her knees. He hikes her skirt around her waist, so her backside's exposed and at our waist level.

"Look at this ass," Ring growls, palming both of her cheeks and spreading them to expose the string of her thong. He rips it off in one sharp yank. "We gotta do this fast before we're interrupted again,"

"Shit," Sunshine yelps. That gets my attention, so I make my way to the side of the desk so I can see her face.

The desk's a little deeper than most, so her face and chest are currently flat on the surface, but not for long. Not giving Ring any mind, I use my right hand to grab a handful of her shoulder length hair and pull her head up to look at me. She meets my eyes with a smile. I kiss that smile off her face so fast. Now's not the time for smiling, it's time for fucking our woman.

"Yessss," she hisses out. I peek back to see that Ring has unzipped his jeans, dropped them down to his boots, and is pushing himself into her pussy.

"That's right. Take him," I say while still distracting her with kisses.

I know the exact moment Ring's all the way inside her because Sunshine inhales to catch a breath. I strike, tangling our tongues together and kissing her through every gasp, whimper, and noise she makes as she's jolted forward by Ring's thrusts.

Next thing I know, her whole body arches from my grasp, her hands slam to the wall in front of her, and she lets out a silent scream. Her eyes are shut and the look on her face is pure ecstasy. I push down on my dick through my sweats, so I don't come just from the sight of her bliss. I need my turn inside of her before I do that.

Ring lets out a string of curses as he comes inside our woman, then wraps himself around her, holding them both upright.

"Alright, my turn." I make my way to Ring's right and nudge him out of my way.

He slowly pulls himself out of her and takes up the position to the left of the desk where I just was.

I turn her head to get one last kiss, then let him take over supporting her.

I push my sweatpants down just enough to let my dick hang out, then push in between her legs. I run one finger down her dripping pussy and push the cum escaping from her channel back in. Some might find it weird that I'm touching my Brother's cum, but in a case like this, it's actually serving a purpose for me. I know Sunshine's on the birth control, but I also know that the pill isn't one hundred percent effective. If we're going to get her to really agree to be our Old Lady, we need all the help we can get.

I have no plans to trap her into having our child, but if this relationship is heading where I think it will, and soon, why not get a jump on step one in starting our family now. I don't care if it's Ring's baby or mine. Even if it doesn't happen today, practice makes perfect in situations like this.

"Are you—" I look up to see Sunshine's head buried in Ring's chest while he watches what I'm doing with wide eyes. "Are you doing what I think you're doing?" he whispers.

"Yup," I answer and nod.

"Fuck yea" is all he responds with before yanking her back up to continue kissing her. I position my tip at her entrance, then push myself up into her heat.

I grab hold of her hips and start pumping fast, with all the strength I've got. I look down where we're joined and listen to our skin clap together with each thrust. The wet sounds her pussy's making from all our joint fluids, makes it sound even hotter and dirtier.

I feel Sunshine start to slide on the desk, so I drop my hands to the wood on either side of her knees, forcing her to stay upright. I keep my hips moving, and before either of us can say a word, she orgasms on my dick. Her pussy grips my member so hard, I start to feel the tingles in my legs. We don't have forever, so I let the feeling take over. I slam into her one more time, hold myself still deep inside her, and explode. My vision goes a little fuzzy.

I blink away the blur in the corner of my eyes just in time to feel her slide forward off my dick, then spin around to face me. She sits her bare ass on the desk in front of me, still bracketed by my hands. The smile she's sporting makes my now lonely cock worth it.

"My knees were starting to hurt. I had to sit down," she explains with a sheepish smile.

"No need to explain yourself, Sunshine. Do whatever you need to." I kiss her quick, then waddle my own behind to the bathroom.

I wet a bunch of washcloths, using one to wipe myself off and tuck my dick away.

Walking back out, I toss one of the washcloths to Ring, then head for Sunshine. She tries to take it from me, but I swat her hand away, wiping between her legs myself. After I clean up the mess we made, I drop a kiss just below her belly button and tug her to her feet. I adjust her skirt back where it belongs and give her a whole body a once-over, pleased with what I see.

"Damn, our woman's fuckin' sexy." I whistle.

"Got that right," Ring agrees as he zippers himself up.

"Not how I thought my morning would go, but I wasn't about to stop you." Sunshine uses a brush from her purse to fix her hair, then slips her purse back over her shoulder. "I hate to fuck and run, but I need to get downstairs. Can I see you two later?"

"I've gotta take Opal to the moms' house tonight because she's spending the weekend there. How about tomorrow night Ring and I take you on that date we've been talking about?"

"Works for me," Ring agrees.

"I'll be boxing more of my mom's stuff for donation tomorrow, but dinner sounds perfect. Where you two gonna take me?"

"That's a surprise, but make sure to wear jeans and closed toe shoes. That way you can ride on the back of our bikes," I get one kiss before she's pulled away by Ring.

"We'll flip a coin to see who you get to *ride* first," the smartass winks before kissing her.

"I like the sound of that." Sunshine untangles herself from Ring, then heads for the door. She opens it but turns our way one more time. "I look forward to riding both of you tomorrow night." And she's gone.

"We're fucked."

"I wouldn't have it any other way."

It looks like we're in for a life of purgatory, but I can't find a reason not to look forward to it. Bring it on.

CHAPTER THIRTY-TWO

SUNSHINE

"Fuck a duck." Shit, that hurt. The bottom of the cardboard box I'm holding is split open and its contents are now scattered all over the kitchen floor. It's just after two in the afternoon and I'm finally almost done with sorting through my mom's stuff for donation. I've kept all the sentimental things, but her clothes can be put to better use than collecting dust in the closet.

I toss the broken box toward the hallway and take a step to my left, only to kick something. "Fuck a duck!" I holler this time.

"Screw a kangaroo?" That makes me scream.

I turn to see Ring in the dining room, hands in his back pockets, smiling at me like I'm the crazy one.

"What are you doing here?" I ask, looking at the floor so I can navigate the mess to get closer to him.

"Since when do I need a reason to help my woman?"

When I'm a few steps away, he reaches out and picks me up, setting me down right in front of him. Since he's so close, I use it to my advantage and wrap him up in a hug. I love both my men equally, but there's something about Ring's hugs that make my heart calm.

Wait a minute . . . love? Calm? When did this happen? Isn't it too soon for that? How did I get here? I'm not one to be so involved without feelings, but I didn't know the L word was on the table yet. Maybe I should keep that to myself for now. Let's see how tonight goes, see if I can get a read on them when it's just the three of us, then I can test the waters.

This relationship, and sharing myself with two men, has gone a lot smoother than I anticipated. The guys said there'd be no jealousy between them, and so far, there hasn't been. Maybe they were right saying this is right for us.

I unwrap myself from his embrace and get back to the silly thing he said when he scared me. "What's this about screwing a kangaroo?"

That gets him laughing. "You never heard that rhyme?"

"What rhyme?" I'm lost.

"I heard you say 'fuck a duck' twice. That's the first line in a nursery rhyme turned dirty. Sam, one of our Prospects, loves to tell jokes. He taught me one that goes like this . . ."

He starts singing, very badly and off-key. "*Fuck, fuck, fuck a duck. Screw a kangaroo. Finger bang an orangutan. Orgy at the zoo.*"

"That sounds like 'Row, Row, Row Your Boat'!" I start laughing hysterically. So hard, I let out a damn snort.

That gets Ring laughing, too. "Glad my horrible singing could bring you some humor."

"I thought it was adorable, but let's refrain from you singing any future lullabies."

His face goes instantly serious, and he draws me back in to kiss me silly. "Any of our babies would love my singing." Another kiss. "In fact, Opal loves when I play her music. She's got her own playlist on my phone that we jam to every time we're in my truck." That earns me another kiss and a slap on the butt.

"Fine, fine, whatever you say." I try and lead our conversation away from babies. We may be having unprotected sex . . . okay, not completely unprotected since I'm on the pill, but that's not always effective. Is it weird that I'm thinking I might want to have their babies? One more thing to add to my 'keep that to myself for now' list.

Duchess wasn't kidding when she said things move fast around here. What is it about these guys that make women fall so fast? And why do I find myself not being freaked out about it?

"Do you need help moving anything?" Ring asks, helping me pick up the scattered items. "I had a quick morning at the brewery, so I swung by to see what you needed."

"Actually, I'm just about done. I was carrying this box out to the garage. There are a few more in the hall that need to go out too, then I'm done."

"Why don't I grab the last couple then meet you out on the front deck? We can relax for a bit before you need to get ready for our date."

"Sounds perfect. I'll call Steel and tell him the plan."

That earns me another kiss before he walks toward the hall. "You just read my mind."

"That's why I'm perfect for you," I volley back at him.

"Damn right you are," he chuckles.

I grab my phone from the charger and call Steel.

"Hey, Sunshine. Did you miss me?" I can hear his smile through the phone.

"Nah. I just wanted to let you know I have to cancel for tonight." I try not to laugh but fail miserably.

"Woman," he growls, sending shiver down my spine. "You're gonna pay for that later."

"I look forward to it, Colt," I tease.

"That's not fair. I'm still at work. Did you call just to tease me?"

"That wasn't my intention, just a bonus. The reason I called was to say Ring's here and that you should come straight here after work. We'll leave for our date whenever you're ready."

"Well, isn't Ring a lucky guy? Skipping out on work to spend alone time with you."

"He's moving some heavy boxes, so don't worry, I'm putting him to work."

"Good. Listen, I gotta go. A customer just walked in to pick up his bike. I should be done in a little over an hour. Okay?"

"I look forward to your call," I whisper, knowing he can hear the teasing in my voice.

"You're gonna be in big trouble, Sunshine. Call you later." Then the phone goes dead.

I shake my head, knowing he's right. I'm asking for trouble by teasing him like that, but I couldn't help myself. I know it'll be worth it later tonight when I'm panting and sweating, exhausted from the loving they're going to give me. It's a lesson I'm more than willing to learn.

I grab two bottles of water from the fridge, then turn to walk toward the front door, but I freeze, unable to take another step. There's someone standing in my living room.

"RING!" I yell.

I see him appear in the screen door, but someone approaches him from the left and knocks him unconscious with a blow to the head.

I step forward, momentarily forgetting the guy standing in front of me. I scream again as he grabs me. I twist and turn, trying to wrestle myself free, but nothing works. Our feet get tangled around each other's and in the area rug under the dining table, and we both fall to the floor. I keep trying to hit and kick him, but he's bigger and smellier than I can stand.

"Quit moving, bitch." He slaps my face and I see stars. "Time to get a little payback for your daddy."

I feel a pin prick in the side of my neck and realize he injected me with something. My eyes start to droop and my body gets very heavy. I try to yell out for Ring again, because I hope he was able to fight off whoever hit him, but I'm losing my own battle to stay awake.

I blink my eyes one more time, only to see the dirty face of my attacker, then I lose the fight. I hope Steel gets here soon.

CHAPTER THIRTY-THREE

STEEL

And another happy customer is off. That guy was one to keep happy for sure. He's a manager at the nearest Harley-Davidson dealership and he sends a lot of business our way. The dealership does have a small shop to work on what they sell, but oftentimes, they don't have enough time to get things done quickly. Perks of being an independent shop, Rebel Repairs doesn't have a corporate time clock to follow.

I bust my ass to do one more oil change, then decide to call it a day. I wash my hands and go find Wrench, who's hunkered in our joint office, looking through some invoices.

"Do you mind if I duck out for the night? I've got plans for dinner."

"Dinner? Who's the lucky dude?" Wrench laughs, giving me shit.

"That's for me to know and you to wish it was you." I flip him off.

"I know you don't swing that way. But really, who's the lady? Is it who I think it is? 'Cause if that's the case, good fuckin' luck. Mountain's gonna kick your ass if you chase her away."

Since he brought it up, might as well put some feelers out and see what another Brother thinks of the conundrum I've found myself in. I sit at my desk and kick my feet up.

"Yes, it's who you're thinking. But we're handling it with kids gloves for now. We'll tell Mountain and Whiskey after we iron out all the details. That's what dinner tonight's for, figuring it all out."

My careful words grab his attention. "We? As in you and her, or as in you and someone else with her?"

"The second one."

"Lemme guess, you and Ring plan on sharing her? I know you two banged chicks together, but I didn't know it was a serious thing."

"We don't like each other that way, but we don't mind sharing one woman. She just does it for both of us, so we're going with it."

"Dude, you're gonna need more than luck."

His concern gets me a little worried, but not a whole lot. Just enough to think about how to approach the topic with my current and former Presidents. "Do you think they know?"

He shakes his head. "I don't think so. I only guessed because I saw you both kiss her the other day. But it's none of my business."

"Thanks." I pull my phone out and bring up Sunshine's contact, since I told her I'd call her.

It rings a few times but goes to voicemail. I try Ring's number and it does the same. I wonder if they decided to start the night's activities a little early. I wouldn't blame my Brother if he snuck in a pre-dinner quickie. I'd do the same if I was in his shoes.

"I gotta shower and hit the road. Tomorrow's your day off, so leave those work orders on my desk. I'll get everything assigned in the morning." I climb to my feet and head for the door.

"Enjoy your dick while it's still attached!" he yells, laughing as I walk out.

I ignore a few club girls as I hurry through the main room, taking the stairs two at a time. I have no use for those holes anymore. It makes me sick thinking about being excited to fuck any of them when I got home from prison. None of them would've made me as happy as Sunshine does. Sunshine, Opal, and Ring are my family now.

I scrub as much as of the grease from my hands as I can, and am done with my shower in less than ten minutes. I toss my towel over the curtain rod and walk back into my room. I grab a pair of green boxers, then search my drawers for a matching green t-shirt. Since Sunshine found it funny that I had matching clothes the one day, I decide to do it again. Hopefully, she'll get a kick out of it.

I hop into a pair of jeans, tie up my boots, slide my cut back on, and I'm out the door. I wiggle the knobs to double check that both mine and Ring's doors are locked, then head down the stairs. No one bothers me on my way out, so I climb on my bike and try calling Sunshine one more time. Neither she nor Ring answer again. I get a sick feeling in my gut, so I fire up my bike and am gone in a flash. I hope I'm overreacting and I'll find them having a post-romp nap.

I cut the normal half-hour ride down to twenty minutes and screech to a halt in Sunshine's driveway. Ring's bike is next to mine and her car's in the garage, so they should both be here.

I hustle to the front porch steps and freeze half-way up. The screen door's open a crack with a boot laying on its side, propping it open. I snap to attention and fly up to the porch. Yanking the door open, I see Ring lying unconscious on the floor. From his bent knees and outstretched arms, it looks like he was trying to crawl in the house when he passed out.

Looking further inside, I see some chairs tipped over, but no Sunshine.

"SUNSHINE!" I yell out, hoping she's maybe hiding somewhere, waiting for me to come find her. I check all the rooms on the main floor, but she's not here. I run upstairs and start to panic when there's still no sign of her.

Jogging back down the stairs, I almost fall on my ass when I see Ring has rolled onto his back and he's holding his head.

"Ring," I drop to my knees next to him, "can you hear me?"

"Quit yelling, asshole," he groans.

"Where's Sunshine? Where is she?" I pick him up by the shoulders, giving him a little shake.

That wakes him from his stupor. "They took her." He looks at me with wide eyes.

I help him over to the couch and he lowers his head back to his hands. I see his shoulders tremble a little, but I've got a phone call to make. I never imagined I'd have to do this.

"What's up, Steel?" Whiskey's voice fills the room because I have my cell on speaker.

"She's gone," I croak.

"Say that again, Brother. Who's gone?" I know I've got his attention, but he's got no idea who I'm talking about.

"Sunshine . . . I mean Penelope. I'm at her house and she's gone. Ring was attacked and someone took her."

I'm met with a few seconds of silence before he explodes. "WHAT THE FUCK DO YOU MEAN SHE'S GONE?"

"I just got here, and Ring was knocked out and she's not here!" Each word gets louder. I can hear the panic in my voice.

"We'll discuss why you're at her house another time, but we're on our way. You best hope she appears before I do." *Click* . . . and he's gone.

Fuck. I make two more laps through the house, upstairs, and even to the basement, but she's still nowhere to be found.

Ring's back to his feet when I walk in the living room. "I don't know what happened."

I throw my arms around him and we exchange the sissiest bro-hug of all time. I could care less if I have to rely on my best friend right now. I know the pain that my heart's feeling, so I can easily imagine he's feeling much the same way. Our Sunshine's missing.

The road outside is quickly filled with the roar of motorcycles. Ring and I make our way to the front porch just as Whiskey runs up the lawn. Doc, Hammer, and Trooper are on his heels. The van pulls into the driveway and I see Mountain struggling a little to hurry out. Sam's at his side as he limps toward us.

We're all standing in a circle, staring at each other, so Mountain's the first to speak. "Where's my baby girl?"

I run my hand over my head, trying to get my brain firing on all cylinders. I need to get my shit together and tell everyone what I know.

Before I can speak, Ring looks at Whiskey and lets it all out. "It's my fault. I was on the porch and got blindsided by a punch. I saw someone in the house, but before I could get to her, I got hit again and was out. I think there were three guys total, but this is all on me."

"Nope. That's not how this is gonna go." Everyone's attention swings to me, so I explain what I found when I got here. About how I found him unconscious and the mess inside the house.

Trooper and Whiskey make their way inside to have another look around while Doc checks on Ring. I find myself alone on the porch with Mountain. The yard's full of my Brothers, but Mountain's all up in my face. If this is a sign of things to come, we're in for one hell of a fucking fight.

"I don't know what's going on with you three, but if my girl doesn't come home in one piece, I'm gonna take it out of both your hides. She comes home or you and Ring can kiss your patches goodbye."

Whiskey comes outside with Sunshine's purse and phone. He gives me a glare sharp enough to slice as he hands me her purse and heads for the lawn. He tosses the phone to Cypher, then straddles his bike.

"Church!" he barks.

I put the purse in my saddle bag and climb on my bike. As we ride back, I find myself not caring about Mountain's threat to take my patch. If we don't find Sunshine, I don't want to step foot back in the clubhouse.

I'll take whatever punishment they give. I'll scoop up Opal and we'll find somewhere new to live. I don't think I could be there without Sunshine. I finally found my reason for joining the Rebel Vipers MC, and it's all been for the woman I might've just lost forever. I thought getting released from prison was going to be my fresh start. Life sure kicked me in the balls on this one.

CHAPTER THIRTY-FOUR

RING

What an epic clusterfuck this day has turned into. Of everything that's just gone down, the thing that bothers me the most is I can't even imagine what would've happened to Sunshine had I not been there when she was taken. We would have gotten to her house later and had no clue about who took her. I'm not one hundred percent sure myself, but based off the quick glance I got of the guy inside the house, I've got a pretty good idea. And it pisses me right the fuck off.

Sam is riding my bike back to the clubhouse, which I'm not very happy about, so I'm stuck in the van with Mountain for a silent ride home. I keep expecting him to start reading me the riot act, but all I'm getting are death glares and him muttering things under his breath. They're probably all threats to kill me if we don't find his daughter. The crazy thing about it is that I wouldn't blame him one bit if he did kill me.

I'm the perfect person to kill and take the fall for her being taken. I have no parents or family. No one would miss me or send out a search party if they didn't hear from me after a few days. I'd just be a ghost name and face in the system, again.

We get back to the clubhouse and everyone marches straight into Church. Before I can get to my chair, a hand grabs me by the shoulder, spins me around, and I get two hard punches in the gut before I can say a word. My head hits the side of the table as I fall to the floor, but I just curl up and wait for the blows to keep coming.

"What the fuck, Mountain?" Steel yells. "You made your intentions clear with me, you don't need to be kicking a man when he's down."

"I'll do whatever the fuck I fucking feel like!" Mountain shouts back. "It's his fault that Penelope's gone! My daughter's gone because of his incompetent ass."

"Pops," I roll to my back and see Whiskey standing next to my legs, "I'll help you beat them down later, but we need him to tell us what he saw first."

"But—" Mountain starts.

"Not now! It's not his fault and you damn well know it. We can blame him all we want, but it won't magically bring her back." He holds out a hand for me to grab, then yanks me to my feet. "Sit your ass down before you pass out again. Start talking."

"I think it was Chaos Squad again." Everyone starts to grumble, but I keep talking. "Based on Duchess's description of the greasy biker we now know as Bullet, I'd bet a million bucks he's the guy I saw in the house. I just know it. I saw his long hair."

I keep my eyes locked on Whiskey and watch as his face goes bright red. If he was a balloon, his head would start getting bigger and he'd explode. He picks up his gavel and chucks it across the room. It sails above everyone's head and crashes into the wall right above Mountain.

"Why would he take her?" Whiskey asks the room.

That's when I realize this might actually be all my fault. What if he followed me to her house and saw it as an opportunity to get another attack on a woman in the club. "This really is my fault. I should've tried harder to get to her. Had I not let the other guy hit me, I could've helped her."

Like the steadfast Brother he is, Steel comes to my defense. "It's not all on you. We had no clue she was on their radar. We've all been relaxed on things lately. You never should've been able to ride to her house alone. This is on all of us."

"Steel's right," Hammer says and nods. He doesn't look happy about it, but apparently, he agrees. "After Tempy came back, we didn't realize they'd still be out looking for more of the girls around here. And it looks like I dropped the ball on the buddy riding rule. That starts again right fucking now. No one leaves here alone. Women are back on lockdown, too."

"I second that," Mountain bangs the gavel he must've retrieved, still giving the whole room an evil look. In all my years in the club, I can count on one hand the number of times I've seen the snarl that Mountain has planted on his face right now. But luckily, it's never been pointed at me, until today that is.

"Back to Penelope. Do either of you have something to say to all of us?" Whiskey asks.

"What are your intentions with my daughter?" Mountain stands up and makes his way toward me and Steel. We both stand and Steel's by my side when he gets in front of us.

"There isn't anything official yet, but we're taking it one day at a time," Steel starts.

"We plan to make her our Old Lady, but only when she's ready. We talked to her about it, and she knows we're not gonna force her to be with us if she chooses to back out," I explain.

"The plan was to take her on a date tonight and ask her how she was feeling about everything, that's why Ring was there. I rode out after work, and we were gonna take her to The Lodge," Steel continues.

I hold Mountain's eyes, so he understands what I'm about to say is the absolute truth. He knows about my past, so hopefully, he gets I'm dead serious. "She's the family I've never had, and I want her to be my future. I swear on everything I've got, she's it for me." I make my last point by pointing toward Steel. "She's it for the both of us."

I can't read Mountain's look, but I take a huge breath when he sets one hand on my shoulder and the other on Steel's. He squeezes his hands tight and just nods.

"When we get her back home, Penelope and I will be having a long talk about this, and if I still can't talk her out of it, I'll step back." His small smile's quickly replaced by his evil smirk again. "But if either one of you hurts a hair on her head while she's under your care, no one in this club will know what happens to you. Do I make myself crystal fucking clear?"

"Yes, sir," Steel and I say at the same time.

"Good. Now, let's get to work." Mountain goes back to his chair and slides the gavel back down to Whiskey. "Let's find our girl and bring her home."

CHAPTER THIRTY-FIVE

SUNSHNE

I think this is the worst headache I've ever had. I can't even open my eyes without feeling like the room's tilting to the side. The wood beams on the ceiling look like they're spinning fan blades.

Wait! Since when does my bedroom ceiling have wood beams? My room has drywall and a ceiling fan. Where the heck am I?

And that's when it all comes flashing back. My house. The man in my dining room. The man outside. Ring! Oh my god! What happened to Ring?

I hold my breath, open my eyes, and force myself to sit up. I'm on a stained mattress directly on the concrete floor. Looking around the space, I see that I'm in what I'd imagine a jail cell would look like. I'm in the corner of a basement, so two of the walls are gray blocks. The other two walls are metal bars that go from floor to ceiling.

That gets me thinking about Steel. If this is anything similar to what he endured the last two years, I owe him a lot more loving the next time I see him. If I ever do see him again. No! I can't think like that. I need to get my head on straight and figure out how to get out of this place. Wherever this is.

The ceiling has beams like the ones in my basement, so I'm guessing this is a basement as well. There are a few small windows up at the top, but they're all boarded over, not allowing me to see out. I don't even know what time of day it is. I don't know how long I've been gone.

The room is mostly dark, but there are a few lights on the opposite end of the basement, illuminating what looks to be a box made of plywood sheets. That's when my hearing kicks in. I didn't realize my ears were ringing until just now, when I started hearing the tiny barks. Are there dogs in that box?

I stand up and walk over to the bars closest to the box. From here I can see over the edge and into where the light is shining. It's filled with puppies. There must be a dozen of them. They look like they're supposed to be solid white, but they're so dirty, their fur is matted down and has a brownish tinge to it. Poor little guys.

"Puppies," I whisper, trying to get their attention.

A few of them start looking around, trying to investigate where my voice is coming from. But one puppy springs to action as soon as it realizes someone is outside of its four walls. I can't see what it's doing, but based on the thumping sounds, I'd guess it's trying to jump over the wall but missing, hitting the board instead.

Whatever it's doing gets the attention of more of the puppies and more start trying to copy him, running into the board. They're so tiny, I hope they don't hurt themselves.

Then, like it was the plan all along, one puppy appears over the board and drops down onto the floor. It escaped! The puppy looks around the basement, then lets out a tiny bark.

"Hi, puppy." I reach my hand through the bars, hoping it can see me.

And it does. The puppy comes running my way. The bars are too close together for me to get through, but it's tiny little body slides between with no problem. As soon as it's through the bars, I pick up the squirming fur ball and hold it to my chest. It starts licking my face and the yippy barks continue.

I turn my body just a bit and lift the puppy so I can see its belly. It's a boy! And he's even cuter up close. I imagine with his fur clean, he'd probably be a giant fluff monster. He doesn't look very old, but based on the fact I don't see a mother dog down here anywhere, they must be old enough to eat on their own. Maybe just a few months old.

Why would anyone be cruel enough to keep puppies like this locked in a basement? They need to be outside where there's room to run and play. Then again, I'd take a wild guess and say that since it's the same people who locked me down here, they have no care for basic human decency.

The door at the top of what I now can see are stairs opens and suddenly the whole space is filled with light, I hold the puppy tight and walk backward to the mattress I woke up on. Slowly, and hopefully quietly, I lower myself and sit against the back wall. The puppy wiggles from my arms and crawls behind my back, hiding from whoever's still at the top of the stairs.

"I know you're awake down there," a voice booms through the space, almost with a mirth to his words. Boots appear on the steps as the person starts walking down. With each step, I see more and more of the man. His boots are caked with mud on the sides, and his jeans are a dark blue, also with mud splattered on them. There are holes ripped in both knees, but not like the jeans you'd buy at the store with holes strategically placed and hemmed to prevent them from ripping further. These holes look like they were worn into the denim after many years of wear and tear.

When he's all the way down, I see he's wearing an extremely dirty white t-shirt and a leather vest, one almost like the cut that all the Rebel Vipers wear. But unlike theirs, this guy's vest is dirty and tattered and looks like it's been run through a meat grinder.

The day Ring explained his cut to me, his voice was filled with honor and pride. He was in a hurry to have sex with me, but he took the little extra time to lay his cut on the counter. He didn't care about any of his other clothes, but he cared where he put his cut.

This guy's skin even looks tore up and scabbed over. Based on my medical knowledge, I'd say this dude is on some serious drugs. His hair is long and so greasy, it makes the black strands look shiny. How can someone let themselves get this nasty? If I don't shower every few days, my skin starts to crawl.

"Welcome to my new hideout," the man announces with a smile, like this is a place to be proud of.

"Where am I?" I try to sound strong, but it comes out in a croak.

"You don't worry about that. I just heard some noises and wanted to come get a good look at you."

"What for?" Maybe if I can keep him talking, he'll accidently tell me where I am. That way, when I figure a way out of here, I'll know how to get back home.

"So, I know who to sell you to." That makes him laugh.

"Sell me?"

"You got it. Your Rebel boys have interrupted two of my sales already, so taking you is just my payback. On top of everything else they've done to me over the years."

This must be the bad guy who took Tempy and Duchess. I've heard bits and pieces of their stories, but never imagined I'd be in a similar situation. Duchess was rescued by the club and Tempy got away on her own. What's going to happen to me?

"The name's Bullet, by the way." He holds a hand out through the bars, but I remain seated.

"Why the hell would I shake your hand? You hurt me, drugged me, and have me locked in this cell. Who the fuck do you think you are?" And with every question, I get angrier.

I had plans for my night. I was supposed to be taken on a date by my guys. I was supposed to finally tell them that I wanted to give our relationship a real shot. I want to get to know my father and brother better. I want Blue and Duchess to show me what it takes to be a woman in the club. I want a family. I want to help raise Opal. I maybe even want to have babies with Steel and Ring. I want a cut with their names on it. I want to wear it proud. I want to be their Old Lady.

Bullet doesn't like my outburst. "I'm the man who holds the keys to your future, so you'd be smart not to back talk and just sit there like a good girl."

"Why should I?" I sass back despite his warning.

He grips the metal bars tight, pressing his face as close as he can, glaring at me like he could set me on fire with his eyes. "If you don't want to end up like my brother did, you need to do what I say and stay the fuck quiet."

He pushes away from the bars and stomps back up the stairs. Less than a minute later, he's back down and pushing a canvas bag through a slot in the bars. The bag hits the floor with a *thump* and he's gone again. This time, when he shuts the door at the top, he leaves the lights on so I can see. I wait a few minutes, listening to footsteps from above. I can hear mumbled voices, but no one comes back down.

I crawl toward the bag and pull it onto the mattress next to me. Only then does my puppy friend come out of his hiding spot and crawl back in my lap. His whole body's shaking like he just went through a tornado. Poor little guy. I can hear barking and whimpering from the box again and wish I could crawl in there and cuddle with all of them.

Looking through the canvas bag, I find a few bags of chips and a six pack of soda. Not the most nutritious of meals, but my stomach now decides it's time to start growling. I open one bag of plain chips and eat a few, then share a couple with the puppy. If he's going to be in here with me, and not his brothers and sisters, I guess I'm going to have to share my food with him. He can't have soda, but I guess chips are better than nothing.

We finish the chips and I drink one of the sodas, then decide to lie back down. I'm still not sure what time it is, but I need to get some rest. That way, when I figure out how to get out of here, I'll have all the energy I need.

CHAPTER THIRTY-SIX

RING

We're on day three of Sunshine being missing and I'm losing my mind. The attack was on Friday, it's now early Monday night, and we still have no clue where she is. We've had Church every day, but all that's been accomplished is us talking in circles, trying to come up with any possible scenarios of what happened.

Because I was knocked out on the front porch of her house, no one really knows what happened to Sunshine inside. We can guess because of the knocked over chairs and kicked up carpet, but anything more is just a guess. The back door was open, so we know that's how they left, but there aren't any tracks or footprints to follow.

"Cypher, anything new?" Whiskey asks. We're back in Church again, basically grasping at straws.

"Nothing new," Cypher responds while typing away at his laptop. "I've been going back and forth looking at the past locations we knew they were, but nothing's popping up."

It's not often that anyone's allowed to have electronics in Church, but when we're dealing with something like this, the rules are a little more lax. No one wants to miss an important call or text, and since Cypher's our resident technology guru, his nose has been buried in his various screens since we got back to the compound on Friday.

"What about the motel?" Hammer finally speaks up. He's been unusually quiet all weekend.

Sunshine being gone has sent all the women in the clubhouse into a bit of a tailspin of their own, Wings especially. Knowing that another woman has been taken by the same men as her, and that she has no information to help, she got extremely upset. When we got back and filled everyone in, Wings threw a lamp across the main room. Then, when Hammer tried to console her, she lost it on him. She was yelling and crying and blaming him for everything that happened to her. She locked herself in her bedroom and no one other than Duchess has seen her since. So, to say that Hammer's been a little out of sorts is a bit of an understatement.

I can understand how he's feeling. The last three nights, Steel and I have been sleeping with our adjoining door open. We've been listening to each other talk about Sunshine until we somehow manage to fall asleep. But when I see him each morning, I see the stress and unrest in his eyes. I recognize it because I see the same in my face when I look in the mirror. We haven't had enough time with her. We need her back, and soon.

Cypher finally stops typing and meets Hammer's angry look with a snarl of his own. "There's nothing at the hotel you guys blew up. The cabin in the woods is dark. And the parking lot at the trail has been nothing but civilians in and out."

I look at the front of the table and Steel's got his head laying on his arms on the table. If I didn't know better, I'd say he was hiding his face because he was crying, but that's not something I think I've ever seen Steel do. He takes a deep breath and sits back up.

"I hate to be the asshole here, but I think we need to call it a night and tell everyone to go to bed early." Whiskey reaches over to Steel and grabs him by the shoulder while still looking at everyone around the room. "We're just sitting in here, twiddling our thumbs. If we don't know anything new by the morning, we'll have Trooper call in the law. I don't know what else to do."

"I agree," Mountain pipes up from the end of the table, "but something like that needs a club vote. Anyone got a motion?"

"I motion we wait 'til eight a.m., then Trooper calls Thomas," Brick speaks up.

"I second that," Bear says.

"All right. Who says 'aye'?" Whiskey asks the room.

"Aye," we all answer at once.

"Any nays?" The room is silent.

"Motion passes." Whiskey slams the gavel. "Let's get out of here and try to have a chill night. Any Brothers who are on watch rotation tonight, report in every hour. Meeting adjourned." *Bang!* One more gavel slam and we all leave the room.

I'm halfway across the main room, heading for the stairs, when the front door slams open and Sam comes running in.

"Why are you running in my clubhouse, boy?" Whiskey's right behind me.

Sam stands up straight, trying to catch his breath. "Jewel's outside. She just pulled in and she's in bad shape."

Just as he finishes, Smoke comes walking inside with his arm around a roughed-up looking Jewel. She's got a black eye, her lower lip is bleeding, and she's holding her left arm to her chest.

"Doc!" Whiskey yells.

Doc appears out of nowhere and helps Smoke lead Jewel to a couch.

Everyone circles around, trying to see what's going on. I keep toward the back of the group, and Steel comes to my side.

"Jewel," Whiskey sits on the coffee table next to Doc, "what happened to you?"

"I was leaving the gas station and was attacked by these two guys," she says through tears. Doc hands her an ice pack and she holds it to her eye.

"Why were you outside the compound?" Steel asks.

"Wait a minute! He's right. She shouldn't have been able to leave. All the women are on lockdown. Why were you out there?" Butch questions.

That makes Jewel a bit defensive. "I needed to get out of here. All these lockdowns are bullshit."

"Whiskey?" We all turn to see Sam still standing by the door. "I let her out earlier because she said you said she could leave."

Whiskey gets all up in Jewel's face, forcing her back further on the couch. She lets out a yelp, still holding her arm. "I don't care what you don't like. If you plan on staying here, you follow my rules. This is your second strike. One more fuck-up and you're gone. Do I make myself clear?"

"Fine," she pouts.

"Now, tell me exactly what happened out there." Whiskey sits back, crossing his arms.

"I came out of the gas station that's a couple miles down the road. These two guys were standing between my car and this truck. I tried to walk past them, but they surrounded me. The guy in the front punched me and I fell. When I was on the ground, they kicked my arm. One of them pulled me up and his breath stunk really bad. He told me he had a message for the club."

Jewel looks down at her lap, tugging a little on her short skirt. Honestly, she looks uncomfortable. I don't know if it's because everyone's looking at her, or that she's scared of what happened to her, but either way, I don't trust whatever's about to come out of her mouth.

"What'd they say?" I ask.

"That they have your lady and to not try and find her. Otherwise, they'll kill her before you do."

Steel and I look at each other in disbelief. If what this bitch is saying is actually true, whoever has Sunshine has made an appearance.

"Holy fuck!" Steel yells. "That means they're watching our clubhouse and following anyone who leaves."

"What did they look like?" Whiskey still has his attention on Jewel.

"They were both wearing cuts, but I couldn't see any patches. They were both average looking guys, short hair, and one had a mustache."

Whiskey stands up and looks around at everyone. "Doc, finish patching her up and get her to her room. Everyone else, back in Church. Cypher—"

Cypher finishes his sentence. "I'll try and hack into the gas station security to see if I can see anything."

Less than fifteen minutes after calling it quits for the night, we're on our way back into Church. What are the chances of that?

Everyone's walking toward the room, but I grab Steel's arm and hold him back for a second.

"What's up, Brother?" he questions me.

"Do you believe her?" I whisper, looking at Jewel out of the corner of my eye.

Steel looks at her and is silent for a bit. "I'm not sure. Knowing her, I wouldn't put anything past her."

"My thoughts exactly."

"Let's just go in there and see what Cypher says, then we'll go from there." Steel heads back to his seat next to Whiskey, and I shut the door behind me.

"What's the word?" I ask, taking my seat.

Cypher pushes his laptop away and sits back in his chair. "I know that gas station has a security system because I've seen cameras when I've been there. But unfortunately for us, either someone turned it off or the system's down, because we've got nothing after six-oh-two p.m. I can see stuff before then, but black screens after."

"What the fuck?" Steel pounds on the table. "Someone has to know something. We need to find her now!"

"I fuckin' agree. We need her." My heart's pumping so damn fast and I'm back to feeling like I'm going to lose it. I thought I was doing good at hiding my emotions tonight, but after the Jewel bullshit, and now that we have even less with no security footage, I'm slipping.

I snap out of my trance when I feel hands on both my shoulders. Hammer's to my right and Brick's at my left. Their silent support brings me back down and I try to relax. It works a little, but I really just need to get out of this room. Normally, being in a room surrounded by my

Brothers makes me happy, but right now, I need peace and quiet.

I wish I was in my room, lying next to my woman, watching her sleep. I would kiss her awake so Steel and I could love on her all night. She'd never doubt that she's all ours, for forever. We'd let her know we aren't ever going to let her go. But someone decided to take a fucking dump on our lives and steal our Sunshine away.

CHAPTER THIRTY-SEVEN

STEEL

After we're let out of Church, Ring makes a beeline for upstairs. I could tell he was getting a little antsy there at the end, so I suggested we hit pause again and continue with our plan to call the cops in the morning if Cypher doesn't find anything new overnight.

I take a seat at the bar and one of the Prospects sets a beer in front of me before I even ask for it. I look up to see that it's Sam and give him a nod in thanks.

I debate going upstairs to talk to Ring but decide to let him have his space. He may be my best friend, and we're obviously pining for the same woman, but that doesn't mean we need to be attached at the hip all the time. I'm still in an adjustment period of my own, trying to figure out how to deal with things here in the real world again. On the inside, I had to learn to deal with things alone, so maybe that's what Ring needs right now. He knows I'll be here for him if he needs my support.

Whiskey and Hammer are down at the other end of the bar, but I keep to myself at this end. After two beers, I decide it's time to go to bed. I need to be up early in case something happens, and I need to be on top of my game.

But before I go upstairs, I pull out my phone and call my moms.

"Steel," Mom Helen answers. "Are you calling for Opal?"

"No, Mom. But I do have a huge favor to ask." I run a hand over my head, trying to figure out how much to tell her.

"What's wrong, son? I can tell something's up."

"I need you to keep Opal for a few more days. There's some stuff going on and I can't have her around it." I decide to keep it vague and simple. It's not a lie, but I don't want to tell them everything. There's nothing they can do out there and I know they'd worry too much. Plus, I really don't want Opal to know about Sunshine being missing.

"I know you're not telling me everything, but I'll let you do your thing. Just promise to keep checking in so we know you're okay." And there's my momma bear coming out. Janie may have been the one to give birth to me, but Helen has always been the leader of our pack.

"I'll text you when I can. That's all I can promise."

"Be safe. Love you, Colt."

"Love you too, Mom." And I hang up.

I head upstairs, grab some pajama pants, close myself in the bathroom, and jump in the shower. I try to scrub the day's worries away, but it doesn't really work. I stand under the spray for a few minutes and just think about Sunshine.

She's made for me. For me and Ring. And for Opal. Tomorrow's a new day and I won't stop until she's back in my arms. I haven't told Ring yet, but I ordered a cut for Sunshine last week. I was hoping it'd be here in case the opportunity came up to ask her to be our Old Lady, but after everything that's happened, I forgot to check if it was done yet. I'll look into it tomorrow.

I slide my pajama pants on, brush my teeth, and shut the light off. Opening the door, I stop dead in my tracks. It takes me a split second to realize that it's not my woman lying under the covers in my bed.

It's Jewel. What the actual fuck?

"What the hell are you doing in here?" I roar.

"I was scared and didn't wanna be alone," Jewel whimpers. She pushes the blanket down, showing she's only wearing a t-shirt and panties. She slithers out of the bed and walks to me. "I figured it'd be okay to wait for you in here."

I feel bad that she got injured, but it's so wrong for her to be in my room. Penelope's missing and I can't think of anything but her. I never want another woman in my bed.

Jewel puts her hands on my chest and tries to kiss me. Ring was right about things with her being a little suspicious. This woman has just pushed my last button.

I grab her wrists and pull back. "Jewel, I'm sorry that you got hurt, but you can't be in here. This isn't your room and you aren't my Old Lady. You have your own room, and I need you to leave."

I barely finish my rant before she goes bat shit crazy. Jewel pushes against my chest and tries to keep hitting me. "I was just beat up by three really bad guys because of you and your whore. I know she's been in here and I wanna know what she has that I don't?"

I take a few steps back, trying to position myself in front of the door, just in case I need to escape this crazy lady. That's when something she said clicks in my head—she said three guys. That doesn't match her earlier story.

"Did you . . . did you just say there were three guys? You said it was two guys earlier." I'm now watching her movements very closely. She's trying to avoid looking directly at me.

"I meant two guys. Did I say three? I don't remember everything because it happened so fast," she stammers. Then she tries to make a break for it.

I get in front of her, grab her by the shoulders, and slam her up against the wall next to the door. "What the fuck's going on, Jewel? What did you do to Penelope? Where the hell is she?"

"You'll never find her, and I'm not saying anything else," she snaps with fire in her eyes.

I bend down to jam my shoulder into her stomach, scoop her ass up, and take off down the hall. As I carry her down the stairs, I yell out to my Brothers, "GUYS! EVERYONE GET UP!" Once I get to the main room, I throw her lying ass down on the floor.

"What the fuck, Steel?" Whiskey yells. He's still sitting at the bar with Hammer.

"This bitch was in my bed and isn't telling the truth about what happened to her tonight." I can barely catch my breath. "Does anyone remember how many men she said attacked her?"

"She said it was two. Why does that matter?" Ring asks as he walks up beside me. He must've heard the commotion in my room because he's now downstairs.

"Because when I asked her why she was in my room, she said she was scared because THREE men hurt her. Three isn't fucking two. The bitch is lying about something. She called Penelope a whore and said we'll never find her. She lied and I wanna fucking know why."

"Where the hell is my daughter?" Oh shit. I look to my left and see Mountain standing at the end of the hallway leading to his room. He's wearing a white tank top and shorts, and he's using his crutches to cross the room. Looks like he was in such a hurry, he didn't even bother to put his prosthetic leg on. "Somebody better start explaining themselves!"

"I don't have to tell anyone anything," Jewel shrieks, still sitting on the floor. "I'm glad the bitch is gone. You're supposed to be mine!"

"Hey, twatwaffle," Duchess suddenly appears. "You obviously don't know how to listen to instructions." She reaches down to grab Jewel by the hair. Before anyone can stop her, she drags Jewel across the floor and slams her face into one of the side tables. I think we're all so stunned to see Duchess acting like this, we're frozen where we stand.

We all hear a crunch and blood pours out of Jewel's nose. Duchess drops her back to the floor and kicks her in the stomach. "You better start talking before I keep kicking your nasty ass."

It's definitely not in our code to hurt women, but since it's Duchess giving the beatdown, no one stops her right away.

"Tell me what happened to Penelope," she yells, delivering another kick to Jewel's leg. "Where the fuck is she?"

"Alright babe, that's enough." Whiskey wraps his arm around her shoulders, pulling her away from the ball of crazy curled up on the floor. "You can't be doing that in your condition. You need to keep the baby safe, and we need the bitch coherent so we can get the information we need."

"I think it's time we take the garbage out to the pit." Hammer says what we're all thinking.

"I couldn't agree more." I turn around and run upstairs. I need to get dressed, then it's time to give this bitch the beatdown that just might end her life.

I tie my boots, put my gun in its holster, and slide my cut on all within minutes. Now's not the time for dawdling.

I almost run into Ring when I open my door to leave. Looks like he was waiting for me.

"When we finish this tonight, we're gonna have a talk. You still on the same page about Sunshine?" I need to hear from him that he's still all in, because even if he's not, I'm going to make her mine.

Ring looks me dead in the eye. "I'm right behind you."

That's all I need to know.

We head downstairs and step outside in time to see Doc and Whiskey literally throw a tied-up Jewel into the back of the van. I head straight for my bike and Ring's right next to me on his. Following the line of other bikes and vehicles out of the lot, we all make a left turn at the corner and ride like a pack on our way to the barn. Time to get some answers about what's been going on around here, and hopefully the information we need to find Sunshine.

CHAPTER THIRTY-EIGHT

STEEL

I shut off my bike but stay on my seat, waiting for what, I'm not really sure. I feel like I should just march into the barn and start swinging on Jewel, but I know that's not going to get us the information we need. I close my eyes and take a deep breath, trying to slow my racing heart. It almost works.

"Steel!" I look up and Ring's standing in front of me. He's still worked up and shifting his weight from foot to foot, side to side. His body looks ready to pounce. "Are you coming or what?"

"Calm the fuck down, Brother," I bark at him while climbing off my bike.

He gets right in my face. "Why? That bitch knows where our woman is, and you want me to be calm. Fuck you!"

I try to be calm, but my anger spits out a little. "I want her back as much as you do, but we need to be smart. We can't go in there with all our cards out."

Ring drops his grumpy attitude and his blank face kicks in. Any emotion he was showing in his eyes is gone in a flash. It won't to be easy to keep our emotions out of what needs to happen in that barn, but we need to put finding Sunshine before our need for vengeance.

While Ring and I have been getting our shit together, our Brothers got Jewel out of the van and set up in the barn we use for situations like this. The first day I saw this barn, I was in awe. I hadn't been prospecting for long when Mountain brought me out here to show me something. Needless to say, I didn't expect to see a guy down in the ten-foot-deep concrete-walled hole. That was the day I realized club life was no joke, and I loved it.

"Let's go see what the bitch has to say." Ring turns and leads the way inside.

We walk up the slight incline, through the two big open barn doors, and stop just inside. All the lights are on and it's as bright in here as it is outside in the middle of the day. There's a bunch of plastic sheets laid over the concrete floor and Jewel's sitting in the middle, chained to a chair. She's wide awake and screaming threats at everyone.

"You won't get away with this! They know where I am! They'll come to save me and kill you all!"

And that makes my first thread snap. I shrug off my cut, throw it at Ring, and make my way to stand in front of the bitch sitting on what she seems to think is her throne. But unluckily for her, this throne is about to be her worst nightmare.

I'm looking straight at the whore, but I ask the room, "Where's the keys to this lock?"

Hammer appears at my side, holding out a ring of a dozen keys. "These ones?"

"Yup." I nod. "I want her off that chair and lowered down in the pit. She doesn't deserve to be sitting in a chair. Chairs are for people who don't betray their club."

Jewel's whole demeanor changes. Her eyes go wide and she starts to freak out. She looks around the room, and when she notices the hole in the corner, she goes feral. She starts trying to kick, but the chains around her legs don't allow much movement. "No!" she screams. "Someone help me!"

"No one's gonna help you now. You lost that right the second you betrayed our woman."

"She's not yours!" Jewel keeps yelling, but I zone out her babble and take the keys from Hammer.

Ring makes his way behind Jewel, and the second she's unlocked, she tries to run but loses her footing and he grabs her first in a reverse bear hug and lifts her clean off the floor. "Stop fighting me, bitch."

"Let's get her hooked to this chain over here." Whiskey's standing a ways to our left, holding the end of a longer chain that's attached to the system of I-beams running the length of the rafters. The longest beam starts at the wall to the right and extends across the room.

I drag the chains that were holding Jewel to the chair and use them to wrap Jewel's body up like a metal mummy. Starting at her shoulders, Ring, Whiskey, and I take turns holding her flailing arms down and pulling the length of chain around her. We wrap her all the way down to her ankles.

Whiskey pulls the chain above us down a bit, attaches a hook that Gunner hands him, and loops the hook through the chain wrapped around Jewel. The chain starts lifting because Gunner's now standing by the wall, pulling the far end of the chain down. This particular chain is looped through a pulley hanging from the beam above, so the more Gunner pulls down on his end, the higher Jewel gets off the floor.

When she's about a foot in the air, I approach her and give her a good shove. The pulley above slides down the beam and Jewel's now midair over the hole.

"What's next?" Whiskey asks.

"Now, we let her down," I reply.

Whiskey chuckles, "Bitch, you're about as useful as a damn slinkie. Some might find you fun to play with, but the best thing about you is getting to watch you fall down."

"Down? Down where?" Jewel starts screeching again.

Gunner slowly lets the chain go, and Jewel starts descending.

"Get some spot lights set up to shine down there," I order, pointing into the darkness. "I'm going in."

"Why not just stay up here?" Ring follows me to the metal ladder hanging on the wall.

I lift it off the wall, drop one end down into the whole, and start to make my way down. But two rungs down I stop and look up at Ring to answer his question. "If she wants to treat all of us like garbage, it's only fitting we return the favor. She betrayed this club and will never see the light of day again." And with that, I make my way down, hitting the ground just as Jewel does.

"What tools do you need down there, Brother?" I look up to see about twenty faces looking down at us. Whiskey's laying down on his stomach, so his head's hanging over the edge.

"Let's start with getting this chain at the right height. I want her upright, but her toes dangling."

"Lift the chain about three feet." I turn fast because I didn't know anyone followed me down. When I see it's Ring, I exhale. "You didn't think I'd let you have all the fun by yourself, did you?"

"The more, the merrier." I laugh.

"What's wrong with you two?" Jewel keeps trying to fight her binds, but it does her no good. "Why don't you just kill me now?"

She's finally in the position I want her to be in. She's suspended just inches off the floor, and her trying to move only causes her body to start spinning slowly. She basically looks like a fish caught on a hook.

"Killing you would be too easy. We want answers, so you'd best start talking before I start removing body parts." I punch Jewel once in the stomach and her whole body swings like a punching bag.

She coughs up a little blood and tries to spit it at me, but I see it coming and move to my right. "I don't have anything to tell you."

"Send down the poultry sheers, a baseball bat, and a needle nose pliers. I've got some things to remove from this bitch's body," I holler up at the crowd. I hear movement but don't take my eyes off Jewel to see who's getting what I asked for.

"I don't need any of that shit to get what I need from this whore." The next thing I know, Ring wraps Jewel's disheveled ponytail around his fist and yanks her head back. He lifts a sharp knife I've never seen before out of his boot and holds it in front of her face. "You tell me where Sunshine is, or I'll cut you and watch you slowly bleed."

Jewel goes dead still and has her eyes locked on the knife. "Steel was supposed to be mine. They promised if I got her out of the way, he'd be all mine."

"Who are they?" Ring questions.

"The same guys who took Wings and her sister," Jewel whispers.

That gets my attention. We suspected this was the work of Chaos Squad, but this is our first confirmation of it being the truth. Duchess told us what Bullet looks like, and Ring thinks he saw him, but this is the proof we needed.

"You're supposed to be loyal to this club. How'd you get involved with them?" I ask.

Ring lets her head go, and she slumps forward, letting the chains hold her up like a puppet.

"I met them through Sydney."

And that's when I go nuclear. I rush forward and lift her head up myself. "What does she have to do with this?"

Jewel says nothing, so I let her go and look up. "Where's that bat?"

Both a wooden and aluminum bat come falling into the hole. I choose the Louisville Slugger and pick it up. I give it a few practice swings to test the weight, then let my anger out full force. I swing and hit Jewel in the middle of her back, right over top of the chains. The bat makes a *thunk* when it hits the metal, but the force behind my swing serves its purpose. Jewel cries out in agony, but Ring and I smile at each other.

"Think she knows we're serious now?" Ring picks up the aluminum bat. Holding it by the handle, he starts looping it through the air.

"I hope so, 'cause I'm getting sick of this." I want to know what my crazy ass, dead baby momma has to do with my missing woman. "Start talking, bitch, or I'll hit you again."

Jewel gasps to try and catch her breath, and I wonder if I broke a rib or two with my strike. "Fine, I'll talk. I'm gonna die anyways."

"Fuckin' right," Ring growls. He starts circling the square space we're in, so I back out of his way, letting him work out his anger his way.

I lean against the wall behind me and get ready to hear whatever Jewel has to say.

"How did Sydney know Chaos Squad?" I start.

Jewel drops another bombshell. "They were her drug dealers."

"So, they're responsible for her dying," I ask, rhetorically. Sydney was the one who shot herself up, but someone in Chaos Squad sold it to her.

Then the hard truths keep coming, only this part rubs me all the wrong way. "I saw her the day before she OD'd and she told me to take care of Opal. She said now that you're back home, I should try to get with you. She wanted me to be Opal's mom."

I charge forward and swing a punch, hitting Jewel in the cheek. Her face flies to the side and the chains clang with the movement. "You'll never be my baby's mother!"

"Sydney said you'd be mine. She promised!" Jewel yells. Her words are a little garbled and there's more blood dripping from her nose. Looks like I just popped whatever Duchess started earlier when she used Jewel's head as a battering ram.

Out of nowhere, Ring swings his bat and it hits Jewel on the front of her knees. If she was standing on her own, I've no doubt she'd be down on the ground with that hit. "You fucked with the wrong Brothers! Where is Sunshine? Tell me NOW!" he shouts out.

CHAPTER THIRTY-NINE

RING

"Tell me NOW!" I shout.

"I've only been to their house once," Jewel says in between her grunts, "but I don't know if she's there."

I drop the aluminum bat and pull the knife back out of my boot. I get as close to Jewel as I can and push the knife's tip between the chains. I push it through her shirt and nick her between the ribs, just enough to break skin. I don't hit any organs. Not yet.

"Where is this house?" I ask through gritted teeth. My anger's about to boil over, so she better answer me.

"It's . . . in Tellison . . . just behind . . . the gas station." Her grunts have turned to heaves for breath.

"Ring, let her go," Steel grabs my shoulder, trying to pull me back. But before I let him move me too far, I push the blade all the way into her rib cage. Only then do I back away from her.

I look at Steel and see the second he realizes the knife's sticking out of her gut. It's about halfway down her left side, and I'd bet the broken ribs Steel gave her from his bat swing are no longer her biggest problem. I knew exactly what I was doing when I decided where to stab her, and I don't regret it one fucking bit.

Jewel's head is flopped back, and her eyes are closed, but I can see movement in her shoulders. I know she's alive for the time being.

"Cypher," Whiskey says from above, "Do your thing and find us the exact address."

There's more shuffling up there, but I see nothing.

"I had to do it," I say to Steel. I turn to see him staring at Jewel, watching her like he's in a trance. "She deserves every ounce of pain she's in," I say to bring him back to the present.

"This better be the truth or I'll yank that knife out and jab it right through her heart." Steel hits himself in the chest with a fist. "She's still gone and we need her back."

His frustration makes my anger boil out of control again. I wish I could kick Jewel, but we can't risk hurting her more until we know if what she said is true. So instead, I turn around and kick the wall. I feel my foot and knee jar with the vibration off the cement, but I could give two shits.

"WHERE'S CYPHER WITH THAT ADDRESS?" I bellow. "I need to end this bitch and go get my woman!"

About five minutes later, he yells out, "I GOT IT!"

"Where is it?" Steel and I echo.

Cypher slides down the ladder like it's a damn slide, his boots riding down the side bars, and he's next to us in seconds. He pulls his phone out of his cut and holds it out. Steel and I surround him to look at what he's seeing.

"She was actually useful for once. This is the gas station." He points to a square on the screen. "And this house," he pinches his fingers and zooms out to show a house a ways behind the gas station, "is supposed to be empty. It was foreclosed on two years ago, but for the last six months, it's been drawing electricity from the grid. Someone's living there and I'd bet it's where we should start."

"Do we need this bitch for anything else?" I look up from the phone and walk toward Jewel.

She's still got my blade sticking out of her ribs, breathing slowly. Either she's unconscious from the pain or she's good at faking it, because she's silent and not moving.

"End her," I hear Whiskey snarl from above.

So, I do what he says. He's our President after all. What he says goes. Doesn't matter that I would've done what I'm about to do even if he'd said not to.

I grab hold of the knife handle, pull it out of her rib cage, and plunge it into her stomach. Her body makes an involuntary jerk and I stab her a second time just below her waist line. This time, I push it in as far as I can and leave the knife embedded deep inside.

My body's moving on its own, so before I can even think about what I'm doing, I have both of my hands on her head and I twist with all my strength. I hear a series of pops and cracks, then she's dead. Letting go of her head, it falls forward so her chin is to her chest.

In the grand scheme of killings, this isn't the worst of them, but I don't give a fuck. We have the information we needed from Jewel, and now that we have our first lead to find Sunshine, we don't need the bitch anymore. Even if what she told us is wrong, she got what was coming to her just for lying to us about sneaking out and being beaten by strangers.

Jewel was supposed to be a loyal club girl and she broke so many levels of trust. She was still friends with Sydney, an excommunicated club girl, and she knew Sydney was doing drugs and didn't say anything. And the worst part of it all, she went somewhere around a rival club. She might not have known all the details of our problems with them, but she should've known better than to have any contact with them.

"Ring." I shake my vision straight and look up to see Whiskey sitting on the edge of the hole. "After we blew the hotel, I told you that you were in charge of the incinerator. This is all on you now."

I totally forgot about that, but hearing him bring it up makes me somewhat happy for the first time in three long days. While I wish I could rush out and get my woman back, I know disposing of this body is important first.

"You heard him, boys," I laugh, kind of creeping myself out a bit. "Let's get her out of this hole and wrapped up."

I slap Steel on the shoulder and continue, "Let's get this done and we'll make a plan to find our woman. You ready?"

"I'm right behind you." He throws my words from earlier back at me.

"Smart ass." I laugh, then start my climb up the ladder.

"Better a smart ass than a dumbass like you!" Steel jokes.

We're both back up on the main level, so I give him a half-ass shove with my shoulder. "If I was a dumbass, I wouldn't have scored Sunshine before you even got out of the slammer."

"I would've gotten her with or without you." He laughs. "Don't forget, I saw her first inside the slammer. So, ha! I win!"

"Speaking of my sister . . ." With that, we both stop our wisecracking and turn to see Whiskey with his arms folded and a very pissed-off look on his face. "What's your plans with her once we get her back? I don't care what my Pops threatened you with, you better have a good fucking answer or I'll throw both your asses in the incinerator with Jewel."

I stand up straight and give him all my attention, hopefully conveying my truth. "Just like we told Mountain, we're gonna make Sunshine our Old Lady. She already would be if she wasn't gone."

"What he said," Steel pipes up, causing half the room to laugh at our expense.

"Fuck," Whiskey swears and drops his tough guy act. "Duchess told me I had to accept this, but just know I'm not happy about it. I never considered her getting with one of my Brothers, but there's two of you, for fuck's sake."

"I may not have any siblings, but I get it. You don't want us scaring her away."

"I'd kill any Brother who tried to get with my sister," Steel says with venom in his voice.

"She just appeared in our lives. When we get her back, because we fucking will, then you guys need to hold on tight. But I still hold the right to burn you fuckers any time I see fit." Whiskey makes his last threat then nods his head toward the body now laying on the plastic sheet behind us.

During our brother to Brothers chat, the guys lifted Jewel out of the hole and got her unwrapped from the chains. Her lifeless body is sprawled on the floor, looking like a broken puppet. Serves the bitch right.

"I'll get the incinerator lit and then we'll toss her in." I head over to the controls on the wall and turn the key to fire it up.

I adjust a few dials and push the button to open the front door to the oven. It lifts up and the heat already roaring from inside makes my face break out in a sweat. I've used this thing a few times over the years, most recently for Loony, the Chaos Squad dumbass who tried to take Stiletto, one of our other club girls. Gunner managed to stop that attack, so we interrogated Loony and heard the name Bullet for the first time.

Unfortunately for Bullet, we've now heard his name way too many times for everything happening in our area to be a coincidence. His club kidnapped Wings, tried to take Stiletto, got Duchess from right under our noses, and now they have the woman I want to make mine forever. I'm not sure what our club did to piss this guy off so bad, but when we find him, he'll learn messing with the Rebel Vipers MC isn't a good idea.

I turn around to see Sam and Smoke each holding an end of the rolled-up plastic sheet. Smoke hasn't been a full patched member for long, so he's still getting stuck with some of the crappy Prospect level jobs.

"Who made Smoke help the Prospect?" I jest, poking fun of him.

"He lost a game of rock, paper, scissors." Hammer laughs. "Dude sucks 'cause he always chooses scissors."

"All right, boys. Toss her on there," I point at the metal table in front of the open incinerator door, "and I'll push her in."

Sam and Smoke swing the garbage up onto the sliding table and Steel tosses both of the bats we used on Jewel on top of her body. I grab some heat resistant gloves off a shelf nearby and slip them on, then grip the handle on the table's end and give it a push into the heat. The sliding table is on rollers, so I walk with the table forward until it's all the way inside the incinerator.

Steel hits the door close button and it slides shut.

Much like when a body is cremated, the oven kicks in full-blast to a temperature of eighteen thousand degrees. It turns the body inside to ash. It'll take approximately three hours for everything to be gone.

"I'm gonna stay here 'til this is done. If everything else is clean, everyone else can head out if they want," I say to Whiskey.

"You heard the man. If you don't need to be here, get the fuck out. Head to the clubhouse and keep your mouths shut. Church is at eight a.m. and everybody better be there on time." Whiskey points to the doors and almost everyone leaves.

Everyone except Whiskey, Mountain, Steel, and myself.

"Is this where you toss us in and pretend you don't know what happened?" Steel chuckles, trying to break the ice.

"Don't think I didn't consider it," Mountain answers with a straight face. It lasts for about ten seconds before he laughs out loud. That breaks the tension, making us all laugh too.

It feels good to release a little after the uncertainty and tightness of the last few hours.

When we all calm down, I remember my cut hanging on a hook on the barn wall. I walk over, hand Steel his, and slide mine back on. I tug it tight around my chest and tap my name badge with my right pointer finger.

"I take Penelope as serious as I take this cut. We'll find her and she'll be wearing one of these as soon as we can order it."

"I kinda already did. It should be here soon," Steel butts in on my serious talk.

"Is that what's in the box that came in yesterday addressed to you?" Whiskey asks with a smile. "I was wondering what it was for."

"Probably. I've never ordered a cut for a woman before, so I don't know what the box looks like."

"When did you do that?" I ask Steel.

"Last week. I wanted to have it here for whenever the right time happened."

"Always on your toes with the quick thinking, ain't ya?" Whiskey half-ass punches Steel in the arm.

"I did keep your ass out of the slammer, so kiss my ass," Steel says and punches him back full force.

"Not funny, asshole. Not funny," Whiskey grumbles back.

We spend the next few hours trading insults, telling old funny stories, and trying to keep the mood as upbeat as possible. I know what's coming tomorrow will send the club on another dangerous mission, so having a little break before the crazy is needed.

Technically, tomorrow is now today. It's about three in the morning by the time I crawl my ass into bed. We've got Church in five hours and I need some shut eye. I spend most of the time dreaming about Sunshine, thinking about the rest of my life with her and our family.

CHAPTER FORTY

SUNSHNE

CLANG! "Time to wake up, you little bitch."

I've been awake for a while now, but have been ignoring the guys roaming around the basement. These idiots have been clomping up and down the stairs for what seems like hours, carrying the puppies upstairs. I don't know where they're taking them, but I'm not very happy about it. As long as those puppies are near me, I know they're safe. Who knows what's going to happen to them upstairs.

Shortly before they all came down here, I managed to convince the puppy who'd been cuddling with me to go back with his brothers and sisters. I know there's food and water in there for them, and my little buddy needed to eat and drink. The snacks I've been sharing aren't enough for his growing little body.

Even though I knew he couldn't understand a word I was saying, I held him and told him he needed to go back in the box. He kept looking at me with his sad eyes as he made his way across the basement. Then with some crazy speed, he took a running start and leaped over the plywood board, and was back inside with his siblings. The barking and yelping and wrestling that went on was so nice to hear.

But it was short lived when the door opened at the top of the stairs and three guys came down. Each one grabbed a puppy at a time and made their way back upstairs. I don't know exactly what they've been doing since, because I rolled over and have been pretending to sleep, but I'm going to miss the little ones. They've never been quiet, except when they're sleeping, but I'll miss the constant companionship, knowing I'm not down here alone.

"I SAID WAKE UP!"

I flop onto my back and look over to see the man who I've learned is Bullet standing outside the bars, staring at me with a pissed-off look. Good, I hope he's mad. I'm not exactly a happy camper myself. And he's about to hear it.

"What the fuck do you want?" I snap back.

"What I want doesn't matter to you, bitch. What I need is for you to put these clothes on." He pushes a plastic shopping bag through the bars and it drops to the floor.

I sit up but keep my ass on the mattress. "And why the hell would I do that?" Hell, even to me, I sound angry.

I've never really had a reason in my life to talk to someone like this, but I almost kind of like it. Maybe I need to start being more assertive in my everyday life. I wonder if Ring and Steel would like it if I tried to be bossy with them in the bedroom? Something tells me they'd try and fight it in the beginning, but eventually, they'd see how it benefits them and they'd let me play a little.

"Your buyer is gonna be here tonight and you need to look halfway presentable. I can't let you shower, but changing your clothes will help with the smell." Bullet sneers.

My panic starts kicking in. "Buyer? Tonight? Why tonight?"

I can't be taken tonight. I haven't figured a way out of here yet. I know I've been down here for a few days, at least, but I'm not one hundred percent sure. Having no open windows can seriously fuck with your internal clock.

"Because tonight's the night he said he'd be here. Why all the damn questions? There's no one coming to save you, so just change your damn clothes and deal with it."

I've got to try and see if he'll tell me what day it is. I need to know how long I've been here. "But why tonight? What's so special about today?"

He stands back and runs his hands through his messy, slimy hair. His frustration with me is growing, but if he plans on me going along with his plan so easily, he's sadly mistaken. If I have to leave his place for another hell hole, I'll be kicking and screaming the whole way.

"Bitch," he growls, "I don't know why it has to be tonight. If the guy wants to pick you up on a random fucking Tuesday night, then I'll let him pay me and pick you up on a Tuesday night. Is that good enough for you?"

Tuesday. I've been here since Friday, so that's four days, five if you count Friday as day one. Is that fast or slow in the kidnapping world? How the hell am I supposed to know?

"Fine," I whisper. I reach forward and grab the bag to see what's inside. I pull out a plain black t-shirt, black leggings, black socks, and black underwear. Hey, looks like I'll be Ring's twin in this get up. He always wears all black, and I wish he could see me.

I'd really hate to go with this new buyer kidnapper person, but maybe getting out of this basement is what I need to figure out where I am. Then I can try to run and find someone to help me get back home.

"Are you gonna change or just stare at the clothes all day?"

Bullet and two of his cronies are now standing next to each other, watching me with hunger in their eyes. How gross. I'd rather stay in my dirty clothes than have to change in front of these sleezeballs.

"I'm not changing my clothes in front of you idiots. If you want me to wear these, you need to leave me alone."

The guys huddle together and argue amongst themselves. I don't know the other guys' names, but I've seen both of them when they brought me food. None of the three look happy at my 'request', but I'm way past caring at this point.

"Hey, assholes," that gets their attention again, "either you leave or I stay just like this." Fuck them and their hush-hush meeting.

"Fine." Bullet gets up close and personal with the bars again, trying to be intimidating. "Your buyer will be here in a few hours. If you're not changed by then, I'll come in there and do it my fuckin' self."

I squint my eyes and try to give him the meanest look I've ever given anyone. "I'd like to see you fuckin' try me, asshole. I'd fight you until my dying breath before I let you get one item of clothing off my back."

The look that drops over his face is priceless. He may have looked angry before, but the shock he's showing now tells me a lot. He's not used to having women talk back to him this way.

The guys behind him start laughing hysterically. "She told you, boss." They sound like cackling hyenas who smoked too many packs of cigarettes, the cackling causing coughing, and I wouldn't be surprised if one of them coughed up a lung. You don't need to know anything medical to know that doesn't sound good.

Bullet spins around and charges at both of them, pushing them against the block wall, hand clamped around each of their throats. "Shut the fuck up or you'll be next up for sale. I know someone who'd be very interested in putting you two to work."

He lets them go and stomps back up the stairs. The two men stay frozen against the wall, trying to catch their breath.

"Bullet obviously doesn't respect you two. What are you doing here?" Maybe I can use the threat against them to my advantage. "If you let me go, I won't tell anyone where this place is. You let me free and I promise the Rebel Vipers won't find you." At this point, if I could just walk out of here, I'd promise these guys the moon.

They look at each other, almost like they're considering it. Maybe it worked. But before they can say anything back, the basement door opens and Bullet yells down. "Get the fuck up here. You two have work to do."

And they're gone.

Since I have no clock, and not knowing when tonight technically is, I make quick work of changing clothes. I don't want to be half undressed when they decide it's time to come down and get me.

Shockingly, everything fits. I don't know who went shopping for this stuff, but they guessed my sizes right. I'm what I'd consider a smaller woman, so maybe they just got lucky. They didn't get me a new bra, so I leave mine on and swap my dirty stuff for the new items. Once I slide my shoes back on, I stand up and stretch.

This cell isn't very big, maybe twenty feet by twenty feet, but it's enough for me to make a few steps before I have to turn around and pace back. I make a few laps around my box, just to get my blood pumping again, trying to wake my whole body up.

If I want to be able to run the second I get outside, I need to start moving now.

After my thirtieth circle, I sit on the mattress and reach my fingers to my toes. I'm mid-stretch when the fireworks start.

Pop pop pop pop pop pop . . . over and over again.

At least it sounds like fireworks.

I can tell the walls of this house aren't soundproof, but being below ground level dampens the sounds coming from outside. If I was a betting woman, I'd place a lot of money on those being gunshots.

Pop pop pop pop pop pop!

I can hear muffled yelling and it doesn't sound good.

I jump up, heave the mattress up on its side, and worm my way behind it. Sliding down to the floor, I use the floppy bulk to cover me. For a tiny mattress, this thing's quite heavy. But I know it's not bullet proof.

I don't know what made me try to use this thing as a shield, but maybe if whoever is shooting up there decides to come down here, and they don't see me, I'll be safe.

What I really hope is that those bullets are coming from guns held by my men. I hope Ring and Steel are here to find me. I hope we all make it out of here in one piece. I hope we can go back to the clubhouse and be together. I hope after all this trouble, they still want me to be their Old Lady.

If I get to see them again, I'll jump in their arms and never let go. I've found my new home, and it's wherever those two men are.

CHAPTER FORTY-ONE

STEEL

"Here's the plan." Hammer points at the projector screen on the wall in Church and everyone watches as he talks about the different points on the map. It's bright and early Tuesday morning and the whole club is in their chairs, listening to their instructions for the day.

Ring, Whiskey, Mountain, and I got back to the clubhouse at about three a.m. and I went straight to bed. I didn't sleep much in the five hours I had, but it was enough that I'm ready to go bust some Chaos Squad skulls. Honestly, it's probably more adrenaline pumping through me than rest, but it doesn't matter. Hammer, our Sergeant-at-Arms, has a solid plan to go find my woman and I'm ready to fucking roll.

Since the screen is behind me, I've got my chair spun around and my eyes locked on every last detail.

"Why no bikes?" Smoke asks from behind me.

"Because we don't want the noise and I'd rather not leave them sitting out in the open in that gas station parking lot," Whiskey answers.

"Makes sense," Smoke replies.

And it really does. Since the house we're going to be ambushing is approximately one hundred yards behind the gas station, we're going to buddy up and drive there in our trucks. That way, if we're spotted, hopefully, the Chaos guys won't suspect it's us. It won't be until we're out of the trucks and across the field, guns pointed their way, that the idiots will know we're coming.

After we know what's going on, a second wave of Brothers will drive across the field and meet us for backup. But by that point, it'll be too late for the dumbasses. They'll have bullets in their faces and we'll be one step closer to finding Sunshine.

"Everyone know their role and who they're riding with?" Hammer asks as he drops into his chair.

The room is filled with positive answers. "Yup." "Got it." "Fuck yea."

"One last thing. I know we did this the other day, but we need one last vote before we head out." Whiskey lifts a finger and points it at me first, then Ring. "These two knuckleheads need their woman back. All in favor say 'aye'."

"AYE!" comes out in a resounding boom.

Bang! Whiskey slams his gavel. "Everyone to the trucks."

The room starts to empty and Ring and I are the last ones out.

"You ready for this?" Ring asks as we make our way through the main room.

"You know I am, Brother." I hold out my fist and he bumps back with his. "Let's do this thing."

"See you there." Ring hops in Whiskey's truck while I drive my own. We debated driving together, but Hammer pointed out it'd be best for us to go separate until we know what we're getting into. Just in case something happens to one of us, the other isn't at risk. It sucks to think of it that way, but going in apart from each other gives us a higher chance of one of us making it to Sunshine.

I haven't had my truck for very long, but it's about to get a crash course in rough driving. I've got Saddle, Smoke, and Buzz in the truck with me and we roll out of the compound parking lot in a hurry. We've got about a twenty-minute drive to the gas station and I plan on driving balls to the wall the whole way.

As soon as we all pull in the gas station, Cypher runs inside to hopefully prevent the employees from calling the cops. We don't plan on being here long, and if the local authorities crash our party, we'll all be in a heap of trouble. I really don't need to be caught with a gun again. I'm a felon on probation for a weapons charge. The guns I've got on me now would send me straight back to prison for the rest of my life.

"Listen up," Hammer speaks up and we all gather around him. "You know your places. Find your buddy and stay by his side no matter what. Once the first team has things secured, I'll whistle and the second team drive over. Any questions?"

Silence.

"Roll out," Whiskey barks and we all pair up.

My partner today is Saddle. Saddle's our Road Captain and probably the best shooter in this club. I've been instructed to stay behind him and move wherever he moves. This is another one of Hammer's instructions for Ring and me to follow. We aren't allowed to initiate any violence, so we can get to our woman in one piece. So, I'm Saddle's shadow like Ring is Tiny's.

We can see the house as clear as day and hustle across the field in no time. There are trees scattered about, so we have plenty of places to duck and hide along the way. It takes everyone less than five minutes to have the house fully surrounded.

I look across the yard and find Hammer, waiting for him to give the second group the signal, when someone comes out the front door and sees all of us. He opens his mouth, but before he says a word, there's a hole in his chest and he falls down the front steps. Two more men come out the front door, but neither makes it more than a few steps.

They're both shot down, leaving all three in a pile on the ground.

Saddle takes a few steps to the right and I follow his every move. I have my gun up, eyes on the house, but my body's making every step all on its own.

All of a sudden, I hear this *pop pop pop pop pop pop* sound coming from behind me. I turn to see a shed in the corner of the yard, surrounded by trees and overgrown bushes. The glass in one of the windows is busted out and the barrel of what looks like a shotgun is sticking out.

"Saddle, behind us."

He turns, and I move with him. "Let's get closer," he orders.

I don't know what this mystery guy is shooting at, but since it doesn't seem to be us, we step back about fifty feet and are next to the shed in no time. I grab the door handle with my left hand, gun still up in my right, and pull it open. Saddle peaks around the door, sees something he obviously doesn't like, and fires a few rounds into the shed.

"Another one down," he chuckles.

"That makes four at my last count."

Still half hiding behind the side of this shed, we look out and see our Brothers still shooting into the house. If Sunshine's really in there, I hope she's heard the commotion and found somewhere safe to hide. If she ends up hurt by one of our bullets, I'll never forgive myself.

"WE GOT A RUNNER!" someone yells.

I say *fuck it* to Hammer's orders to hide out and step into the open clearing. That's when I see Sam, one of our Prospects, running farther away from the house, chasing someone. He's a fast little fucker. Sam quickly catches the guy, tackles him, and they start wrestling. He gets the upper hand and locks the guy in a chokehold, while I blink and almost miss it. He's got the guy pinned to the ground with all his limbs restraining him. Trooper's right on his six and they handcuff the guy, leaving him face down in the dirt.

We all take a breath, but it very soon turns to dread when Ring yells out, "BRICK IS DOWN! DOC!"

That makes the whole club move fast.

Hammer whistles louder than I've ever heard before and a half dozen trucks come barreling our way. They weave through the trees like pros in a maze. The roar of their engines is probably heard a mile away.

Doc, Mountain, Trooper, Ring, and Skynyrd are all down on their knees around Brick. There's so much talking and yelling, I can't make heads or tails of what's happening.

"Where's the damn van?" I see Mountain's head pop up, looking around. He tries to get up on his own, but with his prosthetic and all the craziness, he falls sideways and lands square on his ass. "FUCKIN' HELL!"

I go to rush over to help him but immediately feel a burning sensation in my right leg. I look down and see I've got a rip in my pants and blood running down my leg. I feel myself start to wobble.

What in the actual fuck?

I've been shot.

"Steel!" Saddle catches me and helps me down to the ground. "Let me look at it."

Saddle pokes my leg a few times. Holy hell that stings.

"Quit your whining, boy. It's just a graze. You were told to stay behind me and look what happened when you didn't." Saddle yanks the bandana from my head, wraps it around my thigh, and ties it super fucking tight. "That should stop the bleeding until whatever's going on over there is done. Then Doc can get a look at ya."

He stands up, pulls me to my feet, and we walk—I hobble—closer to the group.

That's when I notice the silence. No one is saying a word except for Trooper and Doc, who are whispering to each other. Whiskey has his head on the ground and Mountain's being held up by Skynyrd. The whole club is standing around just looking at the ground.

"What's going on?" Saddle asks.

Ring gets up, dusts off his hands, and looks our way. "He's gone."

"Who's gone?" Saddle questions. I don't think he's grasping what's happened yet.

"Brick," Ring responds. "He got hit right in the heart."

"Holy shit" is all Saddle can say.

That's when my brain registers what we're doing here and I freak the fuck out.

I grab Ring by the shoulders and get in his face. "Where's Sunshine?"

"Shit," he grabs me back, "we gotta search the house."

"LISTEN UP!" We all turn to see Hammer with a hard look on his face. "We need to search this house and I only want those of you who know you can handle it. If anyone has even the slightest inkling they can't put what just happened out here to the side, I don't want you to step foot in there. Who's going in?"

Ring and I step forward, followed by a dozen more guys. I don't pay much attention to who because my mind's already in that house, finding my woman safe, and holding her in my arms.

"Steel, I hate to say this buddy, but you go in last. I don't need you shot again," Hammer points at me.

"Fine," I answer back, "but when we find her, she rides back with me."

"That's just fine," Hammer tosses back.

With all our guns up, we line up and climb the cement steps. With what I'd imagine is SWAT-level precision, Trooper leads the way into the house. I don't see what's happening inside until I step through the kicked-down door and see the mess.

The bullets we shot through this place make every wall and door look like swiss fucking cheese. In addition to that, there's garbage everywhere. I'm not sure on our final bad guy dead count, but no matter how many people were hiding out here, this level of nastiness is just that, plain nasty.

"There's a basement!" Rings yells. I know it's his voice without seeing him.

I make my way through the house and find the hallway leading toward the back. Stepping into the kitchen just in time to hear footsteps coming from below me, a few people come out of a door, which I see leads to the basement.

I look down and see Ring standing at the bottom with our Sunshine. He's holding her in both arms and they're whispering to each other. She has her arms around his neck and she kisses him, shutting up whatever gibberish he's probably spouting.

All the adrenaline from the day leaves my body and I crash to the floor. My legs give out and I'm down in a flash.

"STEEL!" I'm on my ass so I can no longer see down the stairs, but just as fast as I fell, Ring and Sunshine are up next to me, and Sunshine's wrapping her arms around me.

"Are you okay? Are you hurt?" She must notice the bandana on my leg because she goes ballistic. "What happened? Were you shot? Oh my god! We need to get you to the hospital."

"Hey hey hey." I grasp her face in both hands and hold her directly in front of me. "I'm fine." I pull her in to kiss her for the first time in too damn long.

I'll never be away from her for this many days again for the rest of my life. If I have to be gone for something for the club, I'll find a way to get her to come with me. I don't care what anyone fucking says, this woman's never leaving my side.

She pulls back and I reluctantly let her go. I look at her from head to toe, seeing if I can spot any injuries. If she's hurt, I'll resuscitate every dead man here just to kill them again. "Are you okay, Sunshine? Are you hurt?"

"I'm actually just fine." She looks behind me. "Where'd everybody go?"

I look around and see that it's just Ring, Sunshine, and me left in the kitchen, and we're all sitting on the floor.

"I think they went outside to deal with the mess." Ring grabs one of her hands. "We need to tell you something, Sunshine."

Shit. This isn't how today was supposed to go. We weren't supposed to lose anyone.

"What happened? Did someone else get hurt?" The worry on her face is almost hard to keep looking at. If she wasn't mine, I'd be trying to hide from the scared look I see in her beautiful hazel eyes.

But I keep her gaze and lay it out to her straight. No bullshitting here. Just facts, all out in the open. "It's Brick. He got shot and didn't make it."

"What?" she gasps. "But he's my uncle." And here come the tears.

"Come here." Ring pulls her into his lap and starts rocking her back and forth. "I'm so sorry, Sunshine. I tried to help him. I tried so damn hard."

CHAPTER FORTY-TWO

RING

"I tried to help him. I tried so damn hard." I've got Sunshine in my lap and I'm lost as to what to do next.

When I saw a body lying in the grass, I thought it was one of the Chaos Squad guys. But then I saw the bright green snake on the back of the cut and realized it was one of our guys, so I rushed to him, rolled his body over, and saw it was Brick. His eyes were closed and he wasn't moving.

I noticed the growing blood stain on his gray t-shirt and immediately yelled for help. I have zero medical training, so I was afraid to even touch him. My mind went into 'don't hurt him even more' mode and I just yelled as loud as I could for Doc. I knew he'd know what to do to save Brick. He had to.

I have my head buried against Sunshine's shoulder, so I feel her sobs shake both of us.

"I have no doubt you did everything you could." Steel scoots to my side and wraps his arms around both Sunshine and me.

I feel his arm around my back and just let my worries wash away. I let my Brother and best friend take everything away for this moment and concentrate on giving our woman all the support she needs. As sad as it is that Brick's gone, and I know we'll have to deal with that at some point soon, our woman's needs are what's most important. Brick was her uncle and she needs us.

Sunshine lifts her head from my shoulder and leans back against Steel.

"Are you sure you're okay?" she asks him.

That makes him chuckle. "It's just a graze. I didn't even notice until after the action stopped."

"You were told to stay behind Saddle so this didn't happen." I joke to Steel, nudging him with my shoulder. "How'd you end up with even a graze?"

"No fuckin' clue." He shakes his head.

"I'm glad you're both safe." Sunshine reaches forward and grabs one of each of our hands. "If I lost you both, or even one of you, I don't know what I'd do."

"Sunshine," I lift our joined hands and kiss the back of hers, "we were split up for just that reason. We needed to be sure one of us was safe enough to come find you. Steel getting a graze was just a bump in the road."

Steel lifts their hands and copies my kiss. "I would've walked through fire to get to wherever you were."

"When I started hearing those pops, I hoped it was you guys coming to get me. I hid and just waited. I just knew it was you two." Sunshine looks back and forth between us the whole time.

"Dude," I laugh again, "our lady here had herself wedged underneath a mattress. I almost missed it when I looked around the basement for the first time. She was locked in this cell in the corner, and I didn't see her. All of a sudden, the mattress flopped over, and she was sitting on the floor."

"You shoulda seen the look on his face." Sunshine looks at me, giggling. "I almost thought he was gonna faint."

"I almost did!" I retort. "I had a quick thought that you weren't here and we'd have to start from square one."

"Turns out that bitch actually told the truth for once," Steel growls out. "I'm glad she's fuckin' dead."

That makes Sunshine sit up straight. "Who's she?"

"Jewel," we echo.

"She's dead?"

"Yup. And she deserved that and so much more." I lift Sunshine from my lap and gently set her on Steel's good leg. "We'll talk about this more when we get back home. But right now, we gotta get moving. We've been here for too long." I get up, then lift Sunshine to her feet.

"We need to head outside and see what the rest of the club is up to. I'm sure we've got an interrogation to get to," Steel says as I help him back to his feet.

"Who are you gonna interrogate?" Sunshine questions as we make our way through the house and out into the day light.

"Bullet," Steel replies.

She spins around and stops both of us in our tracks. The look on her face is one of hate and anger. I've never seen this look on her before, and I never want to see it again. "I want in on that."

"No way," I bark.

Steel gives a resounding "Fuck no."

"Yes!" she sasses back. She's got her hands on her hips and her eyes are locked on us. "He did this to me, so I need to see him pay."

"What's going on over here?" Whiskey approaches us and wraps Sunshine in a tight hug. "God, are you okay? You're okay, right?"

"Yes, I'm good," she hugs him back, "but these two blockheads are telling me no."

Whiskey keeps an arm around her shoulders but looks at us. "I think it's a great idea."

"What? We've never had a woman out there." I'm stunned. No woman has ever been anywhere near the pit. As long as I've been around, the club has done everything possible to keep the horrors that happen out there away from our women. "Why start now?"

"I second that. We just got her back. What if she leaves because of what she sees?" Steel is in straight-up panic mode. He's pacing back and forth. If he wasn't limping on that leg, he'd probably pick up Sunshine and run away with her where no one could find her.

"I need to do this." Sunshine approaches me like a quiet church mouse. I'm sure I look panicked too. Thinking about her in that barn is making my heart race. "That asshole, Bullet, has caused way too much pain to this club. Brick was the last straw. I need to see him pay."

"That's why I don't want you to see that place." Steel stops his circles and wraps himself around Sunshine's back. He pushes her forward, and the next thing I know, the three of us are standing in a huddle with her in between us. "Happy things don't happen out there. I can't let that place take away your sunshine."

Sunshine spins around and faces Steel. "If I promise to stay outside the barn during the worst of it, will you let me come with? You two can decide when I come in or have to step out? I need to be there to know he's being handled. I need to do this for Tempy and Duchess and Stiletto. I need to be able to look at them and tell them that the man who caused us so much pain is gone. We need this."

"I don't mean to butt in here," with Sunshine finally back in our arms, I forgot Whiskey's standing next to us, "but I think she's got a point."

"See . . ." Sunshine peeks over her shoulder at me with a smug smile on her face. "Even he agrees with me."

"And as her big brother, and your President," Whiskey's pulling out the big guns, "what I say goes."

"Fine," I huff. I spin her back to face me, grab her face in both of my hands, and kiss her like it's my last day on Earth.

I hold her tight for as long as I can, until both of us need to breathe. Pulling back, I see the smile on her face. She slowly opens her eyes and I'm a fucking goner. I'd give anything to keep her in this state. Anything this woman wants is hers. I'd sell my soul to the devil to give her whatever she asks for.

She lets me out of her grip and leans back into Steel, using him as her support. "I promise I'll stay out of the way and listen to your every word."

"That settles it." Whiskey claps me on the shoulder. "We've got all the garbage loaded in the van, so we need to get moving."

"What's the plan from here?" Steel steps back and takes Sunshine with him, pulling her out of my reach. Asshole. I'll get him back later.

"Steel, Trooper pulled your truck around so the three of you ride together. Head straight to the pit and we'll get everything set up. We'll wait for you to get there before we start any of the fun."

"We'll be right behind you," I say to Whiskey. He turns around and jogs to his truck, hops in, and fires it up.

"Guess that means I'm driving the dumb Dodge. You know I hate that thing. It'll probably die on our way back.

We should've brought my Chevy." I hold out my hand, and Steel tosses me his keys. "But be warned. Because you two get to cuddle in the back seat, I get extra Sunshine time later."

That makes both of them laugh as we walk to the truck.

My back is turned, so I don't see her coming when Sunshine jumps on my back, but I instinctively catch her in a piggyback ride hold. Her legs wrap around my waist and her arms overlap on my chest. "Just for driving the big bad blue truck, I'll let you be big spoon tonight. How's that sound?" she whispers that last part in my ear.

"Oh, you're on," I warn her. I do a little hop to bounce her and she holds on even tighter, laughing the whole time.

"Hey," Steel whines behind us, "wait for the crippled dude."

"I thought it was just a scratch?" I retort. Boy, he's milking his boo-boo for all it's worth.

"I've missed our woman's lovin'. You can't blame me for that."

"Get in the truck and she's all yours." I open the back door, and he climbs in. I tug on the legs around my middle. "And as much as I love you being my backpack, you need to get down so I can drive and we can get this over with."

She loosens her grip and slides down to the ground, then she grabs hold of both my butt cheeks and squeezes. "Thank you for saving me, Ring."

I spin around and kiss her one more time. "Anything for you, Sunshine. Anything for you."

The sparkle in her hazel eyes is in full glow. The first time I saw her, I thought her eyes were a tornado of green and brown. But today, the happiness she's radiating also shows a little gold around the edges. It's like her eyes are a mood ring, showing her feelings to just us.

I hate that we're about to take her to a place I usually have no problem being, but I'll let her get the closure she needs. She says she needs it, so what she says is what goes . . . but just for today.

After today, she'll never step foot in that barn for as long as I'm on this side of the dirt.

CHAPTER FORTY-THREE

SUNSHINE

I know the guys aren't happy I'm outside this barn, but I need to be here. When I told them it was for me and the other girls, I was pulling excuses out of thin air. But I do have to say, my half-ass logic seemed to be all the reasoning Whiskey needed to agree with me. He pulled his 'big brother President card' and my men fell like a house of cards in an earthquake. I have a feeling I'll be paying for my little outburst at a later date, but for now, it's worth it.

"Don't step one foot inside that barn unless Ring or I say so." Steel's in full protector mode. "If I catch you inside, I'll put you over my knee and your backside will be the kind of red none of us would like. Do you understand me?"

I keep my eyes on his and give him my best smile. I run my hands up his front, under his cut, trying to feel every bump and ridge on his chest. Unless I was on top of him in our bed, I couldn't get any closer.

"I'll stay outside." I lift onto my tiptoes and steal a kiss. "But I still want to see him before you end him." I drop back and turn to walk away.

"Woman, you're gonna end me if you keep talkin' like that."

"You like me just the way I am, so deal with it."

Someone was nice enough to put a chair outside the barn door, so I sit on my ass and wait for my turn to go in.

Bullet is the epitome of what's wrong with this world. My men may be part of a biker club, and participate in things that aren't exactly legal, but they'd never do the things that Bullet and his club did.

They'd never lock puppies in a box, they'd never drug people, they'd never kidnap innocent people, and they'd never hurt a woman, unless she did something to deserve it.

"You sure you wanna be out here?" Ring squats in front of me and squeezes my knees.

"I'm sure." I lean forward just a skosh and peck him on the lips.

"If this was anyone else, Whiskey would've said no." Ring stands up and walks toward the doors.

"That's cause I'm his sister and he loves me," I toss out, not even thinking of what I'm saying.

Ring and Steel stop. They look at each other, then back at me.

"He's not the only one," Ring drops his bombshell, and they disappear inside.

Love?

There's that L word again. First, my aunt brought it up while helping her move, but I ignored it. Then, when it popped in my head talking to Ring, I decided to keep it to myself and let the idea simmer.

It's official—I'm in love with two men. Holy crap on a cracker.

When the world stops spinning so damn fast, hopefully, I'll still have the lady balls to say it to their faces. They both deserve to hear it. Those men are my future, and I don't care who knows it. My overprotective father and brother be damned, Ring and Steel, and Opal, are my family now. In that basement, I decided I wanted to be their Old Lady, so if that means telling them I love them, it can't happen a moment too soon.

"I WANT HIM DEAD!" Ring yells out, pulling me from my love haze and back into the present.

I stand up and sneak as close to the door as I can. I lean my back against the wood and listen to what's happening.

"I know you want his head, Ring, but we can't kill him 'til we have all the answers," Whiskey says back.

I'm a bit shocked I can tell who's who by their voices. I haven't been around all that long, but at least I know what my guys and brother sound like.

"He's right." Mountain. I guess I know my dad too.

"This is all your fault anyways." This comes from a voice I'd recognize anywhere—Bullet. His voice is a little muffled, but the evil is still all there.

"All who's fault?" Whiskey.

"Your Pops." Bullet sneers.

"What did my Pops ever do to you?" Whiskey.

"He's the reason I decided to target your club. Did you think I'd waste all this time and money on some random club? You guys made the first move and I fought back."

"I never met you a day in my life. Why target me?' Mountain.

There's some rustling noise. It almost sounds like chains rattling. "Because you had my brother killed!"

"And how am I supposed to know who the fuck your brother is?" Mountain roars back. I can hear the frustration in his voice. I've only seen him uncomfortable once, and that was the day we met. But this tone is totally new to me.

"Does the name Shane Miller ring a bell to you idiots?" Bullet asks.

"That fucker was your brother?" Whiskey asks, and that sets the whole group into a fit of laughter.

I don't know who this Shane person is, or was, but it sounds like the club had a major problem with him.

"He may have been a dumbass, but you assholes had him killed. So, I switched my gears and came after your women with all I had."

"I didn't start this, you no good use of bones." *Punch! Oof!* "Your piece of shit brother started this the day he decided to run me over," Mountain says.

Shane Miller. Bullet's brother. He's the one who tried to kill Mountain. I'd heard the story. He's the one who ambushed him on the road, made him crash his motorcycle, then ran him over with his truck. Shane's the reason my dad only has one leg.

I don't know how he was killed, but just hearing this second hand, I'm glad he was.

"The only reason he did that to you," *Cough!* "was because you let that woman escape him at that gas station."

"All of this is because Mountain stopped Shane from kidnapping a woman? Because he was doing the right thing by not letting you hurt an innocent person?" questions Steel.

"Exactly."

"And you took our women why?" Ring asks.

"I took your women as payback for that one woman you stopped my brother from getting. It was my giant *fuck you* that none of you knew about. Seeing you all run around clueless, well, that was the best part." Bullet tries to laugh, but he coughs every few words and keeps taking deep breaths.

"You took innocent women and put them through all that just to get your giggles? Even for a shithead like you, that's fuckin' low." That came from Hammer, another voice recognition point for me.

But what he said is so true. To kidnap the women the club Brothers have an attachment to just because of some skewed sense of family payback, that's fucked up.

Because the way I'm understanding this, this Shane character's the reason this all started. Shane tried to kidnap someone and Mountain stopped him. Shane decided to chase Mountain down with his truck, and Shane was the one who injured an already down man. Mountain did nothing but try and protect a stranger, and this as retribution is way too much.

"What makes you think we're responsible for Shane being dead?" That's a voice I'm not sure of, but it's still a good question.

"A little birdy in the prison told me a guy with club tattoos came rolling into the infirmary right after he was in a fight with my brother. Shane wasn't smart, but he wasn't dumb enough to try and stab someone with a shank. So, I know it was one of you fuckers," Bullet states.

"Which one of us do you think it was?" Steel asks.

Holy fucking shit. This was the day I met Steel in the prison infirmary. This is the reason we met. Steel killed Shane as retaliation for what he did to Mountain. My world would be so much different had we not met that day.

I would've met him when I came to the clubhouse to meet my mystery father, but we might not have had the connection we formed while I stitched him up. We talked for a good two hours that day. We didn't talk about our families or our jobs or anything really important, but the random questions we asked each other helped build the foundation of our relationship now. His favorite color is green. He loves Cheetos. His favorite movie is *Blazing Saddles*. He even talked about his best friend. I forgot all about that.

This is all because of this greasy, smelly, slimeball.

"I don't give two fucks which one of you it was. What I did wouldn't have changed because of that."

"Since we're gonna kill you and turn you into ash anyways, I guess we'll keep that little tidbit to ourselves," teases Ring.

"Whatever," Bullet retorts.

"I have a question," Whiskey says. "How many of your Chaos buddies are left out there, hiding in the shadows now that we just crashed your party house?"

Oh shit! I never thought of that. What if there are more of them, just waiting to take another woman?

"What was your body count from today?" I can't believe Bullet is asking this. Is he really going to tell the truth?

"We've got seven of your friends waiting to join you in hell." Whiskey.

"Then you got us all. When you torched my motel, a bunch of losers decided to leave the club and run away. I guess they didn't like the risk of being blown to smithereens," says Bullet.

"Ha! That's what you get for leaving a woman on her own. She found a way to escape and got back to us." That's Hammer.

Bullet chuckles. "How's my little Tempy doing these days? Are her boo-boos better? Did she tell you about—" *Whack! Oomph!*

"You keep my woman's name out of your mouth!" Hammer shouts. I'm guessing he hit Bullet, stopping him from saying any more about Tempy.

"Shit, Brother," Whiskey says, "you killed him."

"NO!" I step forward, into the opening, and everyone turns my way.

My feet move me out of my hiding spot. There's no way of stepping back and pretending I wasn't listening to what was going on in here.

In between a few of the Brothers, I finally get my first glimpse of what's been happening.

They have Bullet wrapped in chains, my earlier hearing of the rattling was spot on, and he's hanging midair in the open area. There's a plastic tarp laid out underneath him and it's splattered with blood. I see various tools strewn on the ground, including a hammer, ironically right by Hammer's boots, but I'm too far away to see what anything else is.

I'm facing a wall of bikers clad in denim and leather, and none of them look happy to see me. The feeling's mutual at this moment.

"I said I wanted to see him before you killed him," I kick my attitude up a thousand degrees, letting my anger fly. "You promised me I could see this scumbag before you offed him. I needed to do this for the other ladies and you guys ruined that. You ruined everything!"

My feet get a mind of their own again. I turn around and just start running. I don't know where I'm going, because I don't know where I am, but I run. I don't know which way is the right way back to the clubhouse, so I go around where all the trucks are parked and head straight for the path that led us here. My best guess is this will get me to the road and I'll figure the rest out when I get there.

I'm probably not fifty feet down the driveway when two arms surround me from behind and lift me off my feet.

"LET ME GO!" I scream.

"No!" It's Ring, still holding me up, both arms wrapped around my middle, turning around and marching me back toward the barn.

I start kicking my legs and squirming my body, trying to get down. My arms are free of his grasp, so I beat his forearms with my fists. I'm pissed . . . but pissed is the wrong word. I'm livid. Irritated. Furious. Seething.

How could they let this happen? They promised me if I sat out here like a good girl, they'd let me have my moment. But no. Hammer had to go hammer happy and fuck everything up.

"Sunshine." The second I see Steel standing next to his truck, I deflate like a week-old balloon. Like those ones you get for your birthday, the mylar ones that slowly lose their air and sink closer and closer to the ground. Then one day, you wake up and it's laying on the floor like a dead jellyfish. That's how I feel right now.

I see the morose look on his face and all my anger just sinks. My adrenaline crashes and I deflate. I lean my head back onto Ring's shoulder and close my eyes, my arms feeling like they weigh fifty pounds. I'm tired and ready for this day to be over.

I feel him before I see him. Steel lifts me out of Ring's arms and I latch onto him like he's a lifeline. My arms circle his head, my legs are around his torso, and my feet cross just above his ass.

Ring then closes himself around me and grips my sides so tight, I feel his chest against my back and his head drops to my shoulder. I lean my head toward his and he nuzzles his face in my neck.

"We're so sorry, Sunshine," Steel's voice rumbles through my chest. "I know you wanted your time, but sometimes things in there don't always go to plan."

"Hammer did what he felt was right and we need to be okay with that." Ring presses a few light kisses on my neck and my whole body breaks into goosebumps.

This isn't the time for these feelings, but the tender care my men are showing me right now just goes to show that they understand me. They get my frustration, but they'll also do whatever it takes me bring me down from my emotional cliff dive and help me settle to see the reality of the situation.

"I get it." I lift my head and push up, forcing both guys to stand at full attention to keep me sandwiched between them. I keep my eyes locked on Steel, because I have a feeling he'll understand what I'm about to say more so than Ring will. "I don't really blame anyone for killing him on the spot after what he was saying. I just had it in my head that I needed to be the one to do it."

"What?" And I was right, Ring detaches himself from me and steps behind Steel, forcing me to look at him. "You wanted to kill him yourself? That wasn't part of the deal. Not at fuckin' all!" He rubs both hands over his face. He looks just plain lost.

I reach out my right hand and smooth down his now messy scruff. "If I told you my thoughts back at that house, you would've tossed me in a truck and sent me back to the clubhouse in a flash. You never would've let me come here. And I never would've learned the truth of why we were taken."

"You're goddamn right we wouldn't have let you out here." Steel swats my backside and grips it tight, almost too tight. Apparently, his threat of spankings wasn't too far off.

"We just wanted you safe and away from all this bullshit." Ring waves an arm at the barn.

I turn to see the doors are now closed. I guess anything that's happening in there is now off limits to me. That's fine. Even though I didn't get my secret retribution, I know Bullet's dead. I can go back to the clubhouse and tell the other ladies he's gone for good.

"Can you take me home now?" I look at Ring.

"You wanna go home?" he questions with a sad look on his face.

"Like your house or the clubhouse?" Steel pulls my attention to him.

"The clubhouse." I kiss his cheek. "That's where you two live, right?'

The tension deflates from both of them. I guess my answer was what they were hoping for. Good to know. I want to be wherever they are.

"We'll take you wherever you wanna go," Ring replies with his half smirk smile.

Steel turns around, opens the front passenger side door, and drops me on the seat.

"I thought I was supposed to ride in back with you?" I ask after Steel hops in the back seat.

"I'll let you ride with Ring on the short ride back. 'Cause once we get you home, he'll have to fight me for your attention." Steel leans forward and lets me know his intentions loud and clear.

Ring climbs in the driver's seat just in time to hear Steel's speech. He looks back at Steel and shakes his head. "As much as I hate to say this, no funny business tonight. After everything she's been through, she'd probably like a shower and to rest. We can ravage her when she's ready."

The truck starts rolling and I grab Ring's arm that's resting on the center counsel. He looks at me for a second before turning his attention back to the bumpy path. "Everything okay?"

"Thank you for thinking of me like that." I lift his hand and kiss it.

"Anything for you." He pulls my hand toward him and kisses my wrist.

"I'd wait a hundred days to love on you, just to know you were safe." Steel reaches forward over the seat and drops a hand on my shoulder.

I lay my head back and soak in all the love surrounding me. Because that's what it is—love for my men. They did everything to come and rescue me.

CHAPTER FORTY-FOUR

SUNSHINE

It's a quick drive to the clubhouse, but there's something I need to say before we get there.

"Can I tell you both something?" I turn to see both guys. "I get that what you guys do isn't always on the up and up. But I want you to know I'm behind you one hundred percent." I point at the clubhouse as we pull into the parking lot. "I've got a lot to learn being around this, but I'll do whatever you need me to. Just bear with me while I figure it out."

Ring puts the truck in park. "We'll lead you every step of the way. I know it's a lot."

"This is new for all of us," Steel pipes up. "Just know that if something happens in the club and we get angry, remember that it's not you we're mad at. We just need you to do what we say because we need you safe."

"Duchess gave me the rundown on one of her speeches from Whiskey. He said had they not gone through their shitty situation, they probably wouldn't be together. And while I came here because of my mom dying, I'd like to think I would've found you both regardless."

That makes Ring laugh. I don't know what's so funny about my attempt at a thoughtful speech. "Hey, Steel, remember your talk in Church the day you came home? About how you met a 'hot as fuck nurse' and you were gonna bring her to the clubhouse to show her off?"

"Holy shit. I forgot all about that."

I turn on my knees in the seat, so I can look straight at Steel. "You were gonna come find me?"

"It was a joke at the time, but seeing that not even five minutes later, I was grabbing your ass. I didn't have to hunt you down. You were in my clubhouse and already hooked up with my best friend. It was meant to be."

"Don't you forget it," Ring's still chuckling.

I climb over the center counsel, into his lap. "Forget what? That you ambushed me, taking advantage of me?"

Ring squishes my ass cheeks, tugging me tight to his chest. "I did no such thing. I was trying to see if you were okay. You jumped my bones in that bathroom. You kissed me first, so I had to keep up."

"That's no fair." Steel opens his door and slides out. "If you say we can't fuck her, you two need to stop and get out of the truck. It's not fair if I can't participate."

I push the driver's door open and climb down. I walk to the passenger side and give Steel a hug. "I'm sorry, baby. Do you need a kiss to make it all better?" Now, I'm just teasing him. I can't help it. Poor guy is squeezing his junk through his jeans, probably trying to relieve the pressure.

"You know I like watching you get all hot and bothered," Steel drops a kiss on my forehead, "but only if I can join. So, be nice and cut my dick some slack."

"Fine. Let's get inside so you can give me that shower you two promised." I slap him one time on the backside then head toward the clubhouse.

"Steel!" someone yells, and we all turn around.

Parked at the far edge of the lot is a motorhome. I'm shocked I didn't notice it before. The door's open and this giant steps out, ignoring the tiny steps. And when I say giant, I mean he's so tall, he'd probably make Mountain look like an anthill. This dude has to be seven feet tall.

"Holy hell, Ray," Steel hollers back, and the guy heads our way. "When did you get out?"

"A month after you did. Some overcrowding bullshit bumped up my release. I went home, sold everything, loaded up the wife and kiddo, and here we are."

"This is crazy. With everything going on, I forgot you were coming." Steel shakes his hand. "I got some people I want you to meet."

Ring steps forward on his own. "Nice to meet you, Ray. Steel's told me a lot about you. But he never said he made friends with the Hulk."

Ray's laugh sounds like a boom. "I get that a lot."

"I bet."

"Ray, this is our woman, Sunshine. Sunshine, this is Ray." Steel pulls me to stand in front of him.

I look up, and up, to see the biggest smile on Ray's face. "It's nice to meet you, Sunshine. How'd you end up with these two yahoos?"

That makes me smile. "Let me tell you a little secret," Ray leans down a bit, "when you get stabbed in prison, you get patched up by me."

Ray jumps back to his full height. "This little filly is your naughty nurse? How the hell did you find her out here?"

"She was here when I got home. She's Whiskey's sister," Steel replies.

"What a small world," Ray says back.

"You're tellin' me," Ring comments. "I hate to be a party killer, but we gotta get Sunshine inside. She's had a rough few days."

"No problem." Ray holds up his hands. "I got a run-down from Mountain when I pulled in. We're just gonna plug this rig in and chill out for a couple days. Once you get your club stuff straightened out, we'll catch up."

The guys shake hands and Steel, Ring, and I head inside.

I'm not two steps inside when I'm wrapped up in several sets of arms. But with everyone talking at once, I can't tell who's who.

"Whoa whoa," I wiggle myself from the huddle, "I know you all want me, but one at a time."

They all start talking but stop just as quick, and we all laugh.

"I'm happy you're back," Duchess hugs me again. "When you're ready to talk, I'm all ears."

"Me too." Tempy's hug is next.

"Me three" and "me four." is a joint hug from Stiletto and Raquel.

"Your guys are getting antsy over there, so you better get going." Duchess winks.

"I missed you all too." I head straight for my men.

"Let's get you cleaned up and tucked in." Ring holds my hand as we walk upstairs.

Steel gets Ring's bedroom door open, and as soon as it's shut, I beeline for the bathroom. It just hit me that it's been too long since I've showered. My skin feels like it's crawling.

"Where ya goin' in such a hurry? I thought you wanted help with your shower?" Ring follows me.

I pause with my hands on the bottom of my shirt. "As much as I love wearing black and matching you, I need out of these clothes." I whip the shirt off and throw it in the garbage can. "Bullet gave me these this morning so I could meet my buyer. I want them burned."

"I get it," Steel pushes past Ring and bends down to untie my shoes. He gets one off, looks up at me, and winks. "I'd hate wearing all black too. It's such a gloomy color."

What a silly man.

"I think him wearing all black is hot," I sass back.

Steel gets my second shoe off and stands to toss them in the garbage. He leans in the shower to turn the water on.

Ring gets all up in my bubble, works his hands under my leggings, and uses his giant paws to push them down. I step out and they're gone in a flash. Ring tugs down my panties, yanks my socks off, and stands to unhook my bra.

"She says she likes that I wear all black." He looks at Steel, who's taking his cut off. "I don't know about you, Steel, but personally, I like when she wears nothing at all."

"I second that. Let's get down to our skivvies and get our woman clean."

Steel hands his cut to Ring, who steps out for two seconds, I'm guessing to hang them up, then he's back, already shirtless. I stand there watching my very own double strip show. Now, I get why they like watching me. It's hot as all get out.

"Why do you need to keep your underwear on?" I whine. I totally sound like a brat, but I don't care. Seeing these two in skintight boxer briefs is a temptation I don't know if I can handle.

"You know why." Ring steps in the tub, lifts me up, and sets me down to face him.

"No hanky panky," Steel warns as he steps in behind me, under the shower head. He pulls me back and I close my eyes, just letting the water wash over me. It runs down my face and I soak in the heat.

I feel hands start to roam all over my body. I let them wash my hair, scrub my body, and take care of me like they said they would. Before I know it, the water's turned off, I'm wrapped in a towel, and carried into the bedroom.

Since the day I fully let my guard down, letting these two amazing men completely into my life, they've done nothing but care for me.

Steel hands me a towel and I use it to dry my hair. Ring uses the towel I'm wrapped in to gently dry my body. The guys swap their wet bottoms for dry ones. Someone drops a super large t-shirt over my head and I'm pulled to sit at the end of the bed.

"I know I suck at braids," Steel smiles, holding a hairbrush, "but do you think I could brush your hair?"

"I can do it." I hold my hand out.

"Nope. This is all us." Ring scoots back on the bed until he's against the headboard. "Come up here."

I crawl up and sit cross-legged in front of him.

Steel sits behind me and gently brushes my hair, one little section at a time. "How come you cut your hair?"

"It's been the same length this whole time," Ring states, confused.

"I cut about a foot off not long after I met Steel. That's when my mom was in the worst of her sickness. I chopped it off so it was easier to maintain."

"I like it just the way it is." Ring leans forward for a kiss.

"Me too," Steel agrees. "It's not too long to get tangled but long enough I can grab on while you're riding my dick."

That makes all of us laugh.

Steel sets the hairbrush on the nightstand, pushes me to the right, and I fall to the middle. I roll onto my back. The guys arrange themselves around me, and before I know it, my back's snuggled to Ring's chest and my face is buried in Steel's, and I start to doze off.

There's no sex tonight, but I don't care. There'll be plenty of time for that later. I'm just happy to be back home.

CHAPTER FORTY-FIVE

STEEL

Ring and I stayed up for a few hours, just watching television and holding Sunshine as she slept. She was still out cold when we got up this morning to head to Church. We stayed in bed until ten a.m. but both of us needed to take a leak and get real showers before we went downstairs.

"All in favor of patching in Sam, say 'aye'." Whiskey makes the motion.

"Aye," everyone echoes.

Bang! He slams his gavel and we've got another Brother.

"Any ideas on a road name?" Whiskey asks the room. "I usually know by now, but my brain's fried and can't decide."

"How about Haze?" I throw out a name I've been thinking about.

"What's the significance of that?" Wrecker questions.

"It's a play on Smoke's name."

"Why me?" Smoke sits up, giving me all his attention.

"You both prospected at the same time, so it's almost fitting that your names are themed similar." I look to my right at Whiskey and give him the real reason.

"I heard how Smoke was there when you needed someone to ride your bike after getting Duchess. That took some major balls. Then Sam had Brick's back by chasing down and catching Bullet when he ran away. They were both in the background, doing their prospecting thing, but when needed, they jumped in, no questions asked. Always lingering, but always right there."

"Dude," Hammer lets out a long whistle, "who knew being in the joint would turn you into a philosopher?"

I flip him the bird. "Don't make me go Confucius on your ass."

The whole room busts a gut on that one.

Bang bang! "Alright, settle down, you fuckers. I like the name Haze no matter the psychobabble. Any other ideas?"

The room's silent.

"Then Haze it is. We'll get his cut done up and have a party to tell him this weekend. No telling him 'til then."

That leads to a bunch of fists pounding and boots stomping in celebration.

"Second order of business. Brick's funeral." That makes the room go silent. "I know we don't wanna discuss this, but we have to. Pops, Bear, Skynyrd, Butch, and I talked about it this morning. We'll be waiting a few weeks to have the usual ride and service. We've got clubs around the country to call so people can come pay their respects. When we have a date set in stone, we'll let everyone know."

"I know no one wants to do this, but it's the right thing to do," Mountain speaks up.

"I know the mood sucks big time, but this also leads to my third and final thing for the day." Whiskey reaches inside his cut and sets something on the table. He slides it my way and I lock my eyes on a patch I never thought I'd see not on a cut. It's Brick's Secretary patch.

The look on Whiskey's face shows me he needs me to step into my VP position and do this for him. Telling the club we need to replace his uncle is just too much.

I grab it and hold it up for the room to see. "We need to name a new Secretary."

"I motion that Brewer take the Secretary spot," Bear voices.

"And I second that," Hammer puts in.

"Brewer," I start, "do you have any thoughts on the nomination?"

He stands up and addresses the room. "I'd be honored to serve as this club's Secretary. I know I've got big shoes to fill, but if this is what the club votes, I'll do my damnedest to make everyone proud."

"Then we need a vote, one Brother at a time. I'll start." I stand up. "Aye!"

Whiskey's next. "Aye."

And around the room it goes. Every single one of my Brothers stands and says 'aye'.

Whiskey bangs the gavel. "From this day forward, until the end of his time, Brewer's Secretary of the Rebel Vipers MC."

We wrap up Church pretty quickly, and Ring and I head for the kitchen to find something to eat.

"Let's make some sandwiches, grab sodas, and head upstairs to see if Sunshine's awake. If we let her sleep all day, she won't tonight."

I head for the fridge and grab a bunch of lunch meat, cheese, and other fixings. "Sounds like a plan to me."

When we get upstairs, Sunshine's just coming out of the bathroom.

"Where'd you two wander off to? I woke up and you were gone." Sunshine climbs into the middle of the bed and pulls the blanket over her lap.

"We had Church, then we got some stuff for lunch." I hand her the plate with the sandwiches piled on it.

"Are we feeding an army?" She holds it up, staring at the stack of bread and meat.

"We need to eat. We're hungry, growing boys." Ring sets a soda on each nightstand and puts the rest in his mini-fridge.

We climb in on each side of her, on top of the covers.

"You two are crazy. With how big you made these things, I'll have one and be full until tomorrow." Sunshine sets the plate on her lap and grabs the sandwich on top. She takes a huge bite and groans, letting her eyes roll back. "Thith ith thooo goooood."

I pick one up and take a bite. Damn, these are good.

"I did good," Ring toots his own horn.

"Hey," I say between bites. "I helped."

"You buttered the bread. That's not rocket science. I did the assembly." Ring throws a chunk of crust at me.

"We're not ducks, so no throwing bread," Sunshine scolds us.

"Fine," I grumble.

"Such a buzzkill," Ring mumbles with a mouthful.

"Children," she exclaims. "I'm surrounded by children."

We finish all but two sandwiches, so I get up and put the plate in the fridge.

"Speaking of children. When are we gonna get Opal back?" Ring asks.

"I'll call my moms tomorrow," I answer as I sit back down. "Tonight can be our last night with just the three of us."

"I miss her." Sunshine snuggles into my chest and I wrap my left arm around her.

"Me too, Sunshine." I drop a kiss on her head.

I can't fuckin' sleep.

I slowly slide Sunshine off my chest, gently roll her over, and like she knows just where to go, she wraps herself around Ring's back. He reaches for her arm and lets her surround him like a big spoon. Sometimes, I think he likes it when she holds him like we usually do to her.

As quietly as I can, I sneak out of the bedroom. I make my way downstairs and head for the back porch. Maybe I just need some fresh air.

I've got the screen door half open when I realize I'm not alone.

"If they can share, why can't we?"

"It's just not enough. You need to drop this."

The Prospect, Sam, rushes around me and heads inside. I look to my right and see Smoke standing by a picnic table, hands on his head.

"Is everything okay?"

Smoke startles and looks up. When he sees it's me, he deflates and drops to the table's bench. "I'm not sure."

I step forward and lean against the porch railing, giving him his distance but still trying to show my support. "If you need to talk, let me know."

"Thanks." He nods. "Can I ask you a question and it stay between us?"

"Of course. If you don't want me to repeat it, my lips are sealed."

"How do you do the three people in a couple thing? How does it work? Don't you get jealous?"

I sit across from him at the table. "Not where I thought this was going."

"Sorry, you don't have to answer."

"It's not a problem. I don't know your specifics, but since Ring and I don't like each other sexually, our feelings for Sunshine are separate. I'm sure there are couples out there who do have jealousy issues, but it's something he and I talked about before deciding to really pursue her."

"What about the other guys in the club? Do any of them give you shit for being in bed with another man, even if you're not really with him?"

I think I'm starting to figure out what the problem is. I think Smoke and Sam have feelings for each other, but are having a rough time figuring it all out.

"I'd like to think our Brothers wouldn't have a problem with whatever you decide to do with your personal life. But for us, other than a few funny jokes, no one has given us any real grief about it."

"That's good." Smoke lets out a deep breath.

"I'm gonna say one last thing, then you need to do a lot of thinking. Okay?"

"Throw it at me."

I sit forward and give him the cold, hard truth. "If you have feelings for Sam, you gotta give him time to figure himself out first. If you push too hard, he's likely to buck back and never give you a chance. And if you're thinking of adding a woman to the mix, don't do it 'til the two of you have your shit straight. You can't use a woman as a Band-Aid to help you stay together. That wouldn't be fair to any of you. Does that make sense?"

"It does. Thank you, Steel." Smoke gets up and heads inside.

Oh boy. That was a doozy. I have a feeling he's going to have a rough road ahead of him. I don't envy him one bit.

I drag my ass off the bench, head for the yard, and drop into one of the Adirondack chairs. I look up at the night sky and stare at the stars. Out here, there's very little light pollution, so the stars are bright.

I didn't get to see this from my jail cell. I had a tiny window by my bed, but all the lights surrounding the prison made the night almost as bright as the day.

I only got an hour or two a day to be outside, but there were no stars in the afternoons.

Listening to the crickets buzzing and the trees rustling, I feel my eyes start to close. This is just what I needed, to reconnect with my surroundings, and tomorrow, I'll be back to my regularly scheduled program.

CHAPTER FORTY-SIX

RING

I'm in the hallway outside Steel's bedroom, holding a wiggly bundle in my arms. I give the door a couple light kicks and listen to the voices inside.

"Why do I need this dang blindfold?" Sunshine complains.

"It's a surprise. Hold your horses," Steel replies.

He wasn't exactly happy about this present, but when Sunshine was telling us more about her time in that basement, and the way she talked about this one certain thing, he caved when I pushed.

"Is it a horsey, Daddy?" Opal's excited voice almost makes me want to get her a horse. Almost, but not really.

"It's not a horse. Open the door and see what your Papa has for Sunshine."

Footsteps rush to the door and it swings open.

Opal's the first one to see me and she's staring at the blanket. "What's that?"

"Wanna peek?" I ask.

"You bet!"

I pull back a corner of the blanket and a tiny black nose pokes its way out.

"IT'S A—"

Steel immediately covers her mouth with his hand. "Shh, don't ruin the surprise."

He pulls her into the room, and I follow, shutting the door with my boot.

"Is someone gonna tell me what's going on?" Sunshine's sitting on the bed, arms crossed, a grumpy look on her face.

"One sec." I move to stand right in front of her. I pull the blanket back just a bit, letting my squirming bundle be fully seen.

"It's so cute," Opal whines from Steel's arms. He picked her up, probably to keep her away from our gift.

"You can ditch the blindfold now."

Sunshine whips it off in a flash. When she sees what's in my arms, she loses her mind. Tears roll down her cheeks and her mouth drops open. "It's my puppy friend!"

As soon as he hears her voice, the puppy zeros all his attention on her and starts barking and trying to leap from my arms. I set the bundle of blanket and fluff in her lap.

I sit next to her and watch in amazement as Sunshine and this puppy love up on each other. I don't know which one of them is more excited.

"Look at how fluffy he is. Where'd you find him? Where are his brothers and sisters? How'd you get him here?" The questions flow out, one after another.

Steel sits down laughing, Opal in his lap. "One question at a time."

"When the other guys were cleaning up at the house," I start, leaving out the specifics for the little ears in the room, "they found a dozen of these little white monsters in the back of a van. They couldn't leave the puppies behind, so Buzz took them to the Humane Society."

"I'm so glad they're okay," Sunshine unwraps the little guy from the blanket and slides down to the floor, setting him down to sniff around. "What made you decide to bring one home?"

We all drop next to her, and using our legs, create a barricade so he doesn't wander away from us. Steel, Sunshine, and I are the edges and Opal goes in the middle with the puppy. He starts pouncing at her, and soon, they're rolling and wrestling with each other.

"When you talked the other night about the puppies in the box, I got a feeling you missed this little guy. Yesterday, when I said I was going to work for a few hours, I really went to see if I could figure out which one of them was yours."

"How'd you pick the right one? I know this is him." Sunshine reaches an arm out anytime he's close to pet him.

"Out of the dozen puppies, he's the only boy," I chuckle. "It wasn't hard to figure out."

That makes her laugh too. "I never saw the others close enough to know. But speaking of the other puppies, do you guys know why they were in that basement?"

Steel and I know why they were there, but I'm not sure I want her to know the truth. It's not pretty. I look at Steel to try and figure out what he's thinking.

"We should tell her the truth," Steel starts. "She's gonna find out from someone else if we don't."

"Find out what? What happened?" She focuses her questions on me.

I don't need Opal hearing this, so I lean over to her and whisper in her ear, "Dogfighting."

She pulls back. "What? That's awful!" she gasps.

I keep my tone down. "There were crates stacked in one of the sheds, bloody stains on the floor, muzzles, whips, and other things I'd rather not mention."

"There weren't any other dogs on site, so that's a good sign." Steel tries to spin a positive on the conversation.

"I guess," Sunshine mumbles, feeling the blues about this news.

"No more sad face, Sunshine. What are we gonna name this tiny cloud of fur?" Steel asks as the puppy starts chewing on his boot lace. "Hey, stop that."

"His name's Teddy." Opal pulls the puppy off Steel's leg and into her tiny lap. "He looks just like my teddy bear that Sunshine give'ded me."

"You're right, he does." Sunshine lifts Opal and the puppy into her lap. "I love that name."

"Did they say what breed he was?" Steel asks me.

"Their best guess is Samoyed, based on the pure white. As he gets older, if his fur gets longer, we'll have our answer." I pull the puppy paperwork out of my cut pocket and hand it to him. "He got some shots, but the rest is all you. If I have to remember the other shit they told me, this poor guy's gonna end up blind or eating cat food."

"I knew you'd do this to me." Steel rolls his eyes. "This was your idea, but I have to do all the work."

"I'll help you, Daddy." Opal finally lets the puppy go. She stands up, looks down at her clothes, and tries to brush the fur off. "His fur's all over me!"

"Get used to it." Sunshine shakes out her shirt and the white fur floats into the air. "Looks like we'll need a broom just for our rooms, or there'll be fur in every corner."

We spend the rest of the day showing the puppy all around the clubhouse and compound. Ray, his wife, Sara, and their son, Jamie, join us for a walk in the woods in the backyard. Jamie and Opal take turns holding Teddy's leash and running with him.

By the time night falls, everyone's exhausted. I got a kennel to keep the puppy in at night, but somehow Opal convinced us that Teddy has to sleep with her. He jumped on her bed the second she called his name.

And that's where they are right now. We've got two softly snoring monsters in the corner of Steel's room, so leaving the adjourning door open a crack, the three of us adults make ourselves comfy in my bed for the night.

Steel and I have our backs to the headboard and Sunshine's sitting pretzel style between us, facing us. "Thank you both for the puppy."

"It was our pleasure, Sunshine." I set my left hand on her knee, giving it a squeeze.

"Looks like we got another member of our little family." Steel mirrors my position, setting his hand on her other knee.

"Before we go and make this family thing official, there's something I need to tell you guys." Sunshine laces her hands with each of ours.

"Is everything okay?" I can hear the worry in my voice.

"What's wrong?" Steel's got it too.

"Nothing's wrong."

"Then what is it?" I question.

"I need to tell you both that I love you."

I'm speechless. My eyes are locked on her face and she's bouncing her eyes back and forth between us. The other day, I made a little hint that we loved her, but until now, none of us have come out and said it.

The feelings Steel and I have for her have been there for a while, but neither of us wanted to rush her. I guess now's as good a time as any.

Steel beats me to the punch. "I love you too."

"I love you too," I echo.

"Really?" Like she can't believe us.

I pull on our still joined hands and she scoots closer toward us.

"Hell yea, we do. We've been wanting to say it, but since we never got our dinner date, we didn't get the chance." I use my right hand to pull her head closer to mine and kiss her.

I give her no time to think or try to take control. I flick her bottom lip with my tongue, and she opens for me instantly. We duel each other, and like usual, I win. I don't let her come up for air until I'm good and ready.

I back away a centimeter and she's gone from my grasp. Steel lifts her into his lap, setting her sideways, feet toward me, and he pounces. But unlike my hurried kiss, he takes his slow and sweet. He lets her catch her breath every few seconds, then presses forward again to keep going.

I leave them to their business for a minute and get out of bed.

I barely have both feet on the floor when I hear Sunshine's voice behind me. "Where you going?"

I turn back and give her a wink. "Not going far. Just gotta get something from my desk." I stand up, quickly adjust my half hard dick, and walk to my desk in the corner.

I open the top drawer and grab the black box I stashed in there yesterday. The puppy wasn't the only thing I bought when I was out.

"What's that?" she asks as I get myself back under the covers.

"This is part two of your presents for the day," I hold the box out toward her. She's still sitting sideways on Steel's lap.

"What is it?' she questions again.

"Open it and find out," Steel answers, kissing her cheek.

She slowly grabs the box from my hand. She hesitates opening it, like she's afraid the box will bite her, until the hinge catches and snaps open all the way.

"Wow," she whispers. "It looks almost like Duchess's necklace."

"I got it from the same store Whiskey got hers," I tell her.

"It's so pretty." Sunshine touches the necklace with one finger. "What do the circles mean?"

Steel takes the box from her hands and removes the necklace. He hands me the box and I set it behind me on the nightstand. "The skeleton key part is a new tradition I guess we've started. Whiskey got Duchess hers on a whim, but Ring and I liked the idea of you ladies having something with meaning to symbolize belonging to Brothers."

"The top circle is just for the necklace to hang on. It's the three circles underneath that are important." I reach out and grab her hands in mine. "The circle in the center is you, because you are the center of us. Without you, there'd be no us. Then the circles on each side are Steel and me, because we'll always be by your side. We'll be with you forever."

Steel fumbles with the clasp for a few seconds but finally gets it open. He drapes the chain over her chest and secures it around her neck. "Do you like it?"

Sunshine has tears in her eyes as she picks up the key and holds it in her hand, squeezing it tight. "I love it." She turns to kiss Steel's cheek, then crawls over to me and sits in my lap, facing him.

I tickle her sides and listen to her giggles. "Are you ready for your last present?"

"What else do you think I need? Isn't a puppy and a necklace enough?" She gasps.

"Nope," Steel tells her what's what. "Now that we've told you that we love you, we need to officially make you our Old Lady. The necklace was just part of that."

"Yes, yes, yes," she exclaims.

Sunshine starts bouncing in my lap and raining kisses all over my face. She then yanks Steel's head to her and showers him with her lips.

I pull her back to me and she loops her right arm around my neck. "Does that mean I get a property cut like Duchess and Blue have? I've been wanting one of those so bad."

The excitement in her voice is infectious. I'm sure Steel and I look like smiling buffoons. The happiness is vibrating from her and soaking into both of us.

"You'll be getting one of those, and we're having your name put on it as we speak." I whisper next to her ear, "I thought we were gonna have to fight to get you to agree to be our Old Lady. But seeing you this happy makes me forget all the reasons I had prepared to convince you."

Sunshine gets hold of our hands again. "I knew the time was coming for us to decide where this relationship was going. We'd been physical plenty of times, and I love Opal, so I knew this is where we'd end up. It wasn't until I was in that cell, yelling at Bullet for taking me, that it fully sunk in. I was so angry that he took me and ruined our plans for the evening."

"That date was supposed to be when we asked you," Steel tells her.

"I kinda had a feeling, but I was snatched before we even had the chance."

"I'm sorry for not protecting you. It's all my fault you were taken."

Sunshine shakes her hands free and has ahold of my face in a flash. Her face is so close to mine, our noses are touching. "What happened that day was NOT your fault, Ryan! You were hurt and I don't blame you one bit. It never even crossed my mind. You get that thought out of your head right now. Do you hear me?"

I can't help but smile at her stern face. She's got her eyes squinted and her eyebrows are scrunched low. She's looking at me like what I said is the craziest thing she's ever heard.

"Whatever you say, Sunshine." I grab her face and kiss her like I own her. Full on. All my breath. Just like I will every day for the rest of my life.

"Why do you call me Sunshine?" she asks when I let her go. She crawls out of my lap and sits against the headboard between us.

I give her all my attention. "The day you got here, I just had this random thought that you looked like a ball of sunshine. Then Steel started saying it and I liked it more and more. But the final straw was when Opal called you Sunshine. That's when I decided it was officially your name."

"For me, it was when I walked out of Church and saw you from behind. I had a thought that your hair was the color of the sun." Steel chuckles to himself. "Then you turned around and yelled at me. Your attitude was as hot as the blazing sun. I called you Sunshine for the first time after seeing you again for less than two minutes, and that was it for me."

"You guys didn't talk about it first?"

"Nope." I shake my head. "We didn't plan it, but it fit for both of us."

"Well, I love it."

"Good, 'cause we love you more." Steel leans over and kisses her.

"I think I love her the most," I joke, pulling her away from him to steal a quick kiss.

"Not possible." Steel tries to get her back, but I tug her with me as I lay down on my side. I wrap her in my arms and keep her tight to my chest.

Sunshine's swatting both of us with her hands. "I say I love you both the mostest. HA!"

"That's something I can't argue with." Steel worms his way down, facing us.

"Good, 'cause I'm the Old Lady, so I always win."

We have our woman back in our bed, and she agreed to be our Old Lady. How much better could this day be?

CHAPTER FORTY-SEVEN

STEEL

Now that things have settled into what I'd like to hope is our new normal, daily life and work have started up again. Ring is at the brewery almost every day, and I'm finally working at the garage full time. Between three adults, and Opal's needs, and all the other issues floating around, I'd yet to figure out a regular schedule, until now.

And with us being so busy, Sunshine has delegated herself as Opal's day-to-day caregiver. I told Sunshine she didn't have to, that we'd work out a routine for all three of us adults to pitch in, but she told me it's what she wants. Opal will be going to daycare a few days a week for learning and socializing, but when she's home, she and Sunshine are always up to something.

Like today. They're up to something but wouldn't give me even a hint. My girls kissed me, then shoved me out the front door. They giggled the whole time and said it was a secret. Troublemakers, the both of them.

Sunshine has been super busy this week, working on cleaning and organizing Brick's cabin, so knowing she's taking even one day off to do something fun, I call that a good day. She deserves a little break.

It's finally Friday and I'm ready to get this weekend started. Tonight, once everyone is done working, we'll be kicking off the weekend with a party where we welcome a new Brother into the club. Sam will finally be getting his member cut and new road name, Haze. Then tomorrow, Ring and I have a surprise for Sunshine. It's going to be a crazy couple of days, but I'm looking forward to it.

It's just before noon, time for lunch, so I make my way through the clubhouse and head for the kitchen. Pushing the swinging door open, what I see stops me in my tracks. The kitchen is a disaster. and it looks like a flour bomb exploded.

"What's going on in here?" I turn to see Ring behind me. It looks like he had the same idea of cutting his workday short.

Sunshine and Duchess are standing at the kitchen island, several mixing bowls spread around the surface. Opal is kneeling on a stool, face and shirt smudged with flour.

"We're making cupcakes!" Opal cheers with a smile, clapping her tiny hands, sending more flour into the air.

I make my way around the island, drop a kiss on Sunshine's head, then approach Opal very slowly. She's got her flour-covered hands out, ready to cover me in her mess. "Are you gonna make me any?" I ask, snagging her tiny hands, then tickling her sides.

"Daddy," she replies though her peeling giggles. "We can make your favorite kind next."

"What's your favorite kind, Steel?" Ring questions. I look over and see him wrapped around Sunshine from behind, and she's leaning back on him.

I'm not sure if I want to tell everyone what kind of cupcakes I like, so I whisper it in Opal's ear. Maybe if I tell her, she can tell the other ladies after I duck out of here. But knowing my daughter, my luck won't last long.

She squeals out, "I love sprinkles!"

"Oh my god!" Ring starts laughing so hard, he's got tear rolling down his cheeks. "You like funfetti cupcakes!"

"Be nice." Sunshine smacks him on the shoulder. "What's your favorite kind, Ring?"

Her question gets him to stop cackling enough to respond. "You should know that already, Sunshine. I love the Mountain Dew ones that Duchess makes at the bakery."

"Hey!" Duchess protests, setting down a spatula. "Those are not Mountain Dew cupcakes. Those are lemon pudding. Just because you have a caffeine sugar addiction doesn't mean you get to rename my creation."

"But Duchess," he whines, hands folded, like he's praying for her forgiveness, "I can't help it that your cupcakes taste like my soda."

That makes me laugh, and Opal joins in.

It may sound silly, but hearing Opal offer to make my favorite cupcakes gives me even more hope for our still growing connection. Me being gone for so long really affected her in ways I didn't anticipate. She still has days where she wants nothing to do with me, but every day we grow closer and closer. And just like her newfound love of temporary tattoos, maybe cupcakes can be another step in the right direction.

I know Opal's too young to understand what this all means to me, but this little olive branch from her is just what I needed.

"Enough of your Papa's silliness." I scoop Opal off her stool and carry her over to the open cabinet of baking supplies. "Let's pick out some different sprinkles to put in my cupcakes. What colors should we choose?"

It didn't take Duchess long at all to reorganize everything in the kitchen, and commandeer an entire section of cabinets for her cupcake stuff. Opal chooses orange and black. I don't have the heart to tell her those are typically Halloween colors, and it's barely the beginning of July, but if she wants orange and black, that's what my munchkin's going to get.

"What's going on in here?" Whiskey calls out as he and a bunch of Brothers come barreling into the kitchen. "We can hear your laughing all the way out in the main room."

"We're makin' cupcakes!" Opal announces, like the guys can't see the mess laid out in front of them.

"And Steel likes funfetti cupcakes," Ring announces, laughing again. "He likes sprinkles."

I don't think I'm ever going to live this one down. Now, all the Brothers are razzing me, giving me shit for liking girlie stuff. Kraken even asks if I want Sunshine to paint my fingernails. What a jackass!

He tries to shake a container of rainbow sprinkles over my head, so I use his open stance to my advantage and grab the package of gummy worms from his inside cut pocket. Once he realizes what I did, he starts chasing me around the island. And this leads to pandemonium.

Duchess and Sunshine try to stop the mayhem, but it's too late.

Next thing I know, there's batter and frosting being flung across the kitchen. I'm hit smack dab in the middle of the forehead by a glob of yellow goop, and Opal loses it. She giggles so damn hard, she leans over, landing her hand in a mixing bowl. She then proceeds to smear the chocolate concoction in Ring's face.

He doesn't find it very funny, but I sure do. I whip out my phone and snap a few pictures for future blackmail.

After a few minutes of the slimy free-for-all, Blue appears and whistles so damn loud, we all freeze in place. "For Pete's sake. What's goin' on in here?"

"Sorry, Blue." Whiskey gives her a pouty face, trying to look apologetic but failing. He wipes his chin, leaving a streak of flour behind. "We were just havin' a little fun."

"I can see that." She's standing in the doorway, hands on her hips. "Now, start cleaning up this mess. We've got a party to start here soon." Then she disappears as fast as she came in.

"Party for what?" Sam asks.

Everyone turns to see the Prospect standing in the open pass-through window. I didn't even realize it was raised up. I think the jig is up. We've purposely kept news of the party tonight on the down low so he wouldn't suspect anything, but I think it's time to fill him in.

"Whatchya think, Whiskey? Should we tell the boy the good news?" I ask, nudging him with my elbow.

"I guess we have to now," he jokes. "Blue went and ruined the surprise."

Sam disappears from the window, then pushes his way into the kitchen. "What surprise?"

Messy clothes, frosting and all, I toss an arm over his shoulders and tug him in tight. "Tonight is the night you officially become a Rebel Viper!"

The look on his face is a mixture of shock and plain old happiness. His eyes grow wide, but his smile is infectious. The room breaks out in a deep, vibratory, spirited celebration.

What a weekend this is starting out to be. Let the good times begin!

CHAPTER FORTY-EIGHT

SUNSHINE

I've been helping clean out and organize Brick's cabin for a week now. When I questioned Mountain if it was too soon, he said it was time to pass the torch. I wasn't sure what that meant, but when he told me they'd made Brewer the new Secretary, and they need to pass all the club notes to him, I understood.

Brick's cabin is second in the row of five in the backyard of the compound. Whiskey and Duchess are in the first, Brick had the second, Butch is in the third, and currently the fourth and fifth are empty. They've been used by members in the past, but now are for when people come to visit.

It seems funny that a single man would have a three-bedroom cabin to himself, but he used every room. Brick had the master for himself, but the two spare bedrooms were all club stuff. And they are full. The walls in both bedrooms are lined with bookshelves and file cabinets. I swear there's a store's worth of notebooks, file folders, and plastic totes in here. And it's organized like a library. All the notebooks are in order by date and the totes are labeled with their contents.

I spent the first full day in his bedroom, boxing up his clothes for donation.

It seems like I've been doing this a lot lately. I hate it.

Mountain, Whiskey, Steel, and Brewer have been scouring through Brick's notes for days. As the club's Secretary, he spent every Church taking meticulous notes about the activities happening at the time. The only problem is that no one can make heads or tails of what they say.

Brick had some kind of code that he wrote everything in. Mountain said it was so if someone on the outside ever found one of the notebooks, they wouldn't know the club's business. That was fine and dandy when Brick was the one dealing with them. But now, we're left with thousands of pages of a mix of hieroglyphics and children's doodles.

Steel showed me one page, just to see my thoughts, and I gave up trying after three lines. None of it made sense.

I'm currently on day five of cleaning the cabin and my heart hurts. It hurts deep down that Brick had to make the ultimate sacrifice for me. We didn't get enough time. But in a strange way, I feel his love too.

I'm so happy I got to sit down and talk to him a few weeks ago. Since coming here, I talked to him here and there, but never for long. Until the one day I walked in the clubhouse and saw him sitting alone at the bar.

Both of my guys were busy, so while I waited for them, I hopped up on the stool next to Brick and we talked and laughed for what seemed like hours. We discovered that both our favorite color is orange, and we have a mutual love for the actor Pauly Shore. We started singing the "making a filter song" from the movie *Bio-Dome*, and when Mountain and Blue came out of their room, they found us laughing so hard, we were almost falling off our stools. They stared at us like we'd just escaped the nut house. Just knowing that we both liked something so silly, makes me smile.

But the things I found in Brick's closet have become my favorite. Hill family photo albums.

Because I didn't get to grow up with this side of the family, these names and faces are foreign to me. I didn't get to meet my grandparents. I didn't get to see where their family farm was. I didn't know what my dad looked like as a child.

Flipping through these dozen albums has been a little cathartic for me. Don't get me wrong, I'm still very mad at my mom for keeping this secret my whole life, but getting this connection now is what I needed. Being asked to be part of going through Brick's personal items has settled my heart in a big way.

I'm sitting on the living room couch, flipping through the last album, when I turn to the next page and there's an envelope tucked in the binding. *Andrew* is handwritten on the front. That's Brick's legal name. The envelope is ripped open, so being the nosey person I am, I pull out the single sheet of paper inside, unfold it, and feel like I'm reading in slow motion. I'm in shock at what's written.

> *Dear Andrew,*
> *I know this isn't what you probably wanted to hear, but you have a son.*

I drop the paper to my lap and look around the room to see if anyone's watching me. Is this a prank? Did someone slip this in here to play a trick on me? A kid? Do Mountain and Whiskey know about this?

Holy shit! I need to find Mountain.

I'm just about to get up when Opal comes running in the front door. "Sunshine! Sunshine!"

I slam the photo album shut, paper still in between the pages, and jump up. I set the whole thing on top of the entertainment center. Way up so little fingers can't accidently find it and show this unknown secret to whoever she chooses.

That's one thing I've learned about Opal—this girl has zero concept of personal boundaries. I thought it was cute at first, but when she decided to dig through my purse and start handing tampons out to the Brothers like they were trick or treating, it wasn't so funny anymore. I'm working with her to ask before she touches things, but this four-year-old is so spoiled rotten by these men, it's like talking to a wall sometimes.

"Sunshine! Sunshine!"

I turn to see what she wants. "Why are you running in the house?"

She stops in front of me and grabs my hand, panting to catch her breath. "Daddy and Papa . . . want you to . . . come outside."

I pick her up—okay, so maybe I spoil her too—and head for the front door. "What do they want me for?"

"I don't know," she pouts. "They won't tell me."

I tickle her belly until she giggles. "That's 'cause you tell secrets."

Pushing the screen door open with my butt, I back out on the porch. I turn around and freeze. The yard's full with what looks like every member of the Rebel Vipers MC. Every Brother, Old Lady, kid, Prospect, and club girl. Even Steel's friend, Ray, and his family.

I set Opal down and she runs to Duchess. "What's going on?"

Steel and Ring step onto the front porch and each grab one of my hands.

"We wanted to do this the right way," Steel starts.

"It's time to get your last present," Ring continues.

They pull me forward, down the steps, onto the grass. That's when I notice Opal has rejoined us and she's holding up a black leather cut.

I stare down at it, and when I read what the back says, my tears start flowing.

The top rocker says 'Rebel Vipers'.

The middle patch is the smiling skull wrapped in a green snake.

And the bottom rocker, the most important one of all, says 'Property of Ring and Steel'.

"Here ya go." Opal's holding it up for me to take, but I can't because my hands are still being held.

"Thank you, munchkin." Steel takes it from her and finally lets my hand free.

Ring turns my back to the group so I'm facing them.

"We wanted to give this to you sooner, but with all the hard work you've been doing in Brick's cabin, we decided to wait 'til you were almost done." Steel turns the cut around so I can see the front. "We had your Old Lady name put on a patch on the front."

"Is this still what you want, Sunshine?" Ring squeezes my hand.

I snap out of my fog, yank my hand out of Ring's, and leap at Steel. He catches me midair and picks me up, the cut smushed between our chests.

"Yes," I exclaim, then kiss him. "I want this."

One arm around Steel's neck, I reach out my right hand and grab onto the shoulder of Ring's cut. I pull him to me, and he plasters himself to my back. I turn my head and kiss him. "I want all of this."

That's when the crowd goes wild. Everyone starts cheering and clapping. I hear someone yell, "Get a room!" I look over Steel's shoulder to see Duchess backhand Whiskey across the chest. He grabs her with both hands, kisses her silly, and dips her like in every rom-com movie. It reminds me of when Ring caught me staring at them at their gender reveal. But now, I get the need to be constantly wanting to touch your person. Now, I've got two of those persons who like to fight for my attention, and I love every minute of it.

Steel sets me down and Ring pulls me into his embrace. I wrap my arms around him and nuzzle myself into his chest.

"We've got one more surprise." Ring's vibrating with excitement.

I pull back and look between him and Steel. "Another surprise? What is it this time? A house?" I laugh at my ridiculous guess. I have no idea what they've got up their sleeves, but a house was the first random thing to pop out.

"Well, you're kinda right." Steel holds out a set of key rings. I see my van key fob and the silver keys for my mom's house, but I don't recognize the skull keychain hanging from them.

"What's that keychain for?" I grab the bundle of keys.

"The keychain is for the keys to this cabin," Ring points at the cabin we're standing in front of.

"This cabin? Brick's cabin? Why do I need keys to this cabin?" I'm stumped.

Ring kneels down and waves Opal over to us. He whispers something in her ear and the smile on her face grows so wide. She yells out, for the whole world to hear, "WE'RE MOVING IN TOGETHER!" She starts jumping up and down.

"What?" My eyes flicker between the guys again.

"That's right, Sunshine. The four of us are moving in here all together," Steel answers first.

"If that's okay with you," Ring interjects. "We know you've been having a hard time since you went back to your house, so we wanted to give you a fresh start. We talked to Mountain, and he said the four of us are welcome to live here for as long as we want."

Steel holds the cut up again. "And we want forever."

I turn my back to him and hold my left arm a little out to the side. I feel the leather slide up my arm, across my back, and lift my right arm to finish putting it on. I'm facing the group, my family, and can't hold in my giddiness. I straight-up squeal like a teenage girl. I lift my legs, one at a time, and do a short running in place dance. I'm over the moon.

Duchess rushes forward, and as close as her growing belly lets her get, she hugs me tight. Her and her hugs. I'll never get sick of them.

"Quit trying to steal our woman," I hear Ring sass.

"Yea," Steel joins in. "Just because you've got a new friend, doesn't mean you can hog her all the time."

I turn their way to see them both with their arms folded, trying to be a big and macho, but failing miserably because of their smiles.

I throw an arm over Duchess's shoulder and give them a sneaky smile in return. "Since we're gonna be neighbors now, maybe I should move in with Duchess. Then Whiskey can move in with you two and we don't have to share bathrooms with you smelly dudes."

"Yea," Duchess comes to my defense. "I swear, I live in a frat house sometimes. If Whiskey uses my good towels to dry his dick one more time, I'm gonna start forgetting to shave my legs. Then we'll see how he likes touching all up on my hairiness."

"Woman." Duchess is yanked away from me again. "Don't even start with that again. I said I'd stop using those damn towels. It's just they're so soft and feel nice on my dick."

Oh boy. Time for me to leave this conversation.

The crowd disperses and it looks like a party is well on its way for tonight. The kids are running around, climbing on the playground, and shrieking to the high heavens. The picnic tables are being dragged out into the yard and Wrecker and Hammer are starting up the grills.

I guess we're having another party, two nights in a row. Last night was a late one, because Sam was patched in.

Now he's known by the road name Haze. So, I guess we're in for a whole weekend of good times. I can't complain about that. Just another thing to add to my list of happy moments since I found this new family. I wouldn't trade this for the world.

And I'm moving onto the club compound. How crazy is that? Ring and Steel really have thought of everything. Without me realizing it, they knew I can't go back to my house. Even though I grew up there, the memories of that one fateful day became too much. Being abducted from my childhood home gave me nightmares.

Every night this past week, I've been woken up by one or both of the guys. They've said I'm thrashing and crying, and they didn't know what to do. Looks like they figured it out. A new home. A home that belonged to my uncle. Now, we get to welcome another two generations in on this cabin's story.

Two arms wrap around me from behind, one over my shoulders and the second around my waist. I'm sandwiched in the middle of my two Old Men and can't think of a place I'd rather be.

CHAPTER FORTY-NINE

STEEL

"Thanks for watching her tonight." I hand Duchess a bag of Opal's things, just a change of clothes and her stuffed bear.

"It's no problem. After everything that's happened, I know the three of you need a night to yourselves," Duchess responds.

And she's right. We do need an adult only night. Having Opal home is great, but with the plans Ring and I have for this evening, the little one needs to have a sleep over with the neighbors.

"One of us will call in the morning when the coast is clear." I step off the porch and head for what is now our cabin.

"Just remember," Duchess calls out, "when this baby comes, y'all owe me babysitting time."

"You talk to Sunshine about that," I holler back.

I jog up the front steps, pull open the screen door, and walk inside.

"Talk to me about what?"

I turn to my right, and I'm struck dumb. "Umm . . ." I forget everything I was just thinking about.

"Do you like what you see, Colt?" Sunshine's sitting on the edge of our kitchen island, wearing only her property cut.

"Where's Ring?" I ask, ignoring her question because my brain is mush.

"In the bathroom."

"Does he know what you're wearing?"

"Not yet. You came back from dropping the munchkin off quicker than I thought."

I'm not sure what snaps me from my fog, but I rush forward and kiss her with everything I've got. I slide my hands around her hips, grab hold of her naked backside, push as close to her as I can, and devour her whole. Our tongues battle for dominance, but as usual, I win. I flick the roof of her mouth with my tongue, and she moans like she's in heaven.

Fuckin' right she is.

"Looks like you two started the party without me," Ring's voice comes from behind me.

I quickly yank back from our woman's face and step to the side, leaving one hand on her ass, but out of the way so he can see what I saw when I walked inside.

"Fuck!" he swears, biting a fist. "I don't blame ya, Brother. Our Old Lady is fine as fuckin' hell."

"You got that right."

"That cut looks mighty fine on you, Sunshine." Ring talks as he makes his way forward.

"Why, thank you, Ryan." She tilts her head a little and blushes.

"Quit trying to act all sweet," I tell her while squeezing her butt. "You knew exactly what was gonna happen when we saw you wearing nothing but our leather."

She bites her lip and shrugs. "Maybe."

"Enough of this maybe shit," Ring growls out. He threads his right hand into her hair and pulls her toward him. It's his turn to kiss her until neither of them can breathe. It's all tongue and teeth and grunting from both of them.

I let go of my woman's ass and take one step back. I unbutton and unzip my jeans, push them and my boxer briefs down just a bit, and let my dick have some room to breathe. Because my plan doesn't include him being out in the air for long.

I tap Ring on the shoulder, and he does exactly what I hoped he would. He lifts Sunshine off the island, sets her on her feet, and spins her my way.

"Well, hello there, soldier," she purrs, her eyes looked on my cock.

"Come here," I bark out, demanding her forward. "Right here." I point down at the floor in front of me.

She takes the few steps, eyes on my hardness the whole time.

This time, I grab a handful of her hair and pull down, forcing her head up. I lower my face so our noses are touching and we lock eyes. "Let's move this to the living room, shall we?"

Before she can respond, I start walking backward, still gripping her hair, forcing her along with me.

My jeans around my ass don't allow me to make big steps, so I shuffle back until my legs hit the front of the couch. I let go of her hair, leaving her standing, and sit down.

I get one boot off, then Sunshine kneels between my legs. She yanks off the other boot, then goes to work pulling my jeans and underwear down. As she does this, I slide my cut off and Ring grabs it from me. I look to the side and see he's got his cut in one hand and mine in the other. He walks to the dining room and hangs them on the back of the chairs. I whip my t-shirt off and send it sailing behind the couch.

By that time, Sunshine has me stripped naked and is back to staring at my dick.

"Why don't you climb up here," I tap on my thigh and buck my hips, making my dick jump, "and you can get closer to him."

"Don't have to ask me twice." Sunshine stands up and drops a knee on each side of my hips. She wiggles her way to me and presses her chest to mine. "Want my cut off too?"

"Fuck no," Ring answers for both of us. "You look damn edible with our names on your back. You keep that on 'til we say so."

I slide my hands up her thighs, over her backside, and settle them on her lower back. I can feel the stitching from the patch that holds mine and Ring's names. I can't see it, but I know exactly what it looks like.

"We'll take it off you when we're damn good and ready," I grunt.

Sunshine starts rubbing her hot body all up on mine. Her hands are on each side of my head, her chest still on mine, and her hips grinding down on my lap. I can feel the heat and dampness from her center all over my abdominal muscles.

"Are you wet enough for me to just slide inside you?" I reach my right hand between us and use a few fingers to tease her folds. "Or do you need me to play with your kitty some more?"

She starts raining kisses down the side of my face, then to my neck. "Put him in me now please. You two can play with me more later."

Ring steps up behind Sunshine and pulls her head back. He drops a kiss on her forehead. "How about you turn around, and get settled on his lap that way, so I can see your pretty face?"

"Good plan, Brother."

Using all four of our hands, Ring and I get Sunshine up, turned around, and back in my lap reverse cowgirl style. I slouch down a bit on the cushion and line my dick up with her channel, letting just the tip inside of her.

I grasp her hips and pull her down, making her take all of me at once. I thrust deep inside of her and freeze, holding her ass tight to my lap.

She starts trying to wiggle her bottom, but I dig my fingers in her flesh a bit tighter, pinching her. "If you move," I grunt, "I'll explode before I want to."

"Give me your face, Sunshine," Ring draws her focus to him. "Lick my dick and get it wet."

As Ring gets her attention on him and his needs, her ass stops moving side to side, and I can get a full breath. I lift her up a few inches, just enough so I can go at my speed, and start moving.

Keeping her still, I do all the work. With my feet planted flat on the floor, and my ass deep in the couch, I pump my hips up and down, sliding my cock deep in Sunshine's pussy. I take everything I want from her, and then some. I fuck her so hard and deep, every time I bottom out, she lets out a little squeak.

But it's not a loud or sharp squeak. She can't do that due to the mouth full of Ring's dick she's currently dealing with. He's got both of his hands intertwined in her hair and is blissed out with what she's doing. His head's thrown back, his jaw's locked tight, and I can tell by the tightness of his torso, he's trying not to take over and plow himself into her mouth the way he wants. He's letting her do what she wants right now but he's enjoying every bit.

"That's it," he huffs out. "Keep sucking me."

I pick up my pace and see if I can get her to come quick. In my crouched position, I can't reach around her to play with her clit, so I try something the three of us haven't done yet. I don't know how Sunshine will feel about this, but we're about to find out.

With her back to me, I have a full view of her ass, her legs spread apart over mine, so I can see the puckered star of her back door.

Keeping my left hand on her hip, I lick my right thumb and slide my hand under the bottom of her cut. Using my wet digit, I glide down her lower spine and into the crease of her cheeks. She hasn't made any sudden moves yet, so either she doesn't care or hasn't realized where I'm headed.

Keeping my other four fingers up, I slide my thumb that last centimeter down and tap her star just once. That makes her whole body tense in a flash. She stops moving, mouth still on Ring's dick. I give her hole a little pressure, not pushing in, but a small nudge and she relaxes again.

Taking that as a good sign, I leave my hands right where they are and start my hip thrusts again. She's back concentrating on what's in front of her, so the rodeo continues.

Sunshine's pussy is so damn tight, I'm in fucking heaven. I feel the tingling start in my toes, so I know my time's almost up for this round. I need to get my woman off. And if Ring's anything like me, which I know he is, he could blow at any time with her mouth on his dick.

I kick my hips into high gear and start pulling her down into my upward thrusts. I give my thumb a bit more pressure on her hole, and as soon as it slips past that first ring of muscles, Sunshine comes so hard, her whole body shakes. My thumb's only in her as deep as my fingernail, but that's enough for her to come so forcefully, I can feel her gush against my dick.

Her inner pussy squeezes me tight, pulsating every second, it's almost like morse code to my brain.

I feel the nerves running up my legs set off like fireworks, and as soon as they reach my back, I'm a fucking goner. My dick twitches once and I come harder than I ever had in my whole damn life. I know I've probably said that before, but since every time my dick is inside my woman is the best time, it's the truth.

Her ass starts wiggling again, so I remove my thumb from her dark hole and put both hands on her hips, holding her tight to my lap. We're as close together as we can get, but that doesn't stop my hips from rocking up into hers.

"I'm gonna . . ." Ring starts but doesn't finish his sentence before he blows his load. If the babbling coming from his lips is any sign, she must've sucked his brain out of his dick along with his cum.

Mine and Sunshine's twitching has stopped, so holding her still, I scoot my ass back a little, getting myself sitting up straight. I let my cock slide out of her opening, settle her butt down on my lap, and let Ring finish his work.

Hands still in her hair, Ring takes a step back, taking his deflating member with him. He bends down to kiss her full out, then slowly leans her back against me.

Ring shuffles to my right, turns around, and drops his ass on the cushion next to us. He lays his head back, stretches his arms forward, then interlocks his fingers behind his head. "I think I lost my brain."

That makes me laugh out loud. See, I knew his babbling had a reason.

"Is that a good thing?" Sunshine asks, turning her whole body to the side so she can see both of us.

"Give me two minutes and I'll show you just how good it was." Ring laughs, pulling her legs over his lap.

"I get your mouth next."

Sunshine looks at me with a huge smile, giving me a wink. "Maybe we can take that round to our new bed? I know we slept in it last night, but I'd really like to break it in."

If she wants to break in our new bed, she's on. I stand up, bend over just a bit, toss her over my shoulder, and march toward the hall.

Sunshine slaps me on the ass and grabs and squeezes both of my butt cheeks.

"Be gentle back there," I chuckle.

"But why?" She slaps the other cheek. "You seemed to like playing with my ass just now. Why can't I play with yours?"

I make it to our room and toss her down on our big bed. She bounces a few times, then I pull her up to sit in front of me. "Your ass is mine and his." I toss a thumb to Ring behind me. I drop the funny attitude we had on the walk in here and give her a stern talking to. "Our asses are ours. If you want to play with them, you better ask next time."

She senses my turn in tone of voice and sits up straight. She laces her fingers in her lap and looks up at me under her eyelashes. "Yes. sir."

CHAPTER FIFTY

RING

My legs are still a little wobbly from that killer blowjob Sunshine just gave me, but I manage to get to my feet and follow the laughing duo headed for our bedroom.

Sunshine slaps Steel on the ass a few times, and I shake my head at her feisty attitude. When she lets out the little tidbit about him playing with her ass, my steps falter a bit.

He played with her ass? As far as I know, his dick was in her pussy, so my guess is he used a finger to test her limits. I've thought about breaching her back side a few times, but it wasn't something we've tried yet. Her pussy and mouth have kept us entertained so far. Maybe it's time to kick things up a notch.

My attention focuses back on Sunshine in time to hear her whisper, "Yes, sir."

"That's a good girl, Sunshine," Steel practically purrs at her, stroking her hair back with his hand. She blushes up at him, eyelashes fluttering like a damn butterfly.

Oh, I understand what she's doing. I don't know if Steel realizes it, but I can read her thoughts behind those beautiful hazel eyes with no problem. She's playing him like a fiddle.

I step to Steel's left and grab a handful of Sunshine's bright locks. I set one knee on the bed and jerk her in my direction. She reaches out on instinct, trying not to fall, but my thigh and torso stop her from going anywhere. She grips my leg and holds on tight.

In this position, my dick is practically in her face, but I push him down with my free hand so she can see me.

"I know what you're trying to do, and I don't appreciate it," I snarl. "Steel was telling you how it is and you're acting all innocent. But really, you're thinking naughty thoughts, aren't you?" With every word, I grip her hair a little tighter and lower my head to hers. By the last word, our noses are touching.

"I'm sorry," she answers, eyes open wide. This time, I can see the real apology.

"That's what I thought." I tug her hair a little harder. "Up on your knees and apologize to Steel for trying to trick him."

Once she's kneeling, I let her go. She shifts in front of Steel and looks up.

His walls are up and his expression's guarded.

Sunshine reaches a hand out but stops and drops it to her side. "I'm sorry for trying to fool you, Colt. I didn't mean anything by it."

"Then why'd you do it?" he asks with no emotion.

I start to wonder if I took this too far but decide to let it play out. If it continues too long, I'll step in, but for now, I just crawl into bed and listen.

"I felt you touch me back there and wanted you to do it again," she whispers. Her head drops down as she continues. "But then you said I had to ask to touch yours and thought it was a game."

I see the tension release from Steel's body. It's just a flicker. I don't think Sunshine notices, but I do. Her eyes are on his chest, so when Steel winks at me, I know all is good. But she doesn't need to know that just yet.

"So, how are you gonna make it up to me?" Steel growls, finally touching her again, grabbing her hair like I did, pulling her head back. "What will you do for both of us to apologize for being such a bad girl?"

"Anything you want." The words rush out.

Steel then kisses her full on. His hand's still holding her tight, but his mouth's leading this charge. He leans forward, forcing her back, until she can't stay upright anymore. She lets out a tiny scream, bends her knees, and falls flat on her back. He let go of her hair as she falls, as to not pull it too hard.

"Roll over, Sunshine, and let me watch your ass crawl up into Ring's lap. Show him your apology. Had he not seen the truth in your eyes, you might've just tricked us both."

She does as she's told. Sunshine turns over, flipping her body, repositioning herself to face me.

She crawls into my lap and sets her hands on my shoulders. "I'm sorry, Ryan. I didn't mean for it to happen like that."

I can tell she's trying to keep her eyes on mine, but the uncertainty in her voice tells me I may have pushed a few too many of her buttons with my stern talking. She dropped her wall to Steel, but it looks like I've got some work to do.

My hands have been folded on my torso, so I unlink my fingers and lift my hands to her face. I gently, slowly, slide my palms along her cheeks. My fingers settle on the sides of her neck, my thumbs brush back and forth on the apples of her cheeks, and my palms cup her jaw.

Sunshine closes her eyes, and she nuzzles into my hand. She rolls her neck a few times, just soaking in the gentleness I'm trying to show her.

"Sunshine, look at me please."

She opens her eyes again to meet mine. I see a little of the sparkle she had before, so I hope that's a good sign.

"I'm sorry," she whispers again.

"I know." I sit up and kiss her once. "I saw something in your eyes and needed to correct it fast. I'm sorry if I sounded harsh, but we need to be the ones in charge. Especially if we're going to start playing with you like he started out there. That hole is very tender, and we don't want to hurt you."

"I get it."

"I know we haven't talked about playing with your ass before, but maybe we should. Do you think that's something you'd like to try?"

Sunshine gives a little nod. "I've never done it all the way before, but I trust both of you to teach me. Just maybe not today." She peeks over her shoulder and sees Steel smiling at us. "If just his finger can do that to me, I can't imagine what your monster dicks would do."

We all laugh, and the rest of the tension disappears in a flash. Thank fucking goodness. I couldn't stand one more minute of our woman being scared or afraid of us. We gave her our cut yesterday and I'd hate to see this be something to kill us just as we get started.

Steel walks to the right side of the bed, and Sunshine follows him with her head.

"What now?" she asks, looking back at me.

She's still straddling my lap, so I buck my hips and let my dick brush against her pussy lips. She lets out a little moan. "You played reverse cowgirl already, so how about you climb on my dick, and I'll give you the ride of your life?"

"Yee haw, cowboy." And we're off.

Palms flat on my pecs, Sunshine uses her legs and lifts higher over my lap. She lowers her head to mine and dives in for a kiss. I let her start. Our battle's slow and I take over, still holding her head and directing her so I can kiss her how I want.

Our chests touch as she slides her body even closer to mine. Once she's on top of me, our hips meet. She grinds her slit up and down, over the length of my cock, getting it slick with her wetness.

A few gyrating twists later, she lifts a tiny bit, letting my tip find her center. She lowers down forcing my dick to push apart her folds and slide up into her.

Then, in a move I never saw coming, she drops all her weight on my lap, impaling herself on my cock all at once.

"Fuck," I yell out. I drop my hands from her head and wrap my arms all the way around her body.

She's so much smaller than I am, my hands reach my own arms on the other sides. I slide them down her back and hold on tight.

I scoot my butt forward a few times and lay flat on my back. I bend my knees, essentially locking her whole body onto my chest, I set my feet flat on the bed, and use the leverage I now have to my advantage.

With her head buried in my neck, I start pumping up into my woman with only one thing in mind. *Make her come so damn hard and fast, she's going to scream to the heavens and beg me for more.*

The mattress starts bouncing, so I hold Sunshine tight to me, and close my eyes. I know this round isn't going to last long, but that's okay. I just need to get her off, then I can worry about me.

I jack my hips up and down, just listening to our skin slap against each other's.

"Fuck me hard," she screams. "Make me . . . pay . . . I'm sorry . . ."

Holy fuck, the words coming from her mouth are almost too much.

"That's right, Sunshine," Steel grunts from my left.

I turn my head and see he's now kneeling on the bed next to us. With all the rocking we've been causing, I never felt the bed shift with his movements.

I also notice that Sunshine's leaned her body a bit to the side to get her head out in the open, for Steel to get his dick in front of her face. Her chest is still plastered to mine, but her shoulders, neck, and head are leaning his way.

"If you're sorry," I start, "then suck. His. Dick. Too." I grunt each word as I thrust up, deeper inside her.

Steel wraps one hand around the back of her neck and guides his cock to her face with the other. He flexes his hips toward her, so I set all my focus back on my job, making our woman come on my dick.

I feel the muscles in my back start to twitch, so I know I'm getting close myself.

Wondering if I can make Sunshine come with my finger too, I slid one hand down the back of her cut, the material feels cool, but once I touch her skin, it's on fire. I trace one finger down the seam of her butt cheeks and that makes her body start trembling.

"Do it, Ring," Steels says through clenched teeth. "Touch it and she'll explode."

So, I do. I let my middle finger run over her hole, applying just the smallest pressure, and she detonates.

She pulls back from Steel's hold and lets out what I imagine would've been a scream loud enough to shatter glass had sound actually come out of her mouth. Her eyes roll back, and her face is to the ceiling.

Her left hand slaps down on my chest and her nails dig into my skin. Her right hand I'm guessing is on Steel, but in my attempt to keep my tempo, I'm not paying much attention to anything not happening to me.

Muffled sounds start up again, so he's got her mouth occupied again.

That's when she shocks the living hell out of me and comes again. She comes again, strangling the bejesus out of my cock, I think she's going to squeeze him off.

And I start my flight to the heavens. Tingles flash all over my body and I start pumping rope after rope of heat up into her. I grunt with each jerk, then collapse, losing all my remaining energy.

Steel finishes grunting and flops back, almost falling off the side of the bed.

Sunshine sits up, pushing her weight back on my dick, making me spasm again. I try to hold her tight so she doesn't set me off again, but she's still trying to rescue the flailing Steel. She's trying to catch him, but she's giggling so hard, she snorts. That sends her off balance, sliding off my lap.

Steel rolls to the side and off the edge of the bed, somehow landing on his feet.

Sunshine nose dives to the blanket, where Steel just was, and flops to her back.

And my dick is deader than a doornail, lying flat against my stomach. I reach down to poke him, making sure he's still somewhat alive. That sends both of them into hysterics.

"Did she break you?" Steel puffs between breaths.

"Oh baby." Sunshine keeps giggling, petting my arm. "Is he okay?"

"He's just fine," I grump. "How the hell did you fall off the bed, Steel? We got an Alaskan king mattress for a reason."

Steel pushes Sunshine closer to me, so I grab her and roll to my side, spooning her from behind.

"This damn bed may be a nine-foot square, but our woman's a beast." He crawls up and lays on the other side of her. "She drained me dry for the second time and I couldn't handle it."

"You're such a goof," Sunshine teases him. "I'm glad you didn't hurt yourself like mister crybaby over here." She wiggles her ass into my hips.

I feel myself getting hard again, so maybe it's time to show her what the rest of our night's going to look like.

Since I'm behind her, I push myself forward, and roll her onto her front. I grind my now very quickly growing cock into her ass crack and lean down to whisper in her ear. "Do you want me to show you how unbroken I am?"

Sunshine turns her head so I can see the side her face. "Yes, sir," she whispers.

"Game on," I whisper back.

"I'm ready," Steel responds.

I lift us both up, then wrestle her cut off. Steel sets it on the nightstand and we get back to work.

And that's how we spend the rest of our night, and into the following morning. Breaking in our new bed and loving our woman.

We take breaks in between rounds, getting some snacks and water, and taking turns letting the puppy out. But just after the sun rises, we all pass out in an exhausted heap.

CHAPTER FIFTY-ONE

SUNSHINE

"I want bumpy braids," Opal says out of nowhere.

Ring, Steel, and I are sitting on a couch in the clubhouse main room, and Opal's down on the floor playing with Teddy.

She stands up, walks over to me, and climbs in my lap, displacing the guy's hands that were on each of my thighs.

"Hey, munchkin, that was my hand you kneeled on," Ring grumbles.

"Sorry, Papa," she whispers, but her attention's all on me. "I want bumpy braids like my friend, Pearl, at school."

Now I know what she's talking about. There's a new girl that started at daycare this week and I remember seeing her with Dutch braids in her hair. Looks like our little lady has hair envy. What woman doesn't?

"I don't have any of your hair stuff in here. Can we do it tonight after dinner?" I ask her.

"But I want them now!" she pouts.

"I'll go get whatever you need," Ring gets up, "I need to get the order sheet for Brewer so he can bring stuff from the brewery for the party tomorrow."

"You don't have to." I grab his hand, trying to pull him back down.

"It's okay. What do you need?"

He's such an amazing man.

"Grab her hairbrush and the plastic baggie of the tiny, colored rubber bands."

"I'm on it." And he's gone.

I shift Opal to the vacated couch cushion and stand up to stretch.

"Where you goin', Sunshine." Steel tears his eyes from the baseball game on television.

"Just refilling my water." I grab my cup from the coffee table and start for the kitchen.

Before I make it two steps, yelling from the hallway of the club girls' rooms stops me in my tracks. Tempy comes stomping into the main room, suitcase rolling behind her.

She spins around, and Hammer crashes into her. She pushes him back and shouts, "I said I'm going and there's nothing you can do to stop me!"

"Don't do this again," Hammer practically pleads. "You can't leave again."

"Well, I can't stay here with you around. So, unless you're gonna leave, I've gotta go." Tempy grabs her suitcase handle again and makes a beeline for the door.

"Wait—" Hammer starts to follow her.

I rush to intercept him and shove my empty cup in his hands. "Why don't I go see if I can talk her down. Is that okay?"

Hammer gives me the saddest puppy eyes I've ever seen, except maybe for our real puppy. "Try and talk her into not leaving. Tell her I'll leave her alone now."

"I'll try." I pat his cheek and rush outside, hoping to catch Tempy.

And I'm in luck. Tempy's lifting her suitcase into the back of her new Jeep Wrangler, and I jog across the parking lot.

"Tempy!" I holler.

"I'm not staying." She whips around, deflating when she sees it me. "Oh, it's just you."

"What's going on?" I ask. "Why are you leaving? I thought things were getting better."

"I thought so too, but he hasn't changed. All he wants is a bed buddy and I can't do it anymore."

"I'm sorry." I wrap her in a hug and squeeze her tight.

She pulls back, wiping a few tears. "I'm moving back into mine and Duchess's house until I figure out what to do next. I just started working a few hours at the bakery since she can't be on her feet much right now."

Duchess is getting up there in her pregnancy and her swollen ankles have been a bit concerning, so knowing she's got more help is good to know.

"Hammer asked me to try and get you to stay, but if this is what you really want, I'm behind you."

"Thank you." Tempy shuts the hatch and opens the back driver's side door. She pulls out a three-ring binder with colorful sticky notes hanging out the edges. She holds it out to me, and I hesitantly grab it.

"This is Duchess's baby shower binder. I ordered everything for the party, but can you be the middleman for me as the deliveries start showing up? It's mostly all coming in the mail, so just make sure the boxes don't get lost and check things off the list as they come."

"I can do that."

"Thanks." Tempy gets in her Jeep, starts it up, and is gone.

I flip open the binder as I walk back into the clubhouse. I'm amazed at how organized Tempy has this thing. Each section is color-coded and has a tab to flip to. I wish I was this meticulous.

"What's that?" Ring asks. He must've just come in from getting the stuff I need for Opal's hair.

"This is the baby shower binder." I hold it up. "Tempy asked me to take care of stuff here since she's moving out."

"She's moving out?" Steel jumps up and comes to my side.

"Does Hammer know?" Ring asked.

"Yea. You just missed the show. They were arguing again."

I set the binder on the coffee table, take the stuff from Ring, and pull Opal into my lap.

"Fuck," Ring mutters.

"Papa!" Opal shrieks. "Bad word!"

"Sorry, munchkin," he replies.

The guys resettle themselves at my sides. Just as I finish braiding Opal's hair, the front screen door swings open, slamming into the wall.

"Shit!" We all look up and see Brewer spinning around, trying to catch the door. He finally grabs it and gently closes it.

"What's wrong, Brother?" Ring calls out.

"N-nothing," he stutters back, sounding flustered. He gets himself back in order and heads our way. "Do you have that order list for the Fourth of July party tomorrow? I wanna get that stuff back here before dark."

Ring grabs a folder from the table and hands it to Brewer. "It's all in here."

The screen door swings open, hitting the wall again. "Sorry I'm late!" someone yells.

"Meredith!" Steel jumps up and rushes over to her, scooping her up in a hug.

Opal slides off my lap, running to join the hugs, and Ring follows.

But my focus is all on Brewer. The second Meredith walked in the door, he froze where he's standing. He's got a death grip on the order folder and his eyes are glued on her.

Interesting.

"Who's that?" he whispers.

I stand up and walk to his side. "That's Steel's younger sister, Meredith. She'll be spending a few weeks with us. She wants a little freedom from her folks while she decides what she wants to do next year. College or no college."

He whips his head my way. "She's in high school?"

I chuckle, knowing he's way out of his element. If I was a betting woman, I'd say he encountered her already and rushed in here to get away. But then she came inside, and he's flustered. Looks like someone's got a crush.

"She just graduated, and she's eighteen."

"What are you two starin' at?" Steel turns our way and sees us. He's got an arm around Meredith's shoulder, but her attention is on the floor.

Looks like someone else might have had an instant attraction. This is going to be an interesting few weeks.

"Nothing," Brewer coughs into his fist. "I gotta go. See ya later." And he's out the door.

"What's wrong with him?" Ring questions.

"Looks like he's off his rocker," Steel continues.

"Don't worry about it."

I pull Meredith away from Steel and tug her to the couch. We sit down and I grab the binder, laying it over our laps.

I look up to see the guys staring at us like we've got three eyes. "Either you two sit down and watch your game or go away. Your staring is kinda creepy."

They both harrumph, pouting like toddlers. Steel sits in a recliner and Ring takes the empty cushion next to me. He peeks at the open pages. "Is this the baby shower where we're donating to the hospital for the babies?"

"Yes, it is. Do you still wanna help me?"

"Wherever you need me, I'm all yours." Ring leans in for a quick kiss, then sits back, focus returning to the television.

When I mentioned to my guys that we were going to be using Duchess's baby shower as a collection for supplies to the hospital's NICU, Ring was a little skittish. I cornered him later and asked him what was wrong. He told me it was our local hospital where he was abandoned and he didn't want anything to do with it.

I explained to him that since Duchess already had everything she needed, we were gathering things for babies and families who didn't have anything. Maybe even for mothers like his.

He said maybe if his mother had help like this when he was born, she wouldn't have felt the need to give him away. His whole attitude changed in a second. Ever since, any time I mention the shower, he asks what he can do to help. God, I love this man.

"Everything okay over there?" Steel asks from the recliner he claimed.

"It's all good," I answer, then start flipping through the binder, seeing what's all about to be headed our way.

These last few months have been anything but ordinary. My mother's illness was rough for both of us, but now that she's finally at peace, my heart feels calmer.

It feels like my mother lead me here.

I finally know who my father is. Mountain's a man who lives up to his name. He's strong and tall and unbreakable in my eyes.

I have a brother, and Whiskey's a wild one for sure, but I know he'd do anything for me.

I've got a little munchkin who's decided she needs to be my shadow. I know the next few years in Opal's life won't be easy, but I'll be there for her every step of the way.

And my Old Men. Who would've thought I'd end up falling in love with two men in a motorcycle club? Not me! But I wouldn't go back and change anything.

No matter what life throws at us, I know they'll always be by my side. We'll walk through the pits of hell for each other . . . because that's what a family is supposed to do.

Nothing will come between the three of us. We're unbreakable. And we'll protect this family with a ring of steel for the rest of our lives.

THE END!

EPILOGUE

HAMMER

"You ready to head back?" Whiskey calls out as we're sitting at a red light, an hour from home.

"Fuck yea!" I shout over the rumble of our Harleys. "I need a beer and my woman!"

I see rather than hear him laugh at me, so I flip him the bird.

The light turns green, so I grab my handlebars, pop the clutch, kick into the next gear, and take off, flying down the road and not looking back.

Whiskey quickly catches up and is at my left in no time.

This is how it's been our whole lives. We've both grown up the sons of two of the original Rebel Vipers MC officers, and now we have titles of our own. We were born and bred to live this life.

We're back on the road to the compound in no time. We ride around the last curve and see the fence surrounding our property on the left.

But what's parked at the end of the driveway has us slowing down quick.

The gate is closed, something not usual for the middle of the day, and there's a shiny, black Town Car parked at the approach.

Whiskey pulls in first, and I follow, rolling our bikes around the car. We park between it and the gate. We shut off our motors and swing off our seats.

"What's this car doing here, Diego?" I ask the Prospect who just walked out of the guard shack.

"They wanted to talk to someone in charge, but Whiskey didn't answer his phone. I was about to call Steel." Diego's one of our newest Prospects, but it looks like he's following protocol just fine so far.

Diego has been working for the club for a few years now, over at the salvage and recycling yard. In his time as a club hangaround, he got used to how things work around here quicker than most.

"We got this," Whiskey tells him. "Head back in the shack."

Diego goes back in just as the car's doors open and two men in black suits climb out.

Scary looking dudes too, if I was one to be afraid of anyone.

They look at both of us, look at each other, then start conversing in some foreign language.

"Can we help you?" I ask. I'm this club's Sergeant-at-Arms. If anyone wants something from someone around here, they've got to get through me first.

Their talking stops and they head our way, leaving their car doors open.

The passenger guy tucks his hand into the front of his jacket and pulls out a piece of paper.

"I need to know where I can find this woman." He holds it out, and Whiskey takes it since he's closer.

"What the fuck?" Whiskey shouts. "Why do you need to find this woman?"

"Who?" I ask him.

Whiskey shushes me and waves me off with his hand, his attention on the two men.

"We're just here to pick her up," minion number one replies.

"So, if you Neanderthals would be so kind as to go get our merchandise, it'd be greatly appreciated," minion number two sneers.

Who the fuck talks like that?

"First off, you're on our territory, so calling us names isn't gonna get us doing your bidding." I cross my arms and stand at full attention. "And secondly, your merchandise? I'm sorry, but I don't think we have anything here for you."

I don't know what these fuckers are looking for, but we ain't got it.

"I know she's here, so let's get this over with," minion one growls.

"Who's she?" I bark back.

"You might wanna look at this." Whiskey holds the paper my way, so I yank it from his hand.

I unfold it and look down. My heart drops into my stomach and I feel the blood drain from my face.

What in the actual fucking hell is this shit? This can't be right.

TO BE CONTINUED . . .

ACKNOWLEDGMENTS

Mr. J – When you said I should do this writing thing, I never imagined I'd be writing a whole series. Thank you for dealing with my hours in the writing cave, missed dinners, and late nights. I love you to the moon and back!
Rebecca Vazquez – My book fairy godmother, I hope I did your man Ring justice! You claimed him from almost day one, and here he finally is! #TeamRebelVipers
Kay Marie – My Person! The ying to my yang. We finally got to go to a signing! And the stories we now have from that craziness . . . those margaritas were strong!!! Cristina and Meredith forever!
My KM Alpha friends – Kay, Becca, Heidi, and Olivia – What would I do without y'all? We're still going strong with the TikToks and weather reports LOL! I promise that your stories are coming soon. Becca, you're next!
Charli Childs – And I thought Whiskey's cover was a tough one. This one really pushed your creative buttons,

but you killed it! I promise the next few covers will be easier.

And last, but definitely not least, YOU! THANK YOU, READERS! Thank you for reading Ring, Sunshine, and Steel's story. When I finished book one, I intended on writing a different couple's story, but these three decided it was their turn next. They pushed their way to the front of the line, so I had no choice but to mix some things up and give them what they wanted. But I promise, what's coming next will bring everything going on in the RVMC world full circle.

ABOUT THE AUTHOR

Jessa Aarons was born and raised in the frozen tundra of Wisconsin. She has had her nose buried in books for as long as she can remember. Her love of romance began when she "borrowed" her mom's paperback Harlequin novels.

After experiencing a life-changing health issue, she had to leave the working world and dove back into books to help heal her soul. She would read anything that told a love story but still had grit and drama. Then she became a beta reader and personal assistant to another author.

Jessa is the boss of her husband and their castle. He really is her prince. Thanks to his encouragement, Jessa started putting pen to paper and creating new imaginary worlds. She spends her free time reading, crafting, and cheering on her hometown football team.

SOCIAL MEDIA LINKS

Facebook Author Page

FB Reader's Group

Instagram

Twitter

Amazon

Goodreads

Bookbub

Pinterest

Spotify

TikTok

OTHER WORKS

<u>Rebel Vipers MC</u>
A Mountain to Climb
Whiskey on the Rocks
Ring of Steel
Hammer's Swing
A Smoke Filled Haze
Top of the Mountain

<u>Standalones</u>
Pure Luck – cowrite with Kay Marie

Printed in Great Britain
by Amazon